Praise for Catherine Palmer and her novels

"Catherine Palmer pens a page-turner with a…thought-provoking plot."

—Jill Elizabeth Nelson, *Romantic Times BOOKreviews*, on *Fatal Harvest*

"Veteran romance writer Palmer…delivers a satisfying tale of mother-daughter dynamics sprinkled with romance."

—*Library Journal* on *Leaves of Hope*

"Enjoyable… Faith fiction fans…will find this novel just their cup of tea."

—*Publishers Weekly Religion Bookline* on *Leaves of Hope*

"*Leaves of Hope* is a very emotional tale that's easy to relate to. Ms. Palmer ignites soul-searching conflict and carries her readers on a remarkable journey they will long remember. This is a sharer."

—*Rendezvous*

"Palmer knows how to write about a sensitive subject with wisdom and kindness."

—Patsy Glans, *Romantic Times BOOKreviews*, on *Thread of Deceit*

"Believable characters tug at heartstrings, and God's power to change hearts and lives is beautifully depicted."

—*Romantic Times BOOKreviews* on "Christmas in My Heart"

"*Love's Haven* is a glorious story that was wonderfully told…. Catherine Palmer did a stand-up job of describing each scene and creating a world which no reader will want to leave."

—*Cataromance Reviews*

Catherine Palmer is a bestselling author and winner of the Christy Award for her outstanding Christian romance. She also received the Career Achievement Award for Inspirational Fiction from *RT Book Reviews*. Raised in Kenya, she lives in Atlanta with her husband. They have two grown sons. A graduate of Southwest Baptist University, she also holds a master's degree from Baylor University.

Books by Catherine Palmer

Love Inspired Historical

The Briton
The Maverick's Bride
The Outlaw's Bride
The Gunman's Bride

Steeple Hill Single Title

That Christmas Feeling
Love's Haven
Leaves of Hope
A Merry Little Christmas
The Heart's Treasure
Thread of Deceit
Fatal Harvest
Stranger in the Night

Visit the Author Profile page at Harlequin.com for more titles.

CATHERINE PALMER

FATAL HARVEST

LOVE INSPIRED
INSPIRATIONAL ROMANCE

LOVE INSPIRED®

INSPIRATIONAL ROMANCE

Recycling programs
for this product may
not exist in your area.

ISBN-13: 978-1-335-55110-8

Fatal Harvest

First published in 2003 by Tyndale House Publishers.
This edition published in 2021 with revised text.

Copyright © 2003 by Catherine Palmer

Copyright © 2009 by Catherine Palmer, revised text edition

This edition published by arrangement with Harlequin Books S.A.

For questions and comments about the quality of this book, please contact us at CustomerService@Harlequin.com.

Love Inspired
22 Adelaide St. West, 40th Floor
Toronto, Ontario M5H 4E3, Canada
www.Harlequin.com

Printed in U.S.A.

To Tim Palmer

Thank You, Lord, for blessing me with the gift
of this wonderful man.

Chapter One

Matthew Strong bit the curlicue off the top of his dipped, vanilla ice-cream cone. A shard of chocolate shell came loose and dropped right onto his jeans pocket. He glanced at the Princeton University recruiter in the driver's seat beside him. The man's gray eyes were focused on the turn into Jaycee Park, so Matt flicked the melting chocolate onto the floor of the brand-new Cadillac.

He wished he looked older than sixteen. If he'd known these two men were going to take him out of class today, he might have gone to a barber. As it was, his curly black hair fell well below his ears and over the collar of his shirt. He had on his blue-and-gold striped tie, as usual. His mom had given it to him before she died. He wore the tie every day, and the mustard stain below the knot was impossible to conceal. That, along with the blob of chocolate on his jeans, made him look like a food-fight casualty.

"A perfect score on the ACT," the recruiter said for the second time since they'd left Artesia High School. The man was solidly built and had a blond crew cut. His immaculate red tie stood out against the pin-striped gray of his suit. He drove toward a pair of handball courts that had been built between the empty running track and the deserted softball diamond. "For a sophomore to perform so well is amazing."

Matt eyed his cone, wondering if he should attempt another bite. Why hadn't he ordered a sundae in a plastic bowl? Still, this wasn't too bad a deal. He had gotten out of his trigonometry class and had been treated to ice cream from Dairy Queen. In return, he would spend the next hour listening to this man and his colleague in the backseat tell him how great Princeton was. They'd probably show him some brochures and give him a pep talk. They'd go on and on about how much they wanted him to enroll and how many scholarships they could offer.

For a couple of months now—ever since he had gotten his ACT results—Matt had been flooded with phone calls and letters from universities. He wasn't too surprised at the score. One of his counselors told him he had the highest IQ ever recorded in the school system. These Princeton men were the first two college recruiters who had actually shown up looking for him, but he expected more would follow.

He would have liked his father by his side to help the conversation along. Matt could talk for hours about things that interested him—computers, logarithms, Latin grammar, the shifting of the earth's tectonic plates. Feeding the world's hungry filled his thoughts these days, and he was hard at work on a plan to accomplish that goal. But small talk? Forget it. For chitchat at school, he relied on his best friend, Billy Younger, to fill in his fumbling silences. But Billy was still in class, and Matt's father was never around. He'd be out on the ranch right now, plowing or feeding cattle or something.

"So you're interested in computers," the driver said. He

pulled the Cadillac to a stop behind the solid concrete wall of the handball court. "We understand you're able to do some interesting things with a computer, Matthew."

"Yeah. Especially since I met Miss Pruitt. She's my computer tech teacher." Matt pulled on the door handle and stepped out. At least this way, the chocolate bits would fall onto the ground instead of his jeans. "She doesn't have the latest hardware at school, but her software's okay. The main thing is, she knows the technology."

"Is this Miss Pruitt the one who helped you hack into the Agrimax mainframe?"

Matt paused at the unexpected question. "Uh...no, I didn't..." The two recruiters took a step closer, their eyes trained on his face. "I sent some e-mails.... How did you know about Agrimax?"

"Did Jim Banyon give you those e-mail addresses, Matthew?"

The second man laid a hand on Matt's shoulder. He was tall and beefy, with an acne-scarred face and a football player's thick neck. "Answer our questions, boy."

"What do you mean?" Matt stiffened as the man backed him into the cold gray wall of the handball court. "Questions about my college plans?"

"About Agrimax."

"It's a food company. A conglomerate." Was this some kind of a test? Why did Princeton want to know about his research on feeding the hungry? How had they found out what he was doing?

"Agrimax is one of the world's top three suppliers of food," Matt rattled off, breathless and nervous, feeling like he was at a Scholar Bowl competition. "They have a global network of growers, processors and retailers. They own hundreds of smaller companies, and they—"

"Who gave you access to the Agrimax mainframe?" The beefy man's grip tightened on Matt's shoulder. "Was it Jim Banyon?"

This wasn't what he had expected at all. Recruiters were supposed to lure you with nice offers, weren't they? Suddenly tongue-tied, Matt swallowed hard.

"Did Jim Banyon give you those e-mail addresses?" The blond man shoved him hard into the wall. His shoulders hit the concrete, and he gasped. "Answer me, kid."

"Addresses for the Agrimax executives? No, I—I got those myself. I opened a database. But not the mainframe. I don't hack, sir. I would never break into anyone's private computer system. You can tell Princeton that I—"

"You're writing a term paper. Where did you get your information?"

"How do you know that? Did you hack me?"

"We're doing the asking! Who told you about Agrimax? The genetic developments. The terminator genes. The cloning."

"It's all on the Internet. Anybody can—"

"Do you know Jim Banyon?"

"Yes, sir. He has a ranch near Hope. He used to work for Agrimax before he retired."

"What information did he give you?"

Matt stared down at the cone in his hand. The vanilla ice cream was oozing between the cracks in the chocolate shell and running onto his fingers. "Excuse me, sir," he said. "You're from Princeton, right?"

"Yeah, right." The blond man smirked at his companion. "Maybe he's not so bright after all. Look, kid, somebody downloaded a lot of data from the Agrimax mainframe. Technology. Patented information. Secret formulas. Was that you?"

"I told you I would never—"

"Shut up and answer the questions." The beefy guy grabbed a handful of Matt's hair and yanked his head to one side. Matt jerked in pain, and his cone fell to the ground. "Who has the information?"

Matt's mouth went dry. *Think. Think.*

"Answer me, kid!"

"I don't have it," he mumbled.

"Who does?" The scarred face came closer. "Does Banyon have it?"

"I don't have it! I promise."

"Who's got it?"

The man slammed Matt's head against the concrete. Bright lights swam before his eyes. He thought he was going to vomit. Or pass out. He tried to breathe.

"Search him!" the blond barked.

The beefy man grabbed Matt's arm, swung him around and pushed him up against the wall. With one foot, he kicked Matt's legs apart.

Like a policeman. Like someone trained.

The man was going through his pockets now, taking out the keys to his pickup and then shoving them back. His wallet. They thumbed through it. Thieves? The men studied his driver's license, credit card, student ID. Then they jammed the wallet into his pocket.

"He's clean." The beefy man turned Matt again, one hand pinning his chest to the wall. "Somebody in this armpit town stole our data. Did you take it, boy? Or was it Banyon? Did he give it to you? Answer me!"

"No," Matt managed.

"No, what?"

"I don't have it!"

"Where is it?"

Matt couldn't breathe. He was going to die. "I—I don't have it."

With a roar of anger, the man grabbed Matt's shirt, swung him away from the wall, and then hurled him full force into it. His head smashed against the concrete. The sky flashed a brilliant white. His knees buckled, and the shining light faded to blackness.

"I'm starving."

The familiar bulk of a teenager leaning into Cole Strong's refrigerator could be only one person.

"Hey, Billy," Cole said as the kitchen door banged shut behind him. "Josefina made tamales yesterday. Zap yourself a few of those."

"Thanks, Mr. Strong." A celery stick in his mouth, Billy Younger straightened with the plateful of tamales and a jug of milk. He nudged the refrigerator door shut with his heel as he headed for the microwave oven. "You should have seen what they tried to pass off as lunch today at school. A pretzel with cheese sauce! Can you believe that? Matt and I talked about ditching trig and driving over to the Bell, but we didn't do it."

"You guys better not ditch trig." Cole set his Stetson on the counter and reached for an apple from the bowl. He had been plowing since lunch. The spring had been unusually wet for Southeastern New Mexico, and now, in early May, he was behind. "You both have your sights on Harvard, MIT or Stanford. Can't get into those places if you ditch your high school classes."

"Yeah, Mr. Strong, but you know Matt. He's gonna get in wherever he wants to go." Billy took the steaming tamales out of the microwave. "A couple of college bigwigs were at school today wanting to talk to him. Probably trying to convince him to skip his senior year." He shook his head. "So where is Matt, anyhow? We were gonna meet after school and go to Dairy Queen to talk about the mission trip to Guatemala. My dad doesn't want me to go. I waited for Matt, but he never showed."

Cole glanced down the long hall in the direction of his son's bedroom. It was unlike Matt to back out on anything he'd planned with Billy. The two sixteen-year-olds had been best friends since kindergarten, and nothing could separate them—not peer pressure, girls, sports or even their increasingly divergent interests in life.

"Hey, Matt!" Cole barked down the hall. "Billy's here. You better come get a tamale—they're going fast."

Billy paused in wolfing down his snack and gave a wide grin. "Yeah, Matt," he shouted, his mouth full, "you stood me up, dude! What's with that?"

When his son didn't answer, Cole headed toward the bedroom. In the rambling adobe house that sat at the center of his large ranching and farming operation, terra-cotta Saltillo tiles kept the floors cool in summer and warm in winter. He trailed one hand along the undulating whitewashed wall.

"Matthew?" The door was open, and Cole stuck his head in. As always, his eyes took in a jumble of comic books, telescopes, computer equipment, dirty clothes, athletic shoes and empty pizza boxes spread over every square inch of his son's large bedroom. Matt claimed that he alone fueled the orange soda industry. As evidence, empty cans lay scattered around the room. Trails of ants scurried into and out of the open tab holes.

Josefina had flatly refused to continue cleaning Matt's room. She even made a half-serious vow to quit her job if Cole ordered her to set foot in his son's domain. She adored the boy and had worked for Cole since his wife died eight years earlier. But as she liked to say, "I got my limits, Mr. Strong."

Scanning the room to make sure he could distinguish boy

from junk, Cole shook his head. "He's not here, Billy," he called. "You sure you just didn't miss him at school?"

"No, sir, he was not there. I waited fifteen minutes." Billy joined Cole in the doorway. "I figured those college recruiters messed with his head. You know how Matt gets rattled by stuff like that. And he's been so weird lately anyway, with that research paper he's doing. Weirder than usual, I mean."

From anyone but Billy Younger, this statement would have made Cole bristle. He realized his son was different, but he wished others weren't so aware of it. Reading easily by age three, Matthew had also excelled in math and science. But the boy's social skills were worse than poor. Shy, gawky, nervous, Matt didn't help himself by regularly obsessing over one thing or another. Though he was a good-looking kid, with his mother's dark hair and his father's blue eyes, he had never been on a date and could claim only one close friend.

"What's the paper about?" Cole asked.

"You haven't heard him talking about it?"

"I don't think so."

Cole felt uncomfortable not knowing his son's activities, but he had a ranch to run. Taking control after his own father's death, Cole had barely saved the operation from bankruptcy. Now profitable, it had been cited by journalists and lawmakers as one of the finest examples of a family-owned ranch in the state of New Mexico. But the hard work had taken its toll on Cole's relationship with Matt—not that there had ever been much to build on.

Cole had acknowledged long ago that he and the boy had little in common. When they ate together, dinner was a mostly silent affair. When they went on a road trip, Matt hid behind a pair of sunglasses and the headphones of his portable MP3 player. In church these days, Matt sat with Billy and the rest of the youth group. Summers were no better. Matt spent all his free time parked in front of his computer, and unless it related to ranching, such current technology bewildered Cole. There had never been a strong relationship between father and son, and now it was almost nonexistent.

"He's writing about food or something," Billy said, wading into Matt's bedroom—as if walking across old issues of *MacWorld* and *PC Gamer* were perfectly ordinary. He approached the tangle of cords and computer equipment piled on his friend's desk. "It's like world hunger, you know? The term paper is for English, but we get to choose any subject we want. So Matt gets this idea from Miss Pruitt, who's like his guru. She teaches computers. Miss Pruitt is cool, though. She goes on all these mission trips with her church. And she really feeds the hungry."

"I haven't met Miss Pruitt."

"She's intense." He leaned over Matt's computer and pressed a key. The screen switched from a pattern of morphing colored shapes into a field of text. "You don't want to take her classes unless you like to work. She expects a lot out of you, but Matt's into that kind of thing. He's always going in there and talking to her."

"Does he have a crush on her?"

"A crush!" Billy laughed, and Cole realized the term was a little out of date. "No, sir, you don't get a crush on Miss Pruitt. I mean, it's not that she's ugly, okay? She's just…wow, she's intense. That's all I can tell you."

He peered at the screen. "This is it. This is the first draft of Matt's term paper for English. It's about how these huge food companies are controlling the world."

"What?" Cole frowned. "Food companies doing what?"

"Come on, Mr. Strong—you sell all your beef to Agrimax, don't you? And your chile goes to Selena Foods, which is owned by Agrimax. Your alfalfa? Who gets that?"

"Homestead. Agrimax owns it."

"Okay, Mr. S, you're with me now." Billy was scrolling through text as he spoke. "I wonder where Matt's laptop is."

Cole recalled the minicomputer that his son lugged around along with a graphing calculator and several other gadgets whose names and functions were a mystery to Cole. As with all of Matt's equipment, the laptop was in a constant state of being "upgraded"—which, as far as Cole understood, meant he wrote countless checks, and then Matt bought and installed various circuit boards of all shapes and sizes. "Matt always has it with him," Cole told Billy.

"It's probably in his truck," Billy said. "It has a newer version of his term paper on it. Matt was showing me yesterday. He learned all about these food companies on the Internet, you know? And he went to see that guy who ranches near Hope—what's his name? Who retired from Agrimax?"

"Jim Banyon?"

"Yeah, him. And Matt interviewed Miss Pruitt about her work with famine relief."

"What does famine relief have to do with Agrimax?"

"See, what happened is this. Matt's doing his research, and he gets this big idea that his term paper can be more than just a school assignment. It's a plan for Agrimax to help feed the hungry. So he starts crunching all these numbers on his computer, and he's e-mailing everybody—completely obsessed, you know? He can't talk about anything else. Anyway, the other day he tells me he was wrong about Agrimax helping feed the hungry. He says they're only gonna sell their food to the highest bidders, and they don't even want to hear his ideas. Basically they told him to back off."

A prickle ran down Cole's spine. "Back off? What was Matt doing?"

"Writing to them and bugging them—stuff like that." Billy

straightened. "I told him to chill out. Just forget the whole thing. Write the term paper and get the usual A, and then drop it. But you know how Matt is. He gets these——"

"Obsessions. Yes, I know." Cole raked a hand back through his hair, damp from being under his hat all day. "Do you think Matt is in trouble, Billy? Legal trouble?"

"I don't know, Mr. Strong. He said they were threatening him."

"Threatening him! Why didn't he tell me?"

"I told him he should, but Mr. Strong, you're always out plowing, or on the road to Albuquerque to see your girlfriend. Matt doesn't much talk to anyone but me."

"You and Miss Pruitt." Cole left his son's bedroom and took the long hall in five strides, as Billy followed. "Where's the phone? Why does he always move the blasted phone?"

"Use mine. But I already tried calling him, Mr. Strong. He's got his turned off."

Cole took Billy's cell phone and began searching down the list of numbers Josefina had written on the chalkboard near the refrigerator.

"You don't know Matt's cell number?" Billy asked, a tinge of disbelief in his voice. "Here, give me the phone."

Billy punched a couple of buttons—clearly he had his best friend's number programmed into his phone. "Hey, Mattman, where are you? You said we'd go to DQ after Spanish. I'm out at your place, and your dad's semi-freaking about you. So call me, okay?" He pressed another button. "I left him a message."

Cole hurled his apple core into the trash can. He *did* have to plow. The ranch took most of his time. And yes, since meeting Penny Ames, he had spent what spare time he had in Albuquerque. Now that they were engaged, she required a lot of his attention in planning the details of their fall wedding. She had chosen Tahiti for the honeymoon, and she insisted that Cole go ahead and get his passport, their tickets and a new set of luggage.

Having a woman in his life again took time and energy, but Cole held every hope that Penny would bond them into the family he wanted—for himself and for his son. He felt more than a little guilty about the lousy job he had done as a father. But Matt had never been an easy kid to parent—wandering in a strange world of his own making. Cole had tried to understand the boy, but the older Matt got, the more distant their relationship grew. With the purchase of his first computer, Matt retreated almost completely into a realm of information, entertainment, and communication. Cole had left him alone, grateful his son was occupied and apparently happy.

He sighed. "I've got to finish that field. We plant next week."

"Yeah, sure, Mr. Strong." Billy's brown eyes registered disappointment. "Tell Matt to call me tonight if he shows up."

"What do you mean 'if he shows up'? Of course he'll show up." Suspicion gnawed at Cole. "Where do you think he is, Billy? Tell me the truth."

"I don't know. Maybe he had a wreck. He's not that good of a driver, you know."

Cole clenched his teeth at the image of his son trapped inside a mangled truck in an irrigation ditch somewhere. For years, he had tried to get Matt out in the fields to practice his driving. The boy wasn't interested. But the minute he turned sixteen, of course, he insisted on getting his license. Cole had given his son the use of one of the ranch pickups—an old green Chevy with a rusty bed and balding tires.

"The only road he drives is the one between the high school and the house," he told Billy. "And you just got here. You'd have seen the pickup if he'd wrecked it."

"Yeah." Billy thought for a moment. "He might have gone

out to see Mr. Banyon in Hope. The whole Agrimax thing, you know."

Cole grabbed the phone book from the counter and leafed through the Hope directory. Billy handed him the cell phone, and he dialed.

"Banyon," a voice said on the other end.

"Jim, this is Cole Strong—Matt's dad."

"Oh. Uh-huh."

"Listen, Matt didn't come home from school today, and I was wondering if he might be out there visiting with you."

"No." Banyon breathed heavily into the phone. "Uh, no. Tell him not to come out. Not to do that."

Cole paused, concern working its way up his spine. "You okay, Jim?"

"Uh." There was another pause and more labored breathing. "No. Not...not really."

"Is there anything I can do for you? Do you need a doctor?"

Another silence. "Just...uh...tell Matt not to come. Definitely not to—"

The phone went dead. Cole stared at Billy.

"What's with Mr. Banyon?" the boy asked. "Is he sick?"

"I'm not sure." Cole tapped the phone book, weighing the idea of asking the sheriff to look in on the man. Banyon was in his sixties, but he appeared to be in robust health—not the type to have a heart attack or a stroke. Maybe he was struggling with his farm. On retiring from a white-collar job at Agrimax, Jim Banyon had bought land in New Mexico and was trying to grow cotton on it. Many local farmers had gone belly-up in recent years, and Cole had not predicted great success for his new neighbor. The depression and despair these men felt at the loss of their land and livelihood had led some to alcohol and others to the brink of suicide.

Uneasy over his son's whereabouts, Cole found his thoughts

drawn to his work. It was the one thing that had seen him through his wife's illness and death, the growing estrangement from Matt, and the surge of emotion he had felt on meeting Penny.

"Well, I'm gonna head out and look for Matt," Billy said, grabbing the last tamale from the plate. "He might have gone to the library and forgotten what time it was."

"That would be like Matt."

"Yeah." The boy picked up an apple and dropped it into the pocket of his baggy jeans. "If he's not there, I guess I'll check the computer store. He's been eyeing this tiny USB key he wants to buy. Sometimes he just goes over there and stares at it. Or maybe—"

"Wait. A US… B…what?"

"It's a gizmo that stores information." He paused. "Mr. Strong, Matt's the one who can tell you about computer stuff. Don't you ever ask?"

"I'm asking now. I'm asking you."

"A USB key is a piece of computer hardware, but it's cool because it's so tiny you can hang it on a key chain. Like the size of a pack of gum or something." He held his thumb and forefinger a couple of inches apart. "You plug it into your computer's USB port—" Billy paused, regarded the obviously inept adult before him, and then rolled his eyes "—Universal Serial Bus. A USB port uses hubs to let you attach stuff like printers, digital cameras, game pads, joysticks, keyboards, and mice to your computer. And USB keys."

"All right," Cole said, trying to envision these electronic gadgets that were so commonplace to Matt and Billy.

"So you plug the flash drive, or USB key it's called, into your USB port, and then you can load tons of data onto it— two or three gigabytes of information. Matt wants it because he's got so many programs. I think he's going to ask for it for his birthday."

"I see."

"Maybe Matt's over at the school talking to Miss Pruitt about his paper. He does that a lot. And I guess I could drive out to Hope and see what's up with Mr. Banyon. Or you could go."

Cole considered this option. Surely Matt hadn't gone far. He'd be home soon. "I'd better get back to that field," he said. "Call me when you find him, okay, Billy?"

Resentment flickered in the boy's eyes. "Mr. Strong, you don't even know where your phone is."

As Billy stalked out of the kitchen, letting the screen door slam behind him, Cole sucked down a deep breath. He thought of the field, half-plowed. The ranch hands waiting for his return. The cows ready to calve. The seed that needed planting. The afternoon sun dipping toward the horizon.

Grabbing his Stetson, he headed out the door. "Billy, wait up!" he shouted. The boy braked his pickup.

"I'll check the library," Cole said. "You go to the computer store."

Billy grinned. "I'll meet you at Miss Pruitt's classroom in an hour—207 in the main building. She'll be there—she always works late."

Cole climbed into the car he kept for town trips. "An hour," he muttered. "That shoots this day."

"Please feed me." The small boy, his dirty face streaked with tears, held up a bowl made from an empty gourd. "Give me food, sir."

Josiah Karume could not resist laying his hand on the child's tiny head. How old would this boy be, he wondered. Five... or ten? Malnutrition had so withered and stunted his body it was impossible to tell. His dark skin stretched over the bones of his skull, and his parched lips—ringed with flies—were pulled back from his small white teeth. With a head of sparse orange hair and a swollen abdomen, the boy looked like so many other walking skeletons in the long line of refugees that snaked out behind him.

As Josiah scooped up a dollop of cornmeal mush fortified with protein powder and vitamins, someone tapped him on the shoulder. He poured the mush into the boy's bowl before turning to see who wanted him now.

"A phone call for you, Dr. Karume," his aide said.

Josiah handed his ladle to the man and hurried across the dry, sandy ground toward the makeshift Somalian headquarters of the International Federation for Environmental and Economic Development. As chairman-elect of the organization, he was forced to spend most of his time dealing with mountains of red tape in the African bureau of I-FEED in Khartoum, Sudan. But Josiah relished the rare opportunity to visit the camps where his hard work actually paid off.

"Karume here," he said into the phone that sat on a rickety card table inside the office.

"Josiah, this is Vince Grant."

"Vince! How good of you to phone. What news do you have for me today?"

"I'm just returning your call from Tuesday. Wanted you to know I'm still working on transportation. We've got the cornmeal at our Kansas facility, but the logistics are sticky."

Josiah's heartbeat faltered. "The paperwork in Khartoum is complete, Vince. I'm certain I shall have no trouble with the Sudanese authorities."

"I hear you, Josiah, but I just can't move the product without having all my ducks in a row."

"Ducks?" Though he'd obtained his undergraduate degree

in London and had completed his doctoral work in Texas, Josiah still found American idioms confusing.

"I can't do anything until I've got the official papers in my hand," Grant clarified. "You understand the risk I'm taking with my stockholders. If I move this cornmeal, and it gets stuck in Khartoum…"

"Yes, yes. Of course I understand. Let's see, today is Thursday. I leave tomorrow morning for a conference in Paris, but I shall do all in my power to see that you receive official copies of the documents by the first of next week."

"Great. That's terrific. Well, I've got a meeting here in about five minutes. So how's the family?"

"They are doing well, thank you. And yours?" Josiah stared out the window at the blowing sand. As the sun beat down on the refugees, a young woman suddenly let out a wail and staggered out of line. Falling to her knees, she clasped her baby to her breast.

"Well, both girls are off at college, and my son's polo team won—"

"Excuse me, Vince," Josiah cut in. "I have an emergency here. I shall be in touch."

Setting down the receiver, he shook his head. As he left the office, he could hear the other women begin to keen. But they would not leave their places in line to lend comfort to their comrade. They were hungry, after all, and it had become commonplace to mourn the death of yet another child.

"I'm famished." Jill Pruitt bit into the Big Mac her colleague had carried in from the fast-food strip near the high school. "Mmm. Hey, pass the fries."

"Fries? Jill, I'm surprised at you!" Marianne laughed. "I thought you were strictly a broccoli-and-turnip-greens girl."

"I can go for the occasional lard-soaked French fry," Jill

said, giving the math teacher a sly grin. Jill's fellow instructors at Artesia High School knew all about her dedication to famine relief and her interest in computers and technology. But there was a lot they didn't know, and she enjoyed throwing them off-kilter once in a while.

She scanned the row of grades in her ledger, enjoying the symmetry of the numbers. "You realize most of what we're eating in these burgers was grown outside the United States," she spoke up. "Including the beef."

"Not again, Jill. Could we just finish figuring these midterm grades and go home? It's Thursday. My favorite show is on tonight, and I refuse to miss it."

Jill took another fry. "When you grill a burger, the only part that's American is the fat that drips onto the coals. The rest comes from who-knows where."

"Yeah, yeah, yeah. You told me before." Marianne sipped a soda as she punched grades into her calculator. "You won't be eating any burgers when you get to Pakistan, you know. Holy cows, and all that."

"Pakistanis are Muslims, girl. It's Hindus who don't eat beef."

"Whatever. So when do you leave? Aren't you going to take a break after school lets out?"

"A week, and then I'm outta here." Jill thought about her battered old suitcase—already packed with cool cotton dresses and a pair of sandals. Unmarried at thirty-six—a long-term relationship had ended the year before—she had set aside her longing for a husband and children to concentrate on other interests. Seven years ago a short mission trip to Honduras had lit a fire inside her. She had seen poverty, hunger, homelessness. She had felt the suffering of the people.

From then on, her life had been different. Everything became centered on obeying Christ—on putting her faith in action. The coming trip to Pakistan particularly excited her. As a volunteer with the International Federation for Environmental and Economic Development, she would go to the very heart of the country's most desperate area. She had renewed her passport, gotten her vaccinations, and was champing at the bit to get on with the adventure.

"I'm so pumped about this trip, Marianne," she said. "I can hardly wait. Six weeks in Pakistan! I'll be right across the border from Afghanistan. Can you imagine?"

"You couldn't pay me enough to go there. I can't believe you spend your hard-earned salary to volunteer in places like that. I admire your dedication, Jill, but frankly, I'd be too scared."

"I love it. Did I tell you a group of my computer tech kids signed up to take care of my garden the whole time I'm away? They are so good. It's like they're doing their part, you know?"

Jill tucked a blond corkscrew curl behind her ear and frowned at a row of grades. Matthew Strong was falling behind in website design class again. Matt had so much raw talent, but he typically failed to turn in several assignments each term. She had watched this pattern for two years, and she worried that this time he might bottom out altogether.

"Have you ever had Matthew Strong in class?" she asked Marianne.

"I've got him in trig right now. Weird kid. But brilliant. He could do anything he wanted—if he'd bother to turn in his homework."

"Same thing with me. I hope he hangs in till the end of the year."

"Did you hear about his ACT score? Good grief, he could go to MIT today if he wanted. A couple of college recruiters showed up at my classroom this afternoon to talk with him, and he never came back. So there goes another homework assignment."

"Matt's only a sophomore, for goodness' sake." Jill took another bite of her burger. "These colleges need to back off and let him be a normal teenager."

"Matthew Strong will never be a normal teenager."

"If his father paid more attention to him, he might learn some social skills. His mom died of cancer, you know. The dad is hardly ever around."

"Lots of kids have absentee parents, but they don't turn out like Matt. What about that tie he wears all the time?"

Jill tucked the ringlet behind her ear for the hundredth time that hour. Even as she reached for one last fry, the curl popped back out and bounced around her chin. "It's just Matt's style, I guess."

"Style? That tie is gross beyond belief." Marianne snapped her grade book shut. "Done! I'm taking off. You'll be okay here, I guess."

"No problem. I'm almost through."

As Marianne grabbed her purse, she paused near Jill's chair and leaned down. "Uh-oh. Speak of the devil," she murmured. "I hope this is for you, Miss Pruitt, because I'm gone."

Jill swung around to see a tall, broad-shouldered man step into the classroom. His chambray shirt and faded denim jeans complemented dusty cowboy boots and an old leather belt. He took off his hat to reveal a thatch of short, spiky, brown hair, and he was looking at her with a pair of blue eyes that could belong to only one man.

"Matthew Strong's father." She stood and thrust out her hand. "Pleased to meet you."

"Cole Strong." His grip was firm, his palm callused. A working man.

"I'm Jill Pruitt, computer ed. And that was Marianne

Weston, Matt's trig teacher. You'd better run if you want to catch her."

"You'll do," he said. The blue eyes bored into her. "I'm looking for my boy. Seen him today?"

"He was in my class this morning. Why?"

"He didn't come home after school. Billy Younger tells me Matt likes to stay late and talk to you."

Jill sensed a thread of suspicion in the man's voice. "He drops by between classes or at lunch. He's been working on a term paper—"

"Food, yeah, I know. Billy says you fired him up on it."

"I mentioned my work with hunger relief. Matt was interested, so we discussed it. I gave him some names and addresses to use as sources. Have you checked with Jim Banyon out at Hope? He—"

"Matt's not there." Cole turned his hat in his hands. "Billy says he got crossways with some Agrimax honchos. He was trying to push your ideas on them, and they warned him to back off."

"*My* ideas?"

"My son doesn't know anything about famine relief, Miss Pruitt."

"Oh yes he does, Mr. Strong." She returned his appraising gaze. "He uncovered a wealth of information, and he's very excited about it."

"Obsessed, you mean."

She bristled. "I wouldn't call it that."

"You would if you knew Matt."

"Excuse me, sir, but I do know your son. I know him very well."

"Then where is he?"

She paused to collect herself. In fifteen years as a teacher, she had faced a lot of angry parents. Frustration, concern for a child's GPA, confusion about assignments—all these things drove them to confrontation at the school. Jill had learned to back off, take it slow and insist on civil treatment. But the dominating stance of this man, the hostility in his voice, and the insinuations he had tossed out were getting on her nerves. If he were a more involved parent, she would sympathize with his concern. But she knew for a fact that Cole Strong had shown little interest in his son's life at school before now.

"I'm not sure where Matt is, Mr. Strong," she told him. "Now if you'll excuse me, I'm averaging midterm grades."

"Did he go to all his classes today?" He took a step toward her.

"I'm sorry, but I don't have access to that infor—" Jill caught her breath. "Wait a minute. Two men…college recruiters, I think…asked to meet him during his trigonometry class. Marianne—Mrs. Weston—told me he never came back."

"Who were these guys? Which university?"

"I have no idea."

"Well, look it up." He gestured at her laptop. "You're the computer wizard. Open the file or whatever, and find out who got permission to take my son out of class."

Despite her irritation with Matt's father, she felt a stab of concern about the boy. "I don't have code access to office documents, Mr. Strong."

"Then break the code. Isn't that what you've been teaching my son to do?"

"Sir, I do not appreciate your tone. And I can assure you—"

"Look, lady." He stuffed his hat onto his head. "My son is missing. Do you get that? Matt did not come home from school, and he's not there now. Billy Younger and I have combed this town and haven't found hide nor hair of the boy. Now you're telling me two strangers showed up at school and took my son off someplace—and he never came back? And I'm supposed to be nice and polite about it?"

Jill swallowed. "I'll call Mrs. Weston at home. Maybe she can tell us who the men were."

Chapter Two

Vince Grant gazed at the tray of glazed crullers on the gleaming mahogany desk in his corner office. His new secretary provided him with sweet snacks each afternoon at four, and he wondered if she was trying to give him a heart attack. He didn't like Jennifer, and she didn't like him. But his vision and her efficiency meshed well, and the situation was a lot tidier than it had been with Dawn.

Vince's wife had known about Dawn and the others before her, but this time she refused to tolerate her husband's straying. Maybe it was because their children were growing up and moving on—the two girls away at college, their son busy with polo and soccer. Or maybe it was menopause. Cheryl Grant had grown edgy, moody. He would have to be more discreet.

Tapping his blunt-tipped fingers together, Vince tried to resist the crullers. Things weren't going well on this Thursday afternoon, and food always seemed to calm him. But his tailor—who had used the same patterns for Vince's $4,000 wool suits since he had taken the helm of Chicago-based Agrimax

thirteen years before—had been obliged to take new mea-
surements on his last fitting. Vince didn't like that. At fifty-
eight, he still had a lot of good years left, and he intended to
enjoy every benefit of his position. But he had to look the
part—trim, neatly groomed, well suited and in perfect health.

Vince Grant had great plans for Agrimax. His blueprint—
carefully spelled out in documents to which only he and his
top executives had computer access—was both his obsession
and his pride. Vince had been consumed by the plan for years.
At last, its many components were clicking into place.

In twelve days, the corporation would absorb its two ri-
vals, Megafarm and Progrow. The new conglomerate, with
Vince as its CEO, would essentially control the world food
market—at which time he could begin putting into place the
seed, fertilizer, pesticide and genetic technologies that Agrimax scientists had been developing in secret. The merger and
resulting takeover of worldwide food production would assure
Vince a place in history and make him a billionaire.

The plan had involved skillful diplomacy, hardball board-
room politics, careful public relations and, finally, subterfuge.
His executive board wasn't completely aware of the complex
ramifications of its CEO's plan, though all would benefit im-
measurably. Once in place, the merger would allow Agrimax
to overcome all barriers to power and profitability.

But Agrimax's executive board had found another reason to
be restless. They were unhappy over negative publicity about
the company's genetically modified seed. At the last board
meeting Vince had promised to squelch the problem. He had
his public relations people initiate high-profile food donations
to hunger-relief organizations chosen for their news value. The
newspapers cooperated admirably. Agrimax's media spokes-
woman had appeared on two national morning television pro-

grams and a prime-time talk show. Vince felt confident the company's image concerns were under control.

Until now.

In the past month, someone who identified himself as a high school sophomore had begun e-mailing Agrimax's top executives. Annoyed at first, the executives became nervous when the tone of the e-mails switched from that of an idealist who wanted to end world hunger to the voice of someone who knew the company intimately.

Security had pinpointed the source of the e-mails. They came from a small town in New Mexico near the ranch to which one of Agrimax's leading scientists, Jim Banyon, had just retired. Banyon had been a loyal team player, moving through the ranks until he was awarded a vice president's position. Vince had liked the man, and his work for Agrimax was groundbreaking. The two became personal friends. Their wives even socialized at the country club until Banyon's divorce put his ex out of circulation.

In the past couple of years, the scientist had joined some sort of evangelistic religious group. He grew reclusive, losing interest in golf and absenting himself from the regular happy-hour gathering at the club. Vince hadn't given it too much thought. Last month, Banyon had taken early retirement, and his position had not yet been filled. A week ago, before the e-mails were traced, Banyon returned briefly to Agrimax headquarters in Chicago to clear a few things from his office.

Though the suspicious messages had come from the account of one "Matthew Strong," Agrimax security believed Banyon was the actual source. Vince ordered an investigation into information transferred recently to his former colleague's computer. His worst fears were realized when it was discovered that Vince's own top secret blueprint had been copied from the mainframe.

When his secretary's voice came over the intercom with a call from the head of security, Vince was quick to grab the phone.

"Harwood, what do you have for me?"

"The kid is no problem."

"There really is a kid?"

"Matthew Strong."

"You found him? Talked to him?"

"We took care of him."

"So it's Banyon?"

"There's no question. The two know each other. Banyon's been feeding the boy the data he used in his e-mails to our executives."

"What does the boy have?"

"He's clean. We profiled him before we talked to him. He's a nerd, a Sunday-school-type kid, spends all his time at his computer. Knocked the top off the ACT, but no social life. A wide-eyed innocent—barely sixteen. He's writing a research paper. That's how he got onto us—he interviewed Banyon."

"That's the connection, then."

"Banyon told him a few things, but the kid isn't the source of our trouble. Banyon's got the stolen data on a CD at his house. I'd bet my job on it."

"A CD can't hold that much information, Harwood. Where's Technology? I want them in on this."

"I talked to Technology this afternoon."

"Don't *talk* to them. Get them on the scene."

"Yes, sir." Mack Harwood paused a moment. "I'd rather not wait for Technology to arrive, Mr. Grant. This place is the backside of nowhere. I think we need to look up Banyon today."

"Just get the data, Harwood. Do whatever you have to do."

Vince set down the receiver. He wished he hadn't been

forced to move his former secretary to Agrimax's Wichita branch. Dawn had been good for him. Kept him feeling alive, vital, confident. He reached over and took a cruller from the silver tray.

Seated in his pickup under a cottonwood tree, Matt rummaged in the glove compartment for something to eat. From the debris of torn road maps, ballpoint pens, a pocketknife and the vehicle owner's manual, he rooted out an old Snickers bar and peeled back the wrapper. The candy had gone pale and crumbly, but he wolfed it down anyway. He knew he had to function. Had to keep going. Had to think.

Not fifty feet away, the lights were on in Jim Banyon's house. But who was inside? Hands shaking, Matt gripped the old black steering wheel as he swallowed the last of the chocolate.

Okay, think, think. Think, Mattman!

The two men who had taken him out of trig class said they were college recruiters. Princeton. They wanted to treat him to ice cream. Talk about their computer science program.

So he had gotten into their car.

"Stupid!" Matt slammed his hand on the steering column. *Never get into a stranger's car.* His mom had taught him that. Josefina had echoed it a thousand times. He knew better!

The men had driven him out to the sports complex on the edge of Artesia. That's when they started asking him about Agrimax. About his term paper. About his e-mails to the company. They wanted to know where he got his information.

"Why did I tell them?" he ground out, dropping his forehead onto the steering wheel. "Dumb! I am such an idiot!"

By that time, he had figured out enough to get scared.

They had slammed his head into the concrete wall, and he had passed out. A moment later he came to, crumpled on the ground, aware of blood trickling down the back of his neck. The Agrimax men leaned against their car, talking in low voices.

That's when Matt bolted.

They ran after him. Shouting. Threatening to call the police, send him to prison, put him away forever. He wriggled under the park's barbed-wire fence. Ran down the sidewalk and cut across the yards of several houses. Rounded a corner of the video store. Dashed down an alley. Found a culvert and hid. An hour. Two hours.

Sweating, smelling like dank water, his head throbbing, he ran all the way to the high school just as the last class was letting out. He hid in a clump of bushes and scanned the area for the Agrimax men or their car. Nothing. In the distance near the main door, he saw Billy waiting for him. Checking out the girls. Calling greetings to classmates. Matt wanted to go to him, tell him everything. But what if the two men were watching? Then they would go after Billy, too.

Matt made a dash for his pickup. He sped from the school parking lot, headed out of town. Drove to nearby Hope. Found a thicket of trees near Jim Banyon's house. Cottonwoods, piñons, salt cedar. Not much cover, but he pulled his pickup as far into their midst as he could.

It was beginning to grow dark, so he checked his cell phone. A message from Billy that Matt's dad was worrying about him, searching for him.

That didn't sound right. His dad never cared where he was, did he? Were the Agrimax men holding Billy? Had they made him leave that message?

Shaken, Matt decided to place a call. He pressed the button and listened to the rings on the other end. When Billy answered, Matt barely managed to squawk his own name.

"Mattman, is that you?" Billy's voice had a calming effect.

Yeah, this was Billy. Life was normal somewhere out there. But not here…not in this pickup in the middle of a grove just outside Mr. Banyon's house.

"Listen, Billy," Matt breathed. "I got your phone message, okay? But don't keep looking for me."

"Where have you been, dude? I waited for you after class."

Matt remembered their plan to go to Dairy Queen together. Like always. They each would have ordered an M&M's Blizzard, talked about their classes, planned their weekend. But not now.

"Something bad's going on," Matt said. "Really bad."

"What? You're freaking me out. Where are you?"

"I'm going away. Don't look for me anymore." Realizing he was starting to cry again, which was totally uncool, Matt hung up.

He stared through his tears at Mr. Banyon's house. Nearly paralyzed with panic, he wadded up the Snickers wrapper and stuffed it into the ashtray. What should he do? What was right—and wrong? None of this was supposed to happen! He had just wanted to help feed the hungry.

He needed to talk to Mr. Banyon. Jim Banyon made sense when he explained ethics, when he discussed the difference that Christians could make in the business world. He sounded just like Miss Pruitt when he talked about Christ's command that Christians meet people's needs—no matter what the cost. He understood Agrimax better than Matt ever could. Mr. Banyon would know what to do.

But what if the men were inside the house…threatening him and waiting for Matt? He knew what he ought to do. Leave. Disappear. Get out of town for a while. Isn't that what fugitives did in the movies? But this wasn't a movie. This was no computer game, where he could press a button and start all over. It was real.

He wished he could call Billy again. Billy always had advice—even if it wasn't necessarily right. Matt stared at his phone. Then he threw it out the window into a tangle of tall grass. No phone. No contact. He looked at the laptop lying beside him on the front seat. He was afraid Agrimax had hacked his user account and could read his e-mails and personal information. He should toss that out, too.

No. He could use it to stay in touch somehow. But what if they traced him? Now he was getting paranoid. Matt knew more about computers than those two men did. They weren't Princeton techies, after all. They were Agrimax goons.

All the same, Matt knew if he stayed around, his dad and Billy, and maybe even Miss Pruitt, would get involved. The way the Agrimax men had slammed him against the wall today, they wouldn't hesitate to hurt people if that's what it took to get their data back. Anyone connected to Matt would be in danger, because he had helped Mr. Banyon.

The Agrimax men would soon find out Matt was the one who had told Mr. Banyon that he could copy the incriminating Agrimax information onto a USB key. They would learn that Matt had used his own credit card—which his father had said was just for emergencies—to buy the key. They would discover that Mr. Banyon was going to give the USB key and all its terrible secrets to the chairman-elect of I-FEED, a man named Josiah Karume, who would turn everything over to the right people in government and the media. They would know that, in the name of God, Mr. Banyon was going to ruin them. And that Matthew Strong was helping him do it.

But where could Matt go if he ran? Granny Strong lived in Amarillo. She would take him in. He could drive to Hobbs and cross the state line into Texas. Pick up a map somewhere so he could find the right roads to Lubbock and then Amarillo. Spend what cash he had on gas and food.

He fought the panic that felt like a noose tightening around his neck. *Dear God, please help me! I don't know what to do. I need to talk to somebody. I need help. But You're all I have.*

He forced himself to reason. If God was all he had, wasn't that enough? *God is more than sufficient...a very present help in time of trouble...wonderful Counselor...*

"Okay," Matt breathed out. "Holy Spirit, give me wisdom. And courage, too. Please be my counselor. Help me not to blow this worse than I already have. Amen."

When he lifted his head, he felt calmer. He wasn't in such bad shape after all, he realized. He had about fifty dollars, a laptop, a vehicle. He had youth, energy and brains—more than enough to get him out of this hot water. He even had the credit card his father had given him. What more did he need? Maybe the Snickers had just given him a sugar high, but he was feeling better about the situation. He turned his attention to Jim Banyon's house.

The thing to do was go inside and just talk things through with Mr. Banyon. Maybe everything was really all right. Maybe Mr. Banyon had spoken with the Agrimax men, calmed them down, given them the key, and assured them Matt hadn't done anything wrong. Maybe they would go away, and everything would be normal again. He and Billy would rent a movie and eat four bags of microwave popcorn and drink a twelve-pack of orange soda.

Drawing a fortifying breath deep into his lungs, Matt eased open the door of his pickup. At the squeak, his palms went damp.

It's okay, he told himself. *It's nothing. Be calm, Mattman.*

He edged out of the cab and crept through the cover of trees. The lights were still on in the house. No silhouettes moving around inside. Darkness was falling fast.

Pausing at the edge of the grove, Matt crouched and scanned

the area. There was no way to approach the house without showing himself. He dashed to the front door. It was ajar. He wedged himself against the frame and knocked quickly, quietly. He looked over his shoulder. Was someone moving out beyond the fence?

Gulping down the acid that bubbled up from his stomach, Matt pushed the door open and slipped inside.

"Mr. Banyon?" His voice came out soft and wimpy. Way too high. He cleared his throat and tried again. "Mr. Banyon, it's me, Matt Strong."

Nothing.

His own rapid breaths sounding like a locomotive engine, he moved forward. Down the narrow foyer. His rubber soles made a tump-tump sound on the tile.

Living-room light spilled into the hallway, and he stepped across it onto beige berber carpet. Someone was sleeping on the couch that faced the bank of windows opposite the foyer. An arm lay across the top of the sofa. Mr. Banyon's arm. Matt recognized the turquoise-inlaid silver watchband. Whew. How bad could it be if the rancher was napping? That was normal after a long day's work. His dad was always zonked out on the recliner in the evenings.

"Hey, Mr. Banyon, sir?" Matt said, moving around the couch. "Sorry to wake you up, but I—"

A monster stared back at him. Swollen eyeballs, blackened teeth, a crimson halo. Red stain on the sofa pillow. Bloodstain. Spatters across the back of the couch.

The body was Mr. Banyon's—plaid work shirt, silver belt buckle, jeans, those old boots. But the face. Not the face.

Matt fought to keep breathing. Mr. Banyon's other arm draped down to the floor. Six inches away lay a pistol. Matt's eyes shot back to the face. The blackened teeth and burn marks on the lips...they could only mean...

No. Matt's mouth formed the word, but no sound came out. "No," he said again. "No, God, don't let this be! Don't let this be!"

He fell to one knee, grabbed Mr. Banyon's shirt, and shook him. "Don't do this! Not this!"

The monstrous head rolled, sliding down the pillow toward the shoulder.

Matt jumped backward, stumbling into the coffee table. He reached behind him to steady the large Hopi pot that always sat there. But it was gone—already lying on the carpet, broken into three pieces. Not wanting to look at Mr. Banyon again—and wanting to look just to be sure he hadn't dreamed it—Matt forced himself to scan the room. Books that once lined pine shelves now lay scattered across the floor. A kachina doll's glass case had been shattered. A curtain hung half-torn from its rod.

And Mr. Banyon's desk near the fireplace…the drawers were out, their contents flung around the room…

The Agrimax men had been here. They came looking for it. For the USB key. They must have threatened Mr. Banyon the way they had threatened Matt. And when they left, taking the key and all its forbidden secrets, he had known he would spend the rest of his life in prison. So he had stretched out on the couch and put the pistol in his mouth and…and…

"It's my fault!" Matt knotted his fingers in his hair, squeezed, and pulled. He felt like his own brain was going to come bursting out of his skull. "I did this! Me! It's all because of me!"

He looked back at Mr. Banyon, and his eyes caught the flash of a headlight through the front window. Someone driving along the fence. Approaching the house. The Agrimax men!

Matt pounced on the pistol lying on the floor. He would shoot them. Shoot them both!

No, wait. He couldn't do that. He had never fired a gun in his life. Hated hunting. Hated violence. Billy had teased him— *Come on, Mattman, at least a jackrabbit!* No, Matt wouldn't do it.

Dropping the gun, he couldn't keep his eyes from falling again on the monster. "I'm sorry!" he mouthed, tears wetting his lips. "I didn't mean to do this!"

The crunch of gravel on the drive...then a car door slammed. Matt jerked, and his focus fell on a bulge in the pocket of Mr. Banyon's plaid shirt. It was small, oblong, the size of a cigarette lighter. Only Mr. Banyon didn't smoke.

As someone rang the doorbell, Matt slid two fingers into the pocket. Before he even touched it, he knew what he had found. The key fit neatly in his palm. He dropped it into the front pocket of his jeans and took off for the kitchen.

"Banyon? You in there?"

Matt could hear the voice echoing down the foyer. His foot landed on a small rug, and he skidded halfway across the kitchen floor. The back door stood ajar. Pushing open the screen, he burst through—remembering just in time to grab it so it wouldn't slam shut behind him. Then he started toward the side of the house.

Down on all fours, he peered around the corner. The car parked out front didn't belong to the Agrimax men. It was the sheriff. How had Sheriff Holtmeyer known to check on Mr. Banyon?

Now Matt could see two more vehicles moving up the rutted dirt road, their headlights bouncing. Grateful for darkness, he raced across the yard and dived into the stand of cottonwood trees.

Breathing hard, he yanked open the door to his pickup and climbed in. He turned the key in the ignition, reached for the shift lever, and paused. Leaving the truck idling, he leaned back in the seat and tried to collect his thoughts. If the Agrimax men hadn't found the USB key, then maybe Mr. Banyon hadn't killed himself. Maybe they had been looking for the device and had murdered him in the process. This was bad. Really bad.

Should Matt go to the sheriff, turn himself in, tell him the whole story, hand over the key? The information would go straight back to Agrimax, and that would be the end of everything Mr. Banyon had been trying to do. Had *died* trying to do.

Think, Mattman. Think, think. He wasn't any good at thinking on his feet. Billy said he had no common sense, no street smarts. Give Mattman a logarithm. Give him calculus. Give him a computer to program. Give him Latin grammar or astronomy. He could puzzle through that stuff easily. But not this.

"Dear God, what am I supposed to do now?" he murmured, gripping the steering wheel. This had all been for God to begin with, hadn't it? Feeding the hungry. Convincing Agrimax to turn over some of their excess. Finding a way to really do something for Christ—the way Miss Pruitt did.

But Mr. Banyon was dead now. Everything was over, wasn't it? Matt thought of I-FEED, the organization Miss Pruitt worked with. Mr. Banyon had never heard of it until Matt told him about his teacher's work in famine-stricken lands. Jim Banyon had spent his career in research and technology development for Agrimax. He had climbed the corporate ladder until he was rewarded with a vice presidency—and had lost his marriage and family in the process. But then he found a new life in Christ. Sickened at what he had been involved in through the years, Mr. Banyon told Matt, he was filled with remorse and anger. Finally, he had taken early retirement and moved to New Mexico to start over.

Mr. Banyon said until Matt came along, he hadn't thought

anything could be done to change the corporation's practices. Not until the high school sophomore had knocked on his door to interview him for a term paper. Matt talked to Mr. Banyon about I-FEED. About the starving children. About his passion to feed the hungry. And somewhere in there, he mentioned the tiny USB flash drive he had his eye on at the computer store. Just plug it in and copy anything you want.

Anything? Mr. Banyon had gotten excited then. He knew the password system at Agrimax. He could get into the company's mainframe, couldn't he? He could download technologies still under development, products waiting to be patented, top secret plans that threatened the world's ecology and would keep the poor on the brink of starvation. He could copy the details of Vince Grant's elaborate monopoly scheme, his design for control of the world's food supply and the ensuing global domination. He could blow the whistle on all the corruption—and in doing so, bring attention to the plight of the hungry. Mr. Banyon knew he could make it all happen, he had acknowledged to Matt. He could do this. He would do this for righteousness' sake.

Matt had bought the flash drive and showed him how to use it. Then Mr. Banyon made one last visit to Agrimax, copied the data onto the USB key, and began preparing to deliver it anonymously to Josiah Karume at I-FEED. Once leaked to the media, the information would devastate Agrimax. Mr. Banyon said the company would be forced to its knees by a public outcry. Legal and media pressure would force Agrimax to change its policies and practices. The World Health Organization would get involved, and so would every environmental group worth its salt. Public attention would fall on the corrupt practices of the World Trade Organization and the food companies that controlled global food supplies. Vince Grant's plan to monopolize this system would be exposed and derailed. All this…because of the USB key that now lay in Matthew Strong's pocket.

Matt covered the small shape with his palm. If Jim Banyon had lost his life in trying to do this good work, could Matt do any less than risk his life to finish it? People were hungry. Children were starving. Babies were dying. For months Matt had been able to think of little else.

Now the answer lay in his grasp. What would he do with it? As the two cars pulled to a stop in the driveway, Matt recognized his father's tall profile, his hat, his broad shoulders. Was that Miss Pruitt? How did she get into this? And Billy?

Disbelief twisted through Matt's chest. Had his father really come looking for him? They hardly ever spoke these days. He wasn't sure his dad even remembered he had a son. But there was Cole Strong, striding up to the door of Jim Banyon's ranch house.

Had he decided to suddenly play the concerned parent? Matt frowned. It was a little late now. His son was grown—sixteen—and more than old enough to make his own decisions about his life. Matt had a job to do. As the others went into the house, he shifted the truck into reverse and eased out of the thicket. The gas tank was full, and he could drive all night.

"Hold it, Cole!" Sheriff Holtmeyer came around the corner of the living room in the foyer. "Don't take another step, none of you. I've got a body here."

Cole stiffened. "Is it—"

"It's not your boy. It's the old man—Banyon."

"So where's my son?" Cole started to edge past the sheriff, but Holtmeyer stopped him.

"This is a secured area, Cole. You can't go barging in on it. I've got to get my people out here."

"My boy may be in this house, and I intend—"

"Let us just look around for Matt, Sheriff," Billy cut in. "We won't touch anything."

"I'm sorry, folks. These things have to be done the right way."

"Sheriff, are you sure Mr. Banyon is dead?" Jill Pruitt asked.

"He's dead all right. Suicide, I reckon." The lawman shuddered. "You never get used to this kind of thing."

Cole stared past him at the entrance to the living room. Suicide? Had problems with the farm been that bad for Jim Banyon? And what did Matt have to do with this—if anything? Did he know something about Banyon that had led him to call Billy in a state of panic?

"Cole, you've got to step back outside," Holtmeyer said, hands at his belt. "I don't think your boy's anywhere around here. This looks pretty cut-and-dried to me."

"Come on outside with us, Mr. Strong," Miss Pruitt said, laying a hand on Cole's arm. Her fingers were soft, startlingly warm against his skin. "Surely there's something we can do to find Matt."

Cole stared blankly at the teacher as she followed Billy out into the night. Vibrant with energy that radiated from her wild blond hair and compact figure, the young woman moved as though on a mission. His own body felt stiff, but his brain spun with questions. Where was Matt? Did he know about Banyon's suicide? Who were the two men who took Matt out of class? What had they wanted with him? Did their conversation have anything to do with the suicide? Or had Banyon been just another desperate farmer watching his life savings slip away?

"Mr. Strong?" Corkscrew curls framing her green eyes, Miss Pruitt stuck her head back through the door. "I've had an idea. Why don't you come on out, and I'll tell you what I'm thinking?"

Like a tin soldier, Cole forced his legs down the foyer and out the front door. A dead man lay behind him in that house. Was Matt also in there somewhere? Was he dead, too? Images of his wife swirled upward like dry leaves caught in a dust devil. How ill Anna had looked, lying in bed day after day as the cancer that had begun in her ovaries swept through her body, invading blood and organs and bone. Clouds of dark, curly hair fell out in clumps, but the chemotherapy did no good. How desperately Anna had wanted to live. Not only for Cole, but for Matt. Such a small boy, and so in need of a mother. Cole's greatest fear rose up inside him… Matt…he couldn't lose the boy….

"Mr. Strong, drive me to your house," Jill Pruitt was saying, her hand on his arm again. Touching him, drawing him back. "I'll take a look at Matt's computer. Try to see what he's downloaded recently. Go back over his e-mails, websites he's visited."

"Hey, Miss Pruitt," Billy said, "I just thought of something. Matt probably has his laptop with him. He used to take it to class so he could write programs when he got bored."

"It wasn't in his room this afternoon," Cole said, the realization snapping him back to attention. "Remember, Billy? You mentioned that it had the most recent copy of his term paper."

"Yeah, that's right!" The boy's face broke into the first grin Cole had seen in hours. "If Matt's got his laptop, we can e-mail him!"

"Okay, I'll take you to the house, Miss Pruitt. Billy, you can go on home, and I'll call you if—"

"No way, Mr. Strong! I'm not going home until we find the Mattman. I'm with you guys."

"Billy, there's no point. Go do your homework."

"You think you can just run me off, Mr. Strong?" Billy stepped closer, his chest swelling with bluster. "I know more about Matt than you or Miss Pruitt. I know what he's think-ing, where he likes to go, what he wants to do. And I know what he believes in, too. His mind works weird, and nobody can figure him out any better than me."

"Yes, but, Billy, you're a boy. You don't need to get in-volved in this. I'm not happy you even know about this sui-cide thing—"

"I'm sixteen, Mr. Strong! I'm not a kid. I can drive, and I have a job lined up for this summer. I've already taken the ACT twice, and—"

"Billy, do you know Matt's e-mail password?" Jill Pruitt's hand rested on the boy's arm now.

"Yeah, but I'm not telling." He glared at Cole.

"I do think Billy could help us. He's been Matt's rudder since childhood."

Cole looked from one to the other. He nodded. "All right."

The teacher gave orders. "Call your folks and let them know where you'll be, Billy. We'll see you at Matt's house."

"Okay, Miss Pruitt." Billy gave Cole a last resentful glance. "I'll be there."

As Billy stalked away, Cole opened the passenger-side door for the teacher. She climbed in and immediately took a cell phone from the bag of school papers and books she had brought along. As he started the car, she began to talk. Even her voice was peppy, as though perpetually on the verge of a laugh.

"Marianne, hey, it's me! I'm out with Mr. Strong—Matt's dad." She paused. "Not *out* with him. We're looking for Matt. You know those two recruiters who showed up at your class today to talk to him? Did they take him somewhere?"

She covered the phone and whispered across the front seat. "Marianne says they had gotten a pass at the office, and she assumed they were going to sign him out for an hour or so and take him somewhere to talk."

As Cole drove back down the bumpy road, he passed a couple of deputies' vehicles and the county coroner's car, all heading toward the Banyon place. His fears for Matt were growing by leaps and bounds. Where would the boy go? Matt always came home from school, got to his homework immediately, and then stared at his computer or watched TV. Once in a blue moon, he mowed the grass or took a fishing pole down to the reservoir. Most afternoons, Billy dropped by and ate half the contents of the refrigerator while hanging out with his best friend.

"Okay, call the school secretary, would you?" Miss Pruitt said into the phone. "See if she'll run over to the admin building and get those names off the log for us. I know it's a pain, but we're really concerned." She paused, then glanced at Cole. "What...? No way. Please, Marianne. Give it a rest. Bye."

"Give what a rest?" Cole asked.

"She thinks I should date."

It took a moment for the meaning of her words to penetrate the fog of concern for his son. "Date *me?* Tell her I'm getting married in November. Which reminds me—can I use your phone? Is it all right if I call Albuquerque? I'll keep it short."

"Sure."

As he drove, he punched out Penny's number. How odd that he knew his fiancée's phone number but not his son's. Disturbed, he listened as it rang.

"Hi, it's Penny," she said brightly.

"This is Cole."

"Cole! Hi, sweetie. I was just thinking about you. What's going on at the Ponderosa?"

He grimaced at Penny's name for his ranch. "Listen, this is about Matt. He didn't come home from school today."

"You're kidding! Wow—I never knew he had a social life." She giggled. "So who's the lucky girl that snagged him?"

Unnerved at the lightness of her voice, Cole wondered for the thousandth time whether he was doing the right thing in planning a future with Penny. A successful big-city attorney, she nevertheless seemed to enjoy his ranch and the quiet lifestyle there. Cole had long missed the companionship of being married, and there was no question that Penny was pretty and intelligent. But most of all, he had hoped a wife would help bridge the ever-widening gap between himself and his son before he lost touch with the boy completely.

"It's not a girlfriend," he told her. "We don't know where Matt is. See, he was working on a term paper, and he'd gotten friendly with a rancher out here at Hope."

"Hey, hang on a sec, can you? My microwave just dinged!"

He let out a breath as the phone fell silent.

"She thinks Matt has a girlfriend?" Miss Pruitt asked. "How well does she know him?"

"Pretty well. She's been down here a few times." He knew he sounded defensive, but his own doubts were nagging him.

"I'm back! Popcorn," Penny said. "So what were you saying? Was this one of Matt's obsessive things? This term paper?"

"I guess you could call it that. Anyway, we went out to the rancher's house, and the sheriff was there. Looks like he killed himself."

"Killed himself? Was he a friend of yours? What does this have to do with Matt?"

"We're not sure. I knew the fellow, but—"

"Who's *we?*"

"His computer teacher is with me...uh, Miss Pruitt."

"Jill," she whispered.

"I'm sure Matt's fine, Cole," Penny said. "He's probably at home waiting for you."

"No, Josefina would have called. We gave her the cell number."

"Cole, have you called the police? This is what they do. If you haven't, go home and call them."

"I'm going home." He pulled off the main road into the drive that led to his house. "Miss Pruitt is planning to check Matt's computer. I'll call you when we find him."

"Okay. Call tonight, honey. I'm so worried."

"Penny, there's one more thing." He steered the car up to the front of the house and parked. "If we don't find Matt in a few hours, I'm going looking for him."

"Looking where?"

"If he's scared enough, he may try to drive to my mom's house in Amarillo."

"Cole, don't do this! You need to stay put and let the police find him. You need to be at your house when he comes back—not halfway to Texas. Please, listen to me. You have a ranch to run, and Matt is probably fine. I'm sure he's just off on one of his tangents."

"Yeah, maybe." Cole climbed out of the car. "I'll call you later."

Josefina was running out of the house and across the front porch. She waved a cell phone in one hand. "Oh, Mr. Strong! Did you find him?" Josefina was crying. "You didn't call me! Did you find my baby boy? *Ai, mi bebe!*"

"We haven't found him." Cole took her shoulders. "Have you searched the whole house?"

"Everyplace, Mr. Strong. He's not here. I think he's in a wreck. You should have got him new tires, Mr. Strong. I told you that. He's had a blowout, and he doesn't even have an air bag!"

"Calm down, Josefina. I want you to stop and think of all the places where Matt might—"

The phone in her hand rang, cutting off his words.

Cole grabbed it and pressed the button. "Cole Strong."

"Hey, Cole, this is Sheriff Holtmeyer," the voice said. "Listen, we may have a lead on your boy. My deputy was searching the grounds, and he found a cell phone with Matt's name engraved on it in a stand of cottonwoods near the house. It looks like there was a struggle in the living room. And the blood spatters on the couch—let's just say I'm a little concerned about our suicide theory. We've got tire marks, and we'll be dusting the gun for fingerprints. Cole...you need to let me know if Matt turns up at your place. We'd sure like to ask him some questions."

Chapter Three

Vince Grant swirled the last of his martini and studied the olive that remained in the bottom of his glass. Cheryl had gone to bed hours ago, her Valium performing admirably, as usual.

Vince didn't mind the silence. His wife's presence keyed him up—the thousand questions she threw at him the moment he walked in the door each evening. Can I buy this piece of furniture? Are you planning to go to that gala? What do you think of my dress, my hair, my eyes, my jewelry, my latest chemical peel? Frankly, he didn't know the answers to any of her questions, and he didn't care. But they'd been married forever, it seemed, and so he tried.

He'd been a good husband, all in all. Cheryl had everything she could want or need. Their kids had been educated in the best private schools Chicago had to offer. The eight-thousand-square-foot house sprawled over some of the most exclusive real estate in the city. An indoor-outdoor swimming pool, membership at three country clubs, a regular pew in a dignified church, seven cars, a chauffeur—it was nothing to sniff at. Maybe Vince hadn't always been faithful to Cheryl, but he'd done his job as a provider. Better than most, he reasoned.

He didn't like the idea of anything rocking his boat. Had never tolerated trouble of the sort that dogged him now. Oh, through the years there had been the occasional stirring of the waters. An accountant who had threatened to blow the whistle, transportation snafus, problems with one or another of Agrimax's international divisions, the terrorism threat. Things had grown hotter than usual since the press got wind of the new terminator gene being developed. Vince felt sure he had that under control. But this—the retired scientist and his teenage sidekick—this was making him nervous.

Seemingly nothing more than a fly in the ointment, the problem should be dealt with swiftly and decisively by Agrimax's security division. It had to be. The meeting to finalize the merger was less than two weeks away. But if…if for some reason his people lost track of the data…if it got into the wrong hands…if his executive board learned of the unsavory aspects of the plan he had put into motion more than two years before, and right under their noses… Worst of all, if word of the merger leaked to the media, the public outcry would scuttle the whole scheme.

Vince removed the olive from his martini glass. Tomorrow was Friday, and he'd need to be at the office early. He tipped his glass and drained the last of the drink. Then he stared at his phone. Why hadn't Mack Harwood called? This should all be taken care of by now. Everything under lock and key once again. He slipped the olive from its toothpick and squeezed the pimento onto his tongue. Then he dropped the olive into his mouth and chewed it.

He wouldn't sleep until he'd heard from his security man. Better make himself another martini.

* * *

Cole switched off the cell phone. The three faces staring at him were etched with fear.

"What did the sheriff say, Mr. Strong?" Billy asked.

Cole knew there was no point in trying to keep anything under wraps. The *Artesia Daily Press* would have the story by morning. The *Albuquerque Journal* would print it statewide. It would probably headline the evening's TV news.

"A deputy found Matt's phone in Jim Banyon's yard," he said. "They've got tire marks and a weapon, and they're dusting for fingerprints inside the house."

"They can't possibly think Matt had anything to do with the death," Jill Pruitt said. "That's absurd."

Cole studied the petite teacher with her bouncy, shoulder-length blond curls and bright green eyes. She was the most tightly wound woman he'd ever met.

"Sheriff Holtmeyer is suspicious," he told her. "There was sign of a struggle in Banyon's house. And the blood spatters… something doesn't look right to him. He's not sure it was a suicide."

"Matt did *not* kill Mr. Banyon," Billy said. "There's no possible way! Matt was like Mr. Peace Activist. He wouldn't even touch a gun. I couldn't get him to go hunting with me or nothing!"

"*Es verdad,*" Josefina echoed. "It's true. He wouldn't even kill a cockroach."

"We've got to find out who those two men were," Jill said. "They're involved in this somehow."

"I bet they're from Agrimax!" Billy exploded. "I'd like to blow that company to smithereens!"

"Calm down, boy," Cole said. "Anger isn't going to do us any good. Miss Pruitt, find out what you can about—"

"Call me Jill, for goodness' sake. And I'm already doing all

I can. Marianne will phone me the minute she hears from the high school secretary."

"That's not good enough. Somebody took my son out of school today. I want to know who those men are—and I'd better find out which numskull is responsible for sending a sixteen-year-old kid off campus with a couple of total strangers."

"I'm telling you, if two suits signed in as Princeton recruiters and asked to talk to a top student, they'd get into the building with no problem. It's not like we check credentials or take a thumbprint or anything."

She crossed her arms and glared at Cole as if daring him to respond.

"Well, maybe you should," he said. "Maybe I'll talk to the principal about the flaws in his security system. And while I'm at it, maybe I'll mention the fact that instead of teaching computer science, one of his teachers spends class time filling her students' heads with idealistic tripe about feeding the hungry."

"The principal knows exactly what goes on in my classroom, Mr. Strong. My teaching evaluations are always among the highest—"

"I'm sure they are, Miss Pruitt. I'm sure everyone thinks you're just the cat's pajamas. But you carry the major responsibility in this fiasco, and I'll nail your hide to my barn if I don't find my son pretty soon."

"Mr. Strong—" she set her hands on her hips "—you're the one who just told Billy that anger isn't going to do us any good. Now if you'll excuse me, I'm going to check Matt's computer."

"You do that, lady. And make it snappy."

Jill glared at him.

Before she could speak again, Billy grabbed her arm. "C'mon, Miss Pruitt. Maybe Matt will answer an e-mail."

"Show me what you know, Billy."

Rage curling through his chest, Cole followed the others into the large adobe house. As they stepped into the living room, Jill and Billy turned down the hall to Matt's bedroom. Cole dropped onto a leather-upholstered couch.

"I need to let my mother know what's going on," he told Josefina. "Matt may be headed toward Amarillo."

"Yes," she said, dabbing her eyes. "That's where he would go, Mr. Strong. He would go to his *abuela*. She loves him. She would take care of him if he was in trouble."

"I don't know if that pickup could make it all the way there," he muttered, listening to the phone ring in his mother's house. "The thing's on its last leg."

"I'll fix you something to eat, Mr. Strong," Josefina said. "I made carne adovada today. Does that sound good?"

"Sure, sure." Cole waved a hand to dismiss the little woman. Why did Josefina always think food would fix things? If Matt brought home a B on a report card, out came the empanadas. If a hailstorm damaged the chile crop, nothing would please her until Cole ate a huge plate of enchiladas and refritos. National tragedies were the worst. The attacks on the Pentagon and the World Trade Center had led to three solid weeks of constant cooking. If Cole hadn't ordered Josefina to cease and desist, she would have kept on indefinitely. The freezer stayed jam-packed, and the refrigerator was always bulging at the seams. Thank God for Billy Younger and his appetite.

"Geneva Strong speaking," a woman's voice carried through the receiver.

"Mom." Cole felt a flood of warmth at the familiar greeting.

"Hey there, boy. What's going on with you? How's my little Matthew?"

"That's what I'm calling about. Listen, Matt may be coming to see you, Mom." Before she could respond, he quickly explained the situation. "So if he doesn't turn up here at the house in the next hour or so, I'm going to drive to Hobbs and then on toward Amarillo. I'm concerned he may have broken down on the road somewhere."

"Are you telling me these people think our Matthew may have killed somebody? Are they out of their—"

"Mom, you know and I know that Matt would never harm anyone. Just keep an eye out for him. If he makes it that far, he'll be tired and hungry—and scared."

"I'll look after him. You know that. And if those fools get within fifty feet of my house, I'll give 'em what-for, and you'd better believe it."

"Call the minute you hear from Matt. I'll have my cell phone."

"Don't worry, I'll call you. And I'll be waiting up for Matthew. In fact, I'm going to go put on the coffee now—"

"Mom, he won't make it to your house until early tomorrow morning."

"Well, he might call! Now stay calm, son. We can handle this. I'm going to phone Irene next door. She'll come over and sit up with me. We'll play Skip-Bo."

Cole let out a breath as he said goodbye and put down the phone. Though Geneva Strong could be a handful, he almost wished his mother hadn't moved back to her childhood hometown in Texas. But Cole had been happily married at the time. With a combination of endless hours and backbreaking work, he had rescued the family ranch from the brink of bankruptcy. His degree in agriculture had prepared him to use innovative technology and aggressive marketing strategies, and he held dreams of making the ranch a model of profitability. Though Matt had been a difficult baby, he also was the source of great joy, and Cole had been hoping the boy would have siblings soon. No one had expected Anna to be diagnosed with cancer.

Wondering if his wife's death had erased any natural tenderness he'd ever had, Cole again thought of Matt and all the lonely years his son had spent on this ranch. The aloneness had consumed both of them—so much that they no longer really knew each other. Jill Pruitt, Billy, Josefina, and now Geneva had been quick to deny that Matt could be capable of murder. Why didn't Cole feel that certainty? Why didn't he know his son well enough to be sure?

To him, Matt was distant, odd, almost alien. The things boys were supposed to enjoy didn't interest him—fishing, hunting, horseback riding on the ranch, sports, cars, girls. Actually, Cole didn't know whether Matt was interested in girls yet. They'd never spoken about it. Instead of acting like an average kid, Matt focused on his strange fascinations—math and science mostly. He hadn't wanted a dog. No, he'd bought a mouse and trained it to run through mazes and perform tricks.

Once, Cole had found Matt high in a tree, where he was building a tree house. Wonderful and *normal*. But the tree house had turned out to be a platform for Matt's telescope. The boy was calculating the height of the tree and the distance from his branch to the ground and whether this would make any difference in his ability to observe the stars. At the time, he was seven years old.

Cole stood and stretched the taut muscles in his shoulders. Penny had discouraged him from setting out after Matt. Maybe she was right. He didn't really know where his son might have gone. And the sheriff would put out an all-points bulletin. They probably would locate him in an hour or so.

But the thought of a highway patrolman handcuffing Matt and shoving him into the back of a police car sent a shudder through Cole. His son was just a boy, after all. Barely sixteen, and so naive about the world. There was no telling how he'd react to an accusation of murder.

"We used Miss Pruitt's account and sent Matt an e-mail,"

Billy announced, stepping into the living room. "You should see what she's doing on the computer. She's getting into all Matt's files and stuff. It's awesome! Hey, what's that I smell? Is Josefina cooking?"

"Carne adovada. In the kitchen."

Billy veered in that direction, and Cole grinned in spite of himself. He went down the hall and found Jill Pruitt seated at Matt's desk.

She came across as a bundle of compressed energy in a turquoise skirt and a sleeveless white top. Though she couldn't be forty yet, he figured she ought to be married by now. She was pretty enough, in a frizzy sort of way. He wondered if teaching and famine relief kept her too busy to be interested in marriage. Or was there something else?

"Billy says you sent Matt an e-mail," he said.

"And I'm going through all this data he downloaded," she replied without looking up. Her slender fingers sped across the keyboard.

"What was he copying?"

"Lots of things. The amount of information he compiled on the food industry is incredible. By the way, you'll be happy to know your son is not into pornography. I can't find anything suspicious here at all. The gaming sites are weird, of course, all those mythological characters and fantasy worlds."

"I've watched Matt and Billy play."

"It's a lot of strategy—I think that's what appeals to Matt. The RPGs are a concern, but—"

"Wait. RPGs?"

"Role-playing games." She glanced at him for the first time. "Do you know *anything* about your son, Mr. Strong?"

His hackles rose. Add *abrasive* to the list of Miss Pruitt's attributes. "I know Matt is impressionable," he shot back. "I know he's susceptible to the influence of people he admires."

"Look, I'm aware you want to blame me for his disappearance, but it's not going to work. Matt's interest in famine relief was his own."

"Is that so?" Cole put one hand on the back of her chair, bent down, and tried to read the computer screen over her shoulder. How could anyone who smelled so good be so testy? She was like a rattlesnake hiding in a lilac bush.

"Didn't you tell my son about your little famine-relief jaunts around the world?"

"Of course I did. I talk about a lot of things in my class."

"I thought the subject was computer science."

"If a person has tunnel vision, Mr. Strong," she said, peering at him with those glittering emerald eyes, "then maybe he or she can only do one thing at a time. Some people let their jobs become their lives. They don't leave time for family or hobbies…or volunteering…or ministry. I strive for a *full, balanced life*. And my enthusiasm for it spills over into my job."

He stared back at her. "Some people don't have a job that demands constant vigilance—twenty-four hours a day, seven days a week, and no weekends or summers free to flit around having a full, balanced life."

"Yeah, well, some people have children, and they ought to—"

"They ought to stop listening to people who don't." He reached over her shoulder and touched the computer screen. "Who are all these messages from?"

As she swung around, her curls fluffed out, grazing the hair on his arm. A jolt of adrenaline raced up his skin, shocking him in its intensity. Irked at this as much as at her words, Cole straightened and jammed his hands into his pockets. Miss Jill Pruitt was a stuck-up little do-gooder who thought she knew how to parent Matt better than his own father did.

"I think it's them," she said. "Look at this stuff they've written to him. This is appalling. Poor kid!"

Drawing a deep breath, Cole bent over again and read the message Jill had pulled up on the screen. Whoever wrote it had every intention of intimidating and threatening Matt. The writer informed him that he was in violation of privacy laws and that he had better stay out of the company's business if he knew what was good for him.

Jill closed that message and opened another. More of the same. As she clicked chronologically backward through the long list, Cole saw that the tone of the e-mails had gone from fairly polite to downright hostile. Now she opened another window and found the messages Matt had sent.

"Bingo!" she called out. "It's Agrimax, all right. This is who he's been writing to, see? In this message he's trying to get information. And in this one he's broaching his concept—that Agrimax participate in a global plan to end hunger. I wish we could find that plan."

"It's probably in his term paper."

"No, Billy and I found a rough draft. It mostly addresses the problem of famine. But his solution—that's what Matt was really immersed in. That's what got him into trouble with Agrimax."

"Maybe it wasn't his solution that troubled them. Maybe what burned them was the fact that he'd gotten into their system at all. Obviously, they didn't want him in there."

She gave him a grudging nod. "Could be. He clearly wasn't e-mailing their PR department. This person who's been writing to him has influence. An executive, I think. Matt had gotten further inside the company somehow."

"Can you tell me why you taught him that?" Cole demanded. "What purpose does it serve? He didn't need to learn how to break into a huge company's computer system."

"First of all, I don't teach hacking. Whatever code Matt used to penetrate this level of the company is something he learned from Jim Banyon. Or maybe he taught himself how to get inside their communication network. He's quite intelligent, in case you didn't know."

"Too smart for his own good, it sounds like."

"And second, he hasn't actually accessed the company's mainframe. I doubt Matt would do something like that. He's a very ethical young man."

"Oh, really? I wonder where he got that?"

She shrugged one shoulder. "All right, I guess you haven't totally blown it, Mr. Strong. Matt is a great kid."

Cole wished he could feel better about her compliment. True, he had taken the boy to church every Sunday of his life. They prayed before meals. And Cole had tried to model morality, patriotism and the ideal of the hardworking American male. But how much had he influenced his son in ways that really mattered?

"Okay," Jill said. "I'm going to take a stab at this. I think what happened is that Agrimax felt threatened by Matt, and they sent two men out here to question him."

"Matt—threatening? No way." Cole hooked a thumb in his pocket. "You don't know my son as well as you claim."

"I know he was pushing the company to consider his ideas. That's obvious from the text of his messages."

"Pushing is not threatening. Does Matt write anything that could be called the least bit threatening to the company?"

"I didn't read everything."

"What are you waiting for?"

"Okay, but—"

"Hey, Miss Pruitt, did Matt write you back?" Billy stepped into the room. He had a bowl of thick, red-chile carne adovada in one hand and a spoon in the other. "Did you check?"

"Just a sec. I'll have to access my account." Jill leaned forward and ran through a series of motions Cole couldn't track. In a moment, a message popped onto the screen. "He answered!"

Hope spiraled up through Cole's chest as he bent to read his son's words.

hi miss pruitt im ok dont write again tell my dad dont follow me i will be home when its safe

matt

"He's in trouble, man," Billy said. "He's scared. He thinks those Agrimax guys are after him."

"Does the fact that he wrote us mean he's somewhere with a phone line?" Cole asked.

"Matt's laptop has a wireless modem," Billy said. "You paid for it, Mr. Strong, don't you remember?"

"I don't know what half the stuff he orders is all about."

"A wireless modem works like a regular phone connection," Jill explained. "Matt can use the Internet or access his e-mail account without needing a phone line."

Cole considered this. "Still, maybe he stopped at a motel for the night. Or maybe he's at a friend's house."

"A friend? He doesn't have any friends but me, Mr. Strong. You know that."

"Billy," Cole said, "is there any place Matt would go other than his grandmother's house? Somewhere he'd feel safe?"

"There's places around here where he likes to hang out, you know? Like he spends a lot of time at the cemetery—"

"The cemetery?"

"He goes over there before school and visits his mom's grave. I think he talks to her, but he won't admit it. And he comes over to my place once in a while, but my parents are like—whew. It's bad over there, so we usually come out here to chill. He likes the library, and he likes talking to Miss

Pruitt, but he wouldn't go anyplace around this town to hide, Mr. Strong. Not if he's afraid."

"He does sound scared in that message."

"You know what I think? I think those Agrimax guys might have killed Mr. Banyon, and Matt saw what they did, and now they're after him. I think that's why he took off and doesn't want us to follow him. He thinks we'd be in danger if we got near him."

"You may be right, Billy." Cole studied the computer screen, and then he straightened. "I'm going after him."

"I'll go with you, Mr. Strong."

"No, you won't. Get on home, and I'll call you if—"

"No, sir! I'm going after Matt. You don't understand the Mattman like I do. He's not good at stuff, you know? Regular life is what I mean. Common sense. He doesn't know how to talk to people or do normal junk."

"Now what's that supposed to mean?"

"I mean he needs me, Mr. Strong. If he was blind, I'd be like his seeing-eye dog. I get him through. I help him. I've been doing it since forever, okay?"

"I know you're his best friend, Billy. But you can't go out on the road with me. Tomorrow's Friday. You've got school—"

"You don't get it, Mr. Strong. Matt *needs* me. I gotta go find him!"

"No, Billy, I'm not taking you, and I won't change my mind on this."

"You don't ever bend, do you? You're just like Matt said— like an old dead stump stuck out in the middle of a dry lake, good for nothing. He said there's not a single soft place on you, Mr. Strong. Not inside or out. You're just hard and dead and cold. Well, I'm not like that. Not now, not ever. And if somebody needs me, I'm there. I'm totally there. Do you get that? Do you get it?"

"I get it, Billy. Now, go home."

"I'm already gone." He glanced at his teacher. "Later, Miss Pruitt."

"Later, Billy." As the boy stalked out of the room, she pushed back the chair and stood. "It wouldn't kill you to take him along."

"I don't need another sixteen-year-old on my hands. But I do need somebody who can work a computer. I'll get you back by Sunday night at the latest."

"Me?" She laughed. "Are you kidding? I'm not going anywhere except home. I've got a dog to walk, tests to grade, and a full day of classes to teach tomorrow."

"Yeah, and I've got a missing son who just made contact for the first time since he vanished. Now unplug the computer, and let's go."

"Are you crazy?"

"No," he said. "I'm an old dead stump in a dry lake bed, and the only thing around me that's got any life has disappeared. I'm going to find him, and I expect you to come along."

"If you understood computers, Mr. Strong, you'd realize—"

"But I don't. I understand cattle. I understand hay. I know how to make a ranch productive enough to help feed all those hungry people you care about. But I don't know how to run a computer, and you do. So I'm telling you to pack that thing up, and come with me to find my son."

"I could stay home and check the messages. If Matt e-mails me, then I could call you."

"Miss Pruitt." Cole set both hands on her shoulders and stared into her eyes. "I don't know how to make this any plainer. I'm going to find my son, and you're going to come with me. Bring the computer. Stay in contact with Matt, and tell him what I say. And go through that machine with a fine-tooth comb. Read every past e-mail he got or sent. Read all his reports, all his research, everything. If there's anything else on the computer I need to know, tell me. We'll find my son, and then I'll take you home. Is that clear?"

Her chin stiffened. "I will not do this, Mr. Strong."

"You will do it, because you're the one who caused all this. You put the bug in his ear about famine relief. You fired him up about all the hungry people in the world, and your big mission trips, and your famine-relief projects. And you taught him every technological thing he needed to know to dig himself into this deep hole. So you're coming with me, and you're going to do your dead-level best to stay in touch with my son and help me find him. Do you understand *now?*"

Her nostrils flared as she glared at him. For a moment, he thought she was going to buck him again. But he knew if she did, he'd toss the little fireball over his shoulder, throw her in the truck and make her go with him anyway.

"I will need to make arrangements for my classes," she said through tightened lips. "And perhaps I could be allowed to pack a few things?"

"I'll take you to your house."

"My car is at the school."

"You won't need it." He took her arm. "Let's go."

Chapter Four

Jill stared out at the two-lane road that stretched between Artesia and Hobbs. She could not believe what she was doing. Until this day—this simple, ordinary Thursday in May—her life had been organized and structured. She had graduated cum laude from Texas Tech, taken a teaching position at Artesia High School, joined a church, rented an apartment until she'd been able to buy herself a house, and had been content. She enjoyed her job, her garden, her mission trips, her friends. Everything under control. And then Cole Strong had walked into her classroom.

Now they were jammed into his hot pickup, driving along in the dark, yet they had hardly spoken two words to each other. She could almost feel the rancher seething. Or was it worry that emanated from the clenched fists on the steering wheel, the bunched muscles beneath his blue shirt, the flicker of tension in his jaw? And if he was indeed worried, was it the fate of his son that troubled him—or the unfinished chores he had left behind?

"I'd drive faster, but the antelope are thick tonight," he commented, almost under his breath.

"It would have been a lot quicker if you had dropped down to Carlsbad and taken the highway to Hobbs," she said. "I've done it a hundred times."

"Matt wouldn't go that way. He'd do the straight shot."

"How do you know?"

"I *know*."

Bullheaded old coot, she thought. Okay, maybe Cole wasn't old. In fact, they were probably close to the same age. But he was definitely as hard-nosed and stubborn as they came. Handsome in a weather-beaten, sunburned sort of way, he came across as a man who chose to stand alone—who spoke his mind and hoarded his smiles. A man who didn't need or want anyone.

Right now, though, he needed Jill's expertise. But he certainly didn't want *her,* the idealistic computer teacher who had led his son astray. Well, he was as stuck with her as she was with him.

Jill glanced over her shoulder to where the computer equipment was riding under a billowing tarp in the truck bed. Cole wouldn't hear of leaving it behind, even when she insisted she could communicate with Matt through her own laptop. No, they had to haul the monster LCD monitor and the tower, not to mention the tangle of wires connecting an external hard drive, a CD burner, an optical mouse and the twin speakers. She had tried to draw the line at bringing the printer, but he refused to leave it. So it was jolting behind them, too, no doubt losing bolts and dislodging hardware with every bump in the road.

"I'm supposed to be starting a new unit in my Web-design class tomorrow," she said. "There's no way a substitute can do that for me."

"Why bother starting something new? The kids' brains have shut down for the summer anyway."

"Are you kidding? I never quit until the very end."

"I can believe it."

"What's that supposed to mean?"

"Billy said you were intense. I'd call it hardheaded."

"Me, hardheaded? You're the one who forced me to go with you in spite of all my other commitments."

"It wasn't me who forced you into this truck. It was your guilty conscience."

"I don't feel the least bit guilty for anything I've ever said in my classroom." She crossed her arms, feeling hot and wishing she had a clip to pull her hair up off her neck. No doubt this old truck had never had an air conditioner. "I'm glad I told the students about my famine-relief work, and I plan to keep on telling them until they get the message."

"My son got your message, and now he's missing."

"That's not my fault. Matt has a tendency to take things to extremes."

"And you don't?"

"I suppose your idea of famine relief is mailing a check to some organization you don't even know is legitimate. Or do you even do that much, Mr. Strong?"

"As a matter of fact, I do do that much. My church has a strong missions arm. Part of what we do is feed the hungry. So my monthly tithe check goes toward that, and I'm glad to help in that way. But I don't have time to head off to some godforsaken desert somewhere and ladle out porridge. If you do, that's fine with me. Just don't go foisting your ideas on susceptible young kids who don't have the maturity or wisdom to know what to do with them. And by the way, you can call me Cole."

By now, the tips of Jill's ears were on fire. She rolled down the window and stuck her head out in hopes of cooling off. Never in her entire life had she met anyone as obnoxious and self-centered as this man! How dare he blame her for Matt's disappearance?

"Do you need me to stop the truck?" Cole asked.

"What?" She put her head back inside.

"You look sick. I'll stop if you need me to."

"I am not carsick—I'm angry! Do you have any idea how ignorant you sound? There is so much you could do. But you just sit there, so smug with your little tithe check."

"Where I sit is on a tractor or a plow or a combine. And what I do is grow hay to feed cattle and horses. And what those cattle do is get slaughtered to feed hungry people. So don't tell me I'm not doing my part."

"Who buys your cattle?" Jill asked.

"Agrimax. My chile is processed by Selena Foods, which is owned by Agrimax. And my hay goes to Homestead, a division of Agrimax. Yeah, I owe my soul to the company store. But that's how it goes, Miss Pruitt. If you want to make a living as a farmer or rancher, you sell your product to the company that will keep you in business. For me, that's Agrimax."

This news piqued Jill's interest. She had no idea the man was in league with the devil himself. So Matt's father—like so many others—had been forced to toe the line by one of the three huge corporations that controlled the world's food supply. Softening a little, she drank down a calming breath.

"You're not angry with me," she said. "You're mad at yourself. You know you work for the company that is harassing your son. It's Agrimax that frightened Matt into taking off. Not me."

"A company like Agrimax is not going to pay much attention to some e-mails from a starry-eyed kid who wants to feed the world. He'd be like a gnat buzzing around the head of a bull."

"Then why do you think Matt is on the run?"

He paused. "You really want to know?"

"Yes, I do."

"I think Matt went to interview Jim Banyon for that term paper. I think he got to spending time with the old man, and they became buddies. I don't know whether Matt realized it or not, but Banyon must have seen that his operation was in trouble. I'm sure he had invested all his retirement money into that farm, and even though he hadn't been there long, it wasn't panning out the way he'd hoped. I've seen it happen too many times to count. Men come out here thinking they can make a go of running a small ranch or farm, and then they bottom out. I figure Banyon got depressed and put a bullet through his brain. Matt must have come upon that scene this afternoon and panicked."

Jill mulled over the idea. "But his e-mail made it clear he feels he's not safe. He thinks someone is after him."

For a minute, Cole said nothing. Finally, he swallowed. "You know my son pretty well, Miss Pruitt?"

"Jill. Yes, I think I do."

"Then you know Matt is different. I'll admit that much about him, though I don't like it when people say he's obsessed or weird. When kids call him names and pick on him, I hate that. But the fact is, Billy's right when he says Matt doesn't fit into the normal world. You try to talk to him, and his head is somewhere else. He's always been that way. Just different, you know?"

"I know. That's why he's so wonderful."

At that, he turned to look at her. "You see the good in him?"

"I see more than good. I see brilliance. Genius. I see a future full of possibility for your son. If I had a child, I'd be thrilled if he turned out just like Matt."

"His teachers tell me he has poor social skills."

"Well, they've never heard him talk about things he really cares about. Besides, what sixteen-year-old has good social skills?"

He laughed. "I was a mess at sixteen."

"Me, too. But then, I've always walked my own path in life—trying to go in the direction God leads me. People don't like that sometimes. They don't get it. I stopped caring a long time ago what folks thought. That's how Matt is. He gets his instructions from God, and he's very literal about putting his faith into practice. I love that about him."

"Yeah. So do I." He fell silent again. When he spoke, his voice was husky. "Anyhow, I figure Matt must have the notion that someone's chasing him. You know, he gets these thoughts. He tries to reason things out—but if it's not math or science, it doesn't compute. I think he's running from a phantom."

"I hope you're right. I'm not so sure. The things he told me about companies like Agrimax…well, I was disturbed."

"What's to fear? It's pretty straightforward, if you ask me. Making money is their bottom line, and no one who believes in capitalism can have a problem with that. I realize these corporations run small businesses into the ground and then buy them. I know they force farmers to use their pesticides, fertilizers, seeds—everything. And I know they pay us bottom dollar so they can turn around and sell our produce to the highest bidder. I don't like that, but it's reality."

"You haven't described capitalism—that's a monopoly."

"No way. It's hard-as-steel capitalism. And it's not evil."

Jill felt her ears beginning to heat up again. "How can you say that? You're a relatively small rancher. It's not fair—"

"It's a game. We all play it. Even your famine-relief friends are playing along. These monster food corporations do their bit for world hunger so they can look good. They have their scientists out there developing special breeds of sheep in one remote corner of the world or eliminating a pest in another. Looking good for the newspapers and TV. Your people go along with it to get their handouts. But it's all a big, complex game—and no, it's not fair."

"If it's a game, they ought to know they're playing with the lives of millions of starving—"

"What's that?" Cole cut in. He leaned forward and peered through the windshield at a dark hulk in the distance. "Up ahead on the right side of the road. Do you see it?"

"Slow down. It's a car. No, a pickup. Hey, I think it's Matt!"

Her heart beating double time, Jill unlatched her seat belt as Cole pulled off the roadway.

"What color is it?" he demanded. "Is it—no, it's not Matt's pickup. It's...oh, great."

Jill saw the large shape emerge from the cab at the same moment Cole had.

"It's Billy," they said in unison.

Jill opened the door and stepped out onto the gravel shoulder. She glanced back at Cole. Shaking his head, he remained behind the wheel.

The teenager watched her approach, a sheepish grin scrawled across his face. He took off his ball cap as she neared. "Hey, Miss Pruitt. I was hoping you guys might be coming along."

"Billy, what are you doing out here?" She shrugged. "Why am I even asking that? Did you tell your parents you were going to look for Matt?"

"I called and left a message."

"So why did you stop?"

"I got a...uh...it's a flat. But I don't have a spare. This pick-up's an old clunker, you know. I had already driven a long way past Loco Hills, so I kind of kept going for a while, thinking I could make it to Hobbs."

"Hobbs? That's forty-five miles from here, Billy."

"Yeah." He scratched his head. "I wasn't sure how far it was. Anyhow, the wheel is shot. Like bad. I just kept driving, 'cause this stretch of road is like the desert or something. And then I started seeing the sparks, so I stopped. And that's when it occurred to me you guys might be coming along. And here you are. Think you could give me a ride?"

Jill turned and looked back at Cole's pickup. Just what they needed—a huge sixteen-year-old wedged into the cab with them. If Cole was in a bad humor before, this would make him downright surly.

"I think we'd better call your dad and tell him to come out and pick you up," she told the boy. "He could arrange a tow."

"Miss Pruitt, would you please not do that? My dad is not cool about these things, you know? He'll really ream me. I mean, it could be bad. Mega-bad. If you'd take me into Hobbs, I could try to find another wheel and buy a tire or something, and then—"

"Come on." She laid her hand on his back as they started toward Cole's truck. "It won't be mega-good with Matt's father, but we'll survive."

"Oh, he's nothing like my dad. Mr. Strong is cool. I mean, he's not around much, but he's a good guy, you know? Like he never drinks or cusses or nothing, and he gets Matt whatever he needs—computer stuff and junk like that. And he takes him to church and out to eat. I never saw him get mad—never. Not till tonight. But he would never hit Matt or anybody, you know. He's not like that."

Jill stopped short and caught the boy's arm before they got into the pickup. "Does your dad hit you, Billy?"

"Aw, it's no big deal. I'm bigger than him now." His laugh held no humor. "It used to be bad, and with my mom…well, that's why she's wanting out. I told her to get away, go to a shelter or whatever, but she stays. It's little things like this with my truck—it sets him off, you know, especially if he's been drinking. So if you could just take me into Hobbs, I can take care of it."

She nodded. Opening the door, she climbed in and slid next to Cole. "Billy's coming with us. He had a flat, and his wheel is ruined."

"Hold on a minute now." Cole reached across her and put up his hand. "Whoa, boy. You better just call your dad, and—"

"I told him he could come with us," Jill said. "Hop in, Billy. It's no problem."

"No problem?" Cole grimaced as the boy slammed the cab door, and Jill's elbow sank into his rib cage. "Whose truck is this, anyway?"

"It's yours. But I'm half of the duo, and I promised Billy he could ride along."

Cole sighed as he pulled back out onto the highway. Trying to make herself smaller than she already was, Jill attempted to think of something to say to ease the tension. Unfortunately, Billy smelled like a teenager who had gone too long without a shower and a toothbrush. She was fairly sure she could even catch a pungent aroma emanating from his shoes.

Cole, on the other hand, smelled of something disturbingly masculine. Shaving cream? Or maybe it was the denim he wore. She wished his shoulder weren't so hard. And that she could move her legs.

"There's a truck stop on the outskirts of Hobbs," Cole said. "We'll swing by and ask if they've seen Matt."

Maybe Billy and I can switch places, too, Jill thought. She'd rather have a door handle against her hip than the hard plane of Cole Strong's thigh.

"I hope they have a restaurant," Billy said. "I could eat a horse."

★ ★ ★

The sun had begun its climb through layers of El Paso's brown smog as Matt pulled his pickup into a parking lot near the bridge spanning the Rio Grande. He had spent Thursday night in McKelligon Canyon, with the Franklin Mountains looming around him and an owl hooting in a tree nearby. The concrete tables at the picnic area where he parked were broken and sprayed with graffiti. Litter covered the ground. He hadn't slept, and he'd been too scared to get out and use the public restroom.

In fact, since leaving Hope, the only time he had set foot outside his truck was at a convenience store in Alamogordo. There he had wandered around selecting a road map, some Tylenol for his headache, four Snickers bars, a bag of Cheetos, and an orange soda. While paying for a tank of gas and his food, he had glanced at a television set. His own picture stared back at him on the evening news. Police were seeking the whereabouts of a sixteen-year-old in connection with a possible murder near Hope.

Murder—*him?*

Freaked to the max, Matt had barely made it out of the store without breaking into an all-out run. Luckily, the young clerk had been talking on the phone and hadn't paid much attention to her customer. Still, Matt knew he had been recorded on the video monitor. Every highway patrolman in two states must be watching for his truck.

As he had started across the desert toward El Paso, Matt tried to figure out why the police thought he might have killed Mr. Banyon. How did they even know he'd been out to the house in Hope? It didn't make sense. No one had seen him there. For the hundredth time, he wished Billy were with him. Common sense was Billy's specialty. He never did stupid things.

Matt had turned the situation over and over as he drove, replaying the scene at Mr. Banyon's house and trying to recall what clue he had left behind. He hadn't dropped a shoe or a jacket. He'd thrown out his cell phone, but it was well hidden in the thicket. Surely they hadn't found it. Not this quickly.

He hadn't been inside the house long enough to disturb anything. He'd just stared at that terrible face on the couch... at the bloodstain on the fabric...at the gun....

The gun! He'd picked it up! Matt had groaned as the realization swept over him. Why had he picked up Mr. Banyon's gun? Why had he even touched it? How stupid could you get? Now it had his fingerprints all over it. Next, they would track him to the convenience store in Alamogordo and then to El Paso and then they would get him. If the Agrimax men didn't find him first, the police would, and he'd be charged with killing Mr. Banyon.

How could he prove he hadn't done it? He couldn't. There was no way. He hadn't been at school all afternoon. He hadn't been with Billy. He had no alibi. He was dead meat.

Somewhere along the road, he had pulled onto the shoulder and taken a moment to check his e-mail. Miss Pruitt had written to him again. She and his dad were worried. They knew about Mr. Banyon's death, and they didn't believe Matt had anything to do with it. But if he didn't show up soon, his dad would go looking for him.

Dad? Agrimax could ruin Cole Strong, and it would be his son's fault. He shot back an e-mail warning Miss Pruitt not to write him again and not to go looking for him. He tried to make himself think straight. Tried to be brave and trust in the Lord.

But this wasn't supposed to happen. None of it! Mr. Banyon was going to take care of everything. He was planning to take the USB key to Josiah Karume. The chairman-elect of

I-FEED would be attending some kind of a food summit in France this spring, and Mr. Banyon had arranged to fly over there and meet with him. Now Mr. Banyon was dead and Matt had the key—and everyone thought he was a murderer!

There was no way Matt was going to Europe. The only course he'd been able to think of was to take the key to a different I-FEED official, in the hope that this person would be able to get it into Karume's hands. Miss Pruitt had given Matt the names of several famine-relief workers to contact for his term paper, and he had e-mailed back and forth with Hector Diaz, the man who ran the Mexico division of I-FEED. Diaz's office was in Juarez, just across the river from El Paso. So that's where Matt was headed.

But he probably ought to turn himself in right now and just get it over with. Being held by the police would be better than getting grabbed again by the Agrimax men. At least he could spend his life in prison instead of winding up dead.

All those thoughts and fears had swirled through Matt's head as he drove. He had crossed the state line into Texas, and somehow he made himself keep going. As he inched toward El Paso, he kept glancing in the rearview mirror, expecting to see flashing red lights. The USB key weighed ten tons in his jeans pocket. It was like an Edgar Allan Poe story he had read for English class. Instead of a telltale heart, the key was pulsing away in his pocket. *Boom, boom, boom.* Full of its secret sins.

He hated having the key, but he knew he couldn't just throw it out the window as he'd done with his cell phone. No, he had to carry out Mr. Banyon's plan. He had to do God's will.

And so he had shivered his way through a sleepless night in the canyon. He had dried blood in his hair where the Agrimax men had thrown his head against the wall, but other than that, he felt okay. At dawn, he drove into El Paso and headed for the border crossing into Mexico. Figuring the authorities would be looking for his truck, he parked it and set off on foot toward the bridge, laptop under his arm and the key in his front pocket.

Even at this early hour, the line of trucks and cars waiting to cross into Ciudad Juarez stretched half a mile. Pedestrians bustled along the walkway, few of them tourists. Those would come later. Matt had considered waiting a few hours to blend in better, but he decided to keep moving.

The USB key growing heavier with each step, Matt approached the guard gate. He thought he knew the routine. His parents had taken him to Juarez when he was little, before his mother died and everything changed. And he'd been there a second time on a field trip in fifth grade. He figured he would have to show some identification. He had a passport from a trip he and his dad had taken to Cancún a few years back— the one and only vacation they had ever taken together. He was planning to use it again this summer for the youth mission trip to Guatemala. But it was back home in his desk drawer.

Matt hoped his driver's license would get him into Juarez. He would have to state his business and let the guard know when he was returning. What if they recognized him from the TV news or from police alerts? Would his next stop be a Mexican jail? He imagined the key pulsing, threatening to tell on him. *Boom, boom, boom.*

Matt decided this would be a good time to pray. Protection, guidance, wise counsel—for all these things he petitioned the Lord as he followed the line of people closer and closer to the gate.

"Buenos dias," the Mexican guard said, glancing up at him. "Where are you going so early, my friend? And walking?"

Somehow the Spanish he had learned at Josefina's knee rose

to the tip of his tongue. *"Voy a la ciudad a visitar a un amigo."* I'm going into the city to visit a friend.

"Su amigo?" The man grinned. *"O su amiga?"*

Matt mustered a smile at the reference to a girlfriend. *"Amigo solamente."*

"What do you have there? The box?"

"A laptop computer."

"You going to sell it in Mexico?"

"No, no. It's personal. Games and e-mail, that's all."

The guard shrugged. "Have a nice day, *señor.*"

"You, too."

Matt slipped through the narrow opening onto the bridge. *Boom, boom, boom.* Somehow the USB key had grown so enormous and heavy he wasn't sure he would even fit on the causeway. Hardly able to believe he had passed the guard without incident, he made his way above the fabled river and was swept into the press of people on the Mexican side.

Breathing too hard, Matt lifted up a prayer of gratitude and added another—a request for a taxi. Then the smell of frying sausage hit him, followed by the fragrance of freshly baked bread. Not far from the bridge stood a row of vendors' carts. The snacks he had bought the evening before were long gone, and his stomach churned with hunger. From the vacation with his father, Matt knew the risks of eating and drinking in Mexico. They both had fallen ill after sampling some street food. *"Be careful what you eat in Mexico,"* Josefina had warned them after the fact. *"You'll get a bug."* An amoeba, his father had clarified. Dysentery.

Now, surveying the row of sausages sizzling on an open grill, he tried to tell himself he could go without eating. This mission was all about hunger anyway, wasn't it? Millions of people had nothing to eat, so why did Matthew Strong think he deserved to fill his belly? He passed up the meat and approached a cart loaded with fresh fruit. Could Mexican fruit make you sick? Flies buzzed around a tray of cut mangoes. Forcing himself on, he came to the bread vendor.

"Pan, señor?" a woman asked. She was smiling at him, her eyes as dark and shiny as Josefina's. "You want bread?"

He was salivating by now, so hungry he thought he might faint. Could he at least have bread, the staff of life? "Uh, no," he said. "That's okay. *Gracias, señora.*"

As hungry as he felt, Matt knew he couldn't afford to get sick. Not before he found the man he was seeking. Not before he got rid of the key. Not before he was back home in the safety of his room.

"A leather belt?" a man called out from a storefront. "Leather purse for your girlfriend? I make you a good price, *señor!*"

Feeling light-headed, Matt approached the clerk. "I need a phone book. An address. I need a taxi."

"You come inside. Buy a new wallet!"

"I don't need a wallet. I need a phone book. *Telefono. Yo quiero el direccion de la oficina I-FEED. De Señor Hector Diaz.* I need the address of Hector Diaz."

"Come and see our beautiful leather jackets," the man replied, guiding Matt into the shop.

The scent of polished leather goods swept over him as he stepped through the door. Sandals, purses, backpacks, suitcases, attachés, vests and leather jackets filled countless shelves in the narrow room. Matt shook his head. This wasn't going well.

What would Billy do now? What was the right thing to say? How should he act?

"A telephone book," he told the man again. "I need to find an address."

"No telefono, señor." He held up a pair of cowboy boots. "I make a good price for you. One hundred dollars. Is snakeskin here, you see? Very expensive."

Matt began trying to back out of the store. "I just… I need a phone book."

"Okay, eighty dollars."

The man was holding the boots in Matt's face, shaking them, coming at him no matter how far away he tried to get. Matt saw strange lights around his eyes, and he had a bad feeling he was going to pass out.

"I need something to drink," he mumbled.

"I make you the best price of the day. Sixty dollars. I cannot do better than this. For snakeskin? You will not find this in all of Ciudad Juarez."

"No!" Matt said, slapping the boots out of the man's hand. "I don't want them!"

"*Ai!* What are you doing?" The man swung around and began calling to some men at the back of the shop.

A flurry of Spanish words ringing in his ears, Matt found the door and stumbled outside. He needed a drink. Water. Or a Fanta.

Behind him, three men now stood in the doorway of the shop and shouted in anger. Matt crossed the street, back toward the vendors, back to the old woman with the bread cart.

"Please, *señora*," he said. "I need water. *Agua, por favor.*"

Suspicion flashing from her dark eyes, she glanced at the leather salesmen still hollering at Matt. She shook her head and shooed him away. He dug in his pocket and fished out his wallet.

"I need a taxi!" he called out into the crowded street, waving his wallet in the air. "Where are the taxis? *Donde están los taxis, por favor?*"

People hurried past him, some glancing warily. He knew he wasn't doing this right. He was making a mess of it. He was in his element handling everything by e-mail. Ordering computer parts. Finding information. But now, here in Mexico, there was no one to tell him what to do.

He licked his dry lips and tried to think. He probably ought to move away from the bridge. If the guards saw him causing a ruckus, they might arrest him.

Starting back down the street, Matt turned a deaf ear to all storekeepers who called out to him. *No,* he thought. *Look straight ahead. Don't make eye contact. Just get away from the bridge. Get deeper into the city. Then you can buy a soda.* Bottled—it would be safe, right? Or not? Why hadn't he brought Billy? Billy would know all these things. Billy would joke around, and they'd laugh, and everything would be all right.

In the midst of the cries of the vendors, Matt picked out a word that rang like a blessing in his ears.

"Taxi, *señor?*"

Matt turned toward the voice. "Taxi? *Si!*"

The driver beckoned him toward a line of rusty yellow cabs. He opened the door for Matt, who nodded thanks as he climbed in. The man started the engine, flicked on the meter and turned to his passenger. "Where you want to go?"

"Do you know where I-FEED is? Uh, the International Federation for Environmental and Economic Development?"

The man frowned. "La direccion? Address?"

"No. But I—"

With a sigh, the driver lifted a hefty phone book from the front seat. *"Federacion Internacional de…"*

"Environmental and Economic Development."

"Aha, *si señor.*" He tossed down the phone book and put the taxi in gear. *"Vamonos.* We go."

Matt closed his eyes, clutched his laptop and laid his head back on the cracked vinyl seat. The taxi made several lurching stops, brakes squealing as pedestrians scurried out of the way. Matt couldn't avoid breathing in the choking smog—

diesel fumes, burning tires, industrial smokestacks—and he grew more nauseous by the minute.

"*Señor, aquí.*" The taxi screeched to a halt in front of a barred glass door just off the sidewalk.

Matt handed the man a bill and forced himself to step out into the heat. The key weighing heavy in his pocket, he walked up to the door and turned the knob. Locked. He pressed the doorbell and waited. No one came. Maybe it was too early. What were the hours of business? Blinking away the lights that danced in front of his eyes, he tried to read a message posted on the door.

It was written in Spanish. "I have gone to the International Food Summit in Paris, France," he translated slowly. "I shall return on the thirty-first of this month. Hector Diaz."

Gone? Matt squinted, trying to make sure he had read the message right. He was too late! The man had already left for the meeting in France. What was Matt going to do now? He looked for a mail slot. Maybe he could slip the USB key in there and be done with it.

Nothing. As reality worked its way into his brain, Matt felt his mouth fill with warm saliva. He was going to throw up. He was. He really was.

He stumbled to an adjoining alley. Grabbing the brick wall for support, he bent over and retched. He felt as if he was going to die.

"Too much drinking," a mocking voice said behind him. "*Borrachón!*"

Matt turned his head, but the taunter had gone on by. He clutched at the bricks and braced for a second wave of nausea.

"*Señor.*" A hand tapped his back. "Give me money, *por favor.*"

Matt managed to focus on a pair of bright black eyes nested in a small, filthy face. "What?"

"Money." The hand tugged his shirt. *"Pesos."*

It was a child.

He knew that, and then nothing.

"The boy has it." Mack Harwood's voice on the telephone brought Vince upright in the armchair where he'd sat through the night. "Banyon didn't have any CDs when we searched him."

Vince rubbed his eyes, wishing he hadn't poured himself so many martinis. "What makes you so sure he gave it to the kid?"

"The boy is on the run—Matthew Strong. The police traced him to Banyon's house. They think the boy killed Banyon."

"Jim is dead?" Vince sighed. He regretted what his security men had done, but he hated Banyon's betrayal even worse. "If the police think this Strong kid is a murderer, maybe that's why he's running. Wouldn't you, Harwood?"

"Sir, we believe the boy has the data. We thoroughly searched Banyon's house for CDs or USB keys, and we didn't find a thing. He didn't even own a computer. Banyon must have given the information to Matthew Strong."

"So we have no kid and no data. Is that what you're telling me?"

"I'm reporting on the current situation, sir. We have intercepted phone calls and e-mail messages between the kid and his father. Matthew Strong is on the way to his grandmother's house in Amarillo."

"And I'm assuming you're on top of that?"

"Absolutely."

"Stunning." Vince shook his head. "Just get the CDs, key... whatever, Harwood. Use as many men as you need to do the job. I want that information back in my possession today—

before the weekend—and I don't care what you do to get it. Do you understand me, Harwood?"

"Yes, sir."

Vince pressed the off button on his phone. He didn't ask much. He had no interest in acquiring political power or influence—except where it furthered Agrimax's interests. He had played golf with three presidents, and he knew each one envied his ability to get things done. A handpicked, pliable board of directors was better than a stubborn Congress any day. Democracy was fine, he believed, as long as the outcome of a vote was predetermined.

Military power did not appeal to him, either. He considered the billions spent on arms each year to be an inefficient use of capital. Besides, in the long run, the cumbersome system of separate nations would evolve of necessity into a single world economy. Vince knew he probably wouldn't live to see that day, but he was determined to be remembered as a visionary who had the skills to make his ideas a reality.

But he had to stay on top of anything that could derail him. He was glad now that the threat that terrorists might target America's food supply had led him to build a formidable security force headed by a former Marine with combat experience. To this point, nothing had gotten past them. Harwood was intelligent and physically daunting, with no fears and no morals. As head of Agrimax's highly trained security corps, he had seen the company through more than a few sticky situations. Despite the sick feeling in the pit of Vince's stomach, he would pour himself a cup of coffee and trust Harwood to save his hide.

Chapter Five

The sun lifted into the eastern sky in a blaze of mauve and orange as Cole drove across the flat expanse of the Texas Panhandle. Jill Pruitt's head lay on his right shoulder, her mop of golden ringlets obscuring her features. Beside her, Billy Younger—head back and mouth wide-open—snored loudly enough to startle the jackrabbits on the side of the road. Rising on hind legs, they abandoned their nibbling to stare at the passing vehicle. The morning light shone through their tall ears, translucent pink against the long, pale green grass swaying in the slight breeze.

On any other morning, Cole would have enjoyed this hour. He relished the quiet of dawn. Purple shadows crept from under rocks and the gnarled roots of cottonwood trees to work their way across the grass. Butterflies drifted above the alfalfa—a beautiful bane in his battle to grow high-quality hay. Hummingbirds darted around crimson trumpet-shaped flowers of red-hot poker plants. A coachwhip snake might emerge to test the heat, or a horned toad to seek out a breakfast of insects. Overhead, meadowlarks wheeled across the sky and buzzards circled yesterday's carrion.

This was the land Cole loved, the terrain he relied on to provide him and his son a livelihood. But this Friday morning, he could take no joy in the Creator's display. The night had been long and frustrating as he had driven slowly north, his eyes fruitlessly scanning ditches and underpasses for any sign of his son's truck. He had no idea what the day ahead might bring.

At a truck stop in Hobbs, Cole had asked about his son. No one recalled seeing the youth. A call to Josefina brought the news that a warrant had been issued for Matt's arrest. Cole then phoned his mother, who had not heard from the boy. She didn't answer his second call from Lubbock, and he took this to mean she had gone to sleep despite her determination to stay up and wait for her grandson. Jill sent several e-mail messages to Matt. He didn't answer. Billy had begged to be allowed to continue the search, and Cole had relented under the teenager's persistence.

Somehow the hours had gotten away from him before he remembered he was supposed to call Penny. At one in the morning, she had phoned—upset, worried and angry. Cole had faced her fury more than once, and he didn't like it. The woman he was sure he loved transformed from a confident lawyer and bright, attractive lady into a three-year-old pitching a hissy fit. She called him names and threw things.

Cole had discovered he could provoke these tantrums inadvertently after a hailstorm damaged several acres of his seedlings. When he called to cancel his trip up to Albuquerque to visit her, she became furious, shouting and calling him names. Once she even lunged at him, scratching and slapping. Even now, though he'd been engaged to Penny for almost a year, her sudden explosions of anger still took him by surprise.

On this night when his son was missing and his peace had been shattered, she had flown into a rage over the presence of Jill Pruitt in his truck. Cole glanced at the woman whose head weighed lightly on his shoulder. Penny Ames didn't even know Jill. What did she have to loathe and fear?

Jill's focus remained solely on her students and her ministry passion. She had spent the late-night hours of their long drive talking about the ambitious garden she planted every year, listing for Cole and Billy every vegetable she planned to grow this season and what she intended to do with it. She canned much of her harvest and gave it to her church's food pantry. The rest she sold at the farmers market to help pay for her famine-relief work. Jill also had stories to tell about her experiences as a volunteer in various far-flung places.

Billy had nodded off after they left Lubbock, but Cole encouraged her to keep talking. He told himself he needed the chatter to help him stay awake, but in truth, Jill both annoyed and fascinated him. A bundle of bouncy, blond energy, she was an ornery little thing who wouldn't take no for an answer. With her prickly attitude and thorny assertiveness, she had gotten under Cole's skin like a cactus spine. She irritated him no end. But somewhere in the long hours of the night, he began to enjoy her easy laugh and mesmerizing voice. No wonder Matt had fallen under her sway.

Not only was she dedicated to her missions and her students, but she obviously walked in close communion with God. Every other sentence, it seemed, began, "I felt the Lord leading me to…" or "The Bible says we ought to…" or "If Jesus were on earth today…" Like a filter over a camera lens, everything in her life was tinted by her focus on Christ.

As he drove north toward Amarillo, Cole thought about his own casual faith journey. He did all the right things, of course. Even prayed and read his Bible some evenings. But he didn't have Jill's fire. In fact, he was the sort of lukewarm Christian God would probably want to spit out of His mouth. Cole knew this. But he didn't have the time to change. Each day required so much effort that he didn't have enough energy left for a deeper faith.

As the outskirts of Amarillo came into view, he felt the woman beside him stir. She lifted a hand, rubbed her eyes and made a little mew, like a kitten rising from a nap. Then she must have realized whose shoulder she'd been sleeping on, because she jerked upright, waking Billy midsnore.

"Huh?" he mumbled. "What's goin' on?"

"Where are we?" Jill asked.

"The edge of Amarillo." Cole glanced at her, amazed to find that her hair had not flattened in the night but actually seemed to have sprouted a few hundred more ringlets. "My mother's house isn't far. We'll be there in about ten minutes."

"I'm hungry," Billy said. "Let's get some doughnuts."

"Wow, I had no idea I went to sleep." Jill lifted her purse— a large fabric bag—onto her lap and rummaged around until she found a mirror. "Oh, good grief. Ugh." She poked her hair here and there, frowning at her reflection.

Billy attempted to stretch, which jammed Jill into Cole's shoulder again. "How often do you get a perm, Miss Pruitt?" the boy asked. "It's like mega-frizzy all the time."

"Thanks, Billy." She tossed her mirror back into her purse. "This is natural. I used to put straightener on it and iron it, but I gave up."

"Iron your hair? Whoa…"

"Yeah. Now I just let it go. But since we're on the subject of personal grooming, when was the last time you brushed those chompers, Billy?"

"My teeth?" He clamped a hand over his mouth. "It's been a while."

"Before we start back home this afternoon, we're stopping at a drugstore, and I'm going to buy you some personal-hygiene supplies."

"Miss Pruitt! That's embarrassing."

"Why? It's just a matter of fact, and you know how I feel about factual information, Billy. I insist on it. So we'll scoot you into Mrs. Strong's shower and give you a fresh start on the day. And I'm second in line."

Cole worked to hide the grin on his face. He liked a woman who spoke her mind, even when the subject wasn't exactly tasteful. At least she was honest and forthright. Two of his favorite qualities.

"And as for you, Cole," she began.

"Uh-oh, look out, Mr. Strong. She's gonna start on you. Probably tell you to shave and roll on some deodorant."

Cole winced at the idea that he might rival Billy in body odor. But Jill lifted her hand and ran her fingertip lightly over the stubble on his jaw.

"Hmm. Nope, I have no problem with this," she announced. "It's your relationship with Matt I've been thinking about."

Cole bristled. "What do you mean?"

"He took off without even trying to contact his own father. It's normally only runaways who do that."

"Are you saying Matt ran away from home? From me?"

"I just wonder why he didn't call you. Why he called Billy instead."

"I can tell you one thing for sure," Cole retorted. "Matt didn't run away from home. He's got a good life. I've given him everything he needs and wants—and Billy will testify to that."

"Billy said Matt called you an old dry tree stump." She was staring at him, green eyes boring into him. "I'm just wondering if you've considered the ramifications of everything that has happened. Aren't you bothered by the way your son talks about you? As though you barely exist in his life? I suspect this experience—"

"Excuse me, ma'am," he inserted, the warmth he had felt from her touch evaporating. "You can clean up Billy all you want, but I don't need you acting as my moral compass. I know where things stand with Matt, and I'll raise my son the way I see fit."

"He clearly feels that he can't come to you with things, or he would never have run—"

"Look, you teach him computers. I'll handle his personal life."

"I thought you didn't approve of my teaching methods."

"All I said was that you influenced him."

"And teachers aren't supposed to influence their students? Maybe if his father influenced him more by paying a little attention to him—"

"I pay attention to him. If he ever talks to me, I listen to everything he has to say."

"Do you ever talk to him?"

"I have tried, Miss Pruitt. But I'm not exactly up on the latest findings in genome sequencing and nuclear engineering. Are you?"

"Well...no."

"I don't know a bit from a byte or a RAM from a hertz. And I've learned that if I don't talk his language, he's not interested in communicating with me. Tell me you have deep discussions with the people on your mission trips. Do you speak Pakistani?"

"Urdu. That's the name of the language. And no, I don't. But if I had a son—"

"Well, you don't. And even if you did, he wouldn't be anything like Matthew Aaron Strong. Believe me."

"I still think you ought to—"

"Are you two gonna argue all the way home this afternoon?" Billy spoke up. "If you are, I'll just stay with Granny Strong."

Cole fell silent—irritation joining his worry—as he turned onto his mother's street and pulled into the narrow driveway that led to her one-car garage. Her powder-blue '97 Chevrolet was parked in front, because the garage door was too heavy for her to lift. She refused to let Cole put in an automatic opener for her. He noted that her lawn was neatly mowed, as usual, and her spring bulbs were in full bloom—tulips, daffodils, even a few crocuses left.

At this hour, most of the working adults in the neighborhood had left for their jobs, and the children were on buses headed for school. A couple of minivans and a newer model Lincoln indicated that only moms and retirees might be home at this time of day. Cole stepped out of the pickup and took in the stillness. He'd never been a suburban kind of man. And he could barely stand to spend ten minutes in Penny's downtown Albuquerque condo. Too many people living too close together made him edgy.

"I can't barely walk, I'm so stiff," Billy groaned. "Someone steer me to a doughnut."

"I don't see Matt's truck here." Jill spoke in a low voice, joining Cole as he walked up to his mother's front door. She started to add something, then fell silent.

Cole shook his head. He had tried without success to figure out any other place Matt might have gone. This was it, he thought, pressing the doorbell. His wife's parents had passed away years before he met her, and there were no cousins, aunts, or uncles on either side who were close to Matt.

"Mr. Strong, ring the bell again. I need to use the bathroom." Billy was stepping from one foot to the other. "Maybe it's open."

Cole pressed the button a second time.

He heard chimes from within, followed by silence. His mother rarely left home except to attend church, buy groceries, or play Skip-Bo with Irene. He glanced across the lawn at her best friend's house. Odd. The door stood ajar.

"Go check the neighbor's house," he told Jill. "See if Irene knows where my mother went."

He hammered on the door. Nothing. He tried the knob. The door swung open, and he stepped inside. Alarm pricked through him. Despite the quaint neighborhood, his mother never left her door unlocked.

A blotch of blood on the tan carpet stopped him cold.

"Mr. Strong!" Billy cried out, staring at the dark smear that had seeped into the carpet's thick pile. A curved trail of droplets led away from it toward the front door. "Look—is that… is that…? I'll go get Miss Pruitt!"

"Mom?" A knot in his throat, Cole took off down the long, darkened hallway. "Mom, are you here? It's Cole! Where are you?"

Her bedroom was empty, yellow chenille spread neatly smoothed over the single pillow, Bible near the lamp on the side table. He jerked open the closet doors—clothes all folded and put away. Pale blue house slippers on the floor. Artificial flower arrangement atop a white, starched doily on the dresser.

Beside the bedroom, the bathroom door stood ajar, and he slapped it open. Gleaming porcelain bathtub, sink, toilet. Matched pair of pink towels. Crocheted toilet-roll holder on the tank—a strange, wide-eyed plastic doll emerging from the frills. Fluffy pink rug on the floor. Dove soap, pink hairbrush, Crest toothpaste—everything in order.

The spare bedroom across the hall always stayed shut until Cole and Matt came to visit. Cole threw open the door. The room was dark. Twin beds made, curtains drawn. That familiar musty smell.

His pulse throbbing in his temples, Cole headed back to the living room. He poked his head into the dining room. Oval maple table and matching captain's chairs. China cabinet with rows of pretty flowered dishes. Framed still-life prints of fruit and roses.

"Mom!"

Into the kitchen. Two chairs at the old red vinyl dinette. Skip-Bo cards scattered across the plastic tablecloth. Two glasses of tea sitting untasted, the ice long melted.

"Mom!" he shouted again, returning to the living room just as Jill stepped through the front door.

"No one's over there, but it looks like—" Jill grabbed his arm. "Oh, heavens! Cole, it's—"

"Blood, yeah, I know." He raked a hand back through his hair. "I can't find her. She's not in the house."

"Did you check upstairs?" Billy asked, panting from his run next door to fetch Jill.

"There isn't an upstairs—" Cole remembered the basement. Dashing back into the kitchen, he found the door. It was locked…from the inside. He yanked at it, tried to force the knob.

"Whoa, Mr. Strong," Billy said, edging past. "Leave this to me."

With a swift kick, the boy's foot broke through, splintering wood. For a moment, his shoe stuck in the jagged hole. Jill grabbed his leg and jerked it, and they both tumbled backward, crashing into the table and spilling tea across the Skip-Bo cards.

But Cole had already worked his arm up through the opening in the broken door to slide back the bolt. "Mom?" he called, taking the rickety steps as fast as he dared. "Mom, it's Cole. Are you down here?"

He tugged the cord that hung from a single lightbulb.

"Cole?" The thin voice came from behind a large box labeled Ornaments.

"Mom, what's happened? It's me."

"Oh, Cole! Thank God."

He dismantled a wall of Christmas storage boxes, one at a time, to reveal two elderly women huddled together on the concrete floor. His mother's face was pinched, her mouth drawn into a frightened grimace, her skin as white and transparent as paper. She lifted a hand to him.

"Mom, what's going on? Is that Mrs. Williams?" Cole wrapped his arms around his mother's small frame and helped her up.

"Irene hurt her hip."

"I'm okay, Geneva." The other woman's voice was a whisper. Curled into a fetal position, she had folded her hands under her cheek. Her friend had covered her with a felt Christmas-tree skirt. "I'll be all right. Don't bother anybody now."

"Mrs. Williams, don't move," Cole said. "I'm going to get Mom upstairs, and then we'll call an ambulance."

"Done," Jill said, coming to his side. "It's on its way. Mrs. Strong, I'm Jill Pruitt—can you walk?"

The older woman reached out and laid a hand on Jill's arm. "Miss Pruitt? Why, you must be Matthew's computer teacher! He's told me so much about you. How good of you to—"

"Listen, Mom, what happened here?" Cole cut into the chatter. "Why are you and Mrs. Williams in the basement?"

"We were robbed!" Irene piped up from her crumpled position on the floor. "Those men knocked on the door, and Geneva opened it—"

"Well, I thought it was Matthew, of course, but it wasn't. It was two men, both of them tall and—"

"Big! And they marched right in without being invited. They said they just wanted to talk to us, but I knew it was a robbery, so I yelled for help."

"Irene took to screaming," Cole's mother said, "and I kept telling her to calm down, but these men were like a couple of big ol' Simmental bulls. They sat us down at the kitchen table—"

"Where we'd been playing Skip-Bo, waiting for her grandson, you know."

"And the men started to get angry, what with Irene hollering like that, and they were asking about you and Matthew, and when you were going to get here, and what I knew about Matthew's schoolwork—"

"About his schoolwork!" Irene repeated. "But it was all a trick, because they just wanted to rob us."

"I've been trying to convince her they weren't robbers," Geneva confided in a low voice, "but she won't let it go. What they really were was FBI." As she said this, she gave Cole a firm nod.

"How do you know they were FBI, Mom?"

"Because they already had Matthew's name, and where he lived, and who his teachers were—"

"His teachers?" Jill spoke up. "Did they mention my name?"

"It's those Agrimax men," Billy declared. "They've got everything tapped!"

"And they were trying to rob us!" Irene wailed from the floor. "Only thing that saved us was Geneva's Smith & Wesson!"

"What?" Cole's mouth dropped open. "You used your pistol?"

"I sure as fire did. Winged one of 'em." She stuck her hand down in the pocket of her pink flowered housedress and pulled out the handgun. "One bullet, that's all it took. My daddy always said I was a sharpshooter. I saw one of them fall right there in the living room, and the other one stopped to check on his partner. It gave Irene and me enough time to hightail it down here. I guess we scared 'em off, because they didn't follow us."

"I fell!" Irene whimpered.

"I dragged her over here in the corner and stacked up these Christmas boxes, and we waited it out all night. I knew somebody would show up, but I wasn't sure who. Good thing I've got more bullets—"

"Give me those!" Cole snapped as his mother drew a handful of ammunition out of her pocket. He held out his hand for the gun, as well. "Did the men threaten you?"

"They were going to rob us!" Irene said.

"They said they wanted every letter Matthew wrote to me in the past three years. And they wanted my address book and phone book and all that. They were just plain ugly about it. Rude, you know? I said, 'What's this all about, boys?' They told me Matthew was in trouble for murdering somebody in New Mexico, and they were here to investigate. That's when I figured out they were FBI."

"And you shot at them?"

"I didn't like 'em. Neither one, nor anything they had to say." She shrugged. "I told them Matthew never did a single thing wrong in his life, and I wasn't giving them blim-blam-doodly. They said I better get those letters and that address book quick, or there'd be trouble. So I said okay. Fine. I walked over to the silverware drawer, pretending to fetch my address book. Then I took my Smith & Wesson out from behind the dessert forks and turned around and told them to get their hides outta my house, or I'd show them what trouble really was. When they jumped up and came at me, I let 'em have it. Just like I said I would."

"I bet they robbed us blind after we came down here," Irene added. "I left my door unlocked when I came over to visit with Geneva. They probably took my husband's bowling trophies, all five of them. He was a champion, you know. And the microwave and the mixer. After it got quiet upstairs, I told Geneva to get back up there and call the police. But she wouldn't budge."

"I'm no fool. They were probably lurking outside for a few hours, waiting for Matthew to show up. That's what they do in the FBI. They lurk."

Cole let out a breath. "Jill, will you stay down here with Mrs. Williams, while I—"

"Hello?" A voice called down from the basement door. "Anybody down there?"

"It's them!" Cole's mother grabbed for her gun.

"It's the paramedics." He lifted the weapon above his mother's grasp. "Yes—come ahead!"

In moments, four pairs of soft-soled shoes came padding down the basement steps. The team carried a stretcher and a bag of medical supplies.

"Did you know there's blood on the living-room floor?" one asked.

"I tripped," Irene said as the paramedics surrounded her. "It's my hip. Don't touch it! Oww!"

Cole decided this would be a good time to escort his mother back upstairs.

Someone was pushing Matt. A hand on his back, shoving him.

"Okay, okay, Josefina," he mumbled. "I'll get up."

He forced his eyes open. But instead of a smooth white pillow, his head lay on damp dirt in an alley.

"Huh?" Jerking upright, Matt heard a chorus of squeals and giggles as a group of ragged children scattered. Groaning, he hugged his laptop to his chest as he realized the miniature thieves had been trying to roll him over and steal it.

Ugh…he felt awful. As if he was going to be sick again. As if he might die. The knot on the back of his head hurt again. Why had he even come to this godforsaken—

Awareness shot through him in a shower of pinpricks, and he slammed his hand over his pocket. The lump was still there. The USB key. Thank God! He blew out a sour breath.

Okay, he still had it, but this wasn't going well. Miss Pruitt never had problems like this when she was doing God's work. Confusion and fear. Hunger and barfing and fainting. She didn't have people accusing her of murder or trying to rob her blind. She just trotted over to Afghanistan or wherever and served up healthy, nutritious food to grateful hordes.

Matt checked his watch. Friday morning, 10:20 a.m. He hadn't been out long. A movement caught his eye, and he swung his head to see the group of street children peeking at him around the corner of a building.

"I'm not dead yet!" he hollered in the best Spanish he could muster.

They shrieked and raced away, laughing at him again.

To them, this was a game. Ha. Matt worked himself up into a sitting position and propped his head in his hands. His whole body shook with hunger. Smells of urine and vomit and rotten food swirled through the alley and wrapped around his head.

Maybe I'm dead after all. Maybe I died and went to hell. It couldn't be any worse than this.

He thought of Josefina and her sumptuous breakfasts of fried eggs, frijoles covered with melted yellow cheese, freshly made tortillas spread with butter and fat, greasy sausage links all washed down with orange juice, milk and hot chocolate laced with cinnamon. Right now, he would just about kill for one of Josefina's breakfasts.

Instead, he had to figure out what to do, because he was stuck in Juarez, Mexico, with a USB key full of stolen secrets and a murder charge hanging over his head and two thugs trying to track him down and hurt or kill him. This was not good.

Unbidden tears filled his eyes. He shook his head. He was sixteen and too old to cry. Too smart to sit here in an alley beside his own vomit. Too educated, too rich, too everything. But he couldn't think what to do. Nothing made sense unless he was in his own room with his computer and modem and mouse and all the things he understood.

Not this! Everything happening now was way bigger than he was. Bigger than anything he'd ever imagined when he sat on his soft bed and read Christ's command in Matthew 25: *Feed the hungry.* How hard could that be? Using the research from his term paper, he had formulated a plan that involved the cooperation of major food companies. Agrimax hadn't been the least bit interested in his ideas. But Mr. Banyon had. He thought it was a great idea, and he said he knew how to make it happen.

With Mr. Banyon, everything seemed simple. All Matt had to do was buy the USB key and teach Mr. Banyon how to use it. Mr. Banyon would pull the right strings, and the hungry would get fed.

How had Matt ended up being the one with the Agrimax secrets? This wasn't how it was supposed to happen!

Tears rolled down his cheeks, and he brushed them off as fast as he could, even though he knew no one could see him.

No one except those stupid kids who were peering around the corner again. Laughing at him and pointing.

"What?" he yelled in Spanish. "What's so funny?"

"*Borrachon!* Drunkard!" one of them called back.

"I'm not drunk. I'm sick. I'm hungry." He picked up a pebble and hurled it at them.

They shrieked and scampered away again.

Matt dissolved into full-blown sobs this time, and there wasn't a thing he could do about it. *What am I supposed to do, God? Where am I supposed to go? I came all this way to find Hector Diaz and give him the key so he could take it to Josiah Karume. Now I find out he already left for that food convention in France. Why didn't You tell me, God? Why didn't You guide me better?*

If I go home, I'll have to give Agrimax the USB key, and that will be the end of everything Mr. Banyon was trying to do. Everything You wanted me to do.

His sobs turned to coughing, which stirred up his gag reflex again. The laptop slid onto the dirt as he rolled over onto his hands and knees and retched. Nothing came up. His stomach heaved and heaved, but his tears were the only thing to fall to the ground.

Please help me, God! Please save me!

Collapsing to the ground, he curled into a ball. If the kids stole his laptop and wallet and key, he might as well just die. Die for real. And here they came, three of them, creeping closer. Little street rats, all in rags with their filthy hair hanging down over beady black eyes.

They stopped at a slight distance, elbowing each other and giggling.

"*Señor,*" one spoke up. He thought it might be a girl because of the faded dress she wore, but he wasn't sure. "*Pan?*" She held out a fragment of bread.

Matt stared at it, his stomach whirling and his brain too

fogged to think clearly. This street kid was offering food to him. Was it a trick?

"Bread?" she said again in Spanish. "Eat it."

He clutched his laptop. "For me?"

"Yes." She took a step closer.

Reaching out, he took the gift. The child jumped backward, as if fearful he might grab her.

Breathing hard, he stuffed a bite of bread into his mouth. *Oh, thank You, God!* It was like manna! Melting in his mouth. Caressing his throat. Sliding into his stomach.

He took another bite. Thank You! Thank You!

The little girl smiled at him and tilted her head. "Good, *señor?*"

Matt nodded as he chewed the last bite. "Thank you," he said. "I am very hungry."

"You give us money? Dollars?"

His heart sank. The bread hadn't been a gift after all. They wanted his money. Of course, and why not? He was a gringo, and that meant he was rich. He had the computer under his arm. He had jeans and Nike shoes and everything that said wealthy American. Nodding, he drew out his wallet and pulled out a five-dollar bill.

"Here you go. Thank you."

Eyes wide with excitement, she skipped forward and grabbed the money. With a cry of victory, she and her companions danced out of the alley to rejoin their gang. Matt leaned his back against the brick wall of I-FEED Mexico headquarters, shut his eyes and tried to think.

He should find a phone and call his dad. Cole Strong had to be pretty upset by now. He probably believed Matt had murdered Mr. Banyon, even though the last e-mail said different. Matt's dad had never understood one thing about his son. Didn't even much like him. Every time they tried to do something together, it was a bust. Except church. They did that pretty well. Drove together, side by side, sat through the service, and then went out to eat, because Sunday was Josefina's day off. But they didn't talk—not about anything interesting.

How's school? How's Billy?

Fine, fine.

How's the farm? How's Penny?

Fine, fine.

What did Penny Ames even see in his dad? Matt wondered. Though Matt thought of her as kind of stuck-up, she was young and pretty. Cole was old and sunburned and boring. His hands were callused, and all he ever thought about was plowing or the price his hay might bring. He would make Matt turn over the key. Then he'd get a lawyer—one of Penny's colleagues, no doubt—and try to get his son's name cleared. He would never understand the importance of doing God's will. Of feeding the hungry. Of exposing a company that controlled the world's food supply and refused to save millions of dying children. Children like those little street rats who had fed Matt.

He glanced toward the street and wondered how any wellspring of kindness remained inside their worn-out, dirty little bodies. What made them reach out to a sick, stupid *Americano* and bring him a hunk of bread? And how could he fail to do everything in his power to save kids like that? Jesus had promised that whatever Matt did to the least of his brothers, he was doing that same thing to Jesus himself. And those street kids were surely the least of all.

Even as he thought this, the little ragamuffin girl came tearing around the alley corner, followed by her band of ruffians. With a laugh of triumph, she dropped a large brown paper bag into Matt's lap.

"Open it, *señor!*" she cried as her friends gathered around.

Matt obeyed, and he found himself gazing down at a large loaf of fresh bread, five oranges, a bunch of bananas, two cans of Coke and a string of fat, greasy sausages just like Josefina's.

"Give us," the girl ordered. She and the others squatted in a semicircle around Matt, their hands outstretched.

He reached into the bag and drew out the bread they had bought with his money and returned to share with him. But before he began dividing it among his newfound friends, he held up a hand.

"First, let's thank God for this. *Gracias a Dios.*"

"Dios, señor?" the girl asked. "Who is God?"

Chapter Six

Jill gratefully wrapped her hands around a mug of hot tea and studied the man across the table. The fine lines that weather and sun had etched around Cole's eyes had deepened in the past hours. His large hands, obviously accustomed to hard labor, lay unmoving yet curled with tension.

He lifted one and rubbed it across his unshaven chin. "Well," he said, exhaling a deep breath, "I'm stumped."

"I think Billy's right."

He looked up at her, his eyes flashing blue in the late-morning light. "Agrimax? You really think they'd send two goons to Amarillo to harass my mother?"

"Whoever came here is after Matt. That's all we know for sure."

"It could be the law."

"They'd have shown badges, followed protocol."

"Maybe." He ran a blunt-nailed finger along the thick rim of his own mug. "I wish I knew where that boy went."

Despite her initial dislike of the man, Jill was warmed by

his concern for his son. Maybe Cole did love Matt, but he just wasn't good at showing it. Or maybe he hadn't realized how much he cared until he lost Matt.

"Why don't you call Agrimax?" she asked. "Just confront them."

His eyes caught hers again, and he frowned. "You don't get this, do you?"

"Get what?"

"I work for Agrimax. I might as well be an employee."

"I thought you owned all that land. You run a family farm, don't you?"

"Yeah, and I need to sell what I grow in order to keep it profitable." He took another swig of tea. His face was rigid as he swallowed. "Look, you have a little farm of your own— that garden you babbled about half the night."

She scowled. "Babbled? I never babble."

"Okay, you didn't babble."

"You were interested."

His blue eyes focused on her. "The point is, you ought to understand what I'm saying here. If you want the money to go on mission trips to Pakistan, you have to sell your produce, right?"

"Of course. That's partly why I helped found the farmers market in town."

"Right. Well, I grow a little too much hay and beef for the local farmers market. This is no hobby for me. My livelihood depends on somebody buying my produce. The company that gives me the best deal—the only deal worth the time and effort I put into my land—is Agrimax."

"They buy all your beef? And your hay, too?"

"And my cotton and chile. They tell me what to grow, how much to plant, what kinds of fertilizers and pesticides to use— all based on how much they'll be willing to buy from me at harvesttime. They pay me a fraction of what they'll charge on the other end. Just enough to keep me from going under."

"That's sickening."

"It's business. My crops and beef go through processing plants owned by subsidiaries of Agrimax. Agrimax's ships, trucks, and railcars transport the processed food all around the world. And where does it wind up? Right back at the local grocery store—part of a national superchain—where I spend thirty or forty percent more to buy it than I got paid to grow it."

Stunned, Jill sat in silence for a moment. "You know, this is exactly the sort of thing Matt was saying he had discovered in his research." She looked across at Cole. "Why didn't you tell your son about your work? You could have influenced him so much. You could have explained this all to him firsthand."

"He didn't ask."

"Did you? Did you ever inquire what Matt was studying? What his interests are? His fascination with food companies actually may have been prompted by you and your farm— but you never even knew, because you didn't bother to talk to your son about his life."

He slapped his hand down on the table. "Maybe I didn't want to talk to the boy about what I do. First of all, he's never shown one iota of interest in the farm. And second, the details of the way it runs is not exactly something I like to brag about. Farming and ranching are full of government red tape and restrictions. The food companies have farmers in a stranglehold. We can barely move. Barely hire employees. Barely make ends meet. I do it because I love the work, and I love the land. I'm proud of the farm and everything I've accomplished with it. But I'll be just as happy to see my son find another line of business."

"I don't believe that!"

"You think I want him to have the life of a farmer—a bad back from lifting heavy equipment, hearing loss from loud machinery, skin that looks like leather, and every day the chance of getting a finger or an arm cut off? You think I want him to become a slave to government regulations and the dictates of a company like Agrimax?"

"I think you'd love for Matt to inherit your land. And I think he'd be proud to have the responsibility of carrying on your work."

"Is that what you think, Miss Pruitt?"

Cole might as well have called her Miss Know-It-All. She shifted in her chair. Maybe she didn't know everything there was to know about farming. But surely a man who had worked so hard to build up his enterprise would want his son to inherit it.

"You know that genetically modified, bioengineered seed you find so repulsive?" he was asking now, leaning toward Jill. "I grow that seed for Agrimax. I've sold them tons of it."

"You're kidding."

"No, I'm not—someone has to do it. Why not me?"

"Because it's not right! That seed hasn't been fully tested. We don't know the ramifications for our children and grandchildren. The pure genetic stock may be compromised, and then—"

"That's farming, lady. Agrimax tells me what they'll buy and how much they want, and I grow it. No matter what. It's the system, if you want to succeed as a farmer. And I do."

Jill was breathing hard, trying to comprehend the web that bound this man and other farmers so tightly they could barely move. It was complex and disheartening, so very different from her mental image of the old-fashioned family farm where the farmer planted crops of his choice, harvested them, and sold the produce to nearby retailers.

"So now do you understand," Cole asked, "why I'm not going to call Agrimax and accuse them of chasing off my son and threatening my mother? Who wants to do business with a nutcase? Not Agrimax, I guarantee. They can buy hay, beef and seed from growers all over the world. I'm just one tiny cog in their wheel, and they can easily do without me."

"But you can't do without them."

"Absolutely not. As I said before, I can't sell my hay at your little farmers market. I can't sell my beef to the local grocery store. It doesn't work that way anymore."

"Well, it should. I've set it up so that my church uses its parking lot for a farmers market. We use the huge basement kitchen to can and process all the leftover produce. Any vegetables that don't sell—or are less than perfect—go into jars we can sell at the next market or give away through the church food pantry."

She recalled with satisfaction how well it had worked. Kids from local Christian youth groups had been invited to help with the cooking. Eager to learn from women who had been canning all their lives, young wives and teens crowded into the kitchen each Thursday after the farmers market ended.

"It ought to work that way even with large farms." She looked at Cole. "Then we'd know what we were eating and where it came from."

"Dream away, Miss Pruitt. Large farms need large corporations to back them."

Jill lifted her focus to the small window over Geneva Strong's kitchen sink. Ruffled white curtains trimmed in red rickrack framed the bright blue sky. What had the world come to in the last hundred years since Amarillo was a bustling cow town and farmers sold their produce locally? Was there any hope for a return to those days?

"Well, I got our boy Billy into the shower," Geneva said,

stepping into the kitchen and setting her hands on her hips. "My goodness, he's big. And what an eater! I don't know when I've ever made so many pancakes. Even you never downed that many, Cole, and you used to eat like a horse. I hope you realize this is Friday. That boy ought to be in school, not traipsing around the countryside. Did you know he calls me Granny Strong, just like Matthew? Isn't that sweet?"

"I got hold of the hospital," Cole told her. "Irene's in surgery."

"Surgery! Oh, good night, that must mean she broke her hip. Those FBI devils…we ought to sue them, barging in here like that and scaring two old ladies half out of our wits."

Geneva crossed to the sink and began drying the breakfast dishes she'd insisted on washing by hand herself. Offers to help had fallen on deaf ears, so Jill had taken the opportunity to make the promised trip to the drugstore. She brought back deodorant, toothpaste and other grooming supplies for the Incredible Hulk who had shared the seat in Cole's truck. After Billy showered, they ought to set off for home. But what about Matt?

"Maybe you should try calling Josefina again," she suggested to Cole. "Matt has to be hungry. What if he showed up this morning, and she started feeding him breakfast—"

"It's been less than an hour since my last call, and she has my number. She knows how worried we are."

He tipped his mug for a last swallow of tea. Then he set it on the table and leaned across, his face intense. "Look, Miss Pruitt… Jill…you read my son's research paper. Do you really think Matt's disappearance might have something to do with this food thing?"

"Yes, I do," she said softly.

He looked away, obviously in pain. "I want to believe it was Banyon's suicide that spooked him into taking off, but there's been too much other stuff. Those threatening e-mails. The two men showing up at the high school and taking him out of class. And now those goons coming here asking questions and making threats."

"It was the FBI," Geneva said from the sink. "They think Matthew killed that farmer in Hope. I saw a show on TV where the FBI just came busting through the door and went to shoving people around and asking all kinds of questions the same way they did to me and Irene. Rude. Just plain rude."

Jill stood and carried the two empty mugs across to the sink. "The local police know about Mr. Banyon's death and Matt's disappearance. But I doubt the federal government is involved, Mrs. Strong. Not unless Matt had stumbled onto something that would affect them." She gazed at the stack of gleaming plates. "Anyway, I'm going to check my e-mail one more time."

Frustrated, she walked into the tidy living room and stared at the bloodstained carpet. Earlier, Cole had called the hospital emergency room to ask whether anyone had been admitted for a gunshot wound, but a voice informed him that such information could not be released. The police had arrived shortly after the ambulance. They simply took down the report—confused as it was, with Irene and Geneva each giving a different version of the story—and went on their way.

This whole situation was crazy, Jill thought as she took a seat on Geneva's pale pink sofa. Teenagers like Matt Strong didn't disappear without a good reason. Something terrible must have happened to him. Even if he was guilty of hacking into Agrimax's mainframe or sending someone a flood of e-mails, the most he could be charged with was harassment. Fear of that shouldn't have made him run. No, Jill had an awful certainty there was something more.

Not long after the ambulance sped away with Irene Williams, Jill had set up Matt's computer on the coffee table. So far, she had read through about half of the boy's research for his famine-relief term paper, and she had seen nothing that might cause him to flee. The information he had gathered was fascinating—the underhanded practices of Agrimax and a couple of other major food companies—but all of it was readily accessible by the public. Nothing she had found on the computer would have caused anyone to come after Matt. The term paper itself was even rather pedantic, the sort of essay a sophomore with high ideals and a lot of enthusiasm would write. Nothing groundbreaking or terribly controversial.

Jill logged on to the Internet. She had sent Matt two messages in the past hours—telling him where they were and urging him to do the same. As the hard drive hummed, she prayed again. Not one of her mission trips around the world had brought her this much distress or led to such intensity of prayer. *Please, dear God, please help us find Matt. And keep him safe until we do!*

As a message appeared on the screen, her adrenaline shot up. "Hey, he wrote!" she called out.

Cole was at her side in a heartbeat. "What does he say?"

She read the message:

im ok keep granny safe from them theyre desperate you stay safe too dont come after me but im on the paper trail get it

"Get it?" Cole exploded. "Get what? What does he mean? What's the paper trail? Give me that thing!"

He dropped down onto the sofa, practically sitting on Jill as he grabbed the keyboard and began typing:

Now listen here, boy—

Jill laid her hand over his. "Stop, Cole. Just stop a minute and cool down. We have a message from Matt here, and we need to think it through."

"I've thought it through already. He's playing some kind

of computer game with us. It's like that stuff we talked about yesterday. Armies of trolls and goblins moving back and forth across the screen like some kind of demented chess game."

"What's going on?" Billy emerged from the bathroom, a pink towel cinched around his waist. He was rubbing his mop of thick brown hair with another towel. "Did you hear from Matt? Lemme see!"

He plopped down on the other side of Jill and jammed the two adults into the back of the sofa as he leaned across to see the screen. "Get what?" he asked. "What's the paper trail?"

"You tell us." Jill brushed water droplets from her arms. "You know the Mattman. What's he saying?"

"Well, he's okay, so that's good."

"What do you mean, he's okay?" Cole demanded. "How can he be okay if we don't even know where he is?"

"You're not making sense," Jill said.

"*Okay* means he's safe at home on the ranch," Cole retorted. "Roaming around scared is not okay."

"*Okay* means he's alive, he's not hurt…and scoot over, Billy. I can barely breathe."

"He knows we're in Amarillo, so that means he's been getting your messages, Miss Pruitt." Billy didn't budge. "But he's still freaked out. See, he says *they're desperate.* He saw what they did to Mr. Banyon, and he's afraid they're going to kill him. Or us."

"I still think Banyon killed himself," Cole said.

"You are so stubborn, Cole Strong!" Jill glared at him before giving Billy a mighty push that did nothing to dislodge his damp bulk. "The sheriff said the blood spatters led him to believe it wasn't a suicide. So quit hanging on to that. Somebody shot the poor man, and since it couldn't have been Matt, it must be the people he thinks are chasing him."

"Agrimax?" Cole glared back. "Why would they kill Banyon?"

"He worked for them," Billy said. "Maybe he did something they didn't like."

"Maybe he knew a secret," Jill guessed. "Matt's term paper said these big food companies are developing all kinds of secret technologies. Maybe Banyon knew about those."

"You don't kill someone for knowing a secret that you told them," Cole said.

"You do if they tell," Billy said. "I hate it when people tell my secrets. One time in sixth grade, I liked this girl, Ashley Morris. And I told Jacob Dunn, because he was on my Little League team, and I thought we were buddies. He swore he wouldn't tell, but then he told Ashley's best friend, Dina, and she—"

"Does this story have an end?" Cole asked.

"For goodness' sake, Cole!" Jill snapped. "Don't be so impatient. Billy's telling us something important. Go on, Billy."

The boy looked sheepish. "Well, the end of the story is that Ashley told Dina she liked me, too, so we wound up going out for three weeks."

"And that's supposed to tell us what?" Cole asked.

"It's just that I hate it when people tell secrets after they swear they won't. And if I had a big secret like Agrimax, and if Mr. Banyon knew that secret, and he told Matt, I might go after Mr. Banyon and then go after Matt, too. So maybe that's why Matt ran off."

Geneva, who had been standing over the coffee table and folding her dish towel, let out a loud sigh. "Who cares why the child ran off? The point is that he's gone, and we've got to find him. Now what's this about a paper trail? What does that mean?"

Jill, Cole, and Billy all studied the computer screen, as if the message might suddenly morph into something they could understand. It did feel as though Matt was toying with them, Jill thought. Writing things in code, making them work to find him. Was this all a ploy to get his father's attention? Billy said Matt spent hours at the cemetery. Maybe the boy had realized that he was never going to see his mother again and then decided he'd taken enough of his father's aloofness.

"A 'paper trail' usually means letters and documents," Cole said. "Matt hasn't left us anything on paper. All we have is a couple of e-mails."

"It could be some other kind of paper." Billy scrubbed his head with the towel as he spoke, sending another shower of droplets over Cole and Jill. "Like the newspaper. Maybe there's some kind of clue in the articles about Mr. Banyon's death."

"Albuquerque," Jill said. "New Mexico's largest newspaper is published in Albuquerque. Maybe that's where Matt went."

"If so, he'd have gone to Penny's condo—which would have been smart if he thought he was in some kind of trouble. She's a lawyer, and she could help him. But he's not there."

"Matt's brain doesn't work that way," Billy said, standing. "He has no common sense. I'm sorry to be blunt about it, Mr. Strong, but that's the truth. If it's math, he can think logically. But if it's real life, dude, he's a mess. So we have to think like him, like what he's trying to tell us. When he says paper trail, he means something weird that only we would understand, because he's trying to talk in a code that's just for us. He wants to show us where he is but not let them know in case they're reading his e-mails—which they are, because Granny Strong said they asked her what time we were supposed to get to Amarillo, remember?"

"That's true," Geneva confirmed. "Those FBI men knew it when they walked in that door. They already knew you were on your way to my house before I said a word."

Jill glanced at Cole. "I'd forgotten that. Who did we tell about our trip?"

"Penny," Cole said. "Josefina. Pedro and Hernando, my two foremen."

"I told Marianne Weston. You mentioned it to the sheriff. Billy left a message for his parents. And then...well, we did e-mail Matt."

"Yeah, and that's how they found out," Billy concluded. "They must be tapping into his user account. They've got the Mattman's login name and password, and they're reading everything we write back and forth. Matt's not stupid about things like that, so he's talking in code. He's on the *paper trail*...that's what he said, right? What kind of a trail would be made out of paper?"

"Trees are made into paper," Jill said. "Maybe he's in a forest."

"Maybe he dropped wads of paper on the ground, like Hansel and Gretel." Billy thought about his idea for a moment. "Nah. What kind of thing could he be standing on that you could call a trail? Or what kind of paper is he—"

He paused. He stared at Jill, then at Cole. "Dude. It's his term paper."

Jill lunged for the keyboard and pulled up the famine-relief text Matt had typed in. Cole and Billy leaned in. Geneva came around the coffee table and wedged onto the sofa beside Billy.

"You're still wet!" she exclaimed. "Boy, don't you know how to dry off? I'm going to have to replace my carpet *and* my couch."

"Banyon, that's who he talks about first," Billy said, pointing at the screen. "Look, it's a footnoted interview. It's number one, and that's where he was when all this mess started. Out at Hope with Mr. Banyon. Go to his bibliography page, Miss Pruitt. Who's next on his list?"

She scrolled to the end of the report. "The second footnote refers to Hector Diaz. Matt corresponded with him by e-mail. And it looks like they had one phone interview."

"Who's Hector Diaz?" Cole asked.

"He's the director of I-FEED's Mexico office—the International Federation of Environmental and Economic Development. It's the organization I usually work with on mission trips."

"So you gave Matt this name? Hector Diaz?"

Jill blanched at the accusation. "Well, yes. I provided several names as sources he could contact. For his term paper."

Cole leaned toward the screen and jabbed at the list of Matt's sources. "You had him call people in Mexico, Africa… Pakistan, for crying out loud!"

"Not call on the telephone. I gave him e-mail addresses."

"So now we're supposed to believe Matt went to Mexico?" Cole stood. "He didn't go to Mexico! He's never driven anywhere but the road from the ranch to town."

"And out to Hope," Billy put in. "But I think that's where he went. To Mexico."

"Why?"

"Because it's on the paper trail."

"Billy, use your head! You don't go places because they're in a certain order on your bibliography page!"

"You do if you're the Mattman."

Jill could see that Cole was about to explode. Lack of sleep, combined with frustration and fear, was taking its toll. She rose and walked around the coffee table to where he stood rubbing the back of his neck and staring down at the stain of blood on his mother's carpet.

"I'll e-mail Hector Diaz," she said, laying a hand on his arm.

"E-mail? What good is that—"

"I'll phone him, Cole. Okay? I'll do it right now. I-FEED Mexico's main office is in Juarez, so I'll just pick up the phone and ask Hector if he's seen Matt. Why don't you sit down in that recliner and—"

"Make the call, Jill." He handed her his cell phone. "This is nuts, but let's do it."

Nodding, she picked up her bag and rooted through it until she found her Palm handheld. Flipping open the PDA that contained—among other things—an address book, a schedule planner and e-mail access, she located Hector Diaz's telephone number. In moments, she was listening to the buzz of his phone in Mexico. When the answering machine kicked on, her heart sank.

"*Hola,* this is Hector Diaz. The I-FEED office will be closed until May 31 while I am attending the Third World Food Summit conference in Paris, France, and then taking a short holiday. Please leave your message, and I will—"

She pressed the end button and handed the phone back to Cole. "It's a dead end. Hector's at a meeting in Paris."

"Great. So much for following the paper trail." He punched in a series of numbers. "I'll let Sheriff Holtmeyer know what's happened here. Maybe he has some more information for me."

Billy lumbered back toward the bathroom, leaving a large wet circle on the pink sofa. Geneva let out a cry of dismay and hurried to the kitchen for towels.

Jill walked to the window, leaned a shoulder against the sill, and peered through the openwork lace curtains at the quiet neighborhood. How unthinkable that anything out of the ordinary could ever happen here. What sort of men would barge into the house of an old woman and make frightening demands and threats? Did those people have no conscience?

Hearing the concerned tone in Cole's voice as he spoke on the phone, Jill started to step from the window when a slight movement outside caught her eye. She squinted through the open pattern in the lace.

"Cole?" Her breath shallow, she called into the kitchen. "Mrs. Strong? Does someone in your neighborhood drive a dark blue Lincoln?"

"A what, honey?" Geneva strolled in from the kitchen, her arms laden with dish towels.

"A Lincoln. There's someone sitting in that car out there. A man, I think."

"Let me see." She reached for the curtain, but Jill caught her arm.

"Wait. I don't want him to know we've spotted him. Cole, come here! There's a man sitting in that Lincoln down the street. Did you notice him when we drove in this morning?"

"Nobody in this neighborhood drives a car that nice," Geneva said. "I bet it's those FBI men!"

Cole ended his call and moved to the window. "I did notice that car when we pulled in earlier, but I didn't think… you're right, somebody's sitting in the front seat."

"Call the police," Jill said.

"Forget the police," Geneva announced. "Cole, where'd you put my gun?"

"Now hold on." He set a hand on his mother's shoulder. "We've got to figure out—"

"What's up?" Billy asked, joining the group beside the curtain.

"The FBI's out there watching my house," Geneva told him. "See that blue Lincoln? They've probably tapped my phone and put wires everywhere. We better not say another word. Let's just talk in sign language."

"I don't know sign language, Granny Strong." Billy dropped his bag of toiletries on the sofa. "Tell you what, Mr. Strong.

Let's you and me take off in the pickup and see if they follow. That way we'll know for sure."

"Shh!" Geneva said, putting a finger over her lips. "They'll hear the plan! They've got infrared scanners and listening devices and all that!"

"I'll go," Jill said. "Cole, you stay here with your mother."

"Me and Miss Pruitt," Billy amended. "We'll sashay over to the grocery store and pick up some sandwich stuff, and if the Lincoln follows, we'll know it's those goons from last night."

"I shot one of 'em. He's not in that car, I guarantee. He's in a hospital someplace, because I plugged him good."

"What makes you think he'd follow you?" Cole asked. "I'm Matt's father. I'm the one they're after, because they think I'll be in touch with him."

"So you *do* believe Agrimax is chasing Matt?" Jill asked.

"Sheriff Holtmeyer told me a few things. He couldn't go into much detail because it's a criminal investigation. They're working on the theory that Banyon was murdered. Matt's their number one suspect, but they did discover another set of fresh tire prints near the house."

"I bet they match the tires on that Lincoln," Geneva said.

"The car couldn't have gotten here that fast, Mom. If the man in the Lincoln is the same guy who was here last night, he's not the one who was out at Banyon's ranch."

"Unless he *flew* to Amarillo," Jill said. "Did you ask if the sheriff had checked out flights leaving Roswell and Carlsbad last night?"

"No. But he did tell me something important." Cole paused. "They have a videotape of Matt buying snacks at a convenience store in Alamogordo."

"Alamogordo! That's the opposite direction from the way we went."

"That's because he went to Mexico," Billy said. "He went to find that Hector Diaz guy."

"Maybe. It seems far-fetched to me, but I told Sheriff Holtmeyer about the e-mail and the term paper anyway. I told him about your I-FEED Mexico connection, Jill, and that Matt had that name and address in his paper. Holtmeyer's already following up on what I gave him about the two men who went to the school, Matt's interest in Agrimax, and the other information. He called around, and he's got people checking school records, talking to Matt's teachers, even working with the USDA to contact Agrimax and the other food companies Matt was e-mailing."

"The USDA," Billy said. "Cool."

"Holtmeyer's not happy we took the computer, and he's even less happy that we left town. But the sheriff's a good man. When he heard about what happened here, he was concerned. He's going to look into the Hector Diaz connection right away."

"Wow." Jill's reaction came out as a sigh. "That's great. I feel better knowing someone is working so hard from that end."

"I realize you'd like to go home," Cole said. "But I'm not comfortable leaving my mother here—"

"Stop jabbering, boy, and go find out who's in that car outside!" Geneva cut in.

"Let's go," Billy said. "C'mon, Miss Pruitt."

Jill glanced at Cole. "All right. We'll hit the grocery store and be back in fifteen minutes. But if that Lincoln starts to tail us, I'm coming right back here." She started for the door, then paused. "Give me the gun."

Cole's eyes widened. "No way."

"I'm not going out there without protection."

"What am I?" Billy protested.

"Sixteen. Cole, give me the gun."

He shook his head as he handed over the weapon. "Do you even know how to shoot?"

"No. But I bet I can make it look good." She dropped the gun into her bag and unlatched the front door. "Come on, Billy."

Squaring his big shoulders, the teenager accompanied her to the pickup. "Don't look over there," he said in a low voice. "Don't let him know we suspect anything."

Feeling more nervous than she cared to admit, Jill slid onto the driver's seat and fitted the key into the ignition. A thousand movie images shot through her head—cars blowing up the moment the key was turned, white-knuckle chases down winding mountain roads, people shooting at each other through open windows as they drove, stuntmen leaping from car to car....

Breathing a silent prayer, she turned the key. The pickup chugged to life. She put it into reverse and backed out onto the street.

"Don't look at the guy as we pass," Billy warned. "Just pretend like you don't even see him."

Jill swallowed as they rolled by the navy Lincoln. A quick glance told her the man was still inside the car. Just sitting there, watching. She pulled to a stop at the four-way intersection and signaled left.

"He's not moving," Billy reported. "He's going to stay and keep an eye on the house. He must be waiting for the Mattman."

Feeling as if each tiny tendril of nerve ending was relaxing just a smidgen, Jill drove toward the strip of shops where she'd found the drugstore. Had the Lincoln been on Geneva Strong's street at that hour? Had she driven past it without even noticing? Had it tailed her?

Preparing to change lanes, she glanced in the rearview

mirror and spotted the dark shape behind her. "Billy!" She grabbed his hand. "Oh, Billy, he's following—don't look! Oh, what am I going to do? Why didn't I bring Cole? Where's that gun—wait, don't touch it!"

"Stop freaking, Miss Pruitt!" Billy hollered. "Stop shouting at me! Let's turn around and go back to the house!"

"Be quiet. Don't look back there. Just calm down, Billy." She took two deep breaths. "Okay. We can do this. 'For I can do all things through Christ who strengthens me.' *All things,* Billy. *All things through Christ.* Now think. Should we turn around and go back to the house or go to the store or drive straight to the police station?"

"Go back to the house!" Billy shouted, gripping the seat with both hands. "Let's get Mr. Strong!"

"Billy, good grief, stop yelling at me!" Unexpected tears sprang to her eyes as Jill clutched the steering wheel with stiffened arms and inadvertently drove right past the shopping center. "Oh, no! I missed it, and now I'm lost… Dear God, please help us."

The black plastic wheel grew slippery under her palms. She felt a tear slide down her cheek. This wasn't happening. Really, it couldn't be. She was a computer-tech teacher. She was a gardener and a churchgoer. She didn't get chased by strange men in Lincoln cars.

"Get the gun out of my bag," she told Billy. "Take it out, and whatever you do, don't pull that trigger! And don't look back!"

"Is he still behind us?"

"Yes, he's making every turn I make." She held her breath. "He turned!"

Billy swung around. "Where'd he go?"

"I don't know! He just turned off and went down that street back there."

"Well, let's go after him!"

"Are you crazy?" She rubbed the heel of her hand across her damp cheek. "I'm going to find that shopping center and get back to Geneva's house right now. And put that gun away, Billy!"

"I think we ought to follow him. We need to find out where he's going, so we can see what he's up to."

Jill turned the pickup around in a driveway and headed back the way they had come, making turns that quickly began to seem random. "I'm not going to follow anyone. I may have traveled all the way to Bosnia and Sudan, but nobody was chasing me. Billy, I'm a chickenheart of the first order. Or maybe I'm just smart."

"Nah, you're a chickenheart, Miss Pruitt." He crossed his arms over his chest. "If I'd been driving, I'd have followed him."

She smirked. "Yeah, right."

He gave a sheepish shrug. "Hey, didn't we pass that dough-nut shop on our way into town?"

After negotiating several more wrong turns and stopping at a gas station to ask directions, Jill finally found the shopping center. In moments, she was at the intersection again. But her relief vanished as she turned onto Geneva Strong's street. In the same tree-shaded spot once occupied by the navy Lincoln sat a dark green Mercury Sable with a man in the front seat.

Chapter Seven

Josiah Karume spotted a familiar face descending the curved staircase of the Hotel Batignolle Villiers in Paris. "Hector!" he exclaimed. "I had no idea you were coming to the conference, my friend."

The Mexican trotted across the lobby, his face beaming. "How could I miss the moment when you become our new chairman?"

"You mean the moment when the mountain of paperwork slides from my predecessor's shoulders to my own?"

Hector laughed. "I cannot think of anyone more suited to climb that mountain than you."

"Thank you, Hector. I appreciate your support." Josiah gave his I-FEED colleague a warm handshake. The organization's far-flung employees stayed at this small, inexpensive hotel when attending food summit meetings in France. It gave them the opportunity to share both professional and personal news.

"I've been planning the trip for some time," Hector said.

"The corn has become such an issue this year. I felt I should be here despite the cost."

"Of course, Hector." Josiah laid a hand on his friend's shoulder. "How is your wife? And those two fine sons?"

"All good. But I'm traveling too much these days. Mostly to Oaxaca, of course. The roads are very bad down there. And you—how is your family, *amigo?*"

"Very well, thank you." Newly arrived from the Somali refugee center, Josiah had intended to unpack his bags and leave for the conference center immediately. But registration could wait. "May I treat you to a late lunch, Hector? This corn situation will affect my work, too, sooner or later. I should like to know what you've learned."

"Certainly. I was planning to walk down the street to a café just now anyway. Shall we?"

Josiah left his bags with the hotel manager and accompanied the younger man out into the spring afternoon. The Friday traffic sped past them, not so different from Nairobi, New York, Buenos Aires or any other large city. In Paris, businessmen hurried to appointments, lovers strolled along the Champs-élysées, tourists poured from the Louvre to board sightseeing boats that cruised along the Seine. Everyone moving, talking, honking, pushing, urging. Few gave thought to anything beyond the circle of their own vision. Most in this world, Josiah knew, had very narrow vision.

"Researchers for the Mexican Environmental Ministry recently went into the mountain villages of Oaxaca," Hector was saying as they took a table at a small sidewalk café on Rue des Batignolles. "They were trying to confirm what a team from the UZACHI agricultural center had discovered in November 2000—that the genetically pure strain of corn in the Zapotec Indian village of Calpulapan had been polluted by genetic alterations."

"I read the original study, of course. I was deeply concerned."

"As were we. Our rural indigenous people believe the gods created man from an ear of corn. To alter a religious icon is bad enough, but Mexico has only about sixty pure varieties of native corn—a crop that can be traced back four thousand years. My friend, the whole world relies on our unpolluted genetic stock to ensure biological diversity."

The Kenyan had fallen silent as his colleague spoke. He knew diversity was essential as a hedge against diseases, pests and climate change. But genetically modified strains of corn could contaminate or even displace Mexico's original stock. While there was no evidence that eating these modified crops was harmful, it was clear that they could crowd out—and eventually eliminate—the pure varieties. And without biodiversity, a single pesticide-resistant insect or disease could virtually wipe out the world's supply of corn.

As Josiah tried to imagine Sub-Saharan Africa without its staple food, cornmeal, Hector greeted the waiter. The men ordered sandwiches on baguettes and spoke of other things—the upcoming conference on world food issues, their countries' World Cup soccer prospects, the status of I-FEED.

When their lunch arrived, Josiah was deep in thought. "Tell me, Hector," he said, "were the researchers for the Mexican Environmental Ministry able to confirm the original study on the polluted corn? Or did they find it to be false?"

Hector shrugged. "False, of course. The few polluted strains discovered, they announced, may disappear by themselves or remain at low levels for a long period of time. Ha! Disappear? Can you imagine that? But you must understand, the ministry is under great pressure to deflect attention from the problem. Mexico is a net importer of corn, my friend—more than nine million tons annually, and almost all of it from where?"

"The United States," Josiah said. "Home of the world's giant agrochemical companies and genetically engineered–seed producers. Tell me, have you spoken with Vince Grant about this matter?"

"Why do you place so much trust in Agrimax, Josiah? That company and the two other Goliaths—Progrow and Mega-farm—have far too much control over the world's food supply. And I question whether they are truly competitors. Yes, my friend, we know who fills Señor Grant's bank account."

"But his heart, Hector. I believe his heart is good." The Kenyan sighed. "He has promised a large shipment of corn-meal for my Sudan project."

"And where is this cornmeal now?" Hector held up a hand. "Wait. Let me guess. Still in a warehouse in Kansas?"

"I have to send him the final paperwork."

"We shall see, amigo." He tapped Josiah's plate with his fork. "But eat. Here, you have rich white bread stuffed with roasted chicken and fresh egg and tomato. Soon enough, you return to the land where no rain falls and nothing grows. Where if the people don't perish of hunger, then AIDS will get them soon enough."

"Thank you, Hector," he said. "You have such a way with words. I should nominate you for the chairmanship of the public-relations committee."

Cole slipped the cell phone into the front pocket of his jeans. "Jill and Billy are back," he informed his mother, who was dozing in a recliner. "Mom, I'm going now."

Geneva opened her eyes and let out a deep breath. "Cole, you didn't get a wink of sleep last night, and you're all keyed up. I wish you would just—"

"He followed us!" Billy announced, bursting into the house and tossing Jill's bag onto the sofa. "That Lincoln followed us all the way past the shopping center and up and down a bunch of streets while Miss Pruitt got lost, and then he turned off onto some side street. I wanted to follow, but she wouldn't do it, so anyhow, it took us a while to find our way back. But we did, and did you see the guy in the Mercury out there?"

"Cole, what's wrong?" Jill shut the door. "Something's happened."

"Sheriff Holtmeyer called while you were gone," he said. "The El Paso police found Matt's pickup in a parking lot near the main bridge to Juarez."

"I told you!" Billy crowed, lifting one hand for a high five. No one responded, so he turned it into a victory fist. "Yes! I knew the Mattman went to Mexico! I knew that's what he meant by the paper trail. He went down there to find Hector Diaz!"

"But Hector's not there," Jill said. "He's in Paris."

"We know that, but Matt didn't." Cole picked up the plastic sack of toiletries Jill had bought earlier for Billy. "I can't understand why he thought he needed to see Diaz, and I have no idea where he'll go when he finds out the I-FEED office is closed. But I think I'd better head down there and look for him. I'll take the first flight from Amarillo to El Paso. Then I'll rent a car and drive over to Juarez. Jill, can you give me the address for the Mexico I-FEED office?"

She grabbed her bag off the sofa. "Here," she said, "take my Palm. It's got all my contacts."

"Take the gun, too, Mr. Strong," the boy said. "You might need it!"

"He can't take a gun on the plane." Jill rolled her eyes at Billy.

Cole took Jill's arm. "Will you step outside with me for a minute? I need to ask you something."

"And I need to tell you something."

He didn't like the sound of that, Cole thought as he walked out onto the narrow concrete stoop of his mother's house. He glanced down the street at the Mercury. "Two men in it?" he asked her.

"I'm not positive. Maybe just one." Jill tucked a curly tendril behind her ear. "Listen, Cole, I'm going with you to Juarez."

"What? No, you're not."

"Yes, I am. I know Hector Diaz and his secretary personally, I know right where his office is, and I speak fluent Spanish."

"I don't need your help."

"You might. Besides, I don't have any plans for the weekend, so there's no point in my going home right away."

Cole's irritation over the strangers in the Mercury doubled as he focused on Jill's green eyes. A curl sprang out from behind her ear, but she didn't seem to notice. "No," he said, reaching out and tucking it back, "you're not going with me. In fact, I was going to ask you—and I had intended to be polite about it, too—if you'd be willing to stay here and keep an eye on my mother until I get back. But now I'll just have to tell you what you're going to do, because if I stand here and argue, I'll miss my flight."

"I'd be happy to stay here, but you don't need to be heading off to Mexico by yourself."

"I'm fine by myself. I do everything alone."

"But you and I are a team now. God put us together in this, don't you see? And besides, I'm very worried about Matt. I think if I—"

"No," he said, pointing a finger at her. "No, we're not a team. You're you, and I'm me. I'm the one who asked you to come along, not God. I needed you to work the computer, and now I need you to stay here and watch my mother and keep Billy out of trouble."

"Billy can watch your mother. Those men aren't interested in her. They're after Matt, and that's why I'm telling you that I—"

"Lady, you could drive a man to drink." Irritation surging through him, Cole swung around and stalked down the driveway toward the street. Bad enough he had to deal with a couple of thugs terrorizing his mother. Now he had this stubborn woman on his hands, too.

Well, he'd take care of one of the two this minute, he decided, crossing the street and striding toward the Mercury. He could hear Jill following. Even her shoes on the sidewalk sounded determined. What kind of a female was she? Godfearing, zealous, manipulative, hardheaded...and what was he going to do with her? Why had he touched her hair? He wrapped up his jumbled emotions and prepared to hurl them at the strangers watching his mother's house.

"Hey," he said, rapping hard on the window. "What are you doing here?"

The tinted glass slid down into the car door, and a man with thinning dark hair and round, wire-rimmed glasses blinked at Cole. "Well, I'm lost, to tell you the truth."

He smiled at Jill, and somehow that made Cole even madder.

"What's the problem, sir?" she asked the man.

He held up a sheet of notebook paper on which something had been scribbled. "I'm looking for the home of a Geneva Strong. I was given the street name but not the house number. Do you live in this neighborhood, ma'am?"

"What do you want with Geneva Strong?" Cole demanded.

The man shifted position on the seat, wariness veiling his eyes. "Well, I was told to come here and speak to her."

"What about?"

"Umm...well. It's a private matter, actually."

"I bet it is. I'm her son, buster, so why don't you just spit it out."

"Her son!" The man smiled, opened the car door and stepped out. "That's a relief. They sent me over here from Lubbock. I drove up early this morning, and I seem to have gotten down the address right, except for—"

"Who sent you?"

"The USDA. I'm with the Department of Agriculture." He held out his hand. "Charles Keeling. Friends call me Chuck. Pleased to know you, Mr. Strong."

"You men have any ID?" Cole asked.

"Of course, sir." Keeling motioned to his partner, and both men pulled small wallets from inside their jackets. Keeling held his open, and Cole inspected the familiar green logo— the letters USDA emblazoned above a graphic depiction of rolling farmland.

His anger skulking away like a guilty dog, Cole shook the man's hand. "Cole Strong. This is Jill Pruitt. So why did the USDA send you to Amarillo?"

"I work in security. I'm with the Office of Crisis Planning and Management—the Texas division, of course. I manage technology for the OCPM across the state. We generally deal with larger issues like counterterrorism and biosecurity, but sometimes the department sends us out to help with more localized concerns. I brought along one of our men from the physical security area." Keeling leaned into the car. "Ted? This is Mrs. Strong's son."

A tall, heavy-shouldered man emerged from the passenger side of the Mercury. He had a shock of graying hair, thin lips, and a neck the size of Jill Pruitt's waist. He and Cole introduced themselves.

"Ted works as a security guard, for the most part," Keeling

explained, "though he's had some other training and experience we thought might be helpful."

"Helpful for what?"

"Last night, my supervisor got a phone call from the Eddy County Sheriff's Department in New Mexico. I'm assuming your son is Matthew Strong?"

"That's right."

"We understand there may be a connection between your son's situation and a company called Agrimax. Apparently, a former Agrimax employee, Jim Banyon, was murdered yesterday. We realize your son is being sought in connection with the crime, Mr. Strong, but we believe there may be more to this than first meets the eye. Matthew was taken out of school by two men, am I right?"

"Yes," Cole said.

"And he had been researching Agrimax for a term paper, and he was e-mailing the company?"

"What do you know about Jim Banyon's connection to Agrimax? I thought Banyon had retired."

"I'm not at liberty to divulge classified information about the case. Let me just say that Agrimax's practices have been under investigation for some time by the USDA, and there is cause for concern. We believe your son—perhaps assisted by Jim Banyon, or vice versa—may have stumbled onto some sensitive information. It's possible Matthew got his hands on some technological data that Agrimax doesn't want released—an as-yet-unpatented fertilizer or a new pesticide, for example. Or maybe it was something else. The bottom line is that we believe your son—your whole family—may be in danger. Agrimax is a powerful company, Mr. Strong, and they do not take intrusion lightly."

"This is a food company," Cole said, incredulously. "You're

telling me they'd use strong-arm tactics against a sixteen-year-old kid?"

"Look what happened to your mother last night," Jill reminded him. She turned to Keeling. "Two strangers barged into Geneva's house demanding information."

"We're aware of the incident, Miss Pruitt. The Amarillo police contacted us immediately. Yes, Agrimax is a food company, Mr. Strong. And millions of dollars are tied up in any new technology Agrimax develops. These megacompanies are in serious competition with each other. Money and power are involved—and those are strong motivators. I hate to sound trite, but the truth is very simple—control the world's food supply, and you control the world."

Cole stared down at the pavement, stricken anew by the seriousness of his son's disappearance. If Chuck Keeling was right—and Cole had no reason to believe otherwise—then Matt's panic had a legitimate cause. The boy knew he was in trouble. He had happened upon the body, or perhaps even witnessed, the murder of Jim Banyon. And he knew that anyone who would kill Banyon would kill him, too. Especially if he was still in possession of this technology. Was that why he had been so anxious to find Hector Diaz? Did Matt feel somehow driven to give the technology to I-FEED? What use would that be? I-FEED was some kind of charity, not a corporation that could use technology for good. More important, where would Matt go once he found out Hector Diaz wasn't available?

"The moment we were contacted by the police," Keeling was saying, "the USDA took immediate interest in the case. Ted and I have been sent here, in fact, to protect you and your mother."

"There!" Jill gave Cole a triumphant smile. "This is great.

These men can stay with Geneva and Billy, while you and I go to El Paso."

"I would advise against that," Keeling spoke up. "For security reasons, we'd like to keep the family in one location."

"You can't expect me to sit around twiddling my thumbs while my son's life is in danger," Cole said.

"I can't stop you, Mr. Strong. But the authorities are searching high and low for him—"

"Yeah, and so is Agrimax. I'm going to El Paso."

"I'm going with him." Jill pointed at the house across the street. "Let me introduce you to Mrs. Strong, and we'll—"

"Were any of your people stationed here last night?" Cole asked, suddenly recalling the other car that had been parked there. "There was a dark blue Lincoln right in this spot. It drove off just before you arrived."

Keeling frowned at Ted. "We were given no notification about anyone surveilling this street, were we?"

The larger man shook his head. "You ought to report it, Chuck."

"I'll do that first thing. Listen, Mr. Strong," Keeling said, "I do understand your concerns. I'm a father myself. We realize your son is missing and your mother was threatened. But the USDA—along with other federal and state law-enforcement authorities—is on top of this situation. Your best bet is to stay put. I can assure you of that."

"I won't be sure of anything until I see my son safe and sound."

"Of course. But please understand this case goes beyond a missing teenager. Ted and I wouldn't be assigned to it otherwise."

"What's that supposed to mean?"

"At OCPM, I investigate breaches of security within the USDA—particularly as they pertain to safeguarding our national security. I oversee all Texas employees who work in what we call public trust positions. These are positions that have the potential to compromise national security through access to material classified as confidential, secret or, at the highest level, top secret."

"Are you telling us the USDA sees this situation as a potential threat to national security?" Jill asked.

"We're not sure about that. Not sure at all." Keeling opened the car door and took out a briefcase. "The important thing for you to know is that our people are actively working to resolve this case. Right now we have department agents in Juarez, Mexico, looking for your son. We're also in contact with Mr. Diaz in Paris, but he has not heard from Matthew. When we find him, Mr. Strong, your son will be in good hands, I promise you. So if you'll show me where your mother lives, I'll be more than happy to set Ted up in position outside the house."

Cole wasn't sure whether to feel relief or twice the fear he'd had before. If Matthew had stumbled onto information so sensitive that it might threaten national security, there was no telling what kind of danger he might be in. It appeared that both Agrimax and the USDA were searching for the boy, not to mention the sheriff and who knew how many others.

Who could tell what nefarious types might want to get their hands on Matt's information? As Cole's thoughts raced with visions of terrorists, kidnappers and murderers, his eyes fell on Jill, who was practically radiating blond curls and excitement. Could he leave her here and expect her to protect his mother? Or dare he trust these men to keep an eye on things?

True, Geneva had managed to hold her own against the two intruders the night before. But what about Billy? No telling what kind of trouble that kid might dive into.

"I recommend you all stay here, Mr. Strong," Keeling

repeated. "We'll maintain a protective position outside the house, and the minute your son is found, we'll let you know."

"Good. I'll leave you my cell phone number."

Keeling gazed at him. "It's your decision, of course." He turned to Jill. "Have you had any communication from Matthew since the original phone call to his friend?"

"Two e-mail messages," Jill said. "We brought his computer with us, and I've found some useful information on the hard drive."

"Excellent. Would you mind if I took a look at that?"

"Not at all." Jill started for the house, and the two USDA agents accompanied her. "We were able to read the history of Matt's messages back and forth with Agrimax. It's clear they were threatening him."

Cole stood near the car, uncertainty still weighing on him. He needed to find Matt—and he wanted to do that before anyone else could scare or hurt the boy. But his mother? And Jill and Billy? Cole leaned on the Mercury. Emotionally and physically exhausted, he suddenly realized that he had failed to call on the one source of power that had never let him down. Prayer had gotten him through the deaths of his wife and his father, through the lean farm years, and through the constant uncertainties of trying to parent a boy genius.

How had he let his prayer life slip so badly? Did it take a crisis to bring him close to God? Cole wondered if he truly believed he could manage everything himself—that he only needed to bring in God when the going got too rough. Probably. Not very spiritual…but true.

Now was one of those bad times, and Cole struggled to pray for discernment, for stamina, for patience, for fortitude, and most of all, for finding Matt. As he opened his eyes, he glanced into the car. The front seat was littered with maps and foam coffee cups. There was a laptop, a set of earphones and some other gadgetry he didn't recognize.

National security. Just the thought of it sent a stab of fear through his gut. Certain he had no choice but to go in search of Matt, Cole crossed the street and stepped into his mother's house.

Geneva was serving sweet tea and cookies to Chuck Keeling and Ted, who were explaining their mission on behalf of the USDA. Billy had joined them, his large bare feet propped on a chair despite Geneva occasionally swatting them with a dish towel. In the living room, Jill was throwing things into her bag, poking at her hair, humming a tune Cole didn't recognize. It looked as though he would have no choice but to tolerate her presence for one more day.

"We can't take the computer," he said, moving close to her and speaking in a low voice. "But I want to keep checking messages. Is there a way to do that?"

She looked into his eyes, then glanced at the two men from the USDA. "Why are you whispering?"

"Answer my question."

"I can access my account with my Palm."

"Good." He gestured at the computer. "Put Matt's term paper on one of those keys, and delete it from the hard drive."

"Cole, why? Don't you trust them?"

"I don't trust anybody." He straightened. "Mom, come here a minute."

While Jill sat on the sofa and worked at the computer, Cole slipped an arm around his mother and drew her out of hearing range of the men in the kitchen. "This is serious business, Mom. Everybody involved in this situation is looking out for number one, okay?"

"You're not telling me anything new," she said, eyes sparkling beneath her halo of white hair.

"Chuck and Ted came here to take care of you, but they work for the government. If it comes to a choice between protecting you or national security, you know which they'll choose."

"I wasn't born yesterday."

"All right—and keep a close eye on Billy."

"I can take care of things," she assured him. "Don't you worry about me. And, boy... I'll be praying for you. You and Jill." She punctuated her words with a wink.

He rolled his eyes. "I wish she'd stay here. She's beginning to seem like a parasite."

"I heard that," Jill spoke up from the sofa. "I've had parasites, as a matter of fact. Picked them up at a refugee camp in Sudan, and no, I'm nothing like a parasite. I see myself more as a guardian."

Smiling brightly, she stood and handed him a USB key. "There you go, Mr. Strong. Geneva, it's been wonderful to meet you."

The older woman embraced the younger. "I'll pray for God to give you patience. My son wasn't always this surly. Do what you can to lighten him up."

"Oh, he's just an old, dried-up tree trunk." Jill nudged Cole with her elbow. "But there may be a green sprig or two left in him. Hey, Billy—be good. Don't eat Granny Strong out of house and home while we're gone."

"Adios, Miss Pruitt," Billy called. "Bye, Mr. Strong. Call us when you find the Mattman."

"Done." Cole gave Keeling and Ted a nod and stepped out the door.

"Well," Jill said, "at least we know Billy and Geneva are in good hands."

The smog that hung over the city of Juarez had turned a muddy orange as Cole and Jill drove over the bridge that evening. Cole thought about Matt crossing this span above the Rio Grande, and he wondered again what could have compelled his son to do something so out of character. Matt loved spending hours alone in his bedroom reading comic books or tinkering with his computer. When he wasn't home, he hung out at the library or the computer store. Even the use of a pickup truck hadn't prodded the boy from his usual pattern. Matt reminded Cole of a young calf, always keeping close to the herd, always following the same trails, never straying.

"I can't think what crazy notion could've pushed Matt to drive all the way to El Paso," he said aloud. They had stopped for food near the El Paso airport, and Jill was finishing the last of a green chile cheeseburger. "It's just not like him."

"It's exactly like him," she said. "Matt has a mind of his own. Like that old tie he wears to school every day. The kids make fun of him, but he still wears it. Once he decides to do something, he does it."

Cole drove in silence for a minute. "His mother gave him that tie."

"I'm sorry. I didn't mean to bring up painful memories."

"It's been a long time. Eight years."

"She had a profound influence on Matt, didn't she?"

"On everyone. Anna was a wonderful woman." Again, the image of his wife's beautiful face filtered through his thoughts. He had lost her. He couldn't lose Matt, too.

"Was your wife a Christian?" Jill asked.

"The best kind."

"Then she played a part in developing Matt's faith."

"Not just a part. She was it. She started reading him Bible picture books when he was still a nursing baby. We went to church as a family, but Anna was the one who taught Matt how to pray, taught him to read his Bible every day, taught him to live by his faith."

"And that's what he's doing right now, Cole. He truly believes he can make a difference in the world—for the sake of Christ. He told me that many times. 'Miss Pruitt,' he used to say, 'I want to do something. I want to change the world.' Matt is idealistic, and he's determined."

"He's also just a kid."

"Sixteen—he's old enough to have his own ideas."

"And young enough to be completely naive."

"Maybe Matt's innocent about the ways of the world. But he has his head on straight. He doesn't see the Bible as a book of nice little tales and proverbs. He sees it as a command to action."

"A command to change the world?" Cole couldn't imagine it. He had been content to change one little patch of New Mexico. And even that had been rough going. "Do you think Matt sees Hector Diaz as the answer?"

"Part of it. Matt believed he could actually convince Agrimax to alter its practices, and he saw I-FEED as the agent for change. But his plan seems to have backfired."

"That's an understatement."

Cole checked his rearview mirror. A car had been tailgating him for the past ten minutes, and he was concerned. Almost too tired to think, he told himself it was probably nothing. He reminded himself he was driving in Mexico, where stoplights were generally disregarded, and a single marked lane could hold at least two cars side by side as they jockeyed for position.

He and Jill were driving through a residential area toward the home of Hector Diaz's secretary. Enjoying two weeks' vacation while her boss was out of town, the secretary hadn't wanted to make the trip into the city. But she had agreed to give Jill and Cole the key to the I-FEED office as well as her address book.

"I wonder what Banyon gave Matt before he was killed," Cole said. "Information? Or some object?"

"Oh, I think it's information. Matt must know something, and he's trying to find the right person to tell."

"Why didn't he just tell me? And why is this guy on my tail? He's making me nervous." Cole honked twice and rolled down his window. "Hey, buddy, back off!"

Jill craned to see. "That looks like the Lincoln. How creepy. It couldn't be."

"It's not a Lincoln. I'm sure it's just some driver in a hurry."

"You sure he's not following us?"

"Well, I don't think he's 'following us' like that. This is just how people drive here. He's practically riding my rear bumper."

"I'll tell you why Matt didn't give you the information," Jill said. "Because he couldn't trust you."

"What are you saying?" Annoyed, he rounded on her. "I've never been unreliable a day in my life, and my son knows it. He trusts me."

"Not with this. He figured you'd just turn the information over to Agrimax. Or to the sheriff. Obviously, it needs to get into the hands of the right people. Are you sure that's not a Lincoln?"

Cole could hardly keep up with the woman's train of thought. "It's not a Lincoln, and I wouldn't have turned over the information if Matt hadn't wanted me to. I would have..." He paused, searching for the street that led toward the secretary's home. "Well, I don't know what I would have done. The right thing, I guess."

"The safe thing," she said. "You strike me as someone who thinks it's important to be safe all the time."

"And you don't?"

"The Bible never says we're supposed to have safety as a goal. We're to be righteous, obedient, faithful, long-suffering—"

"Yeah, well, it's a man's job to protect his family and keep them safe."

"But you could reach out once in a while. Go beyond your safety zone. Do something—"

"Look out!" Cole tightened his fists on the steering wheel as the speeding car behind him pulled abreast of their rental car, sideswiping it and sending them careening onto the shoulder. "Hang on!"

"Lord, help us!" Jill grabbed the dashboard as Cole wrestled the fishtailing vehicle back onto the roadway.

"He wrecked our car!" Cole could hardly believe it. "Did you hear the metal crunching? And look at him—he's just driving on past us like it was nothing. Hit-and-run."

"He did it on purpose."

"You think so?"

"Cole, I have a bad feeling. You'd better stop."

"It's too remote out here. I'm going to find the secretary's house and—" He stared in disbelief as a set of headlights came straight at him. "Not again! Jill, hold on!"

Again, Cole swerved off the side of the road, this time striking a concrete post. The rental car skidded from the shoulder in a spray of gravel and went airborne. Gripping the steering wheel, Cole braced for impact, the sound of Jill's scream ringing in his ears. The front end slammed into an embankment and crumpled. The car teetered on its side for a moment, then toppled over.

Cole knew the smell of fuel, the wet drip of something soaking into his shirt, and the silence from the passenger's seat. He was upside down, his seat belt cutting into his stomach, and he couldn't see, and then he couldn't think or breathe, and then…there was nothing.

Chapter Eight

In the wee hours of Sunday morning, Matt slipped through the darkness toward the old adobe house. Even though he'd only been gone since Thursday, he had a feeling he was two inches taller and at least five pounds skinnier than the last time he'd set foot on the Strong ranch. Would Josefina totally freak out when she saw him? More important, would she help him?

Crouching near a scraggly piñon tree, he surveyed the ground of the small, wire-fenced complex where Josefina and her family lived. Her husband, Hernando, was the ranch foreman in charge of cattle. Their children had all grown up and moved away years before, and now Josefina's mother lived with them. She couldn't get out of bed, so Josefina worried about her constantly. A rusty swingset stood in the yard, along with two sheds and a garage. A couple of chickens usually wandered around pecking for bugs, but they must have gone into the shed for the night. Even the dog, Ricky, was nowhere to be seen.

Matt didn't see any Agrimax men or the sheriff lurking

around. In fact, he didn't see any signs of life at all. That gave him a bad feeling.

He checked for the USB key, a habit that was quickly becoming an obsession. It was still there, heavy in his jeans pocket. As had become his custom each time he touched the small piece of hardware, he prayed that God would give him strength to do what he had to do.

Leaving the shelter of the piñon tree, Matt crept toward the open gate in the sagging wire fence. A couple of pickup trucks had been pulled into the yard, and he scampered across barren ground until he was hidden between them. A growl lifted the hair on his neck, but he counted on Josefina's little mutt remembering him.

"Ricky!" he called in a whisper. "Hey, Ricky, it's me. Whatcha doin', boy? C'mere!"

The dog bounded across the yard from where he'd been dozing on the porch. Front paws on Matt's knee, he licked the boy's face. Matt rubbed Ricky behind the ears and relished the comforting feel of thick, warm fur and saggy skin.

"Where's your mama?" Matt murmured. "Isn't she home?"

The dog followed, tail wagging happily, as Matt darted from between the pickups toward the front step. After glancing behind to make sure no one was coming after him, he knocked three times.

"Josefina! It's Matt. Open up!"

He thought he heard a sound from inside the house, but the lights didn't come on. That was probably good, in case there was somebody hidden outside. He knocked again.

"Hey, Josefina! Open the door."

Ricky gave a bark that nearly sent Matt's heart into his throat. He bent down and patted the dog. Standing out here, all he could think about was the last time he had walked into

Mr. Banyon's house. What if someone had murdered Josefina and Hernando, too?

He vividly remembered the moment he laid eyes on that horrible, misshapen face with a bloodred halo spread across the sofa pillow. Mr. Banyon's blackened mouth had haunted him all the way to Juarez. Even while hanging out with the Mexican street kids, trying to figure out what to do next, Matt had been unable to calm down. He thought he was probably going to need a psychologist after this was all over. Then he wondered if it would ever be over.

And then he felt the barrel end of a rifle against his ribs.

"Don't move!" a low voice commanded. The rifle jabbed him harder. "Who are you?"

He was going to throw up. He was going to faint. He was going to die right there on Josefina's porch.

"I'm... I'm..." He ventured a glance out of the corner of his eye. The familiar face with its thick mustache and black hair was outlined by moonlight. "Hernando! It's me, Matt."

"Matthew? Ay-yi-yi. Get in the house!" The man grabbed him roughly by the arm, opened the front door and threw him inside. "What are you doing here, *niño?* Don't you know everybody's looking for you? The sheriff and the police and even the FBI. You're in big trouble."

Matt hauled himself up from the wooden floor where he'd landed. He brushed off his elbows and kneecaps. "I know they're looking for me. Where's Josefina?"

"They say you murdered Jim Banyon."

"I didn't do that, Hernando. Why would I kill Mr. Banyon? I liked him. He was cool."

"Hernando?" Josefina stuck her head around the door frame of the bedroom. "Who's there?"

"Josefina!" Matt had never been so glad to see anybody in

his life. He charged her and threw his arms around her. "Josefina, it's me!"

"Niño?" Her hands clamped around his face, and she forced his head backward so she could look into his eyes. "Matthew! *Mi niñito! Ay, mi bebe!* Where have you been, my baby? Everybody's looking for you. Your father is worried to death! I've been sick to my stomach ever since you ran away."

"Yeah, she's not even hardly cooking nothing," Hernando put in.

"Nothing?" Matt couldn't believe that.

"Sheriff Holtmeyer told us the police found your car abandoned in El Paso!" Josefina grabbed him and hugged him tightly to her breast. *"Ay, mi hijo!* I thought you were dead! I thought somebody killed you for sure!"

"I went to Juarez," Matt managed over the lump in his throat. He'd had no idea he was going to feel like crying just from seeing Josefina, whom he'd seen nearly every day of his whole life. But somehow her round, smooth face and black hair threaded with silver made her look so great. And the way she was holding on to him and rocking him back and forth caused things to well up inside him that he could hardly hold at bay.

"You were in Juarez?" Hernando asked. "You drove that piece of junk all the way to Mexico? What happened, Matt?"

"Somebody towed it. The police, I guess. Maybe they were looking for clues." He swallowed hard, as Josefina made little cooing noises while she patted him on the back and smoothed his hair. "I took a bus to Alamogordo, and then I caught a ride the rest of the way home."

"You hitchhiked!" Josefina exclaimed. *"Ai!* You could have been murdered! They have killers on the highway these days! You don't ever get in a car with a stranger. Didn't I tell you that? They kill you and leave your body in a ditch. *Ai, niñito mio!"*

"Stop your wailing, woman," Hernando told her. "Go fix

the boy some tamales or something. Sit down, Matt. I'm not gonna turn the light on, because who knows? Seems like the sheriff's driving by every hour or two, and other people keep coming over here to ask questions or poke their noses into ranch business."

Matt wiped the stray tear that had found its way down under his eye, and then he took a seat on one of Josefina's saggy couches. The house smelled like red chiles and tortillas and the kind of perfume Josefina always wore. Matt covered the USB key in his pocket with a pillow. Then he picked at the fringe on the pillow while Hernando questioned him.

"So you went to Juarez? What for?"

"I needed to see a man there. But I better not tell you why, in case the sheriff asks."

"Oh, *si*. I got you." Hernando looked confused. "Well, anyway, it's good you're home again. Your father is over in Amarillo, and he's been calling Josefina day and night to see if you came back."

"Cole is not in Amarillo anymore, *mijo*," his wife said, emerging from the kitchen with a plate of biscochitos and a glass of milk. "He went to El Paso to look for Matthew, remember?"

"To El Paso?" Matt felt stunned. "Why did he do that?"

"Because of what we told you—the police found your truck down there," she said. "He's crazy to find you, what do you think? He's your father!"

"Yeah, but…" Matt didn't know how to explain the surprise he felt every time someone told him his father was worried about him. Certainly Matt knew his dad cared for him, maybe even loved him in a detached sort of way. But crazy to find him? Calling day and night? That didn't sound like his dad.

"Now, you just stay right here with us," Josefina said, "and we're gonna call Sheriff Holtmeyer—"

"No, we're not!" Hernando cut in. "He'll throw the boy in jail. You want that? We'll hide him until Cole gets back."

"Hide him? And then what, *mijo?* Then the sheriff will have to come over and get him—and you and me will go to jail ourselves for harboring a fugitive."

"A fugitive? It's Matthew!"

"*Si,* but I saw how they do it on TV. That's what is going to happen, because if we hide him, that makes us guilty, too. Matthew needs to just call up Sheriff Holtmeyer and tell him that he didn't kill Mr. Banyon in Hope."

"It's not going to do any good, because that's not how it works—and I didn't see this on TV. I know it's true, because you remember what happened to my cousin José? First they put the person in jail, and then they get him a lawyer and call out the jury, and then—"

"I have to leave," Matt said. "I'm sorry to interrupt, Hernando. But I have to go. Tonight."

"Go where?" Josefina asked. "You can't run away again, Matthew. You don't have no place to go that's more important than your own family right here. You stay with Hernando and me and Mama. We'll take care of you."

Matt now understood the full meaning of temptation. What wouldn't he give to bundle down into one of Josefina's clean beds and sleep for two days straight? To eat platefuls of good food that wouldn't make him sick? To have Hernando stand at the front door and defend him to Sheriff Holtmeyer? If he just stayed here, everything would work out. And he'd be safe.

Struggling to resist the lure of security and comfort, he accidentally picked off a whole tuft of the fringe on Josefina's sofa pillow. "I can't," he mumbled, pushing on the fringe as if that would make it stick back on. "I can't stay here. There's something I have to do."

"What? What you have to do that's so important?" She clucked. *"Matecito, mi bebé—"*

"No, Josefina." He looked up at her. "I'm not your *bebé* anymore. I'm sixteen now, and God has given me something to do. Something I have to do. I don't want to do it, but—"

"Then don't do it." Hernando slapped his large palms on his thighs. "If you don't want to do it, don't!"

"But that's not how it works with God, Hernando. God called Paul to go on mission trips that ended up getting him shipwrecked and thrown in prison—"

"But God would never want you to go to *prison*," Josefina said.

"How do you know? Paul went. John the Baptist went. A lot of the disciples wound up in prison. And they died, too, Josefina. They died doing what God told them to do."

"But you're not a disciple."

"Yeah, I am. Every Christian is. And if we really listen to God, and if He tells us to do something…then we have to do it, no matter what."

"What is this thing you're so sure God said you gotta do for Him, huh?" Hernando asked.

"I can't tell you." He slipped his hand under the pillow and made sure the USB key was still in his pocket. "It's just something I know."

Josefina looked at her husband. Hernando stared at Matt. Finally he scratched the side of his face and let out a deep sigh. "You're a little bit loco, you know that, Matthew."

Matt grinned. "Yeah, that's what people tell me."

"Well, what can we do for you? I know you didn't come here just for Josefina's biscochitos."

"I need my passport. Billy's, too. They're both at my house. Our youth group was supposed to go on a mission trip to Guatemala. Billy's dad threatened to confiscate his. And don't freak out, Josefina," he added as she threw up her hands in despair. "We'll be okay. I promise."

"But you have to finish the school year," she said. "Don't you wanna be a junior in the fall? And what about Billy? His mama needs him. She threw her husband out, you know? You should stay and let us take care of you."

"I can't do that, Josefina."

"Where are you going to go, Matthew?"

"I'd better not tell you. But I need the two passports."

"I'll get 'em," Hernando said. "I've gotta check on some cows that are calving anyhow. If the sheriff passes me driving around, he won't think nothing about it being two in the morning. Then I'll stop at the big house and get the passports."

"Thanks, Hernando," Matt said.

"They're in the top left-hand drawer of his desk," Josefina told her husband. "I found them when I was cleaning."

"You cleaned my room?"

"What you think? I'm gonna let the FBI look in there with that mess everywhere? Of course I cleaned it. I found where the ants were getting in, too. You won't have to worry about them no more."

Touched, Matt pictured his old room—his comic books, computer, orange sodas—all the things he had thought he loved so much. They seemed far away now.

"How's Billy doing?" Matt asked Josefina as Hernando pulled on his boots.

"He stayed at Granny Strong's house in Amarillo while your dad and Miss Pruitt went to El Paso to look for you. They've got a real guard standing outside the door to protect them. With a gun, too."

"Who sent the guard?"

"The USDA. They sent two, in fact. One is outside, and another one is in the house looking at your computer."

Matt frowned. There was nothing on his computer of interest, but he still didn't like anyone prying into his personal files.

"Why does the USDA think they need to protect Granny and Billy?"

"Something to do with Agrimax," Hernando told him. Chuckling, he reached for the door handle. "The USDA thinks Agrimax is chasing you. If that ain't the stupidest idea, I don't know what is. But that's the government for you."

Cole opened his eyes and stared at the black void surrounding him. Nothing. Nothing but pain. His left arm throbbed. His left leg wouldn't move. As if it had gone to sleep. He tried to think where he was. What had happened.

As he blinked, a faint shaft of light filtered into his consciousness, and he began to distinguish objects. A shape loomed overhead. A bridge? Or a building? Near it, a streetlamp... the source of the light. Brush, reeds, tall grass. Around him, a barricade of twisted metal. He reached up with his right hand and felt it. What was that? A steering wheel? But it had been bent into a distorted oval. Was he inside a car?

A memory shot into his mind. A rental car. A mad race down a narrow road. Mexico. And the woman beside him—

"Jill?" He stretched his arm out, frantically tracing the outlines of the mangled car around him. "Jill, are you there? Jill, talk to me. Answer me. It's Cole. Cole Strong."

That's who he was, he realized. He was Cole, and he'd come to Mexico in search of Matthew. His son. Matt, was missing, had fled in fear. Cole had gone looking for him. But someone sideswiped the rental car. Ran them off the road. Then turned around and came at them again, head-on. A pair of silver headlights bearing down. Cole had fought to stay on the road, swerved at the last instant. The rental flew off the bridge and landed in this ravine.

"Help!" he called out. What was the word in Spanish? *"Ayudame! Ayudame!"*

What day was it? He glanced at his watch. Four-thirty on Sunday morning. The accident had happened late Friday night. Had he been unconscious for more than twenty-four hours?

He had to get out of here! Make sure Jill was okay. Find Matthew. Why didn't she answer him?

"Jill? Hey, Jill, are you there?"

His heart sank. What if she was dead? He thought of Jill Pruitt's pretty face—bright green eyes filled with enthusiasm, brilliant smile, determined little chin. And that hair. All those bouncy golden curls. *"I'm a guardian angel,"* she had told him.

But he hadn't been able to protect her.

Who had been inside that car? The crash had been no accident, of that he was sure. Who would stoop to such reckless action? Someone who had wanted to kill him, that's who. The same person who wanted to kill Matt.

Cole gritted his teeth. He had to get out of this wrecked car. Grabbing the steering wheel, he tried to pull himself from his cramped position. Nothing. He didn't gain an inch. His left leg was trapped. So was his left arm. Maybe if he just started shoving stuff out of the way, he could get loose.

He worked at it for a while, sliding aside everything that would move. A piece of dashboard. Broken glass. The door handle. He found the foam cup from Jill's supper. How had it survived untouched when everything around it was smashed and shattered?

"Jill?" he called again, moving his hand around in the darkness. "Please answer me. Please be okay."

His fingers brushed something soft and silky. He grabbed it. "Jill! Jill, wake up. It's me, Cole!"

Hopeful, he ran his fingertips over the fabric. What had she been wearing? Why didn't he notice these things? He recalled everything about her face. The arch of her eyebrows, the line of her nose, the pretty outline of her lips. But her clothes?

"Jill." He tugged on the silky stuff, pulling it toward him. It was white. White, smooth, billowy...

The air bag.

"Great. Just great."

Exhausted, aching, disappointed, he lay back. His arm ached and burned. The seat belt was cutting into his chest, and he wasn't sure why. He tried to find the release button but couldn't locate it.

As he lay there, hurting and angry, he tried to pray. This was the perfect time to address God, if ever there was one. *Help,* he cried out inwardly. *Get me out of this!*

The sun was coming up, he realized as he prayed. Now he could see clearly through a gap in the metal. The structure overhead and to the left turned out to be a bridge. The streetlight had gone off. The blackness faded to pale purple, and then to shades of orange, pink and blue.

Cole wondered if God ever got tired of hearing him calling out for relief. That's all their communion amounted to. Cole would find himself stuck in a bad situation and then cry for help. *Help me, rescue me, get me out of this mess.* He thought of Jill and her constant chatter about God. Obviously, the Almighty was a regular presence in her life, someone she turned to hourly, if not more often.

Matt must have the same kind of relationship with God, Cole realized. Otherwise, why would he be so committed to feeding the hungry? What else could have made him take the Bible to heart in such a real, concrete way? If you only got around to contacting God when trouble arose, then you didn't think too much about *His* business—you were too busy worrying about your own.

That thought led him to recall his ranch, and he worried

about whether Hernando was keeping a close eye on the calving, whether José was remembering to log the hoe-hands' hours correctly, whether Pete had thought to order pesticide. Were the men watching the irrigation pipes? Had the diesel truck arrived to fill the tank so the employees could keep the tractors running? If only he could talk to them...

The cell phone.

Cole began to search the car again. In the growing light, he could see a lot better. The car lay upside down in a ditch, he realized, but somehow he had ended up on his back. Water seeped along the flattened roof, soaking his shirt and the seat of his jeans. He found the seat belt button and released the pressure that had been cutting into his chest. It did nothing to ease the pain in his arm.

Unable to find the cell phone and too exhausted to keep looking, he called for Jill again. "Jill, are you there? Just say something! This is Cole. Please, just—"

His voice stuck in his throat as he caught sight of two pale fingertips protruding from under a piece of sheared metal right over his head.

"Jill!"

Dear God, please don't let her be dead! Reaching up, he touched the fingers. They were white, bloodless. Nothing. No movement. No life. Her body must be lying directly above him. Sick, spent, he slammed his fist into the car roof. *Not this! Not Jill!* She was too good, too righteous for something so awful. *Why, God? Why Jill and not me?*

And where's my son?

And how am I going to get out of this car?

"Help!" he shouted. *"Ayudame!"*

A truck rumbled across the bridge, drowning his words. Before he could call out again, a car sped past. Then another truck. And another. He looked at Jill's fingers.

"No!" His scream went unheard as a bus roared by. He grabbed the bent steering wheel and pushed as hard as he could. He had to get out. Had to get *out!* His good right leg found a toehold, and he pushed hard against it. In a blinding, shearing flash of pain, his left foot tore free. As agony swept over him, the world went black once more.

Matt got to Amarillo without a bit of trouble, and he had Hernando and Josefina to thank for that. Hernando had given him keys to one of the old ranch pickups that nobody used much—and no one would miss. And Josefina had packed a cooler with bean-and-cheese burritos, roast beef sandwiches, potato chips, plastic Ziploc bags filled with biscochitos and a large supply of Fanta orange sodas. Matt figured he had enough food to last a week. Most of the stuff was frozen when Josefina put it into the cooler, so it would keep awhile.

He didn't make it to Amarillo until late Sunday afternoon, because he stopped at a rest area and took about a five-hour nap. Maybe he was more tired than he knew. He felt weird about missing church, because he hardly ever had, and he wondered what the kids in his youth group were doing. Probably watching TV or playing video games. Or doing homework.

Now, as he took one wrong turn and then another while trying to find his grandmother's house, Matt thought about the little street children who had been so kind to him in Juarez. They sure didn't have a TV or a game system. They didn't have a cooler full of burritos and sandwiches. They didn't even have houses or families. They had nobody but each other.

There were seven in the group that had adopted him—two Marias, José, Pedro, Marcos, Hernán, and their leader, Luz. *Luz* meant "light" in Spanish, and that's what she had been to Matthew. After they ate, she had invited him to stay with them for as long as he wanted. When he agreed, imagining a little house and a mother like Josefina, Luz had led him to the far end of the alley—a dead end that butted up against a concrete-block building. This was where Luz and the rest of the street kids lived—a collection of cardboard boxes protected against rain by pieces of corrugated tin and sheets of tattered plastic.

Luz and the others considered themselves very lucky, she told Matt. Living next to I-FEED's Mexico headquarters, they sometimes got rounded up by Hector Diaz and taken to a feeding station where they ate like kings and queens for a day. Besides that, the restaurant on the other side of the alley emptied diners' plates into a collection of smelly trash cans near the children's cardboard-box houses. This meant lots of half-eaten tortillas, fatty scraps from carne asada, and sometimes burned frijoles. What more could you ask for?

Well, glue, as it turned out. Matt could hardly stand to think about this, and remembering it made him so upset that he ended up back on the outskirts of Amarillo once more. As he started trying to retrace his route back toward Granny's neighborhood, he thought about Luz offering to share her glue with him. She was huffing—inhaling glue fumes. So were all the others, including little Hernán, who couldn't be more than three years old and didn't even have underpants.

It turned out this was what the street children did most of the day when they weren't begging for money. They sniffed glue and then sat around in a daze, destroying their brains before they'd even had a chance to put anything into them. They had never been to school, and they knew nothing. Nothing at all. Didn't know the world was round, didn't know they lived in Mexico, didn't know how to count or read. They'd never heard of God or Jesus. All they knew were the streets where they'd been born and dumped.

Heartsick, Matt had tried to tell Luz how dangerous it was

to huff glue. She just laughed and urged him to try it. He pushed her away and retreated to the farthest corner of the biggest box and tried to sleep. It had been a terrible night.

At one point he woke up and found out that something even worse was going on. Even now, as he drove around and around in Amarillo, Texas, it just didn't seem real to Matt. What happened was that Luz, who told Matt she thought she was eight or nine years old, had found a man. They were under a couple of burlap sacks in the alley. After they were done, he gave Luz money. And then she went out to look for another man. This was what she did every night, she admitted to Matt.

The next morning, Matt had taken Luz aside and had given her nearly all his cash, his watch, and his laptop. He told her to use whatever money she could get from selling his things to feed herself and the others. And not to use it to buy glue. And not to let any more men buy her body. He could barely speak to her without breaking down, but he talked in the sternest way he knew how—like a really firm father.

Luz hugged him, her skinny arms barely able to reach around his waist, and then she went skipping away with the little ones following behind. Matt walked all the way back to the bridge, all the way across to the Texas side, and all the way to the parking lot, where he found that his pickup had been towed. The whole time, he thought about Luz.

Luz was why, in spite of wishing he could be safe with Josefina and Hernando, Matt knew he was going to get that USB key to I-FEED. He understood now that both Hector Diaz and Josiah Karume were at the food summit in Paris. Mr. Banyon had been planning to travel there himself, and he had told Matt he'd scheduled a meeting with Karume, who was chairman-elect of the organization. Mr. Banyon intended to give the information to Karume at their meeting. So Matt decided he would find some way to get to France and complete the mission. He would turn the data over to Karume or die trying. What choice did he really have?

Somebody had to do something. Somebody had to feed Luz—or she would keep on huffing glue in order to dull her brain enough to let men rape her so she could buy food for the children who looked to her as their mother and protector.

And that wasn't right.

It wasn't the way God had planned the world. Jesus had commanded His followers to feed the hungry. He said whatever you do to the least of these, you do to Me. Luz was the least of these. In some mysterious way that Matt didn't quite understand, whatever happened to Luz was happening to Jesus.

The memory of Luz and that creep under the burlap sacks sickened Matt and made him so angry that when he actually turned onto Granny Strong's street, he almost didn't recognize it. But there it was. The boxy little houses lined up in two neat rows on either side of a narrow street. Skinny driveways and one-car garages. Square yards, their new spring grass already withering in the heat.

And right on Granny's front porch, smoking a cigarette, stood one of the men who had taken Matt out of school and threatened him. One of the men who had murdered Jim Banyon.

Chapter Nine

Vince Grant's cell phone chimed the opening notes to "The Battle Hymn of the Republic" right in the middle of the sermon on Sunday morning. Cheryl Grant gasped and threw her elbow into her husband's side. Several in the congregation turned to scowl at him. Vince couldn't care less. Sliding the phone from the case on his belt, he peered at the message.

Mack Harwood.

Abruptly standing, he felt his heavy leather Bible slide from his lap to the polished oak floor. The thud echoed from the high, gilded church ceiling, but the sound barely registered.

It was about time his security man got back in touch. Though he was seething with anger, Vince wore a blank expression as he stalked down the aisle. Harwood had last checked in early Friday morning, and he had promised to have the stolen files in his possession by that evening.

"Harwood, where the devil have you been?" Vince barked as he exited the sanctuary into the narthex. "Tell me you have the data."

"Not at the moment, sir, but I will have it in hand by the end of the day."

"Not at the moment, Harwood? What's that supposed to mean?"

"Sir, the boy has proved to be more elusive than we antici-pated. He's definitely on the run, and it's clear he has a plan in mind. We just have to anticipate his next move."

"Well, where is he now?"

"We believe he left Mexico—"

"You *believe?* You *believe* he left Mexico? Don't you know where he is?"

"Sir, the boy has temporarily vanished from our radar screens, but we expect him to surface at any time. We stopped the father from searching for him, and we've got the grand-mother under tight surveillance. We're also doing—"

"Don't tell me what you're doing, Harwood." Vince could feel perspiration seeping through his starched white shirt. "I don't care what you've already done or what you're planning to do. I care about my stolen files! Your job is to retrieve them, and I expect that to happen. Today!"

"Yes, sir."

"Harwood, you've done good work for me to this point, and I've paid you well. Isn't that right?"

"Correct, sir."

"You have a wife, two grown sons, a nice house, a loyal se-curity force, and an employer who has given you his trust. In a matter of days, your position stands to be upgraded in a big way with twice the salary and three times the personnel. I'm sure you have no intention of letting all this slip out of your hands. But I promise you…if those files are not retrieved…if the information contained on them is leaked to the media… Harwood, you can kiss your future with Agrimax goodbye. Do you understand what I'm telling you?"

"I do, sir. And let me assure you—"

"Don't assure me of anything. Just find the kid and get the CDs, USB key…whatever."

"Yes, sir."

Vince switched off his phone and slipped it back into its case. At the far end of the narthex, an elderly deacon was frowning at him. The man refrained from speaking, unwilling to admonish the CEO of Agrimax.

Organ music swelled to a crescendo as Vince stepped back into the cool quiet of the sanctuary. Good, the service was over. He and Cheryl would make their round of obligatory greetings and then head to the country club for lunch. After that, he would play eighteen holes with his top aide. That would give Vince the opportunity to discuss the situation privately and make plans. At this moment, though, he couldn't see any way out of the mess. If the boy handed those files to the media, Vince might as well put a bullet through his brain.

"Vince Grant!" The pastor pumped his hand as he and Cheryl moved toward the door. "Your phone… I hope everything is all right?"

"His mind is always at work, Reverend White," Cheryl said. "I must have told him a hundred times to turn that thing off!"

"I certainly understand," the minister said. "God bless you both."

Vince knew no one would mention the cell phone again. The church counted on his sizable monthly donations. His money came in handy when the church missions committee started on about feeding the world. Bleeding hearts loved to point out that the world produced enough food to feed everyone. If only the rich nations would share with the poor nations, they whined, everyone on earth could eat.

Vince had nothing but contempt for this line of reasoning. He privately scorned the goody-two-shoes relief organizations that handed out commodities to the Third World's hordes. He knew that only an efficient distribution system would solve world hunger. And when his plan was in place, the people who produced would have food. The others didn't deserve it.

"God bless you, too, Reverend," Vince said, stepping out into the sunshine.

Cole knew two things. Jill Pruitt was dead. And he was trapped. Everything else blurred in and out of his brain, mingling with the pain and fear and rage. As the hours passed, cars and trucks drove over the bridge above him, and not one stopped. He yelled until he was hoarse, and nobody came. Mosquitoes feasted on his bare skin, peppering his ankles where he couldn't scratch. Flies buzzed around his head and sat on his closed eyelids. Jill's fingertips changed color from pale white to a sickly green to purple. And now they were turning black.

Whenever he managed to rouse himself into alertness, Cole used his energy to shout or to try to maneuver his way out of the car. When he was too tired or in too much pain to move, he thought about Anna and how deeply he had loved her. She had been a pretty little spitfire—kind of like Jill, only with dark hair and soft brown eyes and a heart only for her home and family. He missed Anna still, even though years had gone by since her death.

Would Anna know him when they met on the streets of Heaven? No doubt she'd be wearing a many-jeweled crown, and the angels would bless her as they passed by on the golden streets. Cole was certain he would be admitted through those pearly gates. He had accepted Christ as his Savior when he was ten years old. But had his life borne any fruit since that day? Or did he resemble the rich landowner in Jesus's parable—the man who had built big barns filled with grain and had laid up not a single treasure in Heaven?

This startling possibility put Cole's thoughts on a straight track to the truth about his relationship with his son. He had been a lousy father. Some realities became crystal clear when a man was twisted into a mangled automobile and figured he was likely to die pretty soon.

Jill had been right in making accusations against Cole. His sole focus had been the ranch—just like his own father before him. There was work to do, after all. A lot of work. A man could always convince himself that he really was loving his family by doing that work. Children had to be fed, didn't they? And housed and clothed and sent to college?

But it was a lie.

Cole worked because he loved working. Ranching was something he could do well. Very well. He had made a success of himself, unlike his own father, who had let the land suffer until the ranch was threatened with foreclosure. But Cole had saved the place and had built it into a monument to his own ingenuity and fortitude. People praised him for what he had done...and he was proud.

He loved his ranch in the same way a man might love a faithful, well-trained dog. The ranch couldn't talk back or argue. It never asked anything of him he couldn't give. It never made demands that he couldn't meet. It only required time and energy, and then it gave him everything it could in return.

People needed more than that, and Cole never had been sure what to do with those needs. He didn't know how to really talk. Or listen. Both his father and the ranch had taught him to be hard, tough, unbending. Why was it so difficult to be tender?

If he ever got out of this car, he would change that one thing about himself for certain. He would love Matt better.

He would spend time with his son—converse with him, hear him, try to learn what made the boy tick. And then he'd tick right along with Matt the best he could.

Penny Ames filtered in and out of Cole's thoughts now and then. He remembered how much he enjoyed kissing her. He reflected on their first meeting—a water-rights dispute. Penny's law firm had represented the ranchers of Southeastern New Mexico, and somehow during the hours of interminably tedious meetings, Cole had fallen in love with the pretty young attorney.

At least he thought he was in love with Penny. She certainly made him feel alive again, after so many years of dormancy following Anna's death. Penny liked Matt, too, and Cole cherished the hope that she would make his son a good mother.

But lying there in the ditch, he wasn't so sure anymore. Penny didn't really "get" Matt any better than most people. Sure, she teased the boy…even kind of flirted with him. She didn't admire him, though. Not the way Jill had. Penny never had understood where Matt was coming from, or what he meant when he talked about the things that interested him. She thought his obsessions were "funny." He was amusing to her, like a curiosity or a toy that could be put away when it ceased to be interesting.

Cole wished mightily that Jill hadn't died. If they were pinned in here together, she would have many things to tell him. She would argue with him and provoke him and make him laugh. She would talk about God and speculate on why all this had happened. And she would reassure him that God hadn't abandoned them.

Cole found a plastic cup from Jill's supper and let the fetid creek water trickle into it as he'd been doing all day. He poured a little water into his mouth and swallowed. It tasted of coolant and trash and sewage and every other disgusting thing that humans tossed into rivers when they didn't know any better. If he didn't die from his injuries, he'd probably die of typhoid.

And somehow, watching the shadows lengthen and thinking about Jill's dead body above him, Cole wept. Not for where he was and what had happened to him. He wept for what might have been. For Matt. And for Jill. And even for himself.

Matt could not figure out what to do. He felt as if he was frozen in some kind of a space-time warp, and no matter how hard he tried, he just couldn't make a decent plan. He knew the two men with Granny Strong and Billy were posing as USDA agents, but they worked for Agrimax. Three days ago, they had taken Matt out of class, threatened him, and then killed Mr. Banyon. They were murderers! But what could one unarmed kid do to rescue his grandmother and best friend?

After driving past Granny's house, Matt parked the pickup at the far end of the street and turned everybody into mathematical integers. He lined them up on a scrap of paper he'd found in the glove compartment—Granny, Billy, Thug A, Thug B and himself. He gave each person a different letter of the alphabet, and then he started working on the problem. He put the integers into different formulas; then he factored in sets of variables in an attempt to predict the possible outcomes of actions he might take.

It turned out to be another one of his dumb ideas. People couldn't be turned into math formulas, Matt realized after about an hour of this, because they were too unpredictable. One option he came up with was to drive his pickup right through the front door, then grab Granny and Billy and take off. But who knew where everyone was sitting inside the house? What if he plowed Granny and Billy down? Then he'd be charged with killing three people instead of just one. He couldn't bear the thought of having any part in another death of someone he loved.

For a while, Matt considered calling Granny Strong's house and pretending to be somebody else. But if Granny didn't recognize his voice, how would he warn her to get out of the house? Even if he somehow managed to tell her what was happening, how could she and Billy ever slip past the man standing at the front door?

What about the back door? Matt recalled that Granny kept a spare key on the overhead ledge. Could he create a diversion at the front of the house and sneak Granny and Billy out the back way?

Matt looked again at his scrap of paper listing all the integers and variables. His eye fell on the juxtaposition of three numbers. 9-1-1. With a jolt, he sat upright and started the pickup. Telephone. He needed to get to a telephone.

A nearby convenience store had a pay phone outside, he recalled. Fishing in his pocket for change as he drove the four blocks, Matt rehearsed what he would say. He pulled into a parking space, left the truck idling, hurried to the wall-mounted phone, and dropped in the quarters.

"Two armed men have broken into an old woman's home," he blurted out after the dispatcher answered. He gave his grandmother's address and then added, "The men kidnapped a teenager and murdered a rancher named Jim Banyon in New Mexico."

"Sir, how do you know this?" the dispatcher asked.

"Just send the police—and hurry!" Matt hung up and raced back to his pickup. Seconds later, he parked the truck around the corner from Granny Strong's house. Drawing on his memories of playing in the neighborhood as a child, he cut through Irene Williams's yard next door, skirted a swingset and crouched behind a rosebush to wait for the police.

When he heard the wail of a siren, he darted to the kitchen door. He stood on tiptoe and slipped the key from the ledge. He sure hoped he could pull this off. Clutching the key, he leaned toward the window, hoping he wouldn't be seen. Through the glass, he identified Granny and Billy seated at the kitchen table. They were playing Skip-Bo. Granny held a handful of cards and had a victorious smirk on her face. She was winning—like always.

One of the Agrimax thugs stood in the doorway leading to the living room. His big shoulder leaned against the frame, and he was cleaning his teeth with a toothpick. Granny must have cooked her usual fried chicken for their lunch. Matt could almost smell it.

When the doorbell chimed, the man straightened, tossed his toothpick to the floor and left his post. Peering through the living room, Matt saw the front door swing open. An Amarillo policeman stood framed in the afternoon sunlight.

As the thugs greeted the officer, Matt's heart rate sped up to double time. Palms sweating, he inserted the key into the kitchen door. He turned it till he heard the catch click. Then he gripped the handle. As he eased the door open, Billy turned around. His jaw dropped.

Before Billy could speak, Matt held up a warning finger and beckoned. Billy's expression altered from surprise to understanding, and Matt let out a deep breath.

Billy touched Granny Strong's arm. She glanced up. On seeing her grandson, an expression of surprise and joy suffused her face. Billy motioned her to silence. Checking the living room door and finding the Agrimax men still engaged with the police, she and Billy rose from their chairs. Hand in hand, they tiptoed for the kitchen door.

Once all three were outside, Matt caught his grandmother's free hand. "C'mon—we've gotta move it!"

Matt and Billy helped Granny down the steps. As quickly as she could move, they sprinted across Irene's yard. When they reached the pickup, Matt threw open the door. He practically shoved Granny inside and then raced around to the driver's side. Billy made a flying dive into the cab and landed right on top of Granny, who started hollering her head off.

Without waiting for Billy to shut the door, Matt fired the engine and put the truck into drive. Tires squealing, the truck peeled away from the sidewalk. Matt manhandled the large steering wheel in an attempt at a tight U-turn. The truck jumped the curb, taking out Irene's mailbox and clematis vine before jolting back onto the pavement. Matt floored it down the street, turned left, blew through two stop signs, turned right, and got completely lost before braking to a stop in a cul-de-sac.

"Whew!" he breathed out as he leaned back. "That was intense."

Billy shook his head. "Where'd you come from, Mattman? We thought you were in Mexico."

"I drove here to Amarillo to pick you up, but it took me a while to figure out how to spring you from the house."

"Who was that at the front door?"

"I called the cops."

"Dude. That's awesome."

"Get off my lap, Billy Younger!" Granny snorted. "I can't breathe. Good heaven's, boy, you're as big as an ox."

"Josefina told me those guys were with the USDA," Matt said as Billy righted himself. "But she was wrong. Those were the creeps who took me out of school on Thursday. They're the ones who killed Mr. Banyon, man. They're with Agrimax."

"We know. About an hour after your dad and Miss Pruitt left for the airport, Granny Strong and I put two and two together. See, this Keeling jerk was searching your computer when he figured out that Miss Pruitt had deleted your term paper—"

"Young man," Granny cut in, eyeing Matt like she meant business, "we need to get moving. If Keeling catches up to us, our goose is cooked."

"Yes, ma'am." Matt swung the pickup around the cul-de-sac and stopped at the cross street.

"Now then, we're going to get on I-40," Granny informed him.

"But I—"

"Turn right here onto Canyon Drive, Matthew. Right, boy! Didn't you hear me say turn right?"

Matt decided not to question his grandmother's orders. Planning things out hadn't seemed to work too well for him the last few days. Besides, the breeze through the open window felt kind of good, and the clematis vine with its big purple flowers had wrapped around the radio antenna and was waving back and forth like a banner. Matt realized he was actually happy for the first time since the Agrimax men had pulled him out of class.

"My, my, Matthew Strong," Granny Strong said once they were blowing down the interstate, "you sure landed your poor old grandmother in some hot water."

"I'm sorry."

"Well, now, everything's going to be all right. You just settle back, and tell me what's happened. I know you got yourself into a peck of trouble, but don't you worry. I'll take care of you from here on out."

"What do you mean?" he asked. "Where are we going, Granny?"

"Oklahoma City. We'll follow I-40 the whole way. Easy as pie."

Matt swallowed. Oklahoma City. That wasn't part of his plan at all. "Why are we going there?"

"You remember my Aunt Thelma?" Granny asked. "She had a twin, but Velma died a long time ago, back in '56. They were my father's sisters, you know, the only ones he had. Anyhow, Aunt Thelma lives in a quiet little neighborhood there in Oklahoma City. She's ninety-three, can you believe that? Still lives by herself and she's fit as a fiddle. Well, she has a touch of old-timer's disease, I guess, but who wouldn't at that age? Anyhow, she'll put us up, and we can just wait there until this mess sorts itself out."

"Great-Aunt Thelma? Wow." Matt had heard of her, all right. He remembered her, too. She was a giant hawk of a woman, with fiery blue eyes and no-nonsense manners that had kept suitors at bay during her courting years. Unmarried, she had worked for the Oklahoma City telephone company until retirement, and now she lived on her pension. Matt hadn't seen Great-Aunt Thelma since his mother's funeral.

He glanced at Billy, who didn't look too pleased about the situation. But he would perk up pretty soon, Matt figured. Once they got something to eat.

This was probably going to turn out all right after all. They would drop Granny Strong at Great-Aunt Thelma's house and then head for the airport. He and Billy could talk everything through on their way to Paris.

Cole stared up at Jill's fingertips as the sun set Sunday evening. The fingers trapped in the wreck were black now.

He had managed to work both his legs free of the metal that had been tangled around them. His left ankle, he feared, might be broken. At the least, it was badly sprained. He was hungry, too. Famished. He had tried chewing on some of the leaves that floated past him in the creek, but they tasted dead and brackish.

The main reason he couldn't get out of the car was his left arm. It was still trapped. No matter how hard he pulled and twisted, it wouldn't come free. And the pain was so intense that he had passed out more than once from the effort.

As the sky faded from violet to deep indigo, Cole heard something splashing through the creek. Something alive.

"Hey!" he called. *"Ayudame! Por favor!"*

The idea that a child…that any human…might come close enough to hear him and yet fail to rescue him sent a stab of fear through his stomach.

"Help me! Please. *Ayudame!*"

A black, wet snout poked through the broken windshield, and a pair of brown eyes blinked at him. A dog.

Dear Lord, I can't take much more of this.

"Hi, pup," he said, fighting the lump of despair in his throat. "Go tell somebody I'm down here, okay? Ever heard of Lassie?"

The dog's tail wagged. Stretching its head through the window, it licked Cole's free right hand. Then it bounded up onto the car.

Jill. The thought of an animal feeding on her body was more than Cole could stand. He pounded on the metal. "Hey, get away from there! Don't do that!"

The dog leaped down near Cole's head and gave his cheek a lick. Then it trotted off, splashing through the creek, as if finding a man inside a wrecked car were nothing out of the ordinary.

Cole let out a deep breath. At least the dog hadn't disturbed Jill's remains. Come to think of it, nothing had. No carrion birds had been flapping around the car. And really…now that his brain focused on the unthinkable subject…there was no odor. Only the smells of stinky creek water, heated metal and raw vegetation drifted around him.

For the thousandth time, Cole studied Jill's black, dead fingers. And then he realized they weren't her fingers at all. They were his.

Kneeling beside the narrow wooden bed, Jill prayed with every ounce of her being. When she could no longer find the words she needed, she petitioned the Holy Spirit to pray for her, counting on the promise of Scripture that He would intercede for her with groanings too deep to be uttered. As the hours passed and her knees grew cold and began to ache, she found that she stopped being able even to form coherent thoughts. So she simply spoke the names of those who weighed so heavily on her heart. *Matthew Strong… Cole Strong… Billy Younger… Geneva Strong… Irene Williams…*

Several times during her long hours of captivity, she heard the door open. Once a small Mexican woman entered the room bearing a tray of food—fragrant soup, warm tortillas, frijoles. But Jill refused to consider feeding her belly when there was a more critical need—prayer. The situation called for clarity of mind, and that meant fasting was in order.

As in the past two days since the two men pulled her from the wrecked car, they came in and tried to make Jill talk. They asked the same questions over and over.

What did you do with the information that was on Matthew Strong's computer?

You copied it onto a USB key, didn't you?

Where did you put the key on which you copied that information?

What is the password to your e-mail service?

Will you agree to contact Matthew?

Will you lead us to him?

Jill had refused to speak. She had not said a word to either of the men from the moment they had carried her to their own car. They were evil. Her spirit sensed it, and she refused to be compromised by cooperating with them. They had caused the wreck. They had refused to help Cole, who she knew lay badly injured, if not dead. And now she understood they were part of everything that had happened since Matt was taken from Marianne Weston's trigonometry classroom.

Jill lifted her head and gazed at the brilliant stars outside the window of the concrete-block building that imprisoned her. She had heard church bells ring that morning, and she sensed she was still in Mexico, perhaps somewhere near Juarez.

"God, You created those stars," she murmured. "Jesus, You are Lord of the universe. I beg You—"

"*Señorita?*" A tap on the shoulder drew her attention. Absorbed in prayer, she hadn't even heard the door open. The woman who had come to her before stood beside her again, a plate in her hands. "*Comida, señorita?* You eat food?"

Jill glanced over the woman's shoulder at the man who stood guard in the doorway. She shook her head. "I have to pray," she told the woman. "*Jesus es mi pan y mi agua. Yo quiero nada...nada pero Jesus.*"

"Hey!" the man shouted. "What are you saying to Maria?"

"I told her Jesus is my bread and water," Jill said. "I want nothing but Jesus."

"Don't say another word until you're ready to talk to us!"

"You won't keep me from speaking to God," she said, folding her hands and returning to her prayers as Maria hurried from the room. In some strange way, Jill realized, this confinement was exactly what she needed. In the frantic race from Artesia to Hobbs and then on to Amarillo, she had been too preoccupied to spend much time with the Father. Her own adrenaline had taken over, propelling her from one place to the next—finally leading her to join Cole on his flight to El Paso and to Juarez.

Now she was here, in God's hands, and she had plenty of time to address Him. Oddly, in spite of her worries for Matthew and Billy and Granny Strong, she found it was Cole whose rugged face played through her thoughts again and again. In spite of his surly demeanor, she liked Cole Strong. Silent and thoughtful, he was as steady as a rock. Whereas she often found herself swept by her own enthusiasm into one quest or another, Cole had his boots planted solidly in the New Mexico soil. He knew where he came from and where he was going. He understood himself, and—she suspected—he was capable of profound compassion. Though he could change, adapting to loss and growth, in his essence Cole would always be the same. He would be a man she could rely on.

Why had she echoed Matt's words—referring to him as a dry, old tree stump? Cole wasn't anything like that. He was deep, still water. A river of nourishment and life. Suddenly she wished she'd had time to taste that water. To know its comfort, the strength of its currents.

'Lord, keep him alive," she murmured, speaking over a ruckus that had erupted outside her window. The Mexican woman—Maria—was yelling something Jill couldn't understand. A chicken squawked, and a child began to cry. "Father, please protect Cole from harm. Send him help, dear God. Send someone to rescue him. And while he's waiting, Lord, turn his eyes on You. Open his mind to You. Knock hard on his heart, and keep knocking until he hears You."

Jill twisted her fingers into a tighter knot, grateful for quiet again outside. She needed to sleep. She probably should eat, too. But how could she think about such things when lives were in danger? Now she understood that the two men who had passed themselves off as USDA agents must be with Agrimax or some other food company Matt had stirred up. Those men had told her captors about the deleted files. This meant Billy and Granny Strong were in their enemies' hands.

What on earth did Matt know that meant so much to these people? Why were they so desperate to stop him? And where was he?

"Oh, Lord," she began again, "please save Matt. You know his heart, and You understand his motivation. Wherever he is right now, protect him. Wherever he's going, please clear his path. Place a hedge of thorns around him, and keep the enemy from harming—"

"*Señorita!*" The voice at the window startled Jill.

A Mexican man stood outlined in moonlight. She started to rise, and the door behind her flew open. Two men and a teenage boy burst into the room and seized her arms.

"*Vamonos, señorita!*" one of them cried, urging her to accompany them.

Jill had no choice as they dragged her toward the door. Shoved out into the hall, she nearly stumbled over the prone body of one of her captors.

Wrapped from chin to toe with a thick, roughly twined rope, he writhed in rage. "We paid you!" he bellowed through the hood someone had tied over his head. "You can't do this. That woman is a criminal! The United States government will—"

"*Mentidas!*" the teenager cried. "Lies!"

The Mexicans hurried Jill through the front door, where she passed the second captor, who was trussed up like a chicken ready for market. He hung upside down from a metal light fixture on the outside of the little block building. He swung in a circle, his body twitching as he hurled invectives at Jill's rescuers.

Before Jill could even begin to make sense of what was

happening, the Mexican men thrust her through the door of another small house and bolted it behind her. As she reached for something to brace herself, a squat figure scurried from the shadows and threw her arms around Jill. It was Maria, the woman who had been sent earlier to feed her.

Maria's excited flood of Spanish words told Jill that the villagers had noted her fervent prayers and fasting. Though her Agrimax captors insisted she was a spy and paid well for the small house where she had been held, the villagers believed the men had lied. They realized she was a good woman, a holy woman. She had been sent to them by God, they told her. Grasping her hands, they ushered her to a cot where a little girl lay shivering. The child could not have been more than four or five years old.

Jill knelt beside the girl, whose name they said was Celia. Now she realized the truth. These poor people who had seen her praying so fervently must believe she had some miraculous power to heal the sick child. She didn't. Jill closed her eyes and laid her hand on the burning forehead.

"Lord, I can't heal this precious little girl," she prayed softly, "but You can. You are Jehovah Rapha, the God who heals. I beg You now to wrap Your arms around this baby's body and make her well. Take away the fever. Restore Celia's strength. Give her life and vigor and...oh, dear God, I'm all prayed out. I don't know what to say or do. I'm so tired and so..." Jill broke into sobs. "I'm sorry. I can't... I don't—"

"Señorita, señorita." The Mexican woman patted her back.

Jill sucked down a breath. "God heals," she told the woman, speaking in Spanish. "God heals, but we have to do our part, too. You must take this child to a doctor. Take her to the city."

"Sí, señorita. It will be done."

Maria began giving commands, and now Jill realized it was this diminutive but mighty matriarch who had caused the commotion and ordered the villagers to tie up the Agri-max agents. In moments, a red, three-wheeled cycle with a cart welded to the back sped up to the door of the little house. Under Maria's direction, the men bundled both Jill and Celia into the cart.

With silver stars gleaming overhead, a man hopped onto the cycle and began pedaling down the road. Soon they were traveling faster than Jill could have believed possible with such a burden.

"Como se llama?" she called out.

He swung around and gave a wave. "Pedro!"

Pedro. Jill closed her eyes and snuggled the feverish little girl onto her lap. God had heard her prayers and sent Maria and Pedro. Mary and Peter. Wasn't the world a strange and mar-velous place? And didn't she serve an awesome God?

As the three-wheeled cycle sped up and down hills, through thickly vined forest and passed factories belching smoke, Jill sang every praise chorus she could remember. And before long, rays of sunlight began filtering upward through the inky sky one more time.

Chapter Ten

Cole gripped a shard of glass between the thumb and forefinger of his right hand. He had no choice. Not if he wanted to live. Not if he wanted to save his son's life. And he did.

Gritting his teeth, he pressed the sharp glass against the two blackened fingertips—his own fingers. To his surprise, he felt no pain. The flesh was dead, he realized belatedly. The blood had stopped, the nerve endings were numb, the muscle had begun to deteriorate.

This could be my whole body, he reminded himself when the grisly task was done. *I could be dead. I should be dead. But I'm not, because God chose to spare me.*

"Lord, You've given me a second chance at life," he mumbled. "You changed me here in this ditch. You took away something I thought I needed. Now give me what I really need, Father. Make me into the man You want me to be."

Exhausted but unwilling to delay even a moment longer inside the wrecked rental car, Cole reached across his chest with his right hand and grasped his left wrist. He had so little strength left. His muscles were weak, his mouth parched, his nerves raw. Summoning what energy he could, he gave his left hand a jerk.

Blinding blue pain ripped through him as his smashed fingers tore loose from the metal that had pinched them. Agony scorched his arm, and his limp hand dropped onto his stomach. Snakes of searing torment coiled through his flesh, threatening Cole's grip on his mind. He groaned and began to shake violently, the urge to retch welling up inside him like a tidal wave. Curling into himself, he clutched his wounded hand, the blood now pulsing freely.

Barely able to remain conscious, Cole pressed the two stumps against his belly to stanch the flow. "Help me, God," he breathed, "help me, help me."

Terrified he might pass out and drown in the putrid creek, he forced himself to begin the long, slow effort of pulling himself out of the wrecked car. First his head emerged from what had been the driver's side window. He lay back and let the water trickle around his ears. Next he eased his shoulders out of the car, then one elbow. He rolled himself onto his side, grateful for the change in position.

Again Cole rested, cradling his trembling injured hand, wishing he could stop the bleeding, praying for strength. His wet jeans caught on a jagged piece of metal, and they tore as he worked his legs through the opening to the outside. His left ankle burned, swollen and throbbing. Lying prone in the creek bed, he blinked back tears as moonlight cast blue shadows across his bloodied shirt.

As sleep began to overcome him, Cole forced himself to remember Matt. His son needed him. And Jill. Where was she? What had happened to her? He couldn't think it all through.

Now he reached out and grabbed on to a rock that protruded from the shallow water. Grateful for a handhold, he dragged himself with excruciating slowness onto the bank. Cars and trucks drove across the bridge overhead, just as they had for two days, never seeing the filthy man inching like a snail up the side of the ditch.

With his good hand, Cole clutched hummocks of green grass, a broken cinder block that jutted from the dirt, a piece of twisted root. When he couldn't make himself move, he lay with his cheek in the dirt and tried to stay alert. But it wasn't working. Lights moved around his head, shining on the embankment, making him dizzy. He fought the urge to vomit. The pain in his fingers numbed his brain and made his ears ring.

"Cole!" a voice in his head kept crying out. "Cole! Cole!"

He rested on the slope, wondering how much longer it would take to reach the road. Would he make it? Or would some kind of pain-induced insanity overcome him? He wondered if he was bleeding to death.

"Cole! Where are you, Cole?"

The voice was so clear that he knew it must be God calling to him from Heaven's gate. But he couldn't go. Not just yet. Matt needed him. He licked his lips. They felt like old, dry leather against the lump that was his tongue.

"Cole, please answer me!"

"I'm here," he croaked. "Here, God. I'm here."

"*Cole!* Where are you?"

Why did the Lord speak with a woman's voice? That wasn't right. It must be Anna, his sweet Anna beckoning. She wanted him...but Matt needed him more. Didn't she know that?

"Cole, I can't find you," Anna cried. "Please talk to me again!"

"Here," he said. His voice sounded like sandpaper. "I'm right here, Anna."

"Oh, Cole!" Warm hands covered his back. A flutter of

movement blocked the light. "Cole, oh, tell me you're alive. Tell me you're going to be all right!"

Instead of his wife's soft brown eyes, Cole gazed into Jill Pruitt's green ones, her face a pale apparition that hovered just in front of him. The streetlamp behind her transformed blond ringlets into a golden halo. But she wasn't a heavenly being. She carried a flashlight and her tote bag. She was touching him and crying.

She was real.

"Jill." The word came out as a sigh.

Tears flowing, she bent and kissed his cheek. "Yes, Cole, I'm here. Thank You, God! Thank You for preserving his life."

"My fingers are...are... I need a..." He couldn't think of the word, so he pulled his mangled hand from under his stomach. "It's...it's... I need a..."

"Oh, no!" She cupped his hand in her palms. "We've got to get you to a hospital. Pedro, *por favor*—"

"No." Cole forced himself up on one elbow. "Where's Matt? Have to find my son."

"Cole, you've lost a lot of blood. You're dehydrated. Please listen to me."

"Wrap them in a...a..." Why couldn't he think of that word?

As he searched his mind, a second person appeared beside him, a man with dark eyes and a kind face. This time, fresh water trickled across Cole's mouth and down his throat. Jill bandaged his fingertips with a handkerchief. That was the word.

"Bandage," he uttered.

Jill and Pedro didn't listen. Instead, they dragged him up the embankment, his injured ankle knocking against stones and scraping across the pavement. Then they heaved him into some kind of box. Jill crawled into the box beside him and settled his head on her lap. Pedro vanished into the darkness. After that, the box began to move, slowly sliding beyond the streetlamp and past a tree. Gaining speed, it flew along like a magic carpet made of old wood.

Cole knew this must be a dream. A vision of Heaven. Jill's fingers threaded through his hair and her lips softly touched his cheek again and again. A cool breeze played across his chest, drying the wet shirt he had worn so many days. He noticed the stars, chipped ice across a deep blue blanket. And then, most blessed of all, came sleep.

"Tell me the whole story, Josefina," Jill demanded into the cell phone at her ear. "I need to know what happened— every bit of it."

Her voice sounded harsh—so much unlike her that Cole blinked to make sure who sat in the chair beside his bed. In the bright light slanting through a white curtain, he focused on the woman. She wore something he'd not seen in their days together—a pale yellow embroidered blouse, a light green skirt, sandals. The faint scent of perfume drifted near, and he enjoyed it despite the smell of antiseptic in the air.

Where was he, anyway? Cole turned his head. Ten beds marched in a row down the length of the room, each positioned directly beneath a window. At the far end, a woman in a white dress mopped the floor to salsa music from a radio. The only other occupant was a little girl sleeping in the bed next to Cole's. An IV tube ran from her skinny brown arm to a bag of clear liquid.

"Well, I know he's been there, Josefina," Jill said, her pink lips moving against the phone. "So don't even try to deny it. Do you want me to tell your employer that you're keeping the truth from him?"

She glanced at Cole and rolled her green eyes.

"No, you're not protecting him, Josefina," she went on. "You're withholding important information from his father and me—and that's not right."

Cole studied a mound of bandages on his stomach. What was inside it? His brain felt numb, as though he'd been drugged—and he wondered if he had. He didn't hurt. Not much.

"Well, is he still there?" Jill asked. "Is he hiding out with you?"

While talking, she reached over and patted the bandaged lump, which turned out to be Cole's hand. Surprised at this discovery, he began to remember something about a car accident and a piece of broken glass...and cutting off his own fingertips...and Jill coming to save him...and—

"Matt!" He lunged up in bed. "Where's Matt?"

"He's not in Mexico," Jill whispered around the cell phone as she pressed on his chest and forced him down on the bed again. "He went back to the ranch, but Josefina won't give me the whole story. She says she promised Matt she wouldn't tell."

"Give me that phone." Cole reached for it, but Jill waved him away.

"Josefina, please," she said. "We don't even know where to start looking for Matt now. And you know his father is not going to give up—"

Cole swallowed, trying to read Jill's expression.

"Yes, we all thought that about him," she said, "but we were wrong. He loves Matt very much. I've never seen such love. He's determined to find his son. He's not going to quit searching until Matt is safely back home. Now, please—"

Jill's mouth dropped open in astonishment at what Josefina was telling her.

"His *passport?* Are you sure? Billy's passport, too? Oh my word. Well, where were they going? Tell me everything...."

Okay, Josefina, just stay put there at the ranch. We'll be back in touch as soon as we can."

Cole edged himself up into a sitting position as Jill pressed the button to turn off the phone. "Where's Matt?" he asked.

"I have a bad feeling about this."

"He took his passport."

"I think he went to Amarillo to get Billy, and then…but I don't know where he'd get the money for a plane ticket."

"Matt has a credit card I gave him for emergencies."

Her eyebrows lifted. "Cole, why didn't you cancel the card when Matt took off?"

"I thought about it," he replied. "But Matt's my son, and I figure he's in a tight spot."

"Oh, Cole, I'm afraid Matt's planning to fly to France to look for Hector Diaz."

Cole's brain cells snapped to attention. He swung his legs off the bed. "Get my mother on the phone."

"I've tried. She's not at home, and I can't locate her anywhere. I called the hospital and talked to her neighbor. Irene hasn't heard a word from Geneva."

"But those USDA men were supposed to guard them—"

"Phonies. They work for Agrimax. The badges…the whole bit…it was fake. I'm guessing the men in the Lincoln who were watching the house were with Agrimax, too—sent by the two guys who bullied your mother and her friend. When Keeling and his partner arrived in the Mercury, the two in the Lincoln went off duty. We surprised Keeling by confronting him, but he was ready with his cover."

"How do you know all this?"

"Keeling sent two men to Mexico after us. He must have figured out right away that I had deleted the term paper from Matt's computer, and I guess he assumed I'd made a copy and taken it with me. Once he knew that much, his job was just to stay put and hope Matt turned up in Amarillo. But Keeling believes he needs to get hold of Matt's files, so we became a target."

"You're saying Agrimax followed you and me to Mexico?"

"Two men—Agrimax seems to put its security people in pairs—tracked us from the airport rent-a-car place and ran us off the road."

"Why would they do that?"

"They think they need me. Those guys pulled me out of the wreck and didn't touch you. They believed they could get the computer information out of me. Cole, Agrimax sees me as the way to get what they're looking for."

"What they're looking for is my son." He breathed in, trying to think clearly. "Did you give them—"

"Nothing. They held me at a house in a village somewhere near here and interrogated me for hours at a time. I refused to talk—I quoted Scripture at them instead."

"Scripture?" His brows lifted.

"They hated that, especially the Beatitudes. 'God blesses those who are persecuted because they live for God.' That one really got their blood boiling." She grinned. "Anyway, God sent a kind woman who helped me escape. That's when Pedro arrived with his cart and brought Celia and me to this clinic."

She pointed at the sleeping child on the bed next to Cole's. Leaning forward, she whispered, "Celia has dysentery, and they've given her antibiotics and fluids. She's going to be fine. I hope you don't mind that I used your money to pay for her treatment. Your wallet was in your jeans. I have my tote bag, but the Agrimax men emptied it looking for the key, so I'm broke. Those goons never thought to look under the spare tire—so the USB key is safe. Good thinking, by the way. And I found my cell phone in the wreckage."

She smiled, holding it up like a trophy. Cole shook his head, confused.

"Anyway, after we left Celia at the clinic, Pedro pedaled me around trying to find the car," she continued. "But when we spotted it, I couldn't find you—"

"Jill, are you all right?" Cole caught her fingers with his good hand. "Did those men hurt you?"

Her green eyes softened. "I'm all right. They weren't kind, but they didn't rough me up or anything."

Still holding her hand, needing the human touch, he leaned back on his pillow again. A shower was in order. A toothbrush. A change of clothes. But he couldn't think beyond his son.

"Jill, I can't stay here. I've got to find—"

"Matt must have driven to Amarillo to get Billy," she speculated. "From what Josefina told me, I'm nearly positive about that. Two things could have happened once he arrived there. Either Keeling captured Matt and took away whatever Agrimax has been looking for, or Matt and Billy escaped."

Cole shrugged. "A third scenario—Keeling's holding Matt someplace, because the boy won't give him what he wants. My son can be stubborn."

"A chip off the old block." Her lips softened. "I'm choosing to believe they got away."

"And my mother? Where is she?"

"The boys wouldn't abandon her at the house with those creeps. The three of them must be together."

"That's comforting. My mom, my son and his best friend are either being held and tortured somewhere, or they're on the lam in who-knows-what-kind of a car. None of them can drive worth a flip, you know."

She slipped her fingers between his and squeezed. "How are you feeling? You look pale."

"We've got to get out of here."

"Are you hungry?"

"Do you know where we are? Is there a car we can use?"

"You're not listening to me, Cole. You need to eat. You need to rest your ankle and give your hand time to heal. Your fingers—" she grimaced "—the doctor at the clinic is concerned. He cut away the dead flesh and stitched you up, but, Cole—"

"What's the name of this place?"

"We're on the outskirts of Juarez."

"Can you find us a car or something?"

"And just where do you think you're going with a couple of amputated fingers and a sprained ankle?"

"I'm going home."

She stared at him. "To the ranch...to work?"

Cole stroked his thumb across the back of Jill's hand. To him, the idea that he would return to his ranch labors at a time like this was inconceivable now. But Jill could believe it. She had known the old Cole, the dry stump of a man whose whole life was his work. She hadn't yet gotten to know the new fellow—the one who had reordered his priorities while lying inside a mangled car watching his fingers die.

"I'm going home to get my passport," he said. "Looks like I'm headed to France."

Jill's eyebrows lifted, and her eyes sparkled as a grin spread from cheek to cheek. "Well, then...bon voyage!" With that, she leaned over and planted a big kiss right on his forehead.

Cole decided it definitely ranked among the most pleasurable kisses he'd ever had. Top ten, for sure.

Jill glanced in the rearview mirror once every five seconds. Possibly more often. She couldn't help it. Memories of the rental car, the wreck, her interrogation, and her escape haunted her as she drove across the silent New Mexico grassland. Sometimes she saw things—lights, a shape, a car edging too close to the centerline. She gripped the steering wheel and prayed.

Morphine still dulling his senses, Cole dozed beside her in the passenger seat of the car they had rented after an uncomfortable bus ride to downtown Juarez and a taxi across the bridge to El Paso.

How had all this happened to her? And what did God want her to do with it? She could hardly imagine spending tomorrow in her little house with her dog curled up near her feet as she wrote out lesson plans. What day was it, anyway? Monday evening. Good grief, she had prepared nothing for the substitute that day. What had her students done without her? And how would she ever manage the final weeks until school let out for the summer?

The beeping cell phone cut off her thoughts. She picked it up. "Hello?"

"Jill, hi." It was Cole's fiancée. Jill had talked to the woman a couple of times since the accident. "This is Penny Ames. Is Cole available?"

"He's sleeping. I can't wake him right now." She paused and realized she ought to explain. "The doctor gave him painkillers for his hand."

"So you're still at the clinic?"

"We're in a car. I'm driving Cole to his ranch."

"I see. Well, listen, I've decided to take a couple of days off and drive down there. I'm not doing Cole any good just twiddling my thumbs here in Albuquerque. What time do you expect to get him home?"

Jill fretted over how much detail she ought to give on the cell phone. Josefina had told her a lot of information, and now Jill feared she might have erred in forcing the woman to spill the beans. A cell phone wasn't exactly private communication. Had Agrimax been listening? Or was she becoming paranoid? *It's not paranoia when people are lying, shooting and kidnapping,* she decided.

What if Agrimax knew Matt had gone back to the ranch? What if they'd heard Josefina talking about the passports? Even if Agrimax hadn't overheard that call, its thugs might have tapped Penny's phone or staked out her condo. But Jill realized she couldn't evade the woman's question entirely. Penny was Cole's future wife, after all. She deserved to know something.

Jill couldn't deny the tug of resentment down deep in her stomach. Why had Penny thought it was all right to twiddle her thumbs until now? Why hadn't she come to help the minute she knew Matt was missing?

And why did Jill even care?

"I'm not sure when we'll arrive at the ranch," she told Penny finally. "But I'd suggest that maybe...well..."

"Maybe what?"

"I'm not comfortable talking about this on the phone. Drive down if you want, but I'm just not sure...the thing is, Cole might not be around for long."

"Where's he going? Does he know where Matt is?"

"I can't say."

"Listen, I understand your discomfort in revealing too much, but you can at least tell me that. Has Cole found Matt?"

"No." Jill glanced at the man by her side. His eyes were open, watching her. "No, not really. We might have an idea... but, no..."

"*We* might, huh?" Penny was silent a moment. "You know, I appreciate your help, Jill, but you've taken a lot of ownership in a situation that's really not your affair."

"That's true. I operate under a philosophy that says if a man asks for your shirt, you give him your coat, too. If he asks you to carry his burden for a mile, you carry it two."

"Who came up with that brilliant concept?"

"Jesus Christ." Jill again glanced in the rearview mirror. "Look, Penny, Cole insisted I go to Amarillo with him. He needed my computer expertise in order to stay in touch with Matt. I went along to Mexico because I wanted to support him. And I care about Matt a great deal. So I've done my extra mile. Now I'm going home so I can get back to my life. Drive down if you want. This is between you and Cole."

"I'm glad you can see that. Cole is—" she paused "—he's special to me. My feelings for him run very deep. I love him."

"Love is more than just a feeling, Miss Ames. It's toughing it out through thick and thin. Listen, I'd be happy to talk to you again sometime, but I need to concentrate on the road. I'll tell Cole you called."

Jill hung up before Penny could continue her saccharine professions of love. The sun was setting, and Jill had noticed a pair of headlights behind them from the time she answered the phone. She glanced at Cole. One of his big shoulders was wedged against the gap between the door and the seat, and he looked uncomfortable.

"Do you want me to stop?" she asked. "Need something more for the pain?"

"Thank you," he said. He reached across and laid his good hand on her arm. "For the extra mile."

Jill shivered at his touch and made herself focus on the highway. She hadn't wanted to like Cole Strong at all. At first, he had been distant and wooden and demanding. But then she began to see other sides to his character. Things emerged, like green leaves unfolding after a long, harsh winter. His love for his son. His devotion to his mother. His pursuit of justice. His willingness to fight for what he wanted.

It didn't help that Cole had begun to *look* good to her, too. She had become fond of the small curve his mouth made when he didn't want to smile but couldn't help it. She liked his hands—great big strong hands, now scarred in his battle for his son. Cole moved slowly and spoke with deliberation, but his eyes flashed with an inner blaze. He had a lot of life in him. Passion. A man didn't take a bankrupt farm and bring it back to vitality without grit and fire and stubborn determination.

Jill liked Cole's eyes, too. So blue. She glanced again at her passenger, and their gazes locked. Her heart thudded. *Morphine,* she reminded herself. *That look he's giving me right now means nothing.*

Moistening her lips, she stared at the road. She had dated a lot of men in college, and she'd been involved in a long-standing relationship with a football coach at the high school for a couple of years. But he hadn't shared her zeal. Though he professed to be a Christian, his life didn't show much evidence of it. Finally, Jill had realized that he didn't really love people the way she did—not enough to lay down his life.

Cole, she thought, might be different. Though he didn't truly understand his son, he loved Matt. But Jill was beginning to think Cole might actually understand her. He might even like who she was and the way she chose to live out her faith. That was a rare thing.

She looked at him again. He wore that little curve of a smile. "I like your hair," he said. "It's pretty."

Drugs, she told herself. *The man is on drugs.*

"I bet you were a cute little girl."

"And I'm not a cute woman?" she shot back.

"Nah."

"Ah, well—"

"Beautiful."

"So anyway, that was Penny on the phone." Jill kept her focus straight ahead. She couldn't let him continue like this. He would say things he didn't mean, and she would like them.

And then it would hurt. "She's driving down to the ranch to see you."

"You didn't tell her about France."

"I didn't think I should. We don't know how much access Agrimax has to our conversations. Obviously, they've gotten into the computers and some of the phones. I'm wondering if they have some kind of government approval to invade our privacy. Or maybe they're doing it through—"

"It's your hair," Cole said, the words slightly slurred. "I don't know how it does that."

Jill swallowed. "It just grows this way."

"I mean… I don't know how it makes you look like that… like you have a halo."

"It's not a halo. It's frizz."

"You're a holy person. Righteous."

She wished he would fall asleep and let her drive in peace. This intimacy wasn't good. It wasn't safe. "I have many flaws, believe me. I annoy a lot of people, including you."

"Me?"

"Yes, you. In case you've forgotten, you don't like me. You blame me for Matt's interest in Agrimax."

"You help me. I like that."

She glanced over at him, willing him to stop talking. "People say I'm too single-minded. I butt into things all the time. I've even been called boorish."

"But your lips are soft."

Jill smacked her palm against the steering wheel. "Stop this right now, Cole Strong."

"You don't like *me?*"

"Yes, I do. I didn't at first, but now I do. I like you—okay?"

"Really…how come?"

"I don't know." She let out a breath. "I admire you. There."

He tapped her arm. "I admire you, too. You're cute."

"You said I wasn't cute. You said I was…"

"Beautiful. Yeah, that's true." He hummed tunelessly for a moment. "Beautiful, beautiful halo in the moonlight. Green eyes looking down at me…like emeralds…glowing…so, so beauti—"

"Listen, Cole," Jill cut in, "you have a fiancée who's driving all the way down from Albuquerque to see you."

"Emeralds," he repeated.

"Penny has deep feelings for you. She loves you. Now go back to sleep."

"Dormez-vous?" he sang under his breath. "Are you sleeping, are you sleeping, lovely Jill, lovely Jill? *Dormez-vous? Dormez-vous?* I love you… I love—"

"Cole, you don't even know what you're saying. It's the morphine talking. So would you just be quiet? I'm going back to teaching, and you'll find Matt and then marry Penny. And I don't want to have any memories of…of…"

She looked across at him. Eyes closed, he had rolled his head back against the door and was breathing deeply. Sound asleep.

Jill glanced in the rearview mirror. The headlights were gone. The car she had feared was tailing them must have turned off down some country road a few miles back. She studied her reflection for a moment—the riot of curls, the lips, the green eyes, the face she had always considered plain. Then she focused on the highway once again.

Chapter Eleven

"Look older," Matt whispered. "Try to look like we're in college."

Seated beside him on a chrome-and-vinyl chair, Billy bit into a bagel. "It says right in our passports that we're sixteen, dude. There's no way we're going to fool anybody."

"I'm not talking about the airline people. The other passengers. They could be *them*."

"I hate these things," Billy said, eyeing his snack. "They don't have any flavor. Why do people eat them?"

"They're low fat or something." Matt pressed his hand over the USB key in his front jeans pocket.

Things weren't looking too good. Early that morning, he and Billy had driven away from Great-Aunt Thelma's house, leaving Granny Strong there. They had told her they were headed to the doughnut store. They had omitted the fact that they were also going to the airport.

Matt felt lousy about that. He wished he could get his hands on a Bible to see if anyone ever lied in the name of doing

God's work. He knew lying was forbidden in the Ten Commandments. Most of the time when people in the Bible lied, things went from bad to worse. Like a roll call, the characters Matt had studied in Sunday school stood to attention in his mind. First, there was Samson. After he lied to Delilah, his enemies cut his eyes out and made him a slave. Then, there were Ananias and Sapphira. They lied about selling their property, and they both dropped dead. And what about the apostle Peter? At Pilate's house, Peter lied three times about knowing Jesus, and look how that turned out. Jesus knew exactly what Peter had done.

On the other hand, Rahab the prostitute had lied to save two spies, and she wasn't punished at all. In fact, Matt recalled that Rahab wound up being one of Jesus's ancestors. David and Jonathan had cooked up a lie to save David's life. They told Saul that David had gone to Bethlehem when he was really hiding out in a field. And David became king of Israel after that. If the end result was for God's glory, did it make lying okay?

Matt stared at the tile on the terminal floor. Either way, what choice had he and Billy had but to lie to Granny Strong? She never would have let them go to France.

After leaving Great-Aunt Thelma's house, they had driven to the Oklahoma City airport and found an ATM. The credit card Matt's father had given him when he got his driver's license came with the strict instructions that it be used only in an emergency. Well, Matt rationalized, if this wasn't an emergency, what was? Still, he felt guilty as he gathered up the bills from the machine.

Lying. Stealing. What was next?

He'd almost forgotten he was skipping school, too. Here it was Monday evening, and he was on his way to Europe. Who knew when he'd get back home?

Using the credit card, Matt purchased two round-trip tickets to Paris. The airport there was called Charles de Gaulle, a name that didn't ring any bells with either boy, and that was all they knew about where they were headed. They didn't have a hotel reservation or French money. They didn't even know where the food conference was taking place. All this was causing Matt some anxiety, and he couldn't figure out how to calm down.

Their first flight took them to Chicago's O'Hare Airport. Wandering around inside a terminal, they bought bagels, sodas and Cubs ball caps. Then they loitered for a couple of hours in the international waiting area, Billy snacking and Matt getting more and more nervous. Now they were ready to board the jet that would take them across the Atlantic.

What if Agrimax people were on the flight? Matt found something else to fret about. What if they decided to destroy the USB key in some desperate act like blowing up the plane?

Was he becoming irrational? Was he losing his mind? Maybe he was slowly turning into some kind of schizophrenic—

"Low fat, ha," Billy muttered, regarding his bagel with disdain. "Low taste is more like it. These things need a big spoonful of peanut butter or a slab of ham or something. You eat them plain like this, it's a mouthful of foam rubber."

At last the announcement of their flight number echoed across the terminal. The other passengers perked up, grabbing purses, magazines and carry-on bags. Matt realized belatedly that he and Billy should have purchased some luggage, even though they didn't have anything to put in a suitcase. Two kids standing around with nothing but a pair of tickets could attract unwanted attention.

"So when are you going to tell me what they're after, Matt-man?" Billy punctuated the question by slam-dunking the rest of his bagel into a trash can. "Have you got a CD or something?"

"Shh!" Matt elbowed him in the stomach. "They'll hear you, dude. You don't know who's on this flight with us. It might be them."

"Well, it's not Mr. Keeling and Ted, that's for sure. I'd recognize them in a second."

"It could be anybody! And you're just blabbing about whatever you feel like."

"Are you going to be this grouchy the whole way to Paris?"

"I'm not grouchy. I'm just nervous, okay? My dad's going to go ballistic when he finds out I've been running up his credit card. You're only going to get in trouble for skipping school, but I've done all kinds of wrong things."

"Yeah. A murder rap is nothing to joke about."

"Billy, good grief! Why don't you just tell the whole world who we are, huh?"

"Sorry, dude! Don't get so bent out of shape."

Matt stared down at his ticket. He hadn't intended to be irritable with his best friend. How many times had he wished for Billy's companionship in the past few days?

"You're right," Billy admitted in a low voice. "Sheriff Holtmeyer probably told the authorities to look for you in airports. I'm kind of amazed we got through check-in."

"Me, too."

"Agrimax might have found out where we're going, too."

"How could they? Did you tell anybody?"

"I didn't find out about France until this morning, remember?" He shook his head. "It is kind of freaky how they know everything we're doing, though. Do you think Josefina would have told anyone about the passports?"

"No way. She promised."

"What about your dad? She might have told him."

"He's looking for me down in Mexico." Matt pushed his fingers through his hair. He needed a shower. "Billy, I feel so bad about all this. He's gonna kill me…if Agrimax doesn't do the job first."

"Don't worry, Mattman. If somebody wants to hurt you, he's gotta go through me."

Matt nodded, relieved. Billy had always been his protector—all the way up from grade school, when other kids were teasing him or trying to push him around.

"So what are we supposed to be doing?" Matt asked. "Are we supposed to go through the gate now, or what?"

"They're calling us onto the plane in groups." Billy pointed to a spot on Matt's ticket. "You and I are in group five. Look, why don't you just give me that? You're going to bend it, and then it won't go through the machine. You need to relax, buddy."

"I wish I could."

"This is an adventure, okay? It'll be fun."

"It hasn't been so far."

Matt pictured little Luz down in Juarez. No doubt she was out of money by now—probably forced back into prostitution to feed the other kids. And buy their glue.

He thought of Mr. Banyon, too. His life on earth was over, and his ranch would be sold.

Matt's pickup was in a police lot somewhere in El Paso. Hernando's truck was abandoned in Oklahoma City. Granny's best friend had broken her hip. Nope, this had not been fun at all.

"Here's the deal," Billy said, giving Matt a gentle push to indicate that their group finally had been called to board the plane. "Some heavy stuff has happened to you, but you're going to be okay. You're doing the right thing, aren't you?"

"Well…"

Billy halted and took his friend's elbow. "Look, Matt… I

don't want to doubt you, but the stuff we're doing is pretty extreme. This whole food thing isn't one of your obsessions, is it...like tectonic plates or Latin? This is God's will. Right?"

Matt edged forward, his Nike runners moving in little baby steps toward the ramp. The woman in front of him wore bright red high heels with long pointy toes. Weird. He wondered if she was French.

"Mattman?" Billy asked. "We *are* going to Paris because you believe God is leading us, aren't we? You told me you knew this was something you had to do."

"I thought that, but..."

"But what?"

Arriving at the front of the line, Matt showed his ticket and passport one more time. The agent ushered him onto the covered ramp that led down to the plane. Billy came up beside him and grabbed his jacket.

"Matt Strong," he said, "this better not be some wild-goose chase, because if it is—"

"No, no. But it's just that sometimes—" pausing, he looked into his friend's eyes "—sometimes it feels a lot more rational not to listen. Not to pay attention to God. Like it's smarter to be safe."

"Smarter, yeah, I buy that. But remember what our youth pastor always says—God doesn't ask us to be smart. He just wants us to obey. And that's what you're doing."

Matt felt relief pour through him. "'I was hungry, and you fed me.'"

"Yep, that's it." Billy slapped him on the back. "Get on in there, and let's find our seats. I wonder how soon they serve up supper."

"We've pinned the boy," Mack Harwood said.

Vince gripped the phone in his hand. "You caught him? You have the CDs?"

"He's on his way to Paris."

"Paris? Are you kidding me?"

"We have this under control, sir. My men in France are already on it."

Rubbing his forehead, Vince glanced across the restaurant at the table he had just left. His two counterparts—the CEOs of Progrow and Megafarm—were engaged in an animated discussion. The three men planned to meet for most of the next day to finalize plans for the merger. The others looked tense, Vince noted, and he wondered if he appeared equally anxious. The biggest deal in the history of global commerce was just eight days away, and he must not let on that anything was amiss.

"Harwood," he said, flipping open his electronic planner, "I have to finish this dinner. Listen to me. I'm giving you twenty-four hours. If your men don't have those CDs by this time tomorrow, I'm going after them myself."

"That won't be necessary, sir."

"Get the boy, Harwood."

He pressed the phone's off button and took his handkerchief from his pocket. Stepping behind a marble pillar, he blotted his forehead and neck. He felt out of control. Panic gripped his chest. He made himself breathe deeply.

This would end up just fine, he told himself. He was not the CEO of Agrimax for nothing. He had power, could pull strings, could make it work. He trusted in himself—always had.

Lifting his chin and adjusting his collar, he left the security of the pillar and crossed the carpet toward his guests. With a smile and a wave of dismissal, he let them know everything was great.

Cole sat on his couch and surveyed the ring of solemn faces surrounding him. Pedro, his crop foreman, stared with baleful brown eyes. Josefina, a plate of biscochitos on her lap, dabbed at her cheek with a pink tissue. Her husband, Hernando, kept glancing out the window, clearly wishing he weren't there.

And Jill. Perched across from Cole, her eyes tired and her golden halo frazzled, she gazed at him.

Finally, Josefina spoke. "I think you should go to bed, Mr. Strong. You look really bad...like sick, you know? Matthew is gone. You're not gonna see him again till he comes home."

Cole couldn't deny the truth in her statement. Now that the morphine had worn off, he was in pain, and he knew his chances of finding Matt were slim. "I ought to fire your sorry hide, Hernando," he said.

"I know." The ranch foreman shook his head. "I hope you don't, though, because you would have done the same thing if you was me. You would have gotten those passports, and you would have given them to the boy."

"How can you say that? How can you even think I would let my son go flying off—"

"Because he was talking about God. He was telling Josefina and me that he had to do it for God, you know? He convinced us."

"It's true." Josefina blotted another tear. "No sooner had Matthew driven away in Hernando's pickup than we thought we probably made a big mistake. But at the time..."

"It's done now," Jill spoke up. "Looking back is useless."

Cole realized she was right. The moment they had arrived at the ranch, Josefina met them with the news that Geneva Strong had phoned. The day before, she and the boys had made a hair-raising escape from Keeling and his cohort in Amarillo. Then they had driven to Oklahoma City, where she intended to keep them hidden at her Aunt Thelma's house until she located Cole. But early this morning, Matt and Billy had driven off to buy doughnuts and had never returned. She had no idea where they were.

"So you think they really went?" he asked, glancing at Jill.

"Yes, but don't say where." She held up a hand of warning. "It's bad enough that you and I know. It makes us targets. Don't tell the others."

"Ohh," Josefina groaned. "It's someplace bad. They're gonna get killed. They'll die, and it'll be all our fault, Hernando."

"Anyway, the chile is doing okay." Pedro hadn't spoken until now, but clearly he felt this was the time for some good news. "It's up and looking really nice."

"Yeah, we got eight calves since you left," Hernando added. "The livestock is in good shape."

"Can you two handle the place for a few more days without me?"

"Sure," Hernando said.

"*Claro.*" Pedro smiled. "I been doing this half my life, Mr. Strong. Tom Perry from Selena Foods came over from Roswell yesterday to check on our chile, and he says it's looking like the best crop ever. If we don't get hail, we're gonna be great. And the hay—Homestead called me. If it's the same quality as last year, they'll take all we can give them."

Cole felt a warm peace pour through him. "Tell Homestead it'll be better than last year's crop. Phone Tom, too, will you? Let him know I should be back at the ranch by the end of the week, and I'd like to talk to him."

"I'll call him tomorrow morning."

The idea of sitting down over a cup of hot black coffee with his longtime colleague brought Cole a sense of normalcy he hadn't felt since Thursday afternoon, when Matt failed to come home from school. It would be something to look forward to. One day—maybe soon—this mess would be over, and life would start ticking along as it always had. Days and months and seasons slipping by... His focus came to rest on Jill.

She looked away quickly. "Well, I'm bushed. I'd better head for home."

"You don't have to go," he said, wishing he could prevent the inevitable.

"I need to make lesson plans."

"Josefina could make us some dinner. I know you're hungry."

"Do you like enchiladas? I make red ones or green ones."

"I love both kinds." Jill smiled across at the other woman in the room. "But not tonight. Maybe another time."

"Yeah, another time," Cole said. "When we get Matt home, you could come over. Matt would love that. And me... I'd be happy for you to drop by anytime."

She didn't answer, staring at the strap on her tote bag. "Anyway, don't worry about the rental car, Cole. I'll take care of it tomorrow—and I'll handle the paperwork with the wreck in Mexico."

"Thanks. I really appreciate it...everything you've done."

She shrugged. "No problem. Penny should be here soon. I've written her a note about your medicines. You ought to take another painkiller. It's past time. And don't forget the antibiotics, either."

Standing, she picked up her tote bag. Cole watched her, intimate now with this bundle of energy and tireless enthusiasm that had so annoyed him in the beginning. Once a total stranger, Jill Pruitt had stayed at his side. Searched for his son. Cared for his mother. Rescued him from darkness, hunger and the threat of death. He was so used to hearing her voice in the car, to having her near. Somehow, her presence made it seem like everything would work out.

He rose, and with the motion a stabbing pain shot up his arm. Without hesitation, she reached for him. "Are you okay?"

"I'm fine." He winced, hobbling forward on his tender ankle.

"Just stay put. I know my way to the door."

He went after her anyway, feeling a sense of deprivation at the thought of her absence. "I'll call you."

"When you find Matt, yes." She swung around, a small smile pasted on her face. "I'll be praying for you."

"Jill." He stretched out his bandaged hand, but she slipped through the front door. "Jill, wait."

"It's really late. I'd better go."

"But I want to—"

"Your fiancée's coming, Cole." She shifted from one foot to the other. "I need to go home."

"Yeah. Well…thanks. Thanks for going with me."

"Anytime."

Before he could stop her, she hurried away, her sandals crunching on the driveway.

Cole rubbed his eyes as he moved back into the house and shut the front door. He had already thrown a few clothes into a bag. His passport was safely lodged in his pocket. But maybe he could afford a quick shower and a bite to eat.

Matt's framed school pictures hung along the foyer wall, and Cole paused to study his son. He had been a beautiful child—large blue eyes, wavy dark hair, perfect skin. Always solemn, Matt stared into the camera as though this yearly routine bemused him. As though it required him to ponder why the picture must be taken, how the camera worked, what effects the lighting had, and what it would all mean in the end.

What it meant to Cole was that he would not take a shower or eat or do anything else. He would not wait for Penny to arrive from Albuquerque. And he certainly couldn't afford to take any more painkillers. The image of grown men hot on his sixteen-year-old son's trail was enough to recharge Cole. He stepped into the living room.

"Thanks for coming over," he told his three employees. "Keep your mouths shut about the passports, all of you. Don't tell Sheriff Holtmeyer that Matt was here. And whatever you do, don't—" He halted, catching Josefina's stricken look. "Did you tell the sheriff?"

"Well, he came over to the house on Sunday morning right after Matthew left. He wanted to know if we'd seen Matthew—"

"She looked guilty," Hernando cut in. "My wife has never been a good liar. I can always tell if she's—"

"Never mind." Cole gritted his teeth. "Just do the best you can to protect Matt."

The three rose, looking uncomfortable and sad. Cole wished he could ease the situation, but he knew it was impossible. How much information had been leaked already? Who knew about France besides Jill? And what if someone got to her? What if Agrimax—

"Good night, Mr. Strong," Josefina called over her shoulder as Hernando led her toward the kitchen. "You sure you don't want any biscochitos? I baked them today."

Cole stepped forward and took a couple of the small, powdery cookies just to please her. "Josefina, will you do something for me?"

"Anything, Mr. Strong. You know that."

"You used to tell me you had your limits."

She smiled for the first time that night. "Not anymore."

"Me, either," he said.

She touched his arm. "What can I do for you?"

"Will you check on Jill Pruitt? Call her tomorrow, and make sure she's all right. Hernando, you could drive by her house, maybe phone the school, too. These guys—the ones who caused my accident, the men who are after Matt—they know Jill was with me. They interrogated her. They may still think they can get information out of her and—"

"It's okay, Mr. Strong." Hernando laid a hand on his boss's shoulder. "We'll make sure she's all right. I won't let nobody hurt her."

As Pedro, Hernando and Josefina left the old adobe ranch house, Cole let out a deep breath. He could trust them. Maybe they hadn't been as circumspect as he wished, but they were human and therefore susceptible to stress, fear, and all the factors that led people to confess their secrets.

Again his thoughts turned to Jill Pruitt. How had she withstood Agrimax's interrogation for two solid days? Anyone who would run a car off a road and leave a man in the ditch to die could have no conscience. Surely the pressure those men had put on her had been intense. She had prayed, she told Cole. Simply prayed. Was that enough?

Determined to do things the right way, Cole paused beside the couch and knelt. Pressing his forehead against his clasped hands, he begged God to have mercy on his son. *Protect Matthew. Save his life. Lead me to him.*

Was this how Jill prayed? Cole regretted his laziness in remembering to read his Bible, to pray, to commune with the Lord. He was like one of those baby Christians Paul had spoken of—still on the milk of the gospel and not even ready for meat.

"Help me grow, Father," he prayed aloud. He clenched his fists, heedless of the pain in his wounded fingers. "No matter how this turns out, even if I lose my boy like I lost my wife, I want to know You more. I want to be the man You intended when You created me. Grow me like a good healthy crop, like a chile bush loaded with pods. I want to bear fruit. Help me. Teach me. And God...please...please lead me to Matthew. I need to—"

The doorbell cut off his thoughts. Jill? He felt a surge of hope. She had returned. Cole limped toward the door as the bell sounded again. *No, probably it's Penny,* he realized. She must have driven ninety-to-nothing all the way from Albuquerque.

How could he explain that he had to leave her behind? He didn't even have time to talk, to tell her what was happening. Why had she come? Did he want her presence?

The thought of Penny's thousand lawyerly questions, her quick anger, her lack of understanding discouraged Cole as he reached for the door. Had he made a mistake in allowing a relationship to develop between them? Once, he'd been so sure he wanted to marry her. Now that idea seemed foreign and misguided.

He opened the door, but instead of Penny...instead of Jill... Tom Perry stood on the porch. Heavyset, with a friendly face and a rich Texas drawl, the man who bought Cole's chile for Selena Foods stood in the pool of light from the overhead fixture. With a chuckle of surprise, the man held out his hand.

"Cole, I didn't expect to find you here!" He stepped into the foyer and took off his hat. "I was staying overnight in Artesia—getting bored just watching TV at the motel, you know. So I thought I'd drive around the area to take a gander at what's going on with some of my accounts. Your fields are looking real good this spring."

"Thanks." As welcome as the familiar face was, Cole knew he couldn't afford to talk to Tom for more than a moment.

"Anyhow, when I saw the lights on over at your house, I got concerned. Pedro told me you were in Mexico. He says you've had some trouble lately. What's this about your boy? Matt ran off?"

"Something like that," Cole said. "Listen, Tom, I'd invite you in for a cup of coffee, but I'm on my way out."

"At this hour? Whoa, look at your hand. What happened there, buddy?"

"It's not bad, but I really do have to go, Tom. I've got things to take care of. You know."

Tom grew solemn. "Listen, Cole, some of the honchos from headquarters flew down here the other day. I'm not sure you knew that. They're real unhappy about the way things are going. I wanted to warn you that you could have big trouble on your hands. And I'm not just talking about a runaway boy."

Cole belatedly remembered that Selena Foods was owned by Agrimax. Of course. His heart sped up as he studied his old friend. "What kind of trouble are you talking about, Tom?"

"They say your boy stole some information that belongs to Agrimax. Everybody knows Matt is good with computers. It sounds to me like he pirated their patented technology."

"If he did, so what? He's only sixteen. What's a kid going to do with a formula for pesticide or fertilizer? If it's patented, he can't sell it. And he sure can't make the stuff himself. Matt's no threat to Agrimax, Tom. You know that."

"Seems that way, Cole, but all the same…they want to find him."

"Well, so do I."

"Then are you willing to cooperate?"

Standing in the open doorway, Cole noted the car idling in his driveway. Not Tom's old blue pickup. This was a sleek, black luxury vehicle.

"You didn't come out here to check on my fields, did you, Tom? They sent you."

Tom rubbed the back of his neck. "Cole, listen, I need Agrimax just as bad as you do. I've worked for Selena for twenty-three years. Neither of us can get along without our jobs. Why don't you cooperate? Tell them everything you know. Work with them to find Matt. If you help out, they'll make this easy on your boy. I promise."

"I wouldn't give those people the time of day," Cole said. "They tried to kill me, Tom. Down in Mexico, they ran me off the road and left me for dead. They've chased my boy and scared the living daylights out of my seventy-year-old mother. And they killed Jim Banyon, Tom. They murdered him."

As he spoke, two men in dark suits emerged from the car and moved toward the house. "What's going on?" Cole demanded. "Was that a signal? Rubbing the back of your neck like that, Tom?"

The big man stepped aside. "I'm sorry. I tried to talk them out of this."

Cole's numbed brain leaped to alertness. As the men lunged through the door, he grabbed two of Matt's school pictures with his good hand and hurled them. Glass shattered. He ducked into the living room and sprinted for the kitchen. The pain in his ankle shot up his leg as his boots thudded across the saltillo tiles. A shot rang out, and the adobe wall beside his hip exploded in a puff of dust.

Cole flung open the back door and stumbled into the darkness. Shouts echoed. The car in his driveway roared to life, headlights swinging across the alfalfa field behind the house. Curling his wounded fingers against his chest, he dropped to his belly and crawled under a string of barbed wire. Flashlights flicked on, and their beams chased him as he hobbled across the newly mown hay.

Where to run? He could ignore the pain in his swollen ankle, but how much pounding could it take before he collapsed? And where could he hide in flat terrain with few trees and no deep ravines?

Barns? Sheds? He'd be trapped.

Hernando's house was too far away. They'd catch him first.

He could make it to a farm truck...but his keys hung on a peg by the door inside the house.

Another gunshot rang out, and Cole instinctively ducked as the bullet screamed past him. He was starting to panic when his thoughts suddenly focused on his horses. A flicker of hope caught flame. He veered left and rolled under another fence, this one wooden. He knew his property—his pursuers did not. With God's help, he could outwit them.

Ducking to a crouch, he headed across a newly planted chile field, the soft dirt slowing him down. He slipped under a length of irrigation piping that rolled across the crops on large metal wheels. That would deter the car.

Out of breath and in excruciating pain, he forced himself to keep moving forward. *Run for Matt,* he told himself. *Run for the life of Matthew Aaron Strong.*

A dusting of moonlight revealed the saddle horses Cole used for working his cattle. In the corral just ahead, the seven large shapes stood silently, dozing or nibbling on tender green grass. None would expect the burst of activity, and Cole hoped he could use their confusion to his advantage.

As the black car bounced across the fields toward him, he skidded to a stop in front of the corral and threw open the gate. "Hey there, Jack," he called in a low voice. The black gelding was a favorite for Cole's early-morning rides across the range. Steady and powerful, Jack could cover miles without flagging. "How about a run, fella? Come here."

Nostrils flaring, the horse stepped toward him, and Cole caught the animal's mane. He boosted himself up with a foot on the corral fence. His injured hand was useless. Driven by desperation, he threaded his fingers through the horse's mane and mounted.

"Let's go, boy," he yelled, digging his heels into Jack's

flanks. With a howl, he brought the other horses to attention. Nervous, skittish at the unfamiliar disturbance, they whinnied.

As if sensing Cole's distress, Jack took off at a gallop. Cole clutched the mane, leaned forward and did his best to hang on as Jack easily outpaced the other horses, who were making a break for the open gate. The car's brakes squealed as the bolting animals thundered toward it. A gun fired, and a horse screamed.

If they shot one of my animals... Cole gritted his teeth, anger pulsing through his veins. Glancing over his shoulder, he searched in vain for the men who had been chasing him on foot.

At Cole's urging, Jack leaped over a fallen log and kept on course for Catclaw Draw, a shallow creek choked with salt cedar brush. The shrubbery was low, but it would provide some cover. If he could lose the car, it would buy him time—but he couldn't hide in the draw forever. Where could he go? How could he get away once and for all?

Jack's hooves thundered across a stretch of baked earth. The headlights had picked them out again, and the car pulled closer. Cole guided the horse the last few paces and then braced himself as Jack skittered down the five-foot dip into the draw. With his fingers still tangled in the animal's mane, he lowered his head. Salt cedar branches scratched across his thighs and reached for his face. The horse slowed.

Cole glanced behind at the instant the car plunged off the lip of dry ground and plowed straight into Catclaw Draw. Metal crunched, glass shattered, and someone shouted a string of expletives.

"You left me in a ditch," Cole murmured, "and turnabout is fair play. Come on, Jack. Let's head for town. There's somebody I know I can count on for help."

Chapter Twelve

"Two movies, and both of them were lousy," Billy grumbled.

"You should have tried to sleep." Matt followed his friend down one of two narrow aisles between countless rows of seats in the massive jetliner. They were headed for the aircraft's door and the terminal at Charles de Gaulle Airport outside Paris.

"You didn't sleep. You sat there watching that dumb map on the screen. How can you stare at a graphic of a plane moving across a map for seven hours? That's totally boring."

"Better than two lousy movies."

Matt couldn't explain why he was so fascinated by the small digital screen on the seat back in front of him. He didn't know why it intrigued him to watch the airplane graphic as hour by hour it crept from Chicago over Canada, Newfoundland, the Arctic Ocean, and eventually across Ireland, England, and down into France. He hadn't been able to tell his father why he liked to stare at the clock in the kitchen for an hour at a time, either.

Matt just knew he enjoyed precise movement. Tiny increments of space and time compelled him. Mathematical perfection and predictability—things like that were more interesting than movies in which people made long, impassioned speeches or killed each other or performed random actions that made little sense to Matt.

Humans baffled him. He liked girls all right, and he had noticed some pretty ones on this airplane, but he had decided early on in the tenth grade that he would never marry. A wife would drive him crazy in a millisecond—if she could stand to be around him that long.

"I'm beat." Billy shook his head as if that would clear out the fog between his ears. "I don't get how it can be eight o'clock on Tuesday morning. It feels like the middle of the night."

"It is the middle of the night at home. But we've flown through seven time zones, and our circadian rhythms have been interrupted."

"Circadian rhythms?"

"The human body has rhythms which occur in approximately twenty-four-hour cycles," Matt explained as they walked up the covered Jetway to the terminal. "At this point in our circadian oscillations, we should be in bed asleep. But the plane traveled across all those time zones—actually human-imposed geographical regions in which the same standard time is used. Of course, the earth's rotation is the true basis for—"

"Yeah, okay, Mattman," Billy cut in. "Good grief, look at this line of people. I guess we have to go through customs to show we don't have any illegal drugs or vegetables or whatever."

Matt stiffened at the realization they must pass yet another checkpoint. He placed his hand over the lump of the USB key in his pocket and lifted up a prayer for protection. What if they had come this far only to be sent back to the States? Or worse—what if the customs people confiscated the USB key? He hadn't declared it on that little form he and Billy filled out on the plane. Maybe Agrimax had alerted customs to watch for two unaccompanied teenagers without any luggage. This could be really bad.

Billy gazed around the terminal. He edged forward in the line. "Toto, I don't think we're in Kansas anymore."

"I'm freaking," Matt said.

Billy thumped him on the back. "Chill, Mattman. We'll be fine."

It took almost half an hour to inch to the front of the line, but the French customs officials seemed indifferent to the fact that a fugitive from justice was passing into their country. With freshly inked stamps inside their passports, Matt and Billy followed the flow of people out into the main terminal. They stood for a moment, surveying the array of cafés, gift shops and newsstands.

"I'm hungry," Billy said. "Take a look at that bread."

"Baguettes. We need to find a taxi before we can eat. And we have to find out where the conference is going on. I hope Josiah Karume will agree to talk to us."

"Why wouldn't he?"

"He was supposed to be elected chairman of I-FEED at this summit. He's a bigwig now. But maybe if I mention Mr. Banyon, he'll see us. They were scheduled to meet."

"We can't do anything till we change our money. They don't use dollars here."

"They use euros. It's the standard currency in all of Europe." Matt swallowed as a man in dark glasses approached them. He lowered his voice. "Look out, Billy."

"Do you need a taxi?" the man asked in accented English. "I make you a very reasonable price."

"No thanks," Matt said quickly. "We have to figure out where we're going first."

"What is the name of your destination? Perhaps I may assist you."

"It's a food convention," Billy blurted out. "A meeting on world hunger."

"Ah, *oui!* The International Conference on Hunger Relief. At the convention center on Boulevard de la Villette. I know where this is—come with me! I shall take you. A good price—only ten euros."

"We don't have any euros."

"No problem. I accept dollars. You come!"

He turned on his heel and started for the exit. Billy moved to follow, but Matt caught his arm. "How do you know he's safe? Maybe he's with Agrimax."

"Didn't you see his taxi uniform, dude? He's just trying to drum up business."

"But what about changing our money? I read in the airline magazine that you can do it at the airport."

"Just hang with me, Mattman. I'll take care of everything."

Billy set off behind the taxi driver, and Matt had no choice but to tag along. He knew he was being paranoid, but he couldn't get the image of Mr. Banyon's blackened mouth out of his mind. If the Agrimax people would murder harmless old Mr. Banyon, what wouldn't they do? All the same, Matt had to admit he was no good at reading people. He had zero intuition, and as a child, his teachers regularly wrote on his report cards that he needed to work on his "social skills."

The best thing to do was to follow Billy's lead, he decided. They stepped out into a bright spring morning, and the traffic speeding by was unbelievable. Way more congested than Albuquerque or Oklahoma City, and those cities had seemed frenetic to Matt. The taxi driver opened the door of his small black car, and sure enough, there was a meter right on the dashboard. Matt felt a wash of relief.

Another man sat in the backseat, an older fellow dressed in a gray business suit and reading a French newspaper. He barely looked up as Billy climbed in beside him and Matt took a place by the door.

"I am taking this gentleman to Avenue de la République," the driver told his new passengers. "It is near the convention center. No problem."

"*Bonjour,*" the man said, nodding at the boys.

"*Bonjour,*" Billy echoed. He leaned over and whispered to Matt. "I took French in seventh grade. Watch this." He addressed the other passenger. "*Comment allez-vous?*"

"*Très bien, merci. Et vous?*"

"I asked him how he was, and he said he was fine," Billy confided to Matt as the taxi pulled out into traffic.

"What did he ask you?"

"He didn't ask me anything."

"Yeah, he did. He said, '*Et vous?*'"

Billy shrugged. "I don't know that. But here's one. *Monsieur, parlez-vous anglais?*"

"Yes, I speak English," the man replied. "I hail from London, actually."

"London, England?" Matt's thoughts sped through the massive catalog of facts he had absorbed during social studies classes in elementary school. "Why didn't you take the bullet train through the Chunnel?"

"I prefer to fly." He smiled. "And may I ask which of you young men is Matthew Strong?"

At that, Matt gulped down a bubble of air and pressed himself back against the seat. They were dead meat.

"Oh, great," Billy said, his eyes wide as he swung around to stare at Matt. "This is bad."

"May I introduce myself?" the man asked. "I am Dr. John Sloane of Agrimax's Technology Development Department, headquartered in London. My colleague, Pierre Brochant, manages security for the French division of the company."

The taxi driver glanced over his shoulder and smirked at the two boys. "Sorry to mislead you," he said, his broken English suddenly gone.

Matt elbowed Billy. "Did you tell your mom? You told her we were going to Paris, didn't you?"

"I called her from Chicago, because I couldn't very well go clear across the Atlantic Ocean without letting her know. But I didn't tell her—"

"Gentlemen," Dr. Sloane cut in, "I don't believe you've answered my question. Which of you is Matthew Strong?"

Matt stared straight ahead, trying to keep a poker face. He was so mad at Billy he couldn't see straight. How could anyone be so dumb? Thanks to Billy's big mouth, they'd been nabbed in two seconds, like a couple of bozo-brains. So much for counting on Billy for help. Matt would be better off alone.

"I shall assume from the photograph I received by fax last night that you are Matthew Strong." Dr. Sloane looked directly at Matt. "Do not be alarmed. We mean you no harm whatsoever."

"Where are you taking us?" Billy demanded. "We have business at the convention center."

"The conference on world hunger ended last Friday. Hector Diaz is taking a short holiday on the Continent, after which he will return to Mexico."

"We're not here to meet Hector Diaz," Matt said. "We've come to talk to the chairman of I-FEED. He's expecting to have a meeting about...about why we've come."

"I'm afraid you're mistaken. Josiah Karume has already

resumed his post at the Africa headquarters in Khartoum, Sudan."

"You're lying," Matt said.

"No, indeed. What I tell you is quite true. You will find no one with I-FEED in France at this time. They have all returned to their places of service."

"Service. What would you know about that?"

"Are you aware, Mr. Strong, that we at Agrimax work quite closely with I-FEED? Our CEO, Vincent Grant, is a great supporter of humanitarian causes. We're actually one of I-FEED's major suppliers."

"Big deal," Matt said. He lifted his chin. The kids at school thought he was a nerd, but he knew how to talk about things that mattered. "I know how it works. Agrimax donates the surpluses that American farmers grow because of farm subsidies. The U.S. government—the taxpayers—are providing that food, not Agrimax. You funnel it from the granaries to the foreign countries so you can look good."

"And yet, without our services, where would I-FEED be?"

"This is not about I-FEED or any other organization."

"No, indeed. It's about an idealistic young man who has stolen the private intellectual property of a corporation."

"You're wrong, Dr. Sloane. It's bigger than that. It's about hungry, dying children. Starving mothers who can't feed their babies. Fathers who don't have the energy to take care of their families. That's why Mr. Banyon couldn't take it anymore. You people are evil, and he wanted to bring about a change. And that's why I took the USB key."

"A USB key, is that what you have? I should have known." He tapped Pierre on the shoulder. "Find a place to stop. We've got it."

"*Oui,*" the driver said.

"You're not getting the key," Matt said, clutching the solid lump in his pocket. "I won't give it to you."

"What do you mean to do with it—turn it over to I-FEED? They're a humanitarian organization, not a food producer or a media outlet. They can't do anything with it. It's useless to them."

"The stuff on this key is gonna fry Agrimax, and you know it. That's why you killed Mr. Banyon. That's why your people have chased me all over the place. You know that whoever has the information can ruin you. If I-FEED has it, you'll have to cooperate with them, or they'll blow your cover."

"You're saying I-FEED would blackmail us?" Dr. Sloane laughed. "Good heavens, lad, you do have an imagination."

"It's not my imagination. It's what Mr. Banyon told me, and it's not blackmail. He said you're planning things that aren't right—they're not ethical. Your plan is based on technology you've been developing for the past fifteen years. Genetic technology, illegal mergers, hostile takeovers, all kinds of things that will ensure Agrimax control of the world's food supply."

"Pierre, do find a place to stop immediately."

"Dr. Sloane, please, the traffic. We are in the second arrondisement now—very crowded. No parking!"

"Give me the key, Mr. Strong," Sloane demanded, reaching across Billy. "Do so at once."

"No!" Matt gripped it more tightly. "Never."

"You should be grateful we found you before the police did. If you hand over the USB key, I promise that all charges against you will be dropped."

"That's not what I want," Matt replied, unable to see why Dr. Sloane was having such a hard time comprehending this. "I don't care about my own safety. If I did, I wouldn't be doing this. My goal—the goal every Christian should have—is to feed the hungry."

"Young man, Agrimax is doing all it can to make sure that food goes to the needy."

"What's it doing? Tell me what."

"This world is a business. Supply and demand are its pillars. People will always demand food, and we shall always supply it."

"To the highest bidders."

"Of course. Why should we sell to the low bidder? Capitalism doesn't work that way."

Matt tried to think clearly. *Supply, demand, capitalism...* they sounded like words printed on one of his board games—a test of strategy where little plastic pieces moved around on a sheet of colorful plastic. Not real life.

Everything inside the taxi felt surreal, unexpected. None of this had ever crossed Matt's mind when he was sitting with Mr. Banyon and discussing his term paper. Feeding the hungry had been an idea, a workable concept. But it hadn't involved all these terrible things—things that were so out of his control. They couldn't actually be happening to Matthew Strong from Artesia, New Mexico. And yet they were, and he had to do something. Say something.

"You should sell to the low bidders because they need the food," he told the man across from him. "They can't afford to pay high prices. They're too poor, and you're starving them."

"Do you hear the boy, Pierre? Such passion."

The driver glanced over his shoulder. "Passion will never allow you to succeed, Monsieur Strong. Power is what you must seek. To the powerful belongs the victory."

Matt was breathing too hard, nearly hyperventilating. He had to calm down. But how? These men had him in the palms of their hands. They were going to take the USB key away. Mr. Banyon would have died in vain. Nothing would come of his efforts. And people would go on starving.

"It's not about passion or power," he told the Agrimax men. "It's about right and wrong. The world isn't a business—it's a battleground. Good versus evil. And I'm on the side of good."

"How quaint to see the world in black-and-white," Dr. Sloane murmured. "You've been reading too many books, my naive young friend. Heroes and villains, right and wrong, good and evil—this is the stuff of fairy tales."

"It's the stuff of the Bible, which is the only book I've been reading these days, and I can tell you that the forces of good belong to God, and the forces of evil—"

"Calm down, Mattman," Billy said, reaching for him.

"No way!" Without stopping to think, Matt grabbed the chrome door handle. The taxi door swung open, and he hurled himself out onto the street. He landed hard on his shoulder, his head glancing off the pavement and a layer of skin scraping from his arm. Around him, tires screeched, horns blared. Dazed, he lifted his head to see a small blue car bearing down.

This was it. He would die like Mr. Banyon, for the cause of Christ.

Scrambling to his feet, he made a frantic attempt to leap to safety. Too late. The car's fender caught his hip and tossed him into the air. He hit the blue roof, slid across it and landed on solid ground again, his elbow slamming into concrete. He lay on a sidewalk. Cars braked, a waiter dropped a tray of dishes, people ran to see. Coming for him. Reaching.

Matt pushed himself up. A woman with warm brown eyes and bright red lipstick gave him her hand. *"Monsieur, comment allez-vous?"*

"It's the USB key," he said. "They... I have to..."

"Au secours!" she shouted at a man standing nearby. *"Appelez l'samu!"*

"No, no." Matt was on his feet now, watching Pierre drive

the taxi toward him. It had made a U-turn. They were coming back for him. He had to get away.

He grabbed the woman's arm. "I'm in trouble. Can you help me?"

She stared at him. *"Pourquoi?"*

"That taxi. Right there! Those men are trying to kill me!"

She studied the taxi for a moment, and then she looked at Matt again, her coffee eyes assessing.

"Oui," she said. "Come, please."

Grabbing his shoulders, she pivoted him toward the crowded bistro. *"Tout droit,"* she urged. "Straight ahead, we go."

The sea of onlookers parted, and Matt hobbled on his bruised hip through the clutter of café tables and chairs on the sidewalk in front of the restaurant.

"Arrêtez!" someone called from behind as the woman hurried Matt into the cool darkness of the dining room, where patrons looked up from their midmorning coffee, pastries and cigarettes. He glanced over his shoulder to see Billy just ahead of the two Agrimax men, all racing toward him.

"C'mon, Billy!" Matt shouted as the woman shoved him through swinging doors into a busy kitchen.

"Pardon!" she called, giving the chef and his assistants a fluttering wave of her red fingernails.

Hurrying behind, Dr. Sloane and Pierre yelled commands in French, but no one made a move to help.

"Mattman, don't leave me!" Billy called out.

Matt thought about pausing for his friend to catch up. How many times had Billy protected him? But he couldn't risk losing the USB key. Besides, Agrimax had no reason to harm Billy, so his friend was better off without him.

The brown-eyed woman led Matt through the back door of the bistro and into a narrow alley. She moved with surprising speed, her sharp-heeled black shoes clattering on the cobblestones. "Come! Come, *monsieur!*"

Matt gritted his teeth and ran through the pain in his hip and arm. He had to get away. Had to keep the key safe. Had to find the right person to give it to. *Lord, help me!* he lifted up a prayer as he raced around a corner and back out onto the street.

"Mattman, wait up!" Billy's voice carried down the alley. He sounded forlorn, like a little boy.

The woman double-timed it up a set of stone steps, shoved a key into the lock on a tall, gray door, and vanished through the opening. Matt followed, and she slammed the door behind him.

Instead of standing inside a house as he had expected, he found he had slipped into another world. Like Lucy who wriggled through a coat-filled wardrobe into the mystical land of Narnia, Matt had left the smog and traffic of Paris and stepped into the Garden of Eden. A marbled courtyard surrounded him, a large open area with a round fountain in the middle and a statue of a fat naked man spewing water from his mouth. Lanterns hung from trees, and a table with two chairs made an intimate grouping in one corner. Stunned, Matt gaped at the array of potted fruit trees, flowers, hanging baskets, trailing blooms and rows of red-and-pink roses.

A woman's voice interrupted his reverie. "*Voilà!* They will pass." His rescuer brushed a hank of thick brown hair from her eyes and blew out a breath. "Why do you run from these men, eh?"

Matt suddenly felt the pain in his hip, the sting on his arm, the loss of Billy. He lifted his arm to find a swath of reddened, torn skin that was oozing blood. Rats! He had blown it again. Big-time. He had the key, but he didn't have Billy or Josiah Karume. And he didn't have the slightest idea what to do next. Why did God let these things happen to him? Matt was doing the right thing, wasn't he? He had prayed about this almost every minute. So why did nothing ever go the way it was supposed to?

"Monsieur?" The woman stepped closer. She frowned at his arm, then let out a cluck of dismay. "Genevieve! Genevieve!"

A plump older woman wearing a black uniform and a white apron bustled into the courtyard. The brown-eyed woman gave her maid a set of instructions in French, and moments later Matt was ushered into a huge room with long panes of glass, gold couches, gold chairs, deep red rugs, a chandelier with a thousand crystal droplets, and big bouquets of fresh flowers everywhere. Dazed, he stared at the furnishings until Genevieve the maid came back into the room with a tray that held a pitcher of water, a tube of medicine and a white bandage. Before he knew it, she had washed his arm thoroughly and bandaged it up.

"Better?" The thin, brown-eyed woman entered the room and waved him into a chair. Seating herself on one of the sofas, she drew out a long cigarette and lit it from a tabletop lighter. Then she inhaled deeply, tossed her head back and blew the smoke upward. Matt wondered if she was a movie star or a fashion model. She slipped off her black, pointy-toed, pointy-heeled shoes and tucked her long legs under her. The outfit she had on—a brown sweater and tight brown skirt—made her look elegant.

Matt suddenly wished he weren't so scruffy. "Thank you," he said. "Thank you for helping me. Uh...mercy."

"Merci!" She shook her head and rolled her eyes at his attempt to speak French. "Your name, please?"

"Matthew Strong," he answered before realizing he should have made something up.

"Enchanté, I am Clotilde Loiseau. I live here." She swept her hand around the room, and he got the impression there

were a lot more rooms in this fancy house that hid behind a plain gray door. "I take my morning *café* at the bistro where you fell out of the taxi."

"Okay." Matt knew he ought to say something polite, but he wasn't sure what. So he just nodded.

She pursed her lips, and he could tell she wasn't impressed with him in the least. But who ever was?

"Now please explain to me, Monsieur Strong. Why do you fall out of the taxi, and why do the men chase you? Are you a thief?"

"No." He shrugged. "Well, sort of."

"You come all the way from America to steal from taxi passengers? You are a pickpocket?"

He couldn't help but smile at the image. "No...see, I have some data. My friend downloaded it onto a USB key." He didn't know why he trusted the brown-eyed woman, but he slipped the small apparatus from his pocket. "A company— a business—has done some wrong things, you know? And I have the evidence here."

"Let me see."

For some reason, he handed her the USB key. She looked it over. "For the storage of computer *technologie?*"

"Yes," he said. *"Oui."*

"Your friend copied the information about the bad company? And where do you take it?"

"I came to Paris to give it to Josiah Karume. He's the chairman of I-FEED. It's an organization that—"

"Food. Aha." She waved her cigarette around in the air. "A big conference was here in Paris last week. But now, they go."

"You know about I-FEED?"

"Oui, of course. My husband is...how you say?... His company is making helicopters. Not helicopters, eh? Only the..." She spun her finger around and around in a circle.

"The blades?"

"*Non.* The part inside. The machinery to make it turn, *oui?*"

"The rotor."

"These helicopters are purchased by military, private, also I-FEED and other humanitarian organizations. You understand? I-FEED and the others, they use the helicopters for transporting food. We meet these clients sometimes. They come here, or to our home in Provence. It is business only, *oui?* But we hear what they are doing."

She waggled the USB key, and Matt really wished he hadn't let her hold it. "So tell me, Monsieur Strong, why does I-FEED need this *technologie?* And why do they use a young boy to transport such information?"

Matt moistened his lips, his eyes on the key. "I-FEED doesn't know I'm the one who has the information. I'm doing this because…" He realized his whole explanation was going to sound lame to this elegant lady. All the same, he sucked down a breath and launched into it.

"God wants us to feed the hungry. Three big food companies control the world's food supply—Agrimax, Progrow and Megafarm—and all they care about is making money. They make sure the rich get to eat, which leaves the poor to starve. That's wrong."

"*Oui,*" she said.

Heartened by her response, Matt continued. "Jesus said, 'I was hungry, and you fed Me. When you did it to one of the least of these My brothers and sisters, you were doing it to Me!' I believe the only way to really feed the world's hungry is to get these big food companies to stop withholding supplies."

The woman stared at him, her brow creased as she puffed on her cigarette.

"They don't care about Jesus," Matt went on, "and they sure don't care about the starving children. So to get their attention, we have to threaten to expose their practices to the public. Agrimax is planning to merge with the other two companies and take over management of their resources and subsidiaries. This will give Agrimax complete control over the global food supply. And that means they'll have tons of power to do whatever they want."

"Oh, my."

"The trouble is, Agrimax does just enough humanitarian work to look good. Not enough to solve the problem, but enough to get the good PR—that means public relations."

"This I understand."

"My friend Mr. Banyon, he knew what they were up to, because he used to work for them. So he downloaded the evidence, but they killed him before he could get it to the public. They shot him and made it look like suicide. I went to his house and...and...found him. He was dead."

His eyes filling with the dreaded tears, Matt focused on Mrs. Loiseau. She was staring at him like he was an alien or something. As if she'd never met anyone so strange in her whole life.

She drew down a last big lungful of cigarette smoke and mashed the butt in a crystal bowl on a curvy-legged table near the gold sofa. Then she lifted the hem of her sweater, and for a second, Matt thought she was going to take out a gun and shoot him. But it was a cell phone.

Punching some numbers, she studied the USB key in her lap. Matt thought about grabbing it and taking off. That's what he should do. He should snatch it from her lap and run.

"Who're you calling, Mrs. Loiseau?" he asked, feeling anxious. "Don't call the police. Please, I—"

"My husband," she mouthed, her painted lips forming the words. When her husband answered, she began speaking in French, holding up the key as if the man on the other end could see it as she waved her red-nailed fingers around in the air. She said *oui-oui* about fifteen times, and it sounded like *way-way*. After a while, she stopped talking, lit another cigarette and drummed her nails on the table. When she spoke again, it was to say, *"Merci,"* and then she hung up.

"Josiah Karume," she announced. "He is headquartered in Sudan, but he travels everywhere in Africa. My husband finds his current location."

Before Matt could even start to think about what to say next, a butler stepped into the room and told her something, all the while glancing warily at Matt. Mrs. Loiseau let out a bark of anger.

"The men who chase you," she informed him, "they ask about me at the bistro. And now they find the address of my house." She pulled another cigarette from a slim gold case on the table. "They tell my valet they will inform the police. They say you are a fugitive—that you run from America because you murdered somebody."

"I didn't! I swear I didn't kill Mr. Banyon—"

"Arrêtez!" She held up a hand. "I shall send them away. Stay here."

She stood, slipped her long, elegant feet into her pointy-toed shoes and walked across the room carrying the key. Matt thought he was going to faint.

"Wait—you can't give them that!" he said, following her out into the courtyard. "I have to take it to I-FEED. I've come all this way—"

"Go back into the house, Matthew Strong," she hissed. "Do it now!"

Matt couldn't obey. He hung near the fountain with the fat statue and watched as the valet opened the long gray door for Mrs. Loiseau. There stood Dr. Sloane and Pierre—and Billy.

"Billy!" Matt blurted.

"Mattman!" Like a demented linebacker, Billy bulldozed right through the two Agrimax men and barreled past Mrs. Loiseau. She gave a shriek, then began shouting at the men as she jabbed with the USB key. Her valet lunged forward, slammed the door and dropped an iron bar across it. He swung around and went after Billy, but Matt spread his arms to protect his friend.

"It's okay!" he shouted. "He's with me."

Madame Loiseau called off her valet. The man stood back as she struck a pose, lit her cigarette and inhaled deeply. She brushed back her brown hair and tottered across the courtyard, hips swaying in her brown skirt.

"Who is this boy?" She pointed at Billy.

"He's my friend," Matt said. "He came with me from America."

"*Je m'appelle* William Younger, *madame*," Billy said. "*Enchanté.*"

She laughed. "What kind of French do they teach in America? *C'est mauvais!*" Beckoning the boys, she strode toward the house again. "The men will return. I shall take you to the home of my sister. Follow me quickly."

Matt glanced at Billy, glad to have him back. More than glad.

"Mrs. Loiseau," Matt said as she led them through a series of rooms, all of them furnished as if the king of France himself lived there. "Mrs. Loiseau, why are you doing this? Why are you helping me?"

She halted and stubbed out her cigarette in one of the dozens of crystal ashtrays scattered around her house. Her brown eyes clouded for a moment as she gazed at Matt. She glanced away, her lower lip trembling. Then she shrugged.

"You are a boy," she said. "What you have told me is too... how would you say?...too much complication to be a lie."

"Yeah, but—"

"Monsieur Strong—" she set her hands on her hips "—if God chooses to send you help, shall you ask Him why?"

Matt gawked at her, trying to see the chain-smoking, shouting Frenchwoman as a helper from God. But she was vanishing down a staircase, and he knew he'd follow her anywhere.

Chapter Thirteen

Jill woke to the warble of her telephone. For a moment she thought the sound was coming from her TV set. She reached for the remote control, realized she was in her bedroom and lifted the receiver.

"Miss Pruitt, this is Matt Strong," a husky voice said. "I'm in your computer tech class. You know?"

"Of course I know." Jill sat upright and fumbled for the switch on her lamp. "Matt, where are you?"

"Well, I'm in Paris with Billy Younger. Weird, huh? I can tell you that because Agrimax already found out. They thought they'd caught us, but we got away, thanks to a lady who—"

"Matt, where in Paris are you?"

"We're not staying here in France, Miss Pruitt. We're going someplace else."

"Where?"

"I can't tell you. But, Miss Pruitt, will you please talk to my dad and tell him not to come looking for me? I'll be home in a few days. Tell him I'm sorry about the credit card, and I'll get a job and pay him back. And that I feel really bad about him making that trip to Mexico—"

"Matt, your father is already on his way to Paris to find you!" Jill tried to keep a tone of hysteria from her voice. "I mean right now he's driving to Lubbock to get on a plane and fly over there."

"How'd he find out I was in Paris?"

"We knew you went to Mexico to look for Hector Diaz, and we learned that he'd gone to France for a conference. Then Josefina told us you came home and got your passport."

"She *told?*"

"Matt, this isn't a game. You're in a lot of trouble, young man. Your father is flying to Paris, and you have got to stay put!"

"I can't, Miss Pruitt. Billy and I...we just have to do this one thing, and then we can come home. And Mrs. Loiseau—I can say her name because they already know it—she's helping us."

"Who? Who's helping you?" Jill rummaged in the drawer of her bedside table for paper and pen.

"Mrs. Loiseau. Clotilde Loiseau. She's nice, even though she's kind of...well, you'd just have to meet her. Anyhow, this is her phone, and she's not going to make me pay for the call, but it's long-distance, you know? Like *really* long-distance. So I've gotta go—"

"Matthew Strong, don't you dare hang up." Jill put on her sternest teacher voice. "I want to know *this minute* where you're going!"

"Miss Pruitt, they've got your phone tapped. If I say anything, they'll know. It's not like I don't want to tell you, but—"

"Matt—"

"Billy's talking to me...just a sec." He paused. "Okay, Miss Pruitt, you remember the paper trail?"

Jill reflected on the moment in Geneva Strong's house when

they had figured out *paper trail* referred to Matt's term paper on hunger relief. "Yes, I remember."

"Okay, the person we're going to see is my third source."

"I see."

"So you're good?"

"Matt, I wish you would stay in Paris. Please let your father help—"

"No, no. Don't let him come. Do whatever you can to stop him, Miss Pruitt."

"He loves you, Matt. He loves you so much. You know, he nearly died in Mexico."

"Died?"

"We were in a terrible car wreck. Agrimax people drove us off the road, and your father was badly injured. This is not a lark, Matt. This is serious business. You need to stay where you are and let an adult help you."

"Yeah, Mrs. Loiseau is—"

"You need *your father,* not a stranger you just met. And your dad needs you, Matt. He really does. Stay with Mrs. Loiseau until he gets there. Then the two of you can—"

"Dad doesn't understand what this is about. All he cares about is his farm."

"He may not completely understand, but he's learning. He's not like you think, Matt. He's a good man, and you need to give him a chance to be a father to you."

"He already had a chance."

"Give him another one." The phone fell silent for a moment, and Jill worried they had been cut off. "Matt?"

"Yeah, Miss Pruitt, I hear you. But Jesus said you have to be willing to leave your father and mother—leave everything and everybody you love—and follow Him. I'm trying to do what God wants, just like you, Miss Pruitt. Mr. Banyon believed that what I'm doing right now could make a difference. He thought...at least he hoped...we could really feed the hungry."

"Matthew," Jill said gently, "you'll never feed all the hungry. Jesus said the poor will always be with us, remember? This world is Satan's realm. Sin and evil and all of Satan's tools—disease, famine, drought, pestilence, war—these things will last until Christ returns. Do you understand that, Matt? You can't win this battle all by yourself."

"Miss Pruitt—" Matt sounded impatient "—I know that. Jesus didn't tell us to win the battle. That's His job. But He did tell us to feed the hungry—and that's what I'm trying to do. So I gotta go now. I'll see you in a week or so. And Miss Pruitt?"

"Yes, Matt?"

"I really don't want to flunk tenth grade. Do you think you could talk to the principal about me and Billy?"

Jill sighed, knowing this was the least of the boys' problems. "We'll work it out, Matt."

"Okay—bye."

The phone went dead, and she sat on the edge of her bed staring at her bare feet. What to do? Whom to call first? And how had she ended up in the middle of this? *Lord, am I supposed to be involved in this for some reason? Why? What do You expect from me?*

Jill studied her phone again. If Matt was right—and she suspected he was—then Agrimax had indeed put a surveillance device in it. The whole idea gave her the creeps. When had they gotten into her house? And what else might they have done?

What would Agrimax do now, if indeed they had listened in on Matt's call from Paris? Perhaps they had traced it to the home of this mysterious Clotilde Loiseau. If so, they would capture Matt and Billy before Cole's plane ever left the States.

And what about Cole? She had a terrifying flashback to the crash in Mexico. Would the nightmare be repeated on a Texas highway? Should Jill try to reach Cole's cell phone? Was it bugged, too?

Letting out a cry of frustration, she stood and pulled on some jeans, a T-shirt and a pair of tennis shoes. The thing to do, she decided, was to find out where Matt was planning to go and then try to track down Cole. If she drove to Lubbock—if she broke the speed limit the whole way—maybe she could catch up to him in time. But he would still insist on going after his son.

She knew that about him now.

Jill grabbed her bag, took out the key on which she had downloaded Matt's term paper, and slipped it into the slot on her own computer. What if Agrimax had accessed her hard drive somehow? What if they could read everything she had on file? Feeling physically queasy from the thought, she quickly disconnected her cable modem.

The term paper materialized on her screen, and Jill scrolled to the bibliography. As it came up, she suddenly had a terrible feeling that a camera might be watching everything she did. Paranoia filling her, she leaned close to shield the screen with her body and scanned the text. Matt's first source was Jim Banyon. His second was Hector Diaz. And his third...

Jill's mouth went dry. This was insane. Matt Strong couldn't possibly be planning to go to Sudan!

Closing out her computer, she snatched the key and shoved it back into her tote bag. She would have to break every speed-limit law in the state of New Mexico and Texas to catch Cole. But she would. They had to stop Matt.

Jill raced for her front door, her mind filled with images of the country she had visited as a volunteer with I-FEED. Sudan—bordered by Libya, Egypt, Eritrea, Ethiopia and other unstable and hostile governments—was a battleground between rebel armies and the *muraheleen*, the bands of irregular militia backed by Sudan's Muslim-dominated dictatorship. More than four million people had been displaced in a civil war ongoing for more than twenty years. At least two million more had been killed.

Two naive American sixteen-year-olds would stand as much chance of survival as a couple of scrawny chickens in one of Sudan's countless refugee camps. Without protection and an approved escort, Matt and Billy would likely be shot on sight. Or they would be taken hostage and used to extort a ransom from the American government. Their U.S. citizenship would give them little standing in the eyes of the rebels or the militia—envoy John Danforth had visited Sudan on two separate peace missions and had won no support whatsoever from that government.

Her heart slamming against her ribs, Jill threw open her front door and dashed straight into the path of a huge black horse galloping headlong up her driveway. Hooves shooting sparks into the blackness, the animal thundered toward the house at top speed. Transfixed in disbelief, Jill clapped her hand over her mouth in a silent scream.

A shout sounded over the hoofbeats, and the big horse reared. Hooves churning the air, it hovered over her for a single terrifying moment. Then it dropped to the driveway, prancing and snorting, its nose blowing hot steam into the night.

"Jill? Is that you?"

Cole's voice jangled down through her bones, unreal and impossible. She was in some kind of dream, wasn't she? Surely she would awaken, her nightgown drenched and her hair damp.

"Jill, they're after me," Cole gasped. He swung a leg over

the horse and slid to the ground, wincing at his sore ankle. "Listen, can I borrow your car? They came to the house and tried to stop me, but I got away...so would you mind if I took your car to Lubbock... Jill? Are you all right?"

She swallowed. "You have just scared me to *death!*" She pummeled his chest with her fists. "What are you doing riding a horse up to my front door in the middle of the night? And how can you ride, anyway, with that hand—"

"I told you, I—"

"Forget it. Just get in the car. Get in the car!" She stomped over to her little Chevy, whipped open the driver's door, and hurled her bag into the backseat.

"Wait," he said, "I can drive myself—"

"Get in! I'll take you to the airport. I have things to tell you, and besides, you'll never be able to..."

She fell silent, hearing the answer to her own prayer for clarity. *What am I supposed to do, Lord? What do You expect me to do?*

"Just a minute," she told Cole. "And hold on to that horse! I don't want it stomping on my flower beds."

"Can I put him in your backyard? Hernando will come get him."

"Why not?" she answered. "I'm going to be the talk of the neighborhood anyway."

Dashing back into the house, she jerked open her file cabinet, located her travel documents, and lifted the packet from the drawer. In moments, the file had joined her tote bag in the backseat of her car. She scooted in next to Cole and started the engine.

"Jill, where are we going?"

"Sudan," she said. "Listen, did you bring your cell—"

"*Sudan?*"

She wheeled out into the street. "I don't think we should

fly out of Lubbock. I mentioned it on the phone, and Matt says Agrimax has me bugged. Let's head for Albuquerque."

"You talked to my son?"

Cole's voice was rising with every question. Jill glanced across at him. He looked pretty awful. Unshaven, his face was haggard and his eyes bloodshot from lack of sleep. He'd lost his hat somewhere, and twigs were scattered through his brown hair. The bandage on his hand was filthy and tattered. He smelled horsey—a mix of leather and animal—not all that bad, actually. She sensed he was running on adrenaline.

She peeled out of town in the direction of Roswell. With clear roads, they would make it to Albuquerque in time to catch an early flight to a city with an international hub. Perhaps Dallas, or Denver. They would be hard to spot in a huge airport.

"A few minutes ago, Matt called me from Paris," she informed Cole.

"Paris! Why did he call *you?* I'm his father, for goodness' sake!"

Jill reached across and laid a calming hand on his arm. "He's afraid you'll be mad at him. He did use the credit card to buy his and Billy's tickets to France. He wanted me to apologize for that and for all the trouble he's caused you. And he asked me to tell you not to follow him."

Cole rubbed his hand across his eyes, his broad shoulders sagging. "How is he?"

"He's fine. A couple of Agrimax people apparently met the boys' flight, but they escaped. A Frenchwoman is helping them. I don't know if she's trustworthy."

"She might be with Agrimax. They showed up at my house tonight—two of them. Used Tom Perry to get to me. I couldn't believe it. I thought he was a friend."

"They're desperate, Cole. Matt must have something really

big." She ventured another look at the man beside her. Head back on the seat, he was cradling his injured hand. He must be in terrible pain, but he would say nothing.

"So Matt's going to Sudan?" he asked, his voice gravelly.

"Yes."

He gave a mirthless laugh. "I don't even know where the country is."

"Northeast Africa. It's landlocked, except for a little strip on the Red Sea. Sudan is where I-FEED operates a major feeding station. Matt's looking for a man named Josiah Karume. He runs the Africa division of the program out of Khartoum, and he's just been elected international chairman of the organization."

"I thought Matt was hot on the heels of Hector Diaz."

"Sounds like he's changed his tack. Now that Matt's in Europe, Josiah would make a lot more sense than Hector. He has a great deal of power."

"Power for what?" He gritted his teeth. "My son is sixteen! Why is he going to Africa? Why does he need this man?"

"I'm not sure, Cole."

She reached toward him, but he brushed her hand away. "No! Why did you do this?"

"Cole, I—"

"Why has this happened? He's a child. A boy!"

"He's old enough to—"

"No, he's not! If you had a kid, you'd know. He's barely old enough to function on his own. He can't find anything around the house. He's always tripping over his own shoestrings. He loses all his jackets and caps. He doesn't know how to cook or wash his own clothes or balance a checkbook—not one adult thing. He's never held a job or gotten himself to a doctor's appointment. Do you understand that?"

"Yes," she said softly, hurting inside at his words.

"It seems like yesterday he was in diapers," Cole went on. "He was crawling around on his hands and knees. Drinking from a sippy cup. He learned how to walk and then run, and now he thinks he can fly to Africa? No!"

"He's still your baby."

"Yes, he is. He's my baby—and he is a baby."

"Not in his own mind."

"It doesn't matter what's in his mind. I know him."

"Do you, Cole?"

"As a matter of fact, I do. I know him a lot better than you think. I may have spent a lot of time out in the field, but I'm not blind. I've watched him. Josefina talks to me about him, and I listen. You don't have to be with a kid every minute of the day to know what he's capable of—and what he's not. You see these boys in the classroom, so you have a distorted view. If you had a child of your own, you'd know what I'm saying."

"I don't," Jill said. "I don't have a child."

He was silent, his chest rising and falling with emotion. "Well, why haven't you gotten married?"

"Nobody's asked."

"Then they're a bunch of idiots."

She cracked a smile. "You're in a fine mood."

"I'm sorry. I shouldn't have said what I did—about you not having kids and all that. It's none of my business."

"It's okay. There's no big dark secret. I've dated, but I haven't found the right person. Or he hasn't found me. So I don't have children."

"You'd make a good mother."

"I think so, too."

He laughed. "Always the confident Miss Pruitt."

"That's probably why I've turned away potential husbands. I haven't been meek enough."

"Who wants a meek wife? Not me."

She couldn't help looking at him. "You're not the average man."

"Never said I was. You met my mother. I grew up around a strong woman. I like a lady who knows her own mind."

"I guess Penny is a strong woman."

He dropped his head back on the seat. "Penny...she's probably pulling up to my house about now. She'll go ballistic when she finds out I'm gone."

"Strong is good...ballistic is not." Jill studied the road. She shouldn't have said that. Cole had chosen to marry Penny, and he must feel good about his decision. Who was she to cast aspersions on his fiancée?

"She just doesn't get certain things," Cole spoke up. "Like the fact that sometimes I have to take care of other things. Like that I have a life beyond her. I cannot ignore my farm. And I will not stop searching for my son."

"You're willing to follow Matt to Africa?"

"Of course. But I just don't see why he's so fired up to go to this...this..." He paused. "Where is it again?"

"Sudan."

"I do understand why he's running, though. Those men will hurt him, Jill. They'll kill him if they have to. You've seen how far they'll go. Tonight when they came after me with the car—they wouldn't stop. They were shooting out the window. They'd have run me down...."

His voice trailed off, and Jill instinctively touched his arm again. "Do you have your pills, Cole?"

"I can't take anything that would knock me out."

"At least have an Advil." She reached behind the seat and fished in her tote bag. "Here—take a couple of these."

Swallowing the pills dry, he took her hand and pressed it between his, as if that might somehow relieve his discomfort. "Jill, do you know much about Sudan?"

"I've been there."

"How hard is it going to be to get into the country?"

"Hard." She forced herself to switch gears. In a way, she felt relieved to move away from the personal tone of their conversation. Though she couldn't deny she enjoyed talking to Cole, the intimacy of the topic felt dangerous.

"Khartoum is the capital," she explained, "and it's an Arab-dominated government. Tourists are practically unheard of—too much violence and little to see but rubble. The Sudanese people have been at war for twenty years. Civil wars, religious war, tribal war—it's a mess."

He nodded. His hands felt comforting around hers. Despite the uncertainty that lay ahead, Jill sensed security in Cole's presence. Accustomed to taking care of herself, she had expected to reject any man who wore an aura of strength and old-fashioned male protectiveness. But somehow, with Cole clearly so unthreatened by her own bold spirit, she welcomed it.

"Surely they're fighting about something you can point to," he said.

"Oil, mostly."

"Surprise, surprise."

"It was discovered in 1978 in the south," Jill said. "That region is considered African rather than Arab, and it once had a lot of autonomy. When the government moved to control the oil, war broke out."

"So the northern army is trying to take over the southern oil land. Is the southern army legitimate?"

"Guerrillas. The south is controlled by rebel troops, some of which have organized themselves into the Sudan People's Liberation Army. They want full independence."

"How are these people going to react to two American teenagers roaming around their country?"

"Not well, I imagine. Neither side is friendly with the U.S. We passed a law banning trade with Sudan, for one thing. Mostly it's because both sides have committed horrific human rights abuses—scorched-earth raids on villages, abductions, slavery. They use child-soldiers. I met seven-year-olds with battle scars."

"You went to Sudan to feed the kids?"

"Everyone is hungry. When I was there, several relief agencies were operating. But in November 2001 most of them left. They anticipated a big grain harvest that didn't pan out. I-FEED is about the only agency left now. The last time I talked to Josiah Karume, he told me most of the people were down to eating peanuts and nothing else. Whole villages have been deserted for lack of food."

Cole's grip on her hand tightened. "It was all just stories in the newspapers to me. I never even read them. More interested in football scores and commodity prices."

"They're real people, though. Somehow Matt understands that."

"But he doesn't understand reality, Jill. I'm telling you, he doesn't even know how to live in America—he's a fish out of water at the local high school. He'll never survive a place like Sudan."

Jill's stomach tightened as she heard her own fears echoed in his words. She tried to think of something reassuring. The very idea of Billy Younger acting as Matt's guide through the war zone of Southern Sudan gave her nightmares. And this stranger the boys had met...what comfort was an unknown Frenchwoman?

"God is with Matt," she said finally. "We can count on that. We just have to keep praying."

He nodded. "I wish my faith was stronger."

"It's pretty easy to trust God when nothing's at stake. I

guess I've grown my faith by leaning on it through some dicey situations."

"I lost my wife. I ought to be a faith giant."

Jill fell silent, absorbing his words and the pain that accompanied them. "Sometimes normal life takes over," she said. "Teaching school is like that for me. I get into the swing of it, and most of the time I'm just zipping along doing what I do. But the faith that grew inside me during the rough times is still there. I may not be talking with God the way I did down in Mexico when I was so scared you were dead, but my faith in Him hasn't faded."

He didn't respond, and for a moment she wondered if he'd fallen asleep. But when he spoke again, his voice was rough.

"I've prayed more about Matt than I ever prayed for Anna. I loved my wife. Loved her a lot. But maybe my capacity for love is bigger now. Like a field where you get an average harvest one year and twice that the next. Same field, different conditions."

"If your capacity for love has grown, so has your capacity for faith. You have a lot stronger faith than you know, Cole. Just use it."

He gazed at her. She grew uncomfortable, aware of his strong fingers still wrapped around hers. Driving one-handed all this time hadn't been difficult. The road was straight, and the land barely rose toward Albuquerque. But alone with Cole in the darkness, feeling his warmth against her bare skin, Jill knew a sensation she hadn't ever felt. She wanted this man. What would it be like to feel his powerful arms around her, to know the touch of his lips against hers, to revel in the intimacy of his presence? Her desire to slip her fingers through his hair and comb out the bits of grass and twigs made her ache inside. How would it feel to run her hands around the hardened muscle of his shoulders? What would it be like to hear him whisper in her ear?

Jill stared at the short strip of highway illuminated by her headlights. Grounded in reason and educated to admire mathematics and technology, she tried her best to shake off this whirlwind of irrational desire. God had put her and Cole together for one purpose only. They were to join forces in search of Matt. That's all. Cole belonged to another woman. He planned to marry Penny Ames, and Jill had absolutely no right to think of him in any way but as a colleague. A friend. A Christian brother.

There. That was it. She would see him as a brother in Christ. Like the men in her singles' Bible study at church.

"Jill, I've never met a woman like you," Cole said into the darkness. His voice was just above a whisper. "I know I said some crazy things the other night when I was drugged up. Singing and all that. But I do remember what I said to you. It came from someplace real. I do... I have come to care about you."

She realized she hadn't breathed for almost a minute. Obviously, she wasn't hearing him right. He was telling her things, but she was interpreting his words as something different from what he meant. Or not. Or whatever. The main thing was that she had to take in air, and she had to come up with intelligent, logical things to say. Spiritual-sounding things. He was her Christian brother, that's all.

"Well, I care about you, too, of course, as a very good friend," she fumbled, forcing her voice to sound light and cheery. "I mean, look at all we've been through. This has been so crazy." She slipped her hand out of his on the pretense of needing to run her windshield washer. "Wow, that's dusty. Amazing how much dust blows through Artesia in the spring. So I hope Penny didn't run into those Agrimax men. I guess she'll be all right."

"Yeah, she… I probably ought to try to reach her."

"You can use my phone. Here."

He held the cell phone in his injured hand and pressed his fiancée's number with his good fingers. Jill noted she was breathing again. This was better. He would reconnect with Penny, and their love for each other would be so obvious that Jill would be forced to stop misinterpreting his words. Soon he would marry Penny, and Jill would go back to teaching her kids, growing her garden and making mission trips. That's how it had been, and how it would be again. Absolutely.

"Penny?" Cole said into the phone. "Hey, it's me."

Jill fiddled with the vent lever, letting in the night air. Apparently Penny had a lot to say. Cole was quiet a long time, his breath warming her cell phone.

"I'm sorry." His voice sounded so tired. "Yeah, I had to take off in a hurry…. Listen, don't talk to anyone around there, Penny. Don't even stay around my house. You need to just turn around and—"

He fell silent again, listening. Jill tried to remember how it felt to be romantically involved with someone. Good, she thought. At least entertaining. Some of the time. Movies, dinner, football games. Arguments, though. Differences, disagreements, disappointments. She suspected all relationships were like that, even marriages.

"I could not stay at the house," Cole said, his voice harder now. "I had to run, Penny. I barely got away. Dangerous people are after my son, and I'm—"

Jill reflected on how she had felt when Cole was holding her hand a moment ago. That had been new. Heart-stopping. Spine-tingling. She wondered if he knew that sensation when he was with Penny. If so, he shouldn't be saying he cared about Jill. It wasn't right. Not unless he meant it in a generic sort of way.

"I realize you just made a five-hour drive, Penny." He was speaking more gently now. "I'm not going to be at the house for several days....I can't tell you where I'm going... Because—"

Jill thought about turning on the radio. She felt like a Peeping Tom, listening in on his conversation.

"All right." He rolled down the window and let the breeze blow through his hair. Then he rubbed his eyes, still speaking to his fiancée. "Jill Pruitt is driving me to the airport...because she was there. Penny, please don't read into this. Don't get this way. You can't— All right. Yes... I understand. I do."

He nodded a couple of times as Jill switched on the radio and tried to find a signal. How odd to think that Penny was envious of her presence in Cole's life—especially when she'd done nothing but be available to give him a ride.

"Me, too," he said. "Yes, I know. I do, too. I need that.... Okay."

He pressed the button and set the phone on the car seat. Jill located an oldies station and turned the volume up a little. Maybe some bebop-a-loo music would make her feel lighthearted and goofy. She couldn't allow herself to care about Cole Strong and Penny Ames. They belonged to each other, and she was on her own. Single and happy. Yeah-yeah-yeah.

"Penny okay?" she asked.

"Fine."

"That's good." She yawned. "Wow, I'm tired. I need caffeine or a few ice cubes down the back. We'll stop in Vaughn and get something to drink. I need gas anyway."

"Let me take the wheel, Jill. The Advil ought to kick in, and I'll feel better soon. Besides, you made a long drive last night, and I slept most of the way."

"Are you sure? You look like you're in a lot of pain."

"I'll be all right. I want to do this, Jill."

She slowed and pulled over onto the shoulder of the highway. Relieved, she stepped out of the car and walked around the back. There were no other vehicles in sight, and she would doze for a few hours before they hit Albuquerque. She watched Cole unfold himself from the passenger side.

He stood tall before her, the only light coming from his open door. Pausing, she heard her breath catch in the back of her throat. He reached out and touched her shoulder. She swallowed. It was time to think of something light to say. He was her Christian brother, Christian brother....

"Jill," he began, running his hand down her arm. "I know you think I'm a stubborn mule. A dried-up stump of a man."

"No, Cole." She shivered, though there wasn't a wisp of cool air. "That was before. I didn't know you when I said those things. Now I see that you're a caring...wonderful... father to Matt."

His hand closed around her arm, and he pulled her closer. "Jill, I'm not just a father. I'm not just a rancher." His hand slipped behind her back and urged her so close she could feel his breath. "I'm a man, Jill. And I've tried a lot of ways to think of you as anything but a woman who is beautiful and good and perfect."

"I'm not—"

"Yes, you are," he said, and just as she had hoped and feared, he bent his head and brushed his mouth across her lips. A gentle kiss, barely a touch.

"Oh, Cole," she murmured.

"Sometimes it seems like you're all I can see anymore, Jill. When I was lying in that mangled car. When I was riding my horse like a maniac down Catclaw Draw. It was your face that kept me going. You, Jill. Your crazy hair, your bright eyes, your pretty smile."

He kissed her again, this time longer. She let herself be drawn into his arms, and he wasn't her Christian brother or Matt's father or an unfeeling rancher anymore. He was an amazing, disturbing and potent man who crushed her close and woke every hidden flicker of desire inside her heart.

"Cole, I——" She let her eyelids drop shut as his mouth caressed hers and his embrace cradled her.

"Listen, Jill, there's a lot to be said between us. And we've got time." He stepped back. "I'll drive and you rest awhile. Then we'll talk."

"But, Cole, you have to hear me right now. I don't feel right about this. About what's happening here. This isn't how it should be."

"I know. And we'll talk."

"I can say it right now. I'm… I'm a teacher, and I have a whole life that really needs to be solitary, you know? And you. You're marrying Penny. She loves you. She told me that, so you can't be kissing me out here in the middle of the desert."

The shrill beep of her cell phone intruded. Jill reached for the car door. "I've got to get that. It might be Matt."

Cole walked to the driver's side as she slipped into the car and pressed the button.

"I'm sorry, honey," Penny said into Jill's ear. "I was upset and hurt that you left the house without me, but I've thought it all through, and I understand that you did what you had to do. I love you, Cole. Please say you love me, too. Please say you'll forgive me, and we can start over on the right foot. I can't bear the thought of life without you, not even for a minute."

Jill handed Cole the phone. "It's for you."

She turned up the music and closed her eyes. Cole shouldn't have kissed her, and she shouldn't have welcomed it. What she had felt in his arms was wrong. No matter how he had acted, no matter what he had said, it was wrong. He had made a commitment to Penny, and that had to be honored. She concentrated on the radio…one of her favorites… "Song sung blue, weeping like a willow…song sung blue, sleeping on my pillow…"

Chapter Fourteen

"Nothing here is safe." Clotilde Loiseau's brown eyes were fixed on Matt, who sat facing her inside the small charter airplane. "The people have AIDS, tuberculosis, leprosy, oui? The animals, they are wild. They will eat you. Everything is hungry in Africa, even insects. Here is the home of the tse-tse fly. Here mosquitoes bring West Nile virus and malaria. Snakes are many in this country. Some, if they bite, you will die before you take three steps."

Matt clung to the armrests on either side of his seat and hoped he could survive the flight itself. He'd been nauseous ever since they left Kampala, the capital of Uganda. Billy was worse. He'd used three barf bags already. Now he lay spread-eagle in the aisle, moaning and begging Mrs. Loiseau to make the pilot land. Who cared about snakes and mosquitoes when the entire contents of your stomach were threatening to come flying out of your mouth at any moment?

"We shall arrive at the safari camp in one hour," Mrs. Loiseau said, lighting her umpteenth cigarette of the flight. "From there, I shall put you into the hands of Moses. A good guide. He will take you by boat up the Nile River toward Sudan. Ha—funny, you see? Moses in the Nile, like in the Bible."

Matt tried to smile. He couldn't grasp that any of this was really happening to him. Not the plane or the Frenchwoman or even Billy. None of it. It was like some kind of a movie where nothing was what you thought, nobody did what they were supposed to do, everything was warped and strange and unbelievable.

"Before you arrive at the border," Mrs. Loiseau was saying, "Moses will take you by Land Rover to a secret crossing point. But he will not cross over with you. You will have to drive into Sudan alone. Do you understand this, Matthew?"

Matt understood one thing: if he could look into a mirror, his face would be green. The color of lettuce. His hands trembled, and he could barely breathe. It wasn't just the cigarette smoke. The whole cabin felt like the inside of an oven. Didn't they have air-conditioning? Didn't they know people were suffocating inside this miserable little tin can?

"Matthew? Do you listen to me?" Mrs. Loiseau tapped his shin with the sharp toe of her high-heel shoe. "Pay attention!"

"Yes, ma'am," he said, swallowing the warm saline liquid that seeped into his mouth. "Moses. The Nile. Land Rover. Sudan."

"You will be alone," she continued. "You must be careful! Everything in this country is dangerous. The people will be nice in your face, but they will hate you. They will try to rob you and take you as a hostage. You will not be safe, Matthew."

"Okay." He nodded, clutching the barf bag in his hands and wondering if he was going to need to use it.

Mrs. Loiseau shook her head in obvious disgust at his lame response to all her warnings. Matt couldn't figure out why this Frenchwoman had done so much for him. She thought he was foolish and too young and destined to die a horrible death—and she told him so on a regular basis.

Even so, ever since yesterday morning, when she had rescued him from Agrimax, Mrs. Loiseau had done everything in her power to help Matt find Josiah Karume. For some reason, she believed his idea of giving the USB key to I-FEED was a good one, and she had decided to make it happen. She had driven Matt and Billy to her sister's house outside Paris, where they spent that night. Her husband, whom Matt never saw, ordered his private jet to fly the three of them to Uganda the next morning.

In Kampala, Mrs. Loiseau told the customs officials they didn't need visas, because they were going on a very short safari up the Nile—which was true. To ease matters along, she handed out American dollars left and right, explaining to Matt and Billy that these were like gold on the local black market. After clearing customs, they got into this propeller-driven, roller-coaster airplane, and now they were headed for a safari camp on the river.

It was like a theme park in California or Florida, where you went on heart-stopping rides, saw strange and frightening things, and thought you might never escape. Then, when it all became too intense, you got back on the bus, went to your hotel, ate ice cream, and everything was normal. Except none of this was normal, and none of it was pretend.

Everything happening was real, and Matt could hardly believe that it had actually worked out. He knew it must be God's hand behind the whole thing. Mrs. Loiseau really was like an angel the Lord had sent to help out—though if the rest of the angel band were anything like her, Heaven would be a pretty weird place.

"Crocodiles!" she exclaimed, waving her red fingernails

around. "In the Nile River are many crocodiles, and they will attack if you fall from the boat. But the hippos are worse!"

Matt tried to get his brain to focus on what she was saying, but it was difficult. "Uh, Mrs. Loiseau—"

"*Madame* Loiseau," she corrected as the plane made another stomach-churning lurch. "I am French—can you not remember this? *Je suis français. Qu-est-ce que c'est?* What do you wish to say to me, Matthew?"

"Well, um…about the crocodiles and all that. Don't worry so much, okay? I mean, God brought you to that café to help Billy and me yesterday. I wouldn't have escaped from those Agrimax men without you. And you took care of getting us here to Africa. I never had any idea how hard it would be to fly into a foreign country. The way you've helped us with everything reminds me that God is watching over us, and I think we're going to get the USB key to Mr. Karume."

"Not everything," she said in words hardened with anger. "I do not help you with everything, Matthew. When we arrive at the camp, I leave you to go by yourself. I do not protect you. It is because…because I am weak. Myself, I am afraid."

"You?"

"Of course me! Who is talking to you—somebody else?" She jammed her cigarette butt into the metal ashtray in the arm of the seat. "We have been to this camp once—my husband and I. It is very nice, *oui?* Little cabanas for each guest. Delicious food. A boat ride up the Nile. Some fishing. Looking at animals. Tourist things—and always an armed guard to protect us. We have a good time. But you…it will not be like this for you. You must go into the desert. You will have no security, no safety. Sudan is a place of armies and machine guns. I cannot go there, Matthew. I let you go alone. By yourself."

He wasn't sure who she was mad at, but she stared out the

window as though she really wished she could knock some-one's block off. "Well, I'm not by myself—"

"Don't tell me God is with you! God does not always pro-tect the innocent."

To Matt's surprise, she started crying. She reached into her fancy designer purse and pulled out a handkerchief. Dabbing her eyes, she fumbled around for another cigarette. Before she could light it, he reached across and put his hand on her arm.

"Mrs. Loiseau," he said. "I mean, *Madame* Loiseau, the thing is—I'm not really afraid."

"No, because you are young and foolish. You do not un-derstand how fragile is this life. How quickly it can be taken away." She blew her nose into her handkerchief.

"Yeah, but I'm not all that worried about my life, you know?" He wondered why she was crying and whether the things he was saying might make it worse. Despite his roiling stomach, he decided to keep talking. "See, life is like a tiny speck of time," he told her, "but Heaven is forever. My youth pastor says if you're a Christian, your real home is Heaven. Not earth. Earth is where you're sent for a while to try to help other people get to know Jesus. Earth is where you do things for God, like feeding the hungry and stuff—which puts trea-sures in your bank in Heaven. You want your treasures to be in Heaven, because that's where you're going to live forever after you die. But life down here is really not all that big a deal."

Madame Loiseau sniffed, blotting the mascara that was forming dark puddles under her brown eyes. "Oh, Matthew, you are a good boy. I don't want you to die!"

At that, she broke into even louder sobbing. She bent over and wailed into her hands, her shoulders shaking and her breath making little hiccups. Matt wished he hadn't said any-thing. It must have been the wrong thing, as it usually was when he tried to talk to people. He looked down at Billy, who seemed to have passed out in the aisle.

"Madame Loiseau," Matt said, "I'm sorry—"

"*Non!*" She shook her head. "You do not make me cry, Matthew. It is something else."

He scrunched the barf bag as she dabbed at her eyes some more. "Well, what?"

"My son," she said finally, her lips trembling. "He was like you, just a boy. Fourteen."

"I'm sixteen."

"Alain was fourteen. He used the…the inline skates, *oui?*… and he skated every day near my house in Paris. One day, he made a mistake or someone pushed him…we don't know. He fell into the street, and a car struck him. Like you."

"Did he die?"

"*Oui.*" She folded up her handkerchief and dropped it back into her purse. "Three years ago."

"So that's why you helped me."

"I help because you are a silly boy…and a good boy…like my Alain. But you are different from him, also. Alain was a child, you understand? He cared about nothing important, only fun. A happy boy. You, Matthew, talk always about these matters of God." She paused and lit her cigarette. "I rush to you in the street because you remind me of Alain. But I help you go to Sudan because you are you."

"It's because you care about matters of God, too, Madame Loiseau."

"*Pah!* I am not religious."

"But you understand that what I'm saying is true. You believe what I'm doing is right. You'd make a really great Christian, Madame Loiseau."

She exhaled a big cloud of smoke. "Go to sleep, Matthew. You make me tired." With that illogical statement, she pulled a little mirror from her purse and began fixing her makeup. Matt's hands relaxed on the barf bag as he leaned back into his seat. He never knew the right things to say to people. He probably never would.

Cole tucked the blue airline blanket under Jill's chin and gave himself permission to memorize her. Sleeping, she looked like a child—all softness and warmth, her hair drifting around her cheeks and her pearly eyelids almost translucent. Since the moment he had kissed her under the starlight in New Mexico, Cole had seen and done things he never anticipated in his life.

In Albuquerque, Jill had made up her mind to fly with him to Sudan. Though the expense would eat into her hard-earned savings and wipe out her relief trip to Pakistan in the summer, she refused to listen to Cole's objections. She knew Sudan—the land, the customs, the I-FEED people, and even a few words of Arabic. And saving Matt's life had become more important than any other plans she might have had.

A flight to Houston and several hours' layover had eaten up most of Tuesday. While they waited, Jill wrote lesson plans and used her PDA to e-mail them to her colleague Marianne Weston. She briefly outlined the situation to Marianne and asked her friend to let them know of any news on Matt.

That evening, Cole and Jill had boarded a Northwest Airlines carrier bound for Germany. Arriving in the early morning, they hunkered down in an airport waiting room and tried to sleep. Around noon, Jill received an e-mail from Marianne. To their immense relief, they learned that Matt was no longer a suspect in Jim Banyon's death.

Cole's mother had called Amarillo police from Oklahoma City, Marianne wrote. After they drove her home, Geneva Strong confirmed that the two men in police custody had posed as USDA agents and held her and Billy against their will. She said Matt had implicated the same men in his kidnapping and Banyon's murder.

In the afternoon, Cole and Jill had boarded this Lufthansa jet—destination Sudan. They were due to arrive at Khartoum Airport at sunrise.

Throughout the long hours, Jill Pruitt—the little blond dynamo—had stood by Cole's side, eager to tackle every obstacle. Faith shone like a beacon from her bright green eyes. Kindness radiated with every word she spoke. And love... Jill's entire being had been fashioned of love. Her very fiber pulsed with love.

But not for Cole. Not in the way he was beginning to desire it.

He lifted a hand and touched a gold curl near her neck. He had promised to marry Penny Ames. A commitment. A diamond engagement ring. Wedding and honeymoon plans. That was all before God had opened his eyes. His decision to marry Penny had risen out of loneliness, the belief that he ought to provide his son with a mother, and a blind and selfish urge to meet his own needs.

Did he love Penny? Not as he should. He hadn't loved Anna that way, either. He hadn't known how. But in just a few short days, Jill had begun to teach him the meaning of true love. It involved sacrifice, commitment, selflessness, purity, righteousness. All those times he'd read the famous love passage in 1 Corinthians 13—the verses had even been recited at his wedding to Anna—Cole hadn't understood it. Now he longed to live it.

He rubbed his eyes and tried to pray. For Matt... *Lord, keep my son alive, keep him safe, help me find him.* For the ranch... *Guard the land, oversee the crops and livestock, give my men wisdom.* For Penny... *Help me know what to do.*

Could he break their engagement? Should he? Or would it

be best to marry her and work to build the kind of love he'd learned from Jill? If he ended their relationship, Penny would go on without him. Young and accomplished, she would bury herself in her career and eventually marry someone else. But Cole had given his word. Dare he violate that?

What did God want from him? Cole wondered. And how could he find the answer?

The plane began to descend. Jill stirred and made the mewing sound he'd heard before. How could he live the rest of his life and not hear that again? But Jill had made it clear she wanted nothing more than brotherly Christian friendship from him. She refused to discuss their kiss and informed him they had nothing to talk about. He was engaged to Penny Ames. Subject closed.

"Are we there?" Jill sat up and brushed back her cloud of ringlets. "Wow, am I bushed. Did you sleep at all?"

"Maybe a few minutes."

"You'll learn." She reached for her bag, then paused. "I mean…if you ever go overseas again."

"I might." He watched in fascination as she worked on her hair, pushing and twisting, trying fruitlessly to tame the curls. "Maybe I'll take a mission trip someday."

"Really?" She glanced at him, a smile tipping the corner of her mouth. "You'd be blown away by a visit to a refugee camp. It would change your life."

"My life has changed already, Jill."

Her fingers stopped working on the curls. "In a good way. You're not the man who walked into my classroom a few days ago. You're different."

He wiggled his bandaged fingers.

"That's not what I mean, and you know it." She took his hand and examined the gauze wrapping. "How's the pain?"

"I'm in a lot of pain right now," he said. "But it's not from my fingers."

Her eyes darted to his. "I know you're worried about Matt. I am, too. I wish we could contact that Frenchwoman—Clotilde Loiseau. How many times did we call her house in Paris? But they—"

"I'm worried about Matt," he said. "I'm eaten up with it. But, Jill, I've got another concern on my plate."

"Your mom? I'm sure she's—"

"You, Jill." He captured her hand. "I know you don't want to talk about what happened between us the other night, and I'm trying to keep my mouth shut."

"Good. Don't say a word."

"You have to hear this one thing."

"No, I don't." She drew her hand away. "Please, Cole, I'm trying really hard to put it all away. I don't want to—"

"I'm a different man now, Jill. You said so yourself. Those days I spent trapped in the wreck changed me. This all-out hunt for my son has changed me. And you've changed me."

"God changed you."

"Yes, He did. Everything in my life—everything in the entire world—looks different to me now. Including my relationship with Penny."

"She loves you, and you promised to marry her. Those things haven't changed, Cole."

"How do you know?" he demanded. "Those are facts, but you won't let me talk about what's in my heart. You don't understand what I've been thinking. You don't know what I've been praying about for hours while you slept here beside me, Jill."

"I know that when you get home and everything settles down, you'll see the situation more clearly. Right now, it's all blurred by your determination to find Matt. That's the filter you're looking through—as it should be."

"My vision may be filtered, but I'm not blind."

She turned toward the window, her back to him and her voice low. "You can't make decisions at a time like this, Cole. You don't have perspective. Trust me."

He considered her words as the Lufthansa jet thumped onto the runway, reversed its engines, and came slowly to a stop. Africa. Cole looked out the window at the barren ground and scrawny trees. A few days ago, he was sitting on his tractor while he calculated how much chile to plant this spring. Now he was in Africa.

Maybe Jill was right, and things would return to normal when he got back to the ranch. If Matt was safely at home, then Cole could relax. Maybe he would still want to marry Penny and pour his life into his work and give his tithe to the church to spend however they thought best. Maybe he would forget about Mexico and Sudan, about starving people, about relying on God every moment and putting faith into action. Maybe he would forget about Jill Pruitt.

But he doubted it.

Vince Grant stared at his security chief, who sat across from him in the seven-passenger Learjet 55 high over the Atlantic Ocean. He could hardly believe he was traveling to Africa six days before the merger. Mack Harwood had called the night before to report that his men had captured Matt Strong but then let him get away. A Frenchwoman had helped the boy and his friend escape. By strong-arming the woman's sister, the Agrimax agents had learned that the boys and their rescuer were on their way to Sudan.

Vince realized they could have only one purpose in mind. They planned to give a USB key—which Harwood's men had learned contained the stolen files—to Josiah Karume, head of I-FEED operations for Africa. Karume was the last person in the world Vince wanted to have the data, with the possible exception of the press.

Rather than fire Harwood on the spot, which was what he wanted to do, Vince ordered the man to accompany him to Africa. He would deal with Harwood's incompetence later.

"What kind of place is Sudan?" Vince asked.

"Armpit of the world." Harwood held out a thick file. "This is nonclassified CIA information, sir. They're fully cooperating with us in the search for the boy. Sudan has a Muslim government and several known terrorist cells in operation. The CIA keeps a close watch on things, of course."

Vince waved away the file. He didn't care to read about some godforsaken country in the middle of nowhere. Sudan had oil, but no money. It was light-years behind Saudi Arabia and other oil nations eager to do business with the West. Besides, Congress had passed a law banning trade with Sudan. Beyond putting a stop to the kid who had stolen his plans and fled to this armpit of a country, Vince had no interest in the place whatsoever.

"What about airports?" he asked. "Can we take the Learjet to this I-FEED camp in the south?"

"It's doubtful, sir. Except for Khartoum Airport, the country relies on small airstrips, many of them unpaved. We'll have to use the local carrier—Sudan Airways."

Vince swore. "What about renting a car, driving down there? Or trains?"

"Sudan is the largest country in Africa. Most of the roads are little more than dirt tracks. If it rains, they're impassable. The major cities are linked by rail, but train service is unreliable and dangerous."

Looking out the window, Vince tried to calm himself.

There was enough time to return to the States and complete the merger six days hence. His blood boiled at the thought of the trouble and expense that one stupid kid was putting him through. But this mess was nothing compared to the potential damage if the USB key fell into I-FEED's hands.

The kid had gotten into Vince's most sensitive files. His secret merger plans, his lists of clandestine business acquisitions, his classified scientific technologies, and his elaborate designs to control the world food market had all been accessed and downloaded.

Vince knew this information—if leaked—would cause Agrimax irreparable damage. And it would ruin him. He would be accused of plotting to evade antitrust laws. His hostile takeovers of small businesses and farms would be exposed. Protest groups would have a field day with the controversial genetic technologies in development—and actually being used in some parts of the world—by Agrimax. The press would smear his name. The USDA, the FDA and other government agencies would nail him to the wall. Stockholders would flee like rats from a sinking ship. The company would go under, and all his work and dreams would die. The thought of it was enough to knot Vince's stomach and send pains shooting through his chest.

Vince had met Josiah Karume more than once in the past few years, and he knew the African would have no qualms whatsoever about using stolen information for his own purposes. Karume had one agenda, and it wasn't humanitarianism. He was a businessman. Like Vince, he had risen to the helm of a worldwide organization. His goal was to keep the African division of I-FEED solvent, thereby increasing his influence and enriching his own bank account.

Vince had no doubt Karume traveled to refugee camps to distribute some of the produce he wrangled out of Agrimax and others. But the African was no fool. He knew as well as Vince did that food was the key to ultimate power. People had to eat—and they would pay anything to meet that need.

Karume understood the politics of hunger very well. He worked with warlords, tribal chieftains, and anyone else who held the reins of local power in the African countries he serviced on behalf of I-FEED. With the help of greedy middlemen like Karume, the Third World's black market saw to it that humanitarian agencies were efficiently stripped of their "freebies" in order to enrich the coffers of administrators.

Vince was certain Josiah Karume would gladly blackmail him with the stolen Agrimax data. The African excelled at his role in this global food Monopoly game. Agrimax played the game supremely well. I-FEED and other philanthropic organizations played, too. National and local governments played with great zest. The winner was yet to be determined, of course, but the prize was the same for all—money, power, world domination.

As Vince studied his inept security chief, he inwardly fumed. The man he had relied on to safeguard his empire had failed him. Ultimately, this situation was in Vince's hands, and he would resolve it. He would manipulate Josiah Karume. He would put a stop to the father who had chased his son halfway around the world.

And Matthew Strong? Vince gritted his teeth as he thought of the sanctimonious kid who threatened to destroy him. If Vince had his way—and he always did—both Matthew Strong and his little USB key would soon meet a satisfying demise.

Jill stepped down onto the hot runway and drew in a deep breath. Africa! The very smell of the place thrilled her. Unable to resist, she slipped her arm through Cole's and gave it a squeeze.

"This is so exciting! I can't believe I'm here again." She had purchased a pale green scarf in the Frankfurt Airport, and she pulled it over her head as they crossed the tarmac to the terminal. "You're going to love Africa. It's an amazing place. So many cultures and languages. So many animals. So much to see!"

He gave her a tired smile. "I'd settle for seeing Matt."

"We will. But we have to get through customs first, and that could be a hassle. We don't have visitors' visas, inoculations—any of that. I wish I'd been able to reach Josiah by phone. He would have smoothed our way into the country. His secretary here in Khartoum sounded pretty glum about the prospect of tracking him down. He must be way out in the boonies."

"What's the deal with the scarf?" Cole asked her as he limped across the tarmac on his injured ankle. "There's not a rain cloud in sight."

"The northern Sudanese are Muslims, remember? Women cover their heads."

"You're not a Muslim."

"No, but I'm always respectful of local practices."

Jill and Cole accompanied the other passengers through double glass doors into the cool, concrete-and-tile interior of Khartoum Airport. An official met them and escorted the group to a secure area guarded by two uniformed men cradling large automatic weapons.

"Good morning," the customs officer addressed Jill when it was her turn to present her passport. "Welcome to Khartoum, madam."

"Marhaba," Jill said in greeting. She hoped her smattering of Arabic would be taken as an effort to engage in the traditional exchange of small talk the Sudanese people enjoyed at the start of every meeting. "Thanks be to God—*alhamdu lila!*

I'm so happy to be back in Sudan. I came here three years ago to work at a refugee camp with I-FEED."

"Ah, this is good." He gave her a warm grin. "And how do you like Sudan?"

"It's a beautiful country. Very large!" She pointed to her passport. "You can see the stamp of my visit right here. I stayed for six weeks—*sita, naam?* It was a wonderful experience. The Sudanese people are so kind."

"But, madam…" The man looked up, his affable expression suddenly gone. "You do not possess a current visitor's visa. You cannot be permitted to enter Sudan without the visa."

"I realize how difficult this is, but—"

"Not difficult. Impossible." He closed her passport and held it out to her. "You must return to Germany on the first available flight. Next, please."

Jill lifted a hand. "Please…uh, *minfadlak*. My friend and I have traveled a long distance at great expense to search for his missing son. The boy is only sixteen years old. He ran away."

"To Sudan?" The man's dark eyes appeared skeptical.

"He came here to meet with I-FEED officials."

"An American boy?"

"Yes. His name is Matthew Strong."

"And he had a visitor's visa?"

"No, but—"

"Then he was not permitted to enter Sudan. It is forbidden."

"We believe he has found a way to get in—perhaps in the south."

"Ah." The man scratched his head. "We have trouble with the southern borders. The rebels, you know."

"Sir, we must find this boy and take him back to America. *Minfadlak*…please…help us find a way to overcome the problem of the visas."

He looked from her to Cole, his expression grim.

"*Inshaa'allah.* Give me both passports," he said. "One moment, please."

The metal legs of his chair scraped across the concrete floor as he stood. He walked across the secure area to speak with another official, and Jill stepped up her praying. *Dear God, You parted the Red Sea. You knocked down the walls of Jericho. You burst open the prison gates that held Paul captive. Please, please, Lord...*

"Jill, I will not leave this country without my son," Cole said in a low voice. "They need to understand that."

Jill touched his arm, and she could feel the tension in his muscles. "Don't do anything desperate. These Third World countries have a lot of bureaucracy to wade through. You have to be patient."

"I never had much patience to begin with, and what I had is long gone."

She read the steely resolve in his blue eyes. "Pray, Cole. Just pray."

"I'm praying. But I will do what I have to in order to get through those doors and find Matt."

"The machine guns are not for show, Cole. If you make any sudden moves, the guards will kill you. It's that simple. In Sudan, there are no human rights."

"And my son is in this country? He doesn't stand a chance!"

At the despair in his words, Jill couldn't hold herself away from him any longer. She took a step toward Cole and slipped her arms around his waist. Laying her head against his chest, she hugged him gently.

"Relax, relax," she whispered. "We're walking through the valley of the shadow of death, but we don't have to be afraid. God is with us."

She felt his hands slide across her back. His arms tightened around her.

"Jill, I don't know what I'll do if they kill Matt."

"I don't, either," she said. "It's too awful to contemplate."

He heaved a deep sigh. She looked over at the two Sudanese officials. They were using the phone now—a black rotary-dial phone that bespoke the antiquated infrastructure within the country.

"They *have* to let us through," she said. "Getting visas could take weeks. And if Matt made it into the southern part of Sudan somehow, he's in danger. We can't lie to ourselves, and we can't wait on the bureaucracy. Just pray, Cole."

The official moved their way again, and Jill stepped out of Cole's embrace.

"Miss Jill Pruitt and Mr. Cole Strong." He read the names from their open passports. "Yesterday, the United States government alerted Sudanese authorities to the possible presence of a sixteen-year-old, Matthew Strong, who is accused of murder and other crimes. Our security forces are searching for him already. When he is captured, he will be extradited to your country."

"Captured!" Cole barked.

Jill gripped his arm, as if she could hold him back. "That's very good, sir. We're so happy to have the cooperation of the Sudanese—"

"Miss Jill Pruitt and Mr. Cole Strong, you do not have visitors' visas, therefore you are not permitted to enter Sudan." He read from a small paper on which he had written himself a note. "Today is Thursday. The next Lufthansa flight departs from Khartoum Airport on Monday morning. Now you will be taken in a security bus to the Grand Holiday Villa Hotel in the city of Khartoum, where you will stay for three nights at your own expense. You will be kept under guard at all times. You will not leave the hotel even for tourism purposes. On Monday morning, you will be returned to the airport so that you may depart Sudan. Thank you—*shokran*."

He rattled off a string of commands in Arabic. One of the two armed soldiers left his post.

Dismayed, Jill bowed her head and covered her eyes. This was terrible! Impossible! Struggling to hold back tears, she felt Cole's arm around her shoulders. He drew her close and held her for a moment. The guard beckoned, and they had no choice but to accompany him through the terminal toward the exit.

Chapter Fifteen

Cole sat in the rickety bus, his injured fingers aching and every muscle in his body tensed for action. He had made it to Sudan.

The city of Khartoum, built at the convergence of the Blue Nile and White Nile Rivers, stretched for miles in all directions. A guard drove the minibus down an unpaved street lined with one-story houses and shops. Ramshackle stalls displayed stacks of shoes, bolts of fabric, laundry detergent, eggs, fruit and other basic commodities. People glided along the alleys in flowing white robes and flip-flops. Some women wore bright fabrics wrapped around their bodies and draped over their heads.

Though Jill had told Cole that the people were Muslim and spoke Arabic, they had the dark skin and curly hair of Africa. "Brown," Cole commented. "Everything here is brown."

"The color of drought." Jill's eyes reflected her green scarf. "Look, there's a camel!"

He glanced down a dirt lane to see a heavily laden camel

lumber past, with the man who led it moving in equally slow motion. On one street corner, a vendor sat on a short stool and sold coffee from a three-foot-high conical brass urn. Everywhere, groups of ragged children huddled against the houses, their eyes dull and their bodies unwashed.

"What's the story on the kids?" he asked, pointing out one of the clusters.

"They're called *Shamassa*—'Children of the Sun.' They're mostly war orphans, though some are demobilized soldiers who fought in the civil war. They've lost their families, their homes, even their culture. These children flee north to Khartoum hoping for food and work. But they're lucky to stay alive."

"That's outrageous. The government or somebody ought to—"

"Street children live in every major city of the world, Cole. I saw them in Juarez while you and I were down there. I-FEED, UNICEF, and other groups work with these kids in Calcutta, Rio, Nairobi—you name it. It's overwhelming. They just keep turning up, and there aren't enough workers or programs or funds to take care of them all."

Cole shifted on the plastic seat, uncomfortable in the intense dry heat, and angry that such conditions persisted. Why did God allow this kind of suffering? It wasn't right, and it didn't fit with Cole's idea of a loving Creator.

"You know the *Shamassa*, madam?" the guard asked over his shoulder. "You have been to Sudan?"

"*Marhaba!*" Jill said in the greeting Cole had heard several times. She leaned forward, animated again. "*Naam*...yes, I came here three years ago."

"How do you like Sudan?"

"It's very beautiful! The people are so friendly."

Hearing her observation a second time, Cole scowled out

the window at the brown city and its impoverished inhabit-
ants. What did Jill find to like about the place? It didn't even
smell right.

"You visited Khartoum?" the guard asked.

"Only for one day," Jill replied. "Then I flew by Sudan
Airways to the south."

"Where did you go in the south?"

"I went to Rumbek."

"Rumbek!" He looked at her again and beamed. "I am
from Gogrial! It is near Rumbek."

"I've been to Gogrial!" Jill slid her hand across the seat and
grabbed Cole's fingers. "It's a lovely town."

"Not now. Gogrial no longer exists, madam. My village was
destroyed by the Sudanese army. The houses were all knocked
down, and the people were killed. If not killed, they ran away."

"This is terrible news. Was your family harmed?"

"Yes, madam. At that time, I was fighting with the People's
Liberation Army in another area. When I returned to Gogrial,
I learned that my wife and my seven children had been shot.
All of them died."

"Your whole family?" Cole demanded in disbelief.

"Yes, sir, even my parents and my brothers and sisters. The
Sudanese army killed them."

Cole's rage bubbled at the boiling point. "How could soldiers murder women and children?"

"They don't care. Everyone can be the enemy of the Sudanese army. Children become guerrilla fighters. Women feed
the rebel troops. So they must die. After my family was killed
and Gogrial was destroyed, I left the People's Liberation Army
and traveled here to Khartoum to find work. God was with
me, and I took this job as a security guard at the airport. But
every day, I search the faces of the *Shamassa* who live on the
streets. I hope I may see my children among them. I pray to

God they did not die. I pray they escaped and came to the city. Yet, I do not find them. Not even one."

Thinking of Matt—an innocent American teenager in such a place as this—Cole knew an icy fear. "Are there no laws in this country?"

"The Sudan government imposes the Islamic law known as *sharia*. This law has no mercy, only justice. I am a Christian. I try to obey the laws of my country, but I do not follow the teachings of the Koran."

"How did you become a Christian, sir?" Jill asked. "We are Christians, also."

"Everyone in America is a Christian, *naam?*"

"Not everyone," Cole said. "People may say they are, but not everyone chooses to live by the teachings in the Bible."

"Ah." The driver nodded. "This is also true in Sudan. But my mother was a true Christian, and she took me to worship God at the church in Gogrial. Missionaries from Sudan Inland Mission taught my mother about Jesus Christ and built the church before they were forced to leave the country. Now in Sudan it is very dangerous to be a Christian. Many have been killed or sold into slavery. Here in Khartoum, we meet in a secret place. My father practiced our tribal religion—we are of the Dinka people. But I saw the truth in Christianity, and I chose the way of my mother. This is my faith and my practice."

Cole knew he was tired, but that didn't fully explain the emotions swirling through him. How could a man whose entire family had been slaughtered believe in God at all? How could anyone in such a country—a place of hunger, poverty, homelessness and drought—practice any kind of faith? Where was God in Sudan? What was He even *doing?*

"My friend has lost his son, also," Jill was saying. She leaned forward, her arms folded across the back of the seat in front of her. "The boy ran away from America to Sudan because he wanted to help the hungry people here. He has gone to the south to try to find the I-FEED station in Rumbek. We're very worried about his safety, of course, and now we cannot go and search for this child."

"Why can you not go to Rumbek?" the driver asked. "Sudan Airways will take you. Or you may ride in a train."

"We came to Sudan too quickly to wait for the visas."

"This is why you must stay at the hotel?"

"Yes, and then we will be forced to leave Khartoum on Monday. We feel very upset about this, because we need to find this lost child."

The guard fell silent as he pulled the minibus up to the front of the Grand Holiday Villa, a large and elegant hotel with liveried bellmen waiting to greet arriving guests. Cole casually tried the door, but it was locked. No chance of bolting.

The driver shouldered his automatic weapon and walked around to let his passengers out. Jill leaned against Cole for a moment and whispered in his ear. "Pray. This man is a true believer. He may help us."

She stepped out into the bright sunlight, and Cole emerged behind her. Another uniformed guard spotted them. He started across the hotel entryway, his gun strap over his shoulder and the barrel pointing skyward. Cole slipped a protective arm around Jill. He didn't know why he'd agreed to let her come with him. If the Sudanese army had no problem slaughtering women and children, she could be in real danger.

The Christian minibus driver approached his two passengers, blocking their view of the oncoming guard. Only his machine gun separated them as he spoke in a low voice. "God is good. Perhaps you wish to give me your passports for safekeeping?"

Cole glanced at Jill in confusion. She was breathing hard.

She hesitated only a moment, moistening her lips. "Yes," she said, "God is good." She dug into her purse, slipped a folded stack of American currency into her passport, and handed it to the guard.

Stunned, Cole shook his head. "Jill, I'm not going to—"

"Give him your passport." She plucked the blue booklet from Cole's hand. The driver slid the documents into his uniform pocket and turned away without saying more.

"Jill, this is crazy!" Cole whispered. "You gave our passports to a total stranger."

She took his arm just as the hotel guard assumed his station at their side. He introduced himself as Ahmed and indicated they were to enter the hotel.

"You bribed that guy," Cole continued. "That was a lot of money! And for what? He'll sell our passports on the black market. They're probably worth a fortune."

"The thing to remember is that he's our brother in Christ," Jill said calmly. "We have to trust him."

"I don't trust anybody. Especially not in this—"

"People are people, Cole. Some are trustworthy and some aren't. That man took a huge risk in telling us he's a Christian. I think that's significant."

Cole thought the only significant thing was that he was stuck in Africa with an AK-47–toting guard, no visa and now—no passport. And he had no idea if his son was even alive.

"Wow, look at this," Jill exclaimed as they entered the lobby. Bathed in the grandeur of a bygone era, the room gleamed with polished mahogany, marble and brass.

A bellman smiled, apparently oblivious to the fact that the hotel's newest guests were under armed guard. "Welcome to the Grand Holiday Villa." He glanced around. "May I take your luggage?"

"No luggage," Cole said.

"*Marhaba!*" Jill's greeting echoed from the domed ceiling. "What a lovely hotel this is!"

"Thank you, madam. You speak Arabic, I see. You have been to Sudan? How do you like our country?"

"It's beautiful," she said.

"And the people are so friendly." Cole finished her mantra. He stepped up to the front desk. "We need two rooms."

"Two?" The clerk checked his register. "But I was told—"

"We're not married."

"Ah." He looked confused. "Our American guests usually—"

"We're not married," Cole repeated. "We need two rooms."

"I see. A customs official called us to say you would be coming. Upon his instructions, we have prepared a room and hired a guard. Perhaps you will stay together."

"No, we will not."

"Very well. Please excuse me. I must speak to the hotel manager."

He walked into a back room, and Cole turned on Jill. "I can't believe you gave away our passports. You don't even know that guy's name. We'll never find him again, and even if—"

"Cole, can you please learn to trust God?"

"God—who abandons war orphans and child-soldiers to starve on the streets of Khartoum? God—who lets an entire continent suffer under famine and AIDS and who-knows-what-other hardships? I'm supposed to trust that God?"

For the first time since Cole had met Jill, he saw her beautiful green eyes fill with tears. "God is not the author of famine, disease, poverty and war, Cole. Those are Satan's tools."

"God could put a stop to it."

"He will one day. But not yet."

"Jill!" He grabbed her shoulders. "I need my son. I need to find Matthew!"

"Cole, we don't have anyone but God now. We can't rely on anyone but Him. We're at the bottom of the barrel, okay? We have nothing. Nobody. No hope. All we have is God. If we're going to get out of Khartoum, find a way to Rumbek and rescue Matt, we have to trust God. Can you try to do that?"

Cole turned away from her, fighting the emotion that swelled a lump in his throat and tore through his chest like a cancer. While trapped in the wrecked car, he had renewed his commitment to Christ. He had vowed to change his life. To get his priorities straight. To trust God instead of himself.

Now he was being called on to do that. And he couldn't. He couldn't trust. Not enough to hold back the worry and fear. Not enough to hold back the doubt.

"I don't have the faith," he said through clenched teeth. "I told you that."

Jill's hand stroked down his back. "Yes, you do," she whispered, leaning her forehead against Cole's shoulder. "Lord, this man believes in You. Help his unbelief. Help mine, too. We're so scared. We're terrified that Matt might be hurt. We're worried about the passports. I gave them away, and now that I think about it, I probably shouldn't have done that. So here we are, Lord. Just Cole and me. We need You. We need Your help, and we could also use a large infusion of faith. Amen."

"Two rooms!" The clerk held a key in each hand. "And now I must have a credit card to ensure payment. You will stay until Monday? Yes, but I am told no sightseeing is permitted. This is most unfortunate. Only 180 kilometers to the north, we have the pyramids of Meroe. Very interesting! And near Khartoum stands the city of Omdurman with a famous mosque—and a silver dome! At Port Sudan on the Red Sea, visitors may snorkel and dive in the—"

"Sir, I'm so sorry," Jill said. "But we can't leave the hotel."

The clerk eyed their guard. "A great misfortune indeed. But you will enjoy the hotel. We have satellite cable television, a Malaysian restaurant, a grill room, a café overlooking the Nile, a shopping arcade, and three swimming pools. One is exclusively for women!"

"*Shokran,*" Jill said. "We thank you for your kindness."

"*Minfadlak,* please, follow the bellman. He will take you to your rooms."

As Cole moved painfully across the lobby to the elevators, a veil of unreality descended over him. In the midst of such grinding poverty sat a hotel with satellite TV and three swimming pools. And in the midst of utter hopelessness, God had prompted Jill Pruitt to pray for help.

Stepping into the elevator, Cole swallowed down the lump that had wedged in his throat. He would have faith. Against every reality determined to hurl him into an abyss of despair, he would trust in the presence of God.

"Madame Loiseau, Moses is untying the rope." Billy leaned against the rusty railing of the old steam-driven boat. "You better get off now."

Matt nodded, feeling as if the minute the Frenchwoman stepped off, he would lose his last anchor to reality. The Nile was flowing fast, and he knew it wouldn't be but a minute before they were caught in its current. He swallowed down the wad of emotion in his throat. "Thanks again, Madame Loiseau."

"You've been a big help," Billy added. "You saved our lives. Those guys—"

"Enough!" She held up her hand. "I do not say goodbye. These words I cannot speak."

Taking Matt's shoulders, she squeezed them tightly. "You

and William must make me a promise, *oui?* Promise me that you will live. No matter how difficult it may be to stay alive, do not die."

Matt studied the woman who stood before them looking so out of place in her pointy-toe high heels and tight black skirt. "We'll try, Madame Loiseau."

"You make a promise?"

"Oui," he said.

As tears filled her eyes, she smiled. "You are good boys. One day we meet again. I take you to my chateau in Provence. I feed you good food and you swim in my pool. This will make great happiness for you. Oh, William, come to me!"

Billy winced as she wrapped him in her arms and kissed both his cheeks. When it was Matt's turn, he hugged her tightly.

"Thanks a lot," he murmured. "Thanks for all you did."

"Voilà!" As if helping two strange teenagers get to Africa was no big deal, she stepped onto the dock and pushed her cloud of brown hair off her neck. As the boat pulled away, she took out a cigarette. *"Il fait chaud!* I am hot—and close your mouth, Matthew, or you will swallow a fly."

Billy waved. "Goodbye, Mrs. Loiseau!"

"Madame!"

Laughing over getting her goat one last time, he nudged Matt. "She's cool. Weird, though."

"I hope we do see her again." As the boat began its journey up the Nile, Matt turned away, unwilling to watch the woman fade into nothingness. He laid his hand on the USB key and said a prayer for her safety—and his own. Gazing across to the far bank, he noted a dozen or more crocodiles sunning themselves.

Billy squinted in the sunlight. "I hope we don't fall into

the river," he said. "We'd be dead meat, man. Gobbled down like a couple of corn dogs."

"Actually, crocodiles don't eat their prey right away," Matt said. He had read a bunch of books about African wildlife in elementary school. "What they do is drag their victim out into the water and drown it. You don't die from the bite, but from drowning. Then the crocodile hides its prey under a log or a rock in the water until it gets so rotten and decomposed that—"

Noticing the look on Billy's face, he paused. For the first time since they left Amarillo except for when he was airsick Billy looked like he was losing control. He drank down a deep breath of air.

"Matt," he said, "I'm thinking this is, like, really weird. I mean, I'm pretty good at handling most things. And I've helped you through a lot of stuff."

"Yeah, you have."

"But this is definitely not Artesia High School."

"We can do it." Matt said the words with a lot more confidence than he felt. "We'll be fine."

"We're in *Africa,* dude!"

"Don't wig out on me, Billy."

"We're on this little steamboat on the Nile with hippos and crocodiles all around. And hostile natives!"

"Yeah, so?"

"We need to, like, plan how we're gonna keep from getting kidnapped or murdered. Or eaten by something. We don't even have a gun or anything."

"Cool it, Billy. Just relax, okay?" Matt glanced at the front of the boat.

Moses, the tall Ugandan who would take them to the Sudanese border, noted the boys' expressions and left his place at the bow. "How do you find your journey?" he asked as he approached them. When the man smiled, Matt noted a big gap among the white teeth in his lower jaw.

"We're fine," he returned.

Eyeing his gawking passenger, Moses laughed, a deep chuckle that rolled up from the bottom of his chest. "American boys!"

"Yeah, uh…" Matt glanced at Billy, but that gave him no reassurance at all. "So we're going to Sudan, right?"

"Sudan, yes!" Moses laughed again, as he shook his head. "You will die there."

Matt sucked down a breath. "Why do you say that?"

"No food. No Land Rover. Not even water."

"Madame Loiseau said you were going to give us food and water."

"Yes, but you cannot carry enough for a long journey."

"Maybe you should come with us. You could help us."

The African lowered his head and chuckled. "You do not have enough American dollars to pay me for that!"

Matt looked at Billy again. He felt like telling Moses to turn the boat around and take them straight back to Madame Loiseau. They could get on the little airplane and be back in the States in a couple of days.

Billy's eyes held nothing but fear. Fear like Matt had never seen in them.

"You wanna go back?" Matt whispered to his friend.

Billy chewed on his lower lip for a moment. "I wish we could."

"We could."

"But then you wouldn't give the key to that guy."

"I know…but…" Matt wavered, uncertainty rising like tentacles through his chest, wrapping around his throat. "Billy, I'm freaking."

"Me, too."

"What should we do?"

"You decide."

Matt tried to think about starving children and the Bible and Christ's command to feed the hungry. He looked across the river at the crocodiles. He looked at Moses, who was still laughing at the dumb American boys who were going to die. Then he looked at Billy again.

"Will you, like, hate me if we get killed or something?" he asked.

Billy shrugged. "No."

"Well… I think we came this far…so…"

"Okay."

"Are you sure?"

"Not really."

"Me, either."

They stared at each other.

Moses straightened. "You want to go back to the camp?"

Matt shook his head. "No, it's okay. Keep going. We have to make it to Sudan."

Moses regarded him in silence for a moment. "You wait here." He strolled across the deck, reached into a recess near the prow, and withdrew a two-foot-long stick. When he returned to Matt, he held it out. "Take this, American boy. This is a weapon of the Maasai people. A tourist left it here on the boat, and it should be given to you. It is called a *rungu*."

Matt took the stick, which had a large knob on one end. "Thank you."

Without answering, Moses turned and walked back to the bow, where the steamboat's pilot had been watching the exchange.

Billy leaned across and examined the gift. "It's a stick," he said.

"He said it was a weapon," Matt whispered.

"It's a stick."

"Well, it's better than nothing."

Billy rubbed the back of his neck. "Man, I think I'm gonna croak."

At the bow, Moses and the pilot watched the two boys and laughed behind their hands. Matt leaned against the railing, cradled the *rungu,* and wished he weren't here. He thought about his dad and Miss Pruitt, and he hoped they had decided to stay in New Mexico to wait for him. The truth was, Matt missed the ranch—his room and computer, Josefina, good food, clean clothes, his big bed. He even missed his dad. Though Matt resented his father's constant need to work the farm, Cole had always been around.

If his son really needed him—for any serious reason—Cole would leave his work for an hour or two. He would be there. They didn't talk much, and they had little in common. But Matt realized it was good to know where your dad was. It was comforting.

All in all, he had a pretty okay father, especially compared to some kids, like Billy. And right now, Matt really wished he could just look out across the fields and see his dad's truck driving along one of the dirt roads on their farm. That would be nice.

Billy slapped a mosquito on his arm. "I hope it wasn't carrying malaria. Or worse."

"Next time you see one on you, tell me, and I'll mash it with the *rungu,*" Matt said.

"You wish." Billy's mouth curved into a grin. "Touch me with that dumb stick, and I'll break it over your head."

"Hey, watch what you say about my weapon of mass destruction."

Billy laughed. "Dude, you're bizarre."

★ ★ ★

Jill stood on her balcony overlooking the Nile. Everything had come apart—and it was her fault. She never should have given away the passports. Cole was right, of course. The minibus driver had taken them and sold them on the black market. Who could blame him? His job as an airport guard would provide little money for food and housing, and he had lost his whole family. Like every other person in Sudan, he was desperate. Though he professed Christianity, he was human, and Jill had placed too great a temptation before him.

Why had she been so stupid? Why had she trusted the man? People couldn't be trusted—not fully. God was the only one in whom she should put her faith. She knew that, but she hadn't obeyed, and now she, Cole and Matt would suffer the consequences.

Her hair still damp, Jill used her pick to sort out the curls after her morning shower. Cole, whose room was next door, had spent the previous afternoon sleeping. She had napped, too. But she also had made phone calls to the U.S. embassy and I-FEED headquarters in Khartoum, and to the feeding station in Rumbek. All of them dead ends.

The embassy liaison said he would call later with information as to what they should do—but he hadn't. No one answered the phone in the I-FEED office. And the phone lines to Rumbek were out of service.

She did have one bit of good news. In an e-mail, Marianne had assured Jill that the principal had no problem with her absence. He was more concerned that the school had failed to properly protect Matt.

Unable to face Cole, she had ordered room service that evening and had gone to bed early. Now it was Friday, and on Monday morning she and Cole would be deported. Passports or not.

And where was Matt?

Jill had been crying off and on all morning. While praying, showering, eating breakfast, the unexpected tears just came. It was Matt. He would die. There could be no other outcome in a country like this. If Agrimax didn't get to him first, the Sudanese or guerrilla armies would. Or hunger. Or a parasite. Or a wild animal. The possibilities of death were endless, and the hope of life so very tiny.

And her tears came, also, Jill had to admit, when her thoughts turned to Cole. It wasn't just the passports or Matt that hurt every time the man crossed her mind. It was Cole himself. Somehow he had stepped inside her and broken down the "happy single woman" life she had so carefully constructed for herself. She wasn't happy anymore—not the way she had been. A restlessness curled through her, making her want things she had thought didn't matter. Passion. Love. Companionship. A shared life with a man.

She wanted to be soft. She wanted to rely on the strength of another human being. She wanted to be protected and cradled and loved the way a man could love. And the worst of it was—she was soft already, with little to hold her up. She was melting, crumbling, aching inside.

As she watched the boats ply the Nile, Jill gripped the balcony railing and fought the anguish that welled through her. She didn't want just any man. She wanted Cole. His strength and determination and intelligence matched her own. His vitality moved her. Though he kept his emotions under control, with Jill he had been willing to show vulnerability. She had seen his fear and his doubt, and the shared pain had somehow wedded their souls. She felt knitted to him and so utterly comfortable in his presence. How could she bear to return to her old stalwart single life? She couldn't. She couldn't stand the thought of it.

But Cole had promised to marry another woman. He had made a commitment. He loved this Penny Ames enough to want to make her his wife and Matt's stepmother. No matter what Cole said about how the wreck in Juarez had changed him, the fact of his engagement remained.

Though her own feelings for Cole were potent and true, Jill feared his attraction to her couldn't be valid. Every tender word, every gentle touch, even the forbidden kiss that had passed between them was cloaked in the overwhelming blanket of this terrible misadventure. From the moment Jill had met Cole, their interaction had been colored by the search for Matt. Physically, mentally, emotionally, and spiritually, they were stretched thin. These days together had been intense, but not real. The way Cole felt about Jill was the kind of bonding that happened between shipwreck survivors or between prisoners and their guards. And it wouldn't hold up. Not in the harsh light of normal life.

"Hey, there." The voice startled Jill from her preoccupation with her misery. Cole stood on his own balcony next to hers. "How've you been?"

"Pretty good," she said. "No. Bad."

"Me, too."

Pinning her with those bright blue eyes, he searched her face. She saw that he had shaved, showered and combed his hair. He wore a white T-shirt, jeans, boots. And he looked handsome. Heartbreakingly handsome.

"I called the embassy just now," he told her. "They said you'd phoned. They can't get to our case before Monday. But that's the least of our worries. Clotilde Loiseau's sister sent a message through the embassy. Clotilde flew with Matt and Billy to Uganda with plans for them to take a boat to the Sudan border—and then walk inland to find Josiah Karume. Alone. And Agrimax people are on their way to Khartoum."

"Oh, no." Jill's lower lip trembled, and she struggled not to cry. "Cole, I'm so sorry I gave away our passports."

He gazed at her, his eyes tender. "You did what you thought was right."

"It was a huge mistake."

"We'll get back to the States without our documents, I guess." He gripped the railing. "The question is—will we have Matt and Billy with us? Or will Agrimax find them first?"

"I've been praying for the boys."

"Me, too."

"Cole, I never intended to cause you any trouble. You have so much pain…" She couldn't finish.

"I don't blame you for anything."

"You did once."

"That was years ago, wasn't it?" He reached across the narrow space between the two balconies. "Hey…you don't think I still hold you responsible for what Matt did, do you?"

"I am responsible—at least in part."

"You know what you're responsible for? Changing me. Helping me become a better man."

She took his hand. "You changed me, too, Cole. I hardly know who I am anymore."

"I know you. I feel like I've known you forever."

"It's strange, isn't it? In some ways, this time has been so unreal. And yet because of it, I feel like I've gotten to know the real you."

"The condensed version. All of me—shaken, pressed down and running over."

"Isn't that what the Bible says about blessings?" She paused. "Cole, I know I've been reluctant to talk about us…about the things that have happened between us…but I want you to know that you have been a blessing to me. The best thing… the best person that I've ever…"

He squeezed her hand. "Are you crying?"

"Not on purpose."

Laughing, he lifted her hand and kissed her fingers. "Just when I think I really do know everything about Miss Jill Pruitt, I discover yet another side of you."

"This isn't me. It wasn't. But now…now I'm so confused about myself."

"I'm not. I know exactly who I am and what I want."

She focused on him, forcing back the tears. "Cole, how are we going to get to Matt?"

"I've been scoping out the hotel, checking for a way to slip out. The guard followed me everywhere."

She searched for some hope. "Maybe I could lead him off somewhere, and you could sneak away."

"Nah, they've got armed men posted around this hotel as if it were a fortress. I suppose it's to keep thieves out of the tourists' pockets, but it's going to keep us penned in. I thought about climbing down the balcony, but three or four Uzi-toting guys stand watch down there on the street all the time."

"Maybe tonight, we could—" A rap on her door drew Jill's attention. "Cole, someone's knocking."

"Be careful. I'll be right here."

She stepped back into the air-conditioned room. "Yes? Who is it?"

The hotel guard, Ahmed, opened her door. Two Sudanese women garbed in white robes stood beside him in the hallway. Heads covered and eyes averted, each carried a large basket filled with towels, bottles of oil, and brushes.

"You requested a massage in your room," Ahmed said.

Jill shook her head. "No, I—"

"The request for a massage was called to the concierge," Ahmed said. He looked down at a slip of paper in his hand. "I have the chit here."

"But—"

"Please, come." One of the women took Jill's arm and urged her back into the room. The other shut the door and locked it from the inside.

"Listen, I really did not call—"

"God is good," the woman said. She dropped the length of fabric that swathed her head.

"It's you!" Jill gasped, recognizing the guard from the minibus.

"Keep quiet, please." He placed a finger to his lips. "The guard may hear us. Here are your passports with the visas stamped inside. Here are tickets for the train to Rumbek. And this is a photograph of my family, my children. You will please look for them when you are in the refugee camp?"

"Yes, of course!"

"Quickly now...bring the man."

Her heart racing, Jill stepped out onto her balcony. "Cole!" She leaned over and took his hand as the tears spilled from her eyes once more. "God is good!"

Chapter Sixteen

"This is not going to work! I'm blond!" Jill blotted her cheeks with a wad of tissue Cole had brought her from the bathroom. "And I wish I could stop crying. This is ridiculous, and I'm just really so…so—"

"Jill." Cole set his hands on Jill's shoulders as Daniel, the Christian driver of the minibus, wrapped his own white robe around her. "What's upsetting you?"

"Well, you're a man, and there's no way you'll pass for a woman. Besides, you're twice as tall as Daniel."

"Not twice as tall. Maybe a head taller."

"But we have the visas now, so why can't we just—"

"Daniel explained that." Cole couldn't figure out why his curly-haired stalwart pillar of faith and hope was suddenly crumbling before him. "If we show the visas to the guard, he'll wonder how we suddenly got them. And then we'll have to head back to the airport and wade through a mess of red tape. And we could still be deported."

"I know, I know." She sniffed loudly. "God has prepared

this way for us. But everything is just so hard. Why does it have to be hard? Why can't it be easy for once?"

He sighed, hearing his own thoughts reflected in her words. "I guess we're getting a graduate-level course in faith. At least I am."

She nodded, looking miserable in her white outfit. He wished he could scoop her up in his arms and hold her until every sorrow and fear crept out of their hearts. But this wasn't the time or the place. They had only moments before they must escape from the hotel.

"Please understand about this journey you make," Daniel stated as he handed Cole the tickets. "In Sudan, the train from Khartoum to Wau in the south has been used many years for transporting soldiers, horses and supplies to military posts. This train also carried the *mujahideen*—tribal militiamen whose work is to create a security zone along the railway line. While traveling, the train stops often, and these *mujahideen* are permitted to plunder and raid villages in exchange for their protection of the railway."

"That's barbaric," Cole said.

"It is the way of the Sudanese government. The *mujahideen* capture many villagers and sell them as slaves."

Cole turned to Jill in disbelief. She nodded, her eyes sad.

"Recently," Daniel continued, "the United Nations set up a humanitarian train convoy from Kosti to Wau. The World Food Programme operates this. You know it?"

"The World Food Programme?" Cole repeated. "I've heard of it, I suppose." He recalled snippets of TV commercials urging viewers to support hunger-relief foundations. He normally surfed right on past, uncomfortable with the images of skeletal children and their large, pleading eyes. Newspaper and magazine ads had the same effect on him. Seeing pathetic, naked babies holding up empty bowls, he turned the pages quickly.

"These visas I get for you are diplomatic visas," Daniel pointed out. He opened the two passports and displayed the newly inked stamps. "You must not board the military train. You must ride on the humanitarian train. You understand? As soon as you escape from this hotel, take off the robes. When you sit on the train, you must appear to be officials from a relief organization—the World Food Programme or I-FEED or some other. It may keep you safe from the *mujahideen*, who would wish to kidnap you for ransom."

"Kidnap us? This is unbelievable."

"Believe it. Now, here is the weapon I purchased for you," Daniel went on. He lifted the towels out of his basket and presented Cole with a revolver. "It is old, and I could buy only these five bullets. After I obtained the train tickets and the visas, the money was not enough for a better gun. But it will shoot. I tested it."

Cole sighed. A rusty old handgun would hardly protect them from an Uzi or AK-47 carried by almost every adult male in this country, including the marauding *mujahideen*. But it was better than nothing. And it represented another great risk taken by the driver.

"Thank you, Daniel," Cole said softly. "You've been a great help to us."

"I help you because you have lost your son," the African told him. "I understand this sadness. I help you because your son came to Sudan to feed my people. And I help you because I am a Christian."

"You've shown me a greater Christian love and sacrifice than I have seen in my own country, Daniel."

The man smiled. "After you find your son and take him safely to your house in America, you must return to Sudan and help us. You come to feed the people, and then you can tell them about Jesus. There are some Christians here, especially in the south. In Sudan, everyone is hungry for food, yes? But also for hope. Hungry for hope. You will help us, Cole Strong?"

Cole squared his shoulders. "I'll come back to Sudan," he promised. He laid his hand on Daniel's back. "I will feed your people with food and with hope in Jesus."

The sound of a loud sob drew his attention to Jill, who was sitting on the bed in her disguise. Cole studied her in dismay. He'd never been good at understanding women's emotions, and Jill Pruitt's were no exception. The only difference was that now he desperately cared to find out what was bothering her.

He moved toward her, but Daniel stopped him. "We make you a Sudanese woman now, Cole Strong," he said. His companion, Joseph, was unwrapping his own robes. "You must not walk upright. Bend down and turn your eyes away, very shy. Keep the face covered. This is the way of Muslim women in Sudan."

In moments, the men had swathed Cole in white robes. They slipped the pistol back under the stack of towels and handed the baskets of massage supplies to Cole and Jill.

"Daniel, what will happen to you and Joseph?" Cole asked. "Before long, the guard will find you here in the room instead of us. What will he do to you?"

"Aha." From his pocket, Daniel produced three of Jill's ten-dollar bills. "I save these for Ahmed. This is more than two months' wages for a Sudanese man. Ahmed will release us, and then he will run to tell his employer how he was overpowered by fifteen men with guns and knives."

"Why don't we just give Ahmed the money now?" Jill suggested.

"He will never permit you to leave—even for a much

greater sum than this. But if you have escaped already, he will take this bribe and make a story for his employer."

Cole shook the man's hand. "May God bless you and reward you richly for your efforts. We will search for your children."

"God is good," Daniel responded. He laid his hands on Cole and Jill. "In the name of Jesus Christ, may God be with you and keep you safe. May He lead you to your son in safety. May you honor your vow to return to Sudan and bring us hope. Amen. Go in peace."

Feeling a greater sense of God's presence than he'd ever felt in a church service, Cole embraced the two Christian men who had risked so much on his behalf. Then he took Jill's arms.

"Stay close to me," he whispered. "Don't look at the guard. Don't say a word."

He opened the door. Clutching their baskets, they stepped out into the hall.

The guard spotted them and stood from his chair near the wall. *"Kayf haa'lak?"* he asked.

"Keep moving," Cole murmured against Jill's ear. He hurried her down the hallway. "We'll take the stairs."

"Eh?" the guard called after them. *"Kayf haa'lak?"*

"Khal-las," Jill said. *"Ma' Al-Salama."*

They rounded the corner, pushed open the fire door, and fled down the emergency stairwell. At the ground floor, Cole paused. After removing the pistol, he took both baskets and set them against the wall. "What did the guard say to us?" he asked as he shoved the gun under his belt.

"I'm not sure." Jill was breathing hard from their rapid descent. "I think he was asking how the massage went. Or how we were doing. Something like that."

"What did you tell him?"

"I just said we were finished."

He looked down into her pale face and couldn't resist taking her into his arms. "Jill, we're going to find Matt. I have faith."

At that her green eyes brimmed with tears again.

Dismayed, he kissed her forehead. "Tell me what's wrong. Please, Jill, I want to know."

"It's that…that I…that you and I…" She grabbed the corner of her robe and wiped her cheeks. "We have to get out of here. Just never mind, okay?"

She pulled away from his arms and pushed open the exit door of the Grand Holiday Villa Hotel. The heat and odor of Khartoum enveloped Cole as he followed her into the bright morning sunshine. Jill hurried ahead, her shoulders bent. He would never understand women, Cole realized. Never. But if there was one woman he would not stop trying to fathom, it was Jill Pruitt.

A blast of artificially chill air greeted Vince Grant as he stepped into the lobby of the Grand Holiday Villa Hotel in Khartoum. Grateful, he paused and mopped his forehead with a white handkerchief. Just the short walk from the taxi to the front door had been enough to unnerve him.

Khartoum was a disgusting city—filthy, disintegrating and swarming with miscreants. White-robed women hurried by, their heads low and their eyes down, as though they had committed some terrible crime—and they probably had. Men wandered the streets, their skinny arms and gaunt faces stark against their own white garments. Hollow-eyed, they stared at the Caucasian visitors. Vince tried to read what he saw in those dark eyes. Suspicion? Anger? Outright hatred? All of the above, he decided. And the children…they gathered in gangs, no doubt for the purpose of stealing from tourists. The country needed a good welfare system, Vince thought. Schools. And a thousand other things that any civilized nation would take for granted. But what could you expect from the Third World?

"Did you get clearance for the Learjet, Harwood?" he asked as his security chief appeared in the lobby. The man had been on the phone during the ride from the airport, where they had been informed that because they had no visas, they would be detained at the hotel until Monday.

"It's not going to happen, sir." Harwood was sweating. "Sudan has sixty-one airports, but only twelve with paved runways. The airport nearest the Rumbek refugee center is in the town of Juba."

"Then we'll land in Juba."

"Juba is three hundred miles from Rumbek, and the road between them is full of potholes—practically impassable."

"I don't care how far it is or how long it takes to get there," Vince snapped. "Set it up, Harwood. Get us a Jeep or something."

"I'm sorry, sir, but we simply can't take a Learjet 55 into Juba. The town has no electricity. Drought reduced their water supply, and the generators aren't working. They're obsolete anyway. Nobody's got spare parts for anything in Sudan. We won't have radio contact, and a night landing is out of the question. The pilot would have no way to locate the airport."

Harwood rubbed his temples as a guard approached. Uniformed and carrying an AK-47, he stood at attention before them. "I am Ali," he announced. "You may not leave the hotel for tourism purposes."

"Tourism? We don't give a—" Vince bit off an oath and returned to Harwood. "Get the CIA. Get the U.S. ambassador. Do whatever it takes. Check out trains, helicopters, anything that moves. I intend to leave this hotel before the sun sets, Harwood. Is that clear?"

"Yes, sir."

"And what about Karume? Why isn't he answering his phone?"

"I'm not sure, sir. The communications systems in Sudan are—"

"Down? Broken? Out of spare parts? Tell me something I don't know."

"Sir, I left three men at the airport working on the situation. I'm doing all I can to make this happen." Harwood's voice was tense. The veins in his neck stood out like snakes under his skin, and Vince knew he'd pushed his security man as far as he could.

"I'm aware we're in a tight spot here," Vince said. "And I know you're doing all you can. On the other hand, Harwood, we wouldn't be stuck in the middle of Africa if you'd stopped the boy while he was still in New Mexico."

"I won't deny that, sir. And as you know, we made every attempt—"

"Fine, fine. And would you tell the manager to make this Rambo wannabe stop breathing down my neck?"

"Yes, sir." He glanced at Ali and his large machine gun. "Mr. Grant, I'd like to settle you here at the hotel and assure myself of your safety. Then I plan to return to the airport and find out what I have to do to get us out of Khartoum and on our way to Rumbek."

"That's good, Harwood. You do that."

Vince settled into one of the silk-upholstered chairs near a large potted palm in the lobby. Ali took up a position three feet away and cradled his weapon. Vince sighed.

He stared absently at Mack Harwood, who was speaking to the manager at the reception desk. His wife and children hadn't crossed Vince's mind since he'd left Chicago, but now he reflected that Cheryl would approve of this hotel—overtly luxurious and built to cater to the top echelon of the world's wealthy. What a joke. It was like a Mercedes parked in a shantytown.

Vince couldn't deny that a hot shower and a decent meal would do him good. Maybe he could relax enough to take a nap, though he doubted it. He was no longer counting in days the time remaining until the merger. In a mere ninety-six hours, the deal would go down. How infuriating to be stalled by the bureaucracy of an impotent government in a barren wasteland of a country. But his aura of power and control would return soon enough.

He had made up his mind to take care of a few things once he got back to Chicago. Agrimax needed a clean sweep—more thorough background checks of all employees and better technological security. Vince would put these things into place immediately.

Most important, he would ax Harwood and replace him with someone who could do the job. Someone tougher. Someone he could trust to nip problems in the bud.

The image of the boy, Matthew Strong, was imprinted on Vince's brain. Harwood's file contained six photographs lifted from various sources. Unlike Vince's own son, who was handsome and athletic and who possessed his father's gifts of charm and charisma, Matthew Strong could clearly be labeled a geek. A nerd. A loser. He had blue eyes and long, curly black hair that hung well below his ears, and he wore the same out-of-style tie in every photo. Acne-spotted, his long, thin face and his skin looked sallow.

But it was the hint of self-satisfied piety in the boy's eyes that haunted Vince at night when he tried to sleep. What a pleasure it would be to watch the light of holiness fade from those blue eyes. The little pest needed to be taught a lesson in the way the world worked. With murder and theft charges awaiting him, Matthew Strong would have many years to think about it as he read his Bible in a prison cell. And if he never made it safely back to the States, justice would be served.

"I'm hungry, dude." Seated on the hard ground, Billy leaned back against the mud wall of a hut at the edge of the make-shift refugee village. "I can't believe those boys over there are playing soccer. All they've eaten for months is peanuts."

"And that sorghum junk." Matt licked his dry teeth. They felt sticky and gross. He turned his head toward his friend, who was sitting beside him in the scant shade of the hut's thatched roof. Billy's jeans were filthy, and his feet were covered with dust and bites from the tiny red ticks that peppered the grass. Two days before, in a small village they passed, Billy bought a pair of sandals made from the rubber tread of car tires. His sneakers had started rubbing blisters on his heels, but the sandals were worse.

"How long since we left the boat?" Billy asked.

"We crossed the border into Sudan on Friday. Today is…" Matt looked up at the sky and calculated. "Sunday. Sunday morning."

"If we were at home on a Sunday morning, we'd be in church. Our youth group would be in the fellowship center right now."

"Yeah. Eating doughnuts."

"Don't remind me!" Billy groaned. "Dude, do you think that guy is really going to bring a bicycle?"

Matt shook his head, feeling bummed. "I don't think so. I bet he took our money to buy peanuts for his family. He's not going to bring us a bicycle or anything else. I think we're gonna have to walk to Rumbek."

"Walk?" Billy groaned again, louder this time. "I can't walk. We walked for two whole days just to get to this village. And all we've had to eat ever since we got off the boat is peanuts."

"And that sorghum junk," Matt reminded him. "I guess we ought to be thankful though. At least we have something to eat."

Billy gave a snort of disgust.

"Well, it's better than most of these people. Did you see that kid eating grass? Leaves, too."

"I'm gonna die," Billy said. "I'm gonna totally keel over and die right here in this village in the middle of nowhere."

"You're not gonna die."

"Yeah, I am. I'm so thirsty." He grunted. "How can they play soccer? It's blistering hot, and they only ate peanuts!"

Matt rolled his head back around to face the open ground where barefoot boys kicked a ball that had long ago lost its leather covering. They laughed and ran back and forth, as though this game was the most fun they'd had in months. And it probably was. A few of them who spoke English had told Matt they had been soldiers until a couple of weeks ago. Soldiers! And they were younger than Billy and he.

"We're gonna die, both of us," Billy said in a wavering voice. "Just like Madame Loiseau told us."

Matt grimaced. They were both suffering from the hunger, thirst, blisters, ticks, and mosquitoes that had plagued them ever since they got off the boat and walked across the border from Uganda into Sudan. It was hard to see Billy in such bad shape. His best friend looked saggy and sick and totally defeated. The excitement of their adventure had ended long ago, and in only two days in the African bush, life had become a matter of survival.

That's all either of them could think about. The USB key and the mission to save the hungry paled in the face of this all-consuming thirst and hunger. Matt laid his hand over the small hard lump in his jeans pocket. God had brought him so far. The refugee camp at Rumbek lay only twenty miles from this village. But they wouldn't make it. They couldn't. It was impossible.

"You honestly don't think that guy will bring a bicycle, Mattman?" Billy mumbled in disbelief. "We paid him thirty bucks! That was the last of our American dollars."

"I think we got stiffed."

"How hard can it be to get a bike?" Billy groused. "I have three old bikes in my garage. Just sitting around getting dusty!"

"Do you see any bicycles in Sudan?" Matt asked. "Do you see any cars? Any trucks? Do you see food or crops or livestock or shops or any *normal* things? No! Nothing! This place is a desert."

"Mellow out," Billy snapped at him.

"Yeah, right. Like you haven't been griping ever since we got to Africa."

Billy leaned his head back on the wall of the hut. "Aw, Mattman, just try to relax. Just try to stay alive, like you promised Madame Loiseau, okay?"

Matt looked across at Billy, who was swallowing hard, obviously trying not to cry. His parched lips were trembling. Matt patted him on the back. "It's okay, Billy," he said. "We'll be all right."

"I'm never gonna see my house again. Or my mom. I even miss my little sister. And my dad. I don't know why I did such a dumb thing. I don't know why I came with you. Stupid!"

"Hey, man, don't freak out, okay?" Matt patted him on the back some more, this time a little harder. "You came because you wanted to help me find Josiah Karume, remember? And that's what you're doing. You're helping me, just like you always have. You found the guy who sold us those peanuts. You tried to buy a bicycle. And now, we're both just going to have to figure out how to take the next step."

"I can't take another step," Billy said. "You saw my feet, dude. The blisters have popped, and my skin is all raw and bloody."

Matt studied his best friend's tick-bitten legs, blistered feet and sunburned nose. A tear had escaped his eye and started down his cheek. What was Matt going to do if Billy really did die? He couldn't even think about it.

"Look, Billy," he said, giving his friend's shoulder a shove, "stop moaning. You're a really strong guy, and you can't let this stuff get you down."

"I'm not strong," Billy mumbled, wiping his nose on his sleeve. "I'm weak."

"No, you're not. You're the person I've always counted on, right?"

"Yeah, so what? You can't count on me now. I can't even stand up."

"Yes, you can. You know why? Because you're like my mom."

"Your *mom*?" Billy frowned. "What do you mean by that?"

"She was really strong down inside. But when she first found out she had cancer, she cried all the time and got depressed. I remember it—it was awful. She said she didn't want to die and leave my dad and me. She wanted to see me grow up—she wanted to hold her grandbabies. All that. Later on, though, after she got used to the idea of having cancer, her strength came back. She had a lot of faith in God, see. Not faith that she'd get well, but she believed He was with her through all the pain and sadness. And she knew He was going to be with my dad and me after she was gone. That was really important for me to see—how she got through it all because of the strength inside her."

"Is that how come you wear this dirty old tie?" Billy picked up the end of Matt's tie and studied it sadly. "To remind you of how strong she was?"

"Partly."

"I don't have that kind of strength, Matt. Strength from God. I'm too hungry."

"I don't think God takes hunger and suffering away," Matt said. He had thought about this a lot. "Not always. My mom didn't get well. That's not the deal God promised. It's like the Twenty-third Psalm, you know? We don't get to avoid the valley of the shadow of death. But while we're walking through it, we don't have to be afraid because He stays close beside us. His rod and His staff protect and comfort us."

"Mattman, you're gonna be a preacher one of these days," Billy said. "All I can think about is that feast He's prepared for me in the presence of my enemies. Where's the food? I'm ready to eat! Lord, send down the manna!"

Matt couldn't hold back a chuckle. "You idiot."

"Hey, here comes that kid who keeps asking us to play soccer. Why don't you see if we can get some more peanuts?"

"Hello, Santino," Matt said as the boy approached. Earlier that day, Santino had told them he was fifteen, but he looked about ten. He had narrow eyes and very white teeth, and he seemed to think these two white boys sitting on the ground in his village were pretty hilarious.

"Why you cannot play football with us?" Santino asked. "Come!"

"We can't." Matt had already told him this, but it wasn't getting through. "We're too weak. Our feet hurt, and we're hungry. Besides, we need to go to Rumbek."

Santino grinned, his teeth gleaming in his ebony face. "You gave your money to Aken Amuon for a bicycle!"

At this, he bent over and laughed as though this was the

funniest thing he'd ever heard. His pals had edged closer by this time, and they all joined in, yukking it up—ha ha ha.

Matt looked over at Billy, who was scowling, then back at the boys. "If you give us peanuts," Matt suggested, "we'll play football with you. American football."

"American football?" Santino's dark eyes widened. "Can you teach baseball?"

"Yeah, and basketball. But—" Matt thought for a moment "—but we don't have time for that because we need to get to Rumbek. Do you know the way to Rumbek?"

"Of course!" Santino chuckled. "It is there." He pointed off in the direction of the same nothingness that surrounded the whole village.

"We don't know the way. And we can't walk that far because of our sore feet. So I guess we'll just sit here and not teach you how to play American baseball or football or basketball."

Santino spoke to his buddies, and they all chattered for a while. They pointed one direction and then another. They yelled at each other, shoving back and forth. And finally Santino stepped out of the group.

"Why do you tell us a lie, American boy?" he asked Matt. "You say you come to Sudan to feed us, but you have no peanuts even for yourselves."

This was a logical question, and Matt realized how dumb he and his companion must look to these natives. "I don't have food, but I have this," he said, taking the USB key from his pocket. "This is a machine with secrets inside it. And this machine may help bring food to Sudan. I have to take it to Rumbek and give it to Josiah Karume, the director of I-FEED."

"This is a machine?" Santino peered at the key. "It is a gun?"

"No, it's part of a computer."

"Computer? I do not know this machine."

"It's very powerful."

"Ah." Santino explained this to his comrades. Then he nodded at Matt. "You may teach us to play American football, and then we shall take you to Rumbek."

"No way. You take us to Rumbek, and then we'll teach you how to play football."

"Eh!" Santino smacked him on the back. "Good! You come now."

He and the other boys filed off toward one of the huts in the distance. Matt helped Billy to his feet, and they stepped out of the shade and into the blazing sunlight.

"Do you think they've got a car in that hut?" Billy asked.

"I don't know." Matt stepped gingerly, trying not to injure his feet further. "I hope it's—"

"Oh, boy. Oh, great." Billy stopped in his tracks. "What is that thing?"

"A horse." Matt laughed. "I think it's a horse!"

Santino proudly led the bony animal across the clearing. The other boys wheeled out a small cart made of tree branches and bare bicycle tire rims. They hitched the horse to the cart with ropes and pointed for the boys to climb in.

"This horse I capture from the *mujahideen*," Santino explained. "After my village was attacked and my parents were killed, I was taken by the *mujahideen* to be a slave."

"A slave?" Billy turned to Matt. "I thought slavery was abolished."

"In America, dude."

"My work was to tend the horses of the *mujahideen* who raid the villages," Santino continued. "One night, I steal this horse and escape. This is now my horse."

He looked so proud of the broken-down old animal that

Matt wanted to laugh. But he knew this was serious business. "Are you guys going to walk?" he asked.

"We walk." Smiling, Santino dug around in his pocket and pulled out a handful of roasted peanuts. He offered them to Matt and Billy, and then he beckoned his friends. "Let us go to Rumbek and learn to play American football!"

Chapter Seventeen

"A helicopter?" Vince gripped the telephone. "Is it reliable?"

"My men will check it out as soon as it arrives in Khartoum, sir, although we'll have to use the native pilot." Mack Harwood sounded weary. Agrimax's security chief had stayed at the airport well into Friday night, trying without success to get Sudan's visa and inoculation requirements waived and to arrange a flight to the refugee camp in Rumbek. Saturday had proven equally futile. Finally, early this Sunday morning, he was calling from the airport to say he had received clearance and found transportation.

"And you tell me Josiah Karume authorized the use of this helicopter?" Vince asked.

"His office staff here in Khartoum gave us permission, sir. It's an old Soviet-made chopper that I-FEED uses to transport food to remote areas. It's been over near the border with Chad, which is…uh…west of here. It's supposed to arrive back here around noon, and we're trying to find fuel—"

"Trying to find fuel?"

"Basic supplies and parts are scarce, Mr. Grant, and the bureaucracy is a nightmare."

"Have you talked to Karume himself?"

"No, sir. Evidently, he's down at the refugee camp in Rumbek, but we're not getting a phone connection. They tell me the camp does have service off and on, but Karume usually stays in touch with his staff by computer, using a wireless modem with satellite—"

"So is Karume answering your e-mail messages?"

"Not yet, sir. We weren't able to find his office until yesterday morning, and then it took us most of the day to locate his secretary and the other staff. Businesses shut down early on Fridays for religious reasons, and you also have to work around their prayer times. We've just now managed to get permission to use the helicopter, and we'll keep trying to connect with Karume in Rumbek."

"Does the office staff know anything about the boy? Has he made it to Rumbek?"

"No one has heard from Karume. He flew into Khartoum from Paris last week and immediately took the train down to the camp."

"Get me out of this hotel, Harwood." Vince tossed his wet towel on the bed. He'd been swimming that morning, trying without success to distract himself from the fact that the merger meeting was now forty-eight hours away. "Send a limo for me. I'll be bringing Ali along. He's a good bodyguard."

"Well, sir, about the limo—"

"I want to be at the airport when the chopper arrives, Harwood. And keep trying with Karume. E-mail him. Tell him the boy is coming his way, and warn him not to do anything until I get to Rumbek. Make sure he understands the seriousness of this, Harwood."

"Yes, sir."

"You work on patching me through to the refugee camp by phone. I want to talk to Karume."

"I'll do my best, sir." Harwood paused. "Mr. Grant, I won't be able to send a limo for you. There aren't any in Sudan. It'll be another taxi."

"A taxi?" Vince raked his fingers back through his damp hair. "Just get me out of here, Harwood."

Jill leaned against the metal window frame of the old bus and stared out at the African grassland beyond the dirt road. Despite Daniel's dire warnings, she and Cole had changed back into their regular clothes, boarded the humanitarian train and made it safely to Wau. After baking for several hours in the extreme heat, they boarded this bus bound for Sudan's southern capital city of Juba. It would stop in Rumbek that afternoon—providing its bald tires didn't burst, it didn't bottom out in a pothole, and its radiator didn't explode. Every two or three miles, the driver stopped the bus and added fluid. Engine coolant? Water, more likely, Jill surmised. As they rolled along, steam and smoke drifted steadily from under the hood.

"What are you thinking about?" Cole asked when she let out a sigh. He was wedged up against her, because two other passengers had decided the three-person seat had plenty of room for all. In fact, humans and livestock all competed for space in this packed menagerie on wheels.

"I'm hoping this bus makes it to Rumbek," she told Cole. "I'm thinking about Matt and Billy, too, wondering where they are. I pray they're safe at the camp with Josiah Karume."

He shook his head. "If they're there, it'll be a miracle. I don't see how two kids from small-town America could survive this."

"With God all things are possible." She shrugged. "Sounds nice, doesn't it?"

"Yeah. Got another one?"

"Probably. My brain is too tired to have an original thought. It's reeling with verses I learned in Vacation Bible School and proverbs my grandpa used to say. 'All's well that ends well. The early bird gets the worm. Hate the sin but love the sinner. Be in the world but not of the world.'"

"You're beautiful."

She caught her breath, then tried to laugh. "That can go on my list."

"Fine, but I've never meant it more."

Stunned, Jill realized she was actually blushing. Thank goodness for the scarf. Not only did it hide unwashed and frizzled hair, but maybe it would shield her pink cheeks. This was the first time Cole had mentioned his feelings for her since they left Khartoum. Jill had tried to tell herself she didn't care. On the train, they had been separated—men in one car and women in another. But Cole had had ample time to talk to her at station stops, and he'd said nothing. She decided she must have convinced him that the weirdness of this time and place had distorted his outlook. After all, they were a long way from his ranch and Penny Ames.

"Do you ever think what it will be like when we get home?" she asked him now. "You'll be ranching, and I'll be teaching. We never ran into each other before. So I guess I won't see you. I've gotten… I'm used to us. Being together, you know."

She could feel his eyes on her, the blue intensity. "I want it to be that way, Jill. Us together."

"But Penny would—"

"Don't talk about Penny, okay?" He let out a hot breath. "I know everything you want to say. Yes, I asked Penny to marry me. I know this is a strange time for you and me. And if I lose Matt…"

Unable to hold back, she took his hand and held it tightly. "Cole, you don't have to—"

"No, let me say this. If I lose Matt, things will be hard for me. I didn't believe I would ever get through the months after Anna's death, but I did. Eventually, I made it to the place where it doesn't hurt every day. I don't think about her constantly, not the way I once did. But a child... Matt... I don't know how you could ever get over losing a child. I can't see how I could live through one day after another knowing... knowing he was gone."

Jill blinked back tears.

"Maybe if I lose Matt, or even if I don't," Cole continued, "maybe I'll realize I ought to go ahead and marry Penny. I might stop thinking about you. I might go back to the man I was and be okay with letting you go. But I don't think so, Jill."

She took the end of her scarf and blotted the tear wandering down her cheek. "I hope not."

"Really?" He took her hands. "Is that why you've been crying so much? Is it because you don't want to let go of what we have here? Tell me, Jill."

"I can't talk about it. It feels wrong. Like adultery, or something."

"I'm not married to her!"

"I know, but you are promised. If you promised to be my husband, and then you went off to Sudan and started wooing—"

"Wooing? I'm not wooing you, Jill. I never intended for this to happen with us. I'm an honorable man. God put us together to find Matt, and along the way, I realized I can't imagine living without you."

Tension rippled through his shoulder, pressed so hard against her own. The man was amazing, Jill thought once again. Maintain your integrity, her grandpa had advised. And integrity was Cole Strong's guiding principle.

"I trust you," she said. "I know you were loyal to your wife, and I believe you intended to marry Penny. And…and I do understand about how this experience has changed you. It has changed me, too."

"In what ways?"

"I've always been so big on mission work. Doing my part, and all that. But all I do is go in and help—an outsider swooping in, doing good, and then winging her way back home again. I never stay and dig into relationships. I've been that way with everything. I help my students, try to influence them and then shuffle them out the door to their next class. My friends know I won't really get involved in their lives. A lunch or a party, maybe. But nothing serious."

"Why?"

"I don't want to get hurt. I've watched marriages end. I've seen kids rebel and leave home. Friends have lied to me and betrayed me. Relationships are risky—and you know that, too. I've accused you of being distant, but it was the pot calling the kettle black."

Cole gave a tired laugh.

"It's true," Jill said. "I've always been wary. And then…you came barging into my classroom and ordered me to go with you to Amarillo."

"Ordered you?"

"Yes, you did. And once I let you in, I started to like you. And admire you. And care about you."

"And love me?"

Startled, she glanced up. His eyes were depthless. "I can't imagine my life without you," she said.

"I love you, Jill Pruitt." He lifted her hand and kissed it. "Here on a bus in Southern Sudan, I love you. And I think…

I believe that back in New Mexico on my ranch, I'm still going to love you."

"Okay," she said softly.

"Okay, what?"

"I love you, too." Her voice shuddered with the emotion of speaking words she held so dear. "Here on the bus, I mean. And probably... I expect... I imagine that back in New Mexico in my house, I'm still going to love you."

"It's enough, Jill. It's enough for me to know you feel this way now. I still have to work things out with Penny, but I've known for a long time what I need to do. I see God's path in front of me, and I want to walk it, Jill. I want to walk it with you. When we get back—" he kissed her hand again "—*if* we get back, we'll take the first steps together."

Jill leaned her head on Cole's shoulder and let the tears fall. She was so happy and so miserable and so scared. It was all too much, and she had a terrible fear that this fragile thread of love between them would snap. Danger, loss, pain, even guilt—any of these might sever the thread. They hadn't had time to weave a thick cord that could bind them together through everything that would pull at them. They had known each other such a short time, and their love had been spun on the unstable loom of this strange pursuit.

Jill nestled against Cole and drank in this moment of union between them. He wrapped his arm around her and brushed his lips across her forehead. She lifted her head and kissed his cheek. For now, this would have to be enough.

As the bus rolled into Rumbek, the sun was settling into the tops of the thorny acacia trees surrounding a collection of thatched huts and white tents. Cole searched the clearing, hoping to see Matt. The barren ground was deserted except for a few people gathered around a fire.

"Why have they lit a fire in this heat?" Cole asked Jill as they waited their turn to step down from the bus.

"Roasting peanuts, I imagine."

Cole groaned. Though he and Jill carried some packaged cookies and fresh bread from Khartoum, they had run out long before the train station at Wau. Expecting to replenish their supplies, they had discovered that roasted peanuts were the only food available. In fact, at every station and bus stop, only peanuts awaited them, and the price rose as they journeyed south.

"Do you see Matt and Billy?" Jill asked, peering over his shoulder. "I don't see them."

"They're not out in the open." He climbed down from the old bus and started toward the fire.

"Wait, Cole!" Jill caught his arm. "What's that sound?"

He glanced upward, recognizing the distinct *thunk-thunk* of helicopter blades.

"Sounds like a chopper. I wonder if—"

"Oh, look, there's the relief center! Maybe the boys are in there with Josiah."

They hurried hand in hand toward the small block building. Cole's heart clenched. *Please, God, please let Matt be here. Please let him be safe!*

He hammered on the door. "Josiah Karume? Are you in there? Matt?"

"It's my dad!" The voice was filled with disbelief.

Cole threw open the door as his son barreled into his arms. "Matt!"

"Dad!" Matt hugged him hard, jumping up and down. "Dad, you came! And, Miss Pruitt—whoa!"

"Miss Pruitt!" Billy threw his arms around her. "Awesome! Hey, Mr. Strong!"

As Billy pumped Cole's hand, a cloud of dust blew over

them. Squinting, Cole turned to see the helicopter setting down in the clearing. He pushed the boys and Jill back inside the building and shut the door against the whirlwind.

"Dad, this is Mr. Karume," Matt said, hauling his father across the room to where a distinguished-looking African man worked at a small laptop computer on his desk. "Mr. Karume, I want you to meet my father, Cole Strong."

"Welcome to Rumbek, Mr. Strong." The African stood and held out his hand. "Your son and his friends arrived not fifteen minutes before you. We were just discussing his journey. How did you come this way, also? And Miss Pruitt—is it you?"

"Josiah!" Jill grasped the man's hand. "It's wonderful to see you again."

Caught up in the joy of finding Matt safe and healthy, Cole struggled to hold back tears as his son beckoned him to the desk in a corner of the room. "Look, Dad, Mr. Karume has the greatest laptop. He's got new software and a USB port, so we plugged in the key. And it works! All the information is on there! I was afraid that with everything it had been through— airport scanners and that trip to Mexico and then on the way to Sudan we had to— Dad, are you hurt? Miss Pruitt said you were in a wreck in Juarez."

Cole held up his bandaged fingers. "I'll live, Matt, did you really have to—"

"Yeah, Dad, I had to come here, because Mr. Banyon was planning to give the USB key to Mr. Karume, and I had to finish the job after he...after they..."

"We've been eating peanuts ever since we got to Africa," Billy cut in. "And they have this nasty sorghum junk that—"

"Well, well, well!" The office door opened to a middle-aged American in a business suit. "Josiah, great to see you!"

"Vince Grant?" Karume stepped around the desk to greet the man. "This is a great honor indeed."

Startled at the intrusion, Cole slipped one arm around his son and the other around Jill. A Sudanese guard shouldering an Uzi joined the businessman, and another man stepped into the room beside them. He and the two who waited behind him wore shirts emblazoned with a familiar logo. *Agrimax.*

"It is my pleasure to introduce Mr. Vince Grant," Karume announced, turning to Cole and the others. "Mr. Grant is the chief executive officer of Agrimax—"

"Agrimax!" Matt made a dive for the laptop.

"Stop him," Grant barked. To Cole's horror, he grabbed the Uzi from the African guard and trained it on Matt. "Back off, boy! Don't touch that computer!"

Cole jerked his pistol from his belt and took aim at the executive. "Put down your gun, Grant."

"You're way outnumbered, Strong, and your son's in my sights. Harwood, get the key."

"Please, Mr. Grant," Karume spoke up, raising his hands to halt all movement in the room. "Tell me what is happening here."

"It's the USB key, Mr. Karume," Matt called out. "It's what I was showing you. Agrimax has been developing secret technologies—things that could harm crops and destroy pure genetic stock. And there's some kind of plan on the key. It's a scheme to buy out other companies and merge—"

"Quiet, boy!" Grant yelled, brandishing the Uzi.

"Matthew, get over here!" Cole barked.

"He wants to build a monopoly, Mr. Karume!" Matt kept talking, the words pouring out of him. "He wants to dominate the global food supply. He wants the power to control the world. Mr. Banyon told me about the plan before they shot him!"

"Control the world," Grant scoffed. "It's all nonsense,

Karume. You know my reputation. I've worked with I-FEED for years. I've provided countless shipments of food and—"

"It's just a ploy to get good PR!" Matt hollered.

"What do you know about anything?" Grant snarled. "You're just a kid. Just a stupid boy! Step away from that computer now, before you get hurt."

"I'm not leaving the USB key. You can't have it!"

"Matthew, come here!" Cole grabbed his son's arm, but Matt clutched the desk.

"No way, Dad. I brought the key here, and Mr. Karume is going to show the world what Agrimax is doing. This is why I came. This is what God wants!"

"Please, please—everybody." Karume stepped to the center of the room, blocking Matt from the Uzi. "Mr. Grant, put down the weapon, I beg you. And, Matt, go with your father. We must sort this out in a civilized way."

"The boy stole the information on that key," Grant said, talking down the barrel of the Uzi. "Karume, hand it to me."

"Mr. Grant, please. I must understand why the young man has taken such trouble to bring me the USB key. And why have you traveled all the way to Sudan? Surely this tells me the information is significant."

"It's significant, all right. It contains Agrimax's confidential plans and technologies—information this boy pirated from our computer system."

"That's not true," Matt said. "Mr. Banyon copied the data onto the USB key. And you killed him because of it. You murdered him."

Grant ignored Matt. "This information cannot go public—"

"Yeah, because it would destroy Agrimax!" Matt blurted. "You know it!"

"Karume, I have the power to make or break you." Grant continued speaking to the I-FEED director. "You understand how things work in this business. Give me that key, and I'll see that you never want for anything."

"You're trying to bribe him!" Jill cried out. "How can you do that?"

Grant smiled, his expression humorless. "Mr. Karume knows how things work in the Third World. Nothing gets done without money under the table. Nothing happens unless you know the right people. Karume, you work with warlords and chieftains, don't you? You understand that for people to eat, palms have to be greased."

"Josiah's a Christian!" Jill retorted. "He would never accept a bribe."

"Christians don't engage in bribery? Then tell me how you got to Rumbek." He paused for effect. "We heard about your escape from the hotel, Miss Pruit. You and Mr. Strong didn't have legal paperwork to be roaming around in Sudan. Somebody helped you get your visas. Somebody took bribes on your behalf. So don't try to goody-two-shoes me, lady."

"And yet you are wrong on one matter, Mr. Grant," Karume said. "I never bow to coercion. It is true that I have learned to work with governments, warlords, tribal chiefs—and even a company as difficult as Agrimax. But Miss Pruitt is correct in her estimation of the strength of my faith. I am a Christian, and thus I must act with integrity."

"Integrity demands that you turn over my property."

"Yes, yes. Put down the weapon, and I shall assess the information on the computer. If I judge it to be of value to the relief work here in Africa and around the world, I shall make use of it as I see fit. If not, I shall return it to you."

Breathing hard, Cole hadn't let go of his son's arm. But the boy refused to budge from the desk. "Do as I say, Matthew," he insisted. "Come over here!"

"Dad, help me get the key out of the laptop!"

"Don't lay a finger on that laptop," Grant snarled. "No one touches the USB key!"

He leaned to shove Karume out of the way, and Cole lunged for the laptop. As his fingers touched the keyboard, the screen exploded in a hail of bullets.

Dropping to the concrete floor, Cole grabbed Matt's tie and yanked him down. The boy fell in a tangle of cords.

Amid shouts and screams, another spray of gunfire erupted. Chunks of concrete wall dropped to the floor. The pop-pop-pop deafened Cole. He struggled to cover his son.

The computer sparked and burst into flames. An acrid odor filled the air. Windowpanes shattered, charts fell from the walls, chairs tumbled over and splintered. A cloud of chalky dust fogged the room.

Cole shoved Matt into the desk's kneehole. The boy had gone limp—with fear? Or was he injured? Someone coughed, and then an eerie silence descended.

A groan led Cole's focus to the corner, where Jill slumped against the wall. One sandal had come off. Her head hung low. A blossom of blood darkened her green scarf.

Cole felt cold fear surge through him. Had God brought them together only to let death snatch her away now? He cocked his pistol. *Dear Lord, don't let Jill die. I love her. Please don't let her be dead!*

"Is the laptop destroyed?" a voice asked. "Get what's left of the key, Harwood."

"It's melted, sir. It's a lump of plastic."

Cole heard the voice just overhead. *Vince Grant.* He crouched low behind the desk, his muscles tensing.

"Are you, uh…planning to contact someone about the injuries, sir?" The voice of Grant's flunky. "This I-FEED guy is pretty bad off."

"Are you suggesting we transport these people to a hospital, Harwood? Save their lives so they can testify against us?"

"Sir, I just don't believe it's right to—"

"I don't believe *you,* Harwood!" Gunfire again shattered the room. The man's body toppled backward onto the desk, his head dangling over the edge where Matt was hiding.

Cole tried to think. The helicopter. Yes, that was how they could get everyone out. Karume was injured. Jill lay bleeding in the corner. And where was Billy?

"You men, get the chopper going," Grant barked. "Ali, help me gather up this computer mess."

As the door slammed shut, Grant's arm with its gray sleeve and clean white shirt cuff appeared at the top of the desk. Cole reached up and clamped his fingers around the man's wrist. Leaping to his feet, he jammed his pistol against Grant's forehead.

"Drop your weapon!" he roared. "Drop it!"

"You fool!" Grant raised the Uzi. Bullets peppered the wall as he swung the submachine gun toward Cole.

Cole squeezed the trigger of his pistol. *Click.* Nothing happened.

Grant reared away, trying to aim the Uzi at Cole. Still holding the man's wrist, Cole flipped the pistol around and slammed the butt end into Grant's temple.

As Grant staggered backward, Cole jumped the desk and threw himself at the businessman. Again, he smashed the handgun against Grant's head. The Uzi skidded across the floor.

"Stay away from my boy!" Cole shouted, struggling to pin the writhing man's arms. "Leave my family alone!"

Grant freed one arm, shoved Cole against a filing cabinet, and leaped for the Uzi. Cole straightened in time to see a dark hand snatch the Uzi first. A line of red dots erupted across Grant's chest. He jerked violently for a moment, and then he fell still.

"What?" Cole looked up in confusion.

Ali stood over him, the Uzi cradled in his arms. "I am Sudanese," he said simply. "This man tried to prevent the other one from feeding my people."

Cole glanced at Josiah Karume, who lay moaning on the floor, his body riddled with bullets. Then he turned to Jill. She was bent over, holding her head. He leaped to his feet. Folding her in his arms, he held her close. "Jill, are you all right?"

"It's a scratch," she sobbed. "I'm okay, but…"

"Thank You, Lord."

"Oh, Cole. Everybody's hurt." She squeezed his shirtsleeves. "Josiah. He's bleeding a lot!"

The next minutes were a blur as Cole and Jill worked their way around the room. Matt was shaken but unharmed. Billy had a bloody contusion from throwing himself to the floor and hitting his forehead on a metal file cabinet. Josiah Karume's injuries were the most severe—three bullet wounds, one of which had cut through his abdomen and another through his arm. He was groggy, groaning in pain. Cole used Matt's tie to form a makeshift tourniquet for the arm wound.

In the camp, chaos reigned. At the sound of gunfire inside the I-FEED command center, armed refugees had poured from huts and tents. They tied up the Agrimax security team and then rushed the small office. Amid shouts, shoving and a hundred random commands called from every direction, Cole managed to see that Josiah Karume was carried onto the helicopter. Jill, Matt and Billy climbed in behind him. Finally, Cole jumped aboard.

The Sudanese pilot had been apprehended along with the Agrimax men. After his release, he decided to make a thorough check of the helicopter—which had been swarmed by countless refugee children during his brief captivity.

While the pilot examined the helicopter's frame, wheels, tail pylon and stabilizer, Cole checked Jill's injury. A bullet had grazed her scalp and caused profuse bleeding. She shuddered as he wrapped an arm around her and kissed her cheek.

"We could have been killed," she sobbed. "Any of us. And two people died."

"Grant got what he deserved," Matt said with uncharacteristic venom as he blotted the contusion on Billy's forehead. "He tried to shoot my dad, and he killed one of his own guys. He's the one who ordered his men to murder Mr. Banyon."

"Yes, but what was it all for?" Jill leaned on Cole's shoulder. "He destroyed the USB key."

"He trashed it," Matt said. "We lost everything."

"Come here, son." Cole pulled the boy into a bear hug. "The important thing is that you're alive. You scared us to death."

"I'm sorry, Dad." Matt gave up the battle to hold in his tears. "I didn't think you would come after me, and I never thought people would get killed. It was for nothing. Now Agrimax will go on doing terrible things, and people will keep starving. Nothing changed. I don't know why God let it happen."

"But things have changed, Matt," Cole said. "A lot has changed."

"Yeah," Billy said. Till now, he had been unusually quiet. "Like you and Miss Pruitt are all...like, kissing and hugging."

"Huh?" Matt leaned over, squinting in the darkness. "Miss Pruitt? You and my dad?"

"It just..." She shrugged.

Cole took Jill's hand. "Yeah, we've gotten to know each

other very well while we've been chasing you guys halfway around the world. And I like what I see. A lot."

Jill smiled at him.

Matt rubbed a knuckle under his damp cheek. "Well, I'm glad you won't be with Penny anymore, Dad. She bugs me."

"I never knew that," Cole said. "There are a lot of things I didn't know. Maybe it's because I wasn't really paying attention. But I do see that Penny isn't right for me. It's like I'm seeing through different eyes." Cole leaned his head back as the pilot climbed into the cockpit and began checking the instrument panel. How little he had understood his son. "If you'll start telling me what you're thinking, Matt, I promise I'll do a better job of listening. You've already taught me to listen more closely to God. I want to do His will—just like you did when you brought the USB key to Mr. Karume."

"Hello?" Karume mumbled from the blanket on which he lay. "Did someone call me?"

As the rotor blades began to turn, Cole knelt down and took Karume's wrist to check his pulse. "We were saying that Matt intended well when he brought you the key, even though Vince Grant destroyed it."

"Ah yes." He grunted in pain. "Destroyed...but not lost."

"What did you say?" Jill asked, speaking over the growing roar of the helicopter's engine. "The Agrimax data was stored on the USB key."

"But the satellite link—the wireless modem. All files from the laptop transfer automatically to my office in Khartoum."

Jill gasped. "Oh, Matt!"

"Miss Pruitt!" He threw his arms around her. "The data is intact! It went to Khartoum! Billy—we did it!"

"Dude!" Billy shouted as the chopper lifted into the night sky. "This is too cool! We gotta celebrate. When we get home, let's go to Dairy Queen and get, like, a Blizzard, or maybe fifteen, and—"

"And a drink of water," Josiah called up from his spot on the floor. "With ice."

"As much ice as you want," Cole said. "Just hang in there, okay?"

"Yes," he muttered. "Okay. Everything is okay."

"Yeah." Matt draped his arm over his father's shoulder. "Everything is okay."

Jill slipped her hand into Cole's. "God is good," she said.

He smiled. "God is very good."

★ ★ ★ ★ ★

Acknowledgments

Several years ago while riding on a shuttle bus, I met the man who was the inspiration for this book. William Heffernan, Ph.D., teaches in the Department of Rural Sociology at the University of Missouri in Columbia. But he is more missionary than professor. His blue eyes lit with a flame, and his words were zealous as he talked to me about the world's hungry people and the need to feed them. Later, on the MU campus, Dr. Heffernan outlined for me the dire implications of consolidation in the global food system. His passion for the American farmer and his work with the Food Circles Networking Project stirred my heart as I thought of Christ's many parables and teachings centered on agriculture. While any errors in this book are my own, I wish to thank Dr. Heffernan for teaching me so much about the food systems and for sharing with me his own ideas about how to save the small farmer while also helping to feed the hungry.

Others who assisted me with information about world hunger and relief programs include Harold Cummins, Kristie Mc-

Gonegal, and Sharon Buchanan-McClure. Geoffrey Palmer, my then seventeen-year-old son, explained computer technology to me. He and the other boys who once filled our basement with laughter, snores and the constant aroma of pizza provided the inspiration for Matt and Billy. These wonderful young men include Ian Campbell, Charlie Thompson, Mark Resner, Mark Johnson, Evan Lowery, and Nathan Jentsch.

With this book more than any other, I've realized the vital importance of those who helped me shape it into the final story you hold in your hands. Karen Solem believed in the project from the onset, and her enthusiasm brought it into existence. My husband, Tim Palmer, is my strength and encouragement. Without his listening ear and the countless hours he spent reading and redlining this manuscript, it would not exist. I am so grateful to God for putting these and so many other important influences into my life. Thank you all.

A Note from the Author

Dear friend,

One summer, I was walking from our cabin to the lake when I spotted a retired friend of mine watering his yard. In one hand, he held a dinner plate. I greeted him and asked why he was carrying around a plate. He told me he had just picked it up from an elderly neighbor who lives alone. "My wife always cooks a little extra every day," he said, "and I take a meal over to him in the evening. It's just as easy to cook for three as it is for two, you know."

This may seem like an insignificant deed, but in this way, my friend and his wife are obeying Christ's teaching in Matthew 25:31–45. *The Life Application Study Bible* tells us that "God will separate his obedient followers from pretenders and unbelievers. The real evidence of our belief is the way we act." My friends' act of obedience doesn't require wealth, great skill, or high intelligence. But in their own way, they are feeding the hungry—and Christ, as well. As He said, "I assure you, when you did it to one of the least of these my brothers and sisters, you were doing it to Me!"

What have you done to obey Christ's teaching? Have you made a meal for a sick friend? Did you volunteer for a Meals on Wheels program? Did you send a donation to a trustworthy hunger-relief organization? Or did you, like the characters in my book, try something extraordinarily risky and bold in your efforts to feed the hungry?

Thank you for being a part of Christ's body and for joining me in the important task of feeding those who hunger.

Blessings!

Catherine Palmer

IF YOU ENJOYED THIS BOOK
WE THINK YOU WILL ALSO LOVE

LOVE INSPIRED SUSPENSE
INSPIRATIONAL ROMANCE

Courage. Danger. Faith.

Find strength and determination in stories
of faith and love in the face of danger.

6 NEW BOOKS AVAILABLE EVERY MONTH!

Brad whipped into a parking lot, left his truck idling and grabbed his phone. He didn't know whom to trust. So what were his options? He saw only one and took it.

"Springfield Medical. How may I direct your call?"

"Nurse Janie Kirkpatrick in the ER, please."

"Sorry. She's clocked out."

"Okay, listen, this is Officer…Tucker," Brad said, hoping his memory for names was as sharp as ever. "I misplaced her phone number after that ER incident today. It's vital that I reach her ASAP. Can you help me?"

"I'm sorry, Officer. Why don't you contact the cops who were on scene?"

He was about to start pleading when she added, "Hold on. Here's one of them."

A genial male voice came on the line. "Hey, Tuck, up to your old tricks? If you wanted her number you should have just asked her for it."

Brad couldn't believe he'd gotten this far. "Yeah, yeah. Give a guy a break."

"Okay. But you'll owe me one." Reciting a phone number, the cop chuckled.

All Brad said was "Thanks" before ending that call and punching in Janie's number.

He'd almost given up when a sweet voice said, "Hello?"

"Ms. Kirkpatrick? Janie Kirkpatrick?"

"Yes. Who is this?"

"A friend. You're in danger. Don't ask questions, just hit the road. Now. And don't tell anybody where you're going."

"Why should I believe you? Who are you?"

"The guy from the ER."

He heard her loud intake of breath. "Brad?"

"Yeah. My boss is coming after you. You need to run. It's not safe for you in Springfield. Keep this number in case you need help and let me know you're safe once you get far enough away."

"Oh, *right*."

"Wait!" Brad was desperate. "You have to believe me."

"Why should I?"

"I can't give you any details," he said soberly.

"Then goodbye."

"No! Think. You met me. Did I seem like the others?"

There was a brief hesitation before she said, "No," but Brad wasn't satisfied so he resorted to pleading. "Please, you know I didn't belong with those other men. You could sense it. I'm sure you could."

"You're assuming a lot," Janie replied.

"Because a lot is hanging on this conversation," Brad said.

"Like what?"

He blew out a noisy sigh before he spoke. "Like your survival."

Don't miss
On the Run *by Valerie Hansen,*
available January 2021 wherever
Love Inspired Suspense books and ebooks are sold.

LoveInspired.com

LOVE INSPIRED

INSPIRATIONAL ROMANCE

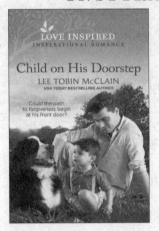

Child on His Doorstep

LEE TOBIN McCLAIN
USA TODAY BESTSELLING AUTHOR

Could the path to forgiveness begin at his front door?

Save $1.00

on the purchase of ANY Love Inspired or Love Inspired Suspense book.

Available wherever books are sold, including most bookstores, supermarkets, drugstores and discount stores.

Save $1.00

on the purchase of any Love Inspired or Love Inspired Suspense book.

Coupon valid until August 31, 2021.
Redeemable at participating outlets in the U.S. and Canada only.
Limit one coupon per customer.

52616916

5 65373 00076 2   (8100)0 12478

LICOUP0820TRADE

LOVE INSPIRED

INSPIRATIONAL ROMANCE

UPLIFTING STORIES OF FAITH, FORGIVENESS AND HOPE.

Join our social communities to connect with other readers who share your love!

Sign up for the Love Inspired newsletter at **LoveInspired.com** to be the first to find out about upcoming titles, special promotions and exclusive content.

CONNECT WITH US AT:

 Facebook.com/LoveInspiredBooks

 Twitter.com/LoveInspiredBks

Facebook.com/groups/HarlequinConnection